Strategic Compromise

STRATEGIC COMPROMISE

A NOVEL

William Nixon

A Birch Lane Press Book
Published by Carol Publishing Group

A Birch Lane Press Book
Published by Carol Publishing Group

Editorial Offices
600 Madison Avenue
New York, NY 10022

Sales & Distribution Offices
120 Enterprise Avenue
Secaucus, NJ 07094

In Canada: Musson Book Company
A division of General Publishing Co. Limited
Don Mills, Ontario

Queries regarding rights and permissions
should be addressed to: Carol Publishing Group,
600 Madison Avenue, New York, NY 10022

Manufactured in the United States of America
10 9 8 7 6 5 4 3 2 1

Library of Congress Cataloging-in-Publication Data

Nixon, William (William Holladay)
    Strategic compromise : a novel / William Nixon.
        p.   cm.
    "A Birch Lane Press book."
    ISBN 1-55972-026-3
    I. Title.
PS3564.I96S77   1990
813'.54--dc20   89-77828
                                                        CIP

To Tammy with love

Strategic Compromise

Chapter One

Villa Taverna was storybook beautiful, an elegant estate in the exclusive Pariolo section of Rome. It was the official residence of American Ambassador Andrew Scott Markum, and at night, when the ground lights burned, the looming belvedere-tower held vigil over the sculptured gardens filled with sarcophagi and marble capitals and statues from the court of Caesar. Beneath the gardens, tunneled deep and still unexplored, lay the ancient catacombs, where legend says the Roman matron Sabinilla entombed St. Valentine on 14 February 269 A.D. However, on this November evening, two embassy security officers stood on either side of the southern entrance to the catacombs. Another shivered beneath the arched trusses of the tower and monitored the compound gate where four Marine guards, in their dress-blue uniforms, saluted the arriving limousines.

Daniel McBride, the ambassador's chief of staff, stood in front of the Marines, closer to the street. His eyes were bloodshot, and they burned from fatigue and the late hour. In his hand, he held the only copy of the closely guarded guest register, and as the cars pulled to the gate, he checked off the names and nodded to the Marines to let them pass.

Inside the Villa, the ambassador stood beside his wife, beneath the cross-vault ceiling of the entrance hall, and greeted his distinguished visitors. His smile was sincere, more so than the strained smile of Mrs. Markum, a fragile woman in her seventies, who ushered the guests into the reception rooms at the left of the receiving area. With each new arrival, she turned slowly, almost painfully, and gestured toward the spacious rooms decorated with lacunar ceilings and ancient marble fireplaces.

Guests filled the villa with motion and color, sequined gowns, and black tuxedos purchased on the Spanish Steps, Fifth Avenue, and Faubourg Saint-Honoré. They included politicians, multinational businessmen and women, celebrities and foreign service officers representing each of the sixteen NATO nations. As the bossa nova of Stan Getz livened the air with the sounds of saxophones and brushed snares, the ambassador's guests helped themselves to Italian wine, saucy hors d'oeuvres and polite conversation.

Robert Thomas Hamilton, a man known to his friends as Malibu, stood alone in the far corner of the east reception room feeling uneasy and looking at a seascape by Emilio Gola. The picture was entitled "Spiaggia di Alassio," and Robert did not know why he was studying it so intensely, except that it gave him the prop he needed to avoid the uncomfortable ritual of socializing. From time to time, he glanced about the large room, looked at the beige sculpted marble, the Murano glass chandeliers, and the faces and body language of the dignitaries.

Most of the people appeared natural, laughing, talking and tasting, as if they had come of age within social circles and possessed innate charm. But not Robert. He thought of the many places he would rather be, and how, were it not for his job with the *Washington Post*, he would never subject himself to such demoralizing affairs.

He turned back to the Gola and wondered why the woman sitting on the beach in the foreground of the painting wore a white dress while those around her wore dark bathing suits. She, too, looked out of place, and for a moment Robert liked the painting. He smiled to himself and took a drink of orange juice.

"Had Emilio not died so young, his name would be synonymous with Picasso or Rembrandt." A sweet voice from behind caught Robert's attention.

Without turning to see who was speaking, he answered: "But it says here that he lived to be seventy-two." He pointed to the artist's brief biography hanging next to the work and then turned to see Diana Sillito, a model-turned-actress whose startling beauty translated well in any country.

"See what I mean," she said.

Her million-dollar smile made the journalist self-conscious. He had seen the same smile many times in magazines and movies, but there was something unsettling about seeing it for the first time in person, a feeling of nervous delight. He found himself using both hands to steady his drink. His posture felt awkward.

"My name's Diana Sillito," she said. Her voice was animated with personality. She extended her jeweled hand, a hand so ornate Robert was not sure whether to shake it or kiss the rings.

"I know." He settled for the less chivalrous of the two gestures. "My name's—"

"Don't they call you Malibu?"

"—Malibu," he finished, flattered that she knew his nickname. "How did you know?"

"I like to think I'm not your average cardboard starlet." Diana rolled her eyes and shook her head. Her face looked funny, yet it was bright with character and elegance, and Robert swore that her sculpted hair moved in slow motion just as it did in the shampoo commercials. "I've read all your stuff."

"You mean fluff."

"And you're so humble."

"Not really," he said, continuing to study her face. He believed she was more beautiful in person, and he had never before met a celebrity who was. "You can't afford to be humble when you're a journalist. Confidence bordering on arrogance. That's the secret."

"I've heard the same said about actors." She appeared sincerely interested in what Robert had said.

"Then what happened to you?"

"To me?"

"You don't seem too arrogant."

"That's because you don't know me. Yet."

"Sounds portentous." He smiled and winked and took an uneasy sip of juice, surprised by his own audacity. *Portentous? Where did that come from? Pompous and awkward, not to mention forward*, he thought and hoped she would not pick up on it.

"You talk like you write," she said with a laugh timed to overcome the uncomfortable moment.

Robert was impressed that she chose to let his remark drop, and he was flattered that she knew his work well enough to venture such a comment. He was also relieved when a white-tied waiter, bearing a sterling silver compote brimming with caviar, interrupted long enough to let him reorganize his thoughts.

"What are you doing in Rome?" he asked when the waiter left. Diana had been as friendly to the man as she was to Robert, and the journalist had the impression that her sweet personality was genuine.

"The Girl from Ipanema," she said excitedly.

"What?"

"They're playing 'The Girl from Ipanema.' Come dance with me." She took Robert's hand, and he followed with a reluctant step before admitting that he didn't know the first thing about dancing, especially the formal kind of dancing that these occasions demanded. "It's easy," she persisted, taking the glass of orange juice from his hand and leading him to the marble floor next to the ebony grand piano. "Like making love to music."

"Excuse me?" he laughed.

"You heard me. Just put your hands here—and—here. Now move slowly, like this, from side to side, and let the music fill your mind and—"

"I'm beginning to understand," Robert smiled and looked down on her small, gently curved nose and high tanned cheekbones. "But you still haven't answered my question."

"Your question?"

"What you're doing here in Rome."

"A remake of *The Agony and the Ecstasy*. How about you?" she asked, and then, with a shake of her gorgeous mane and a deep breath, interrupted before he could answer. "No. I promised myself I wouldn't play games. I mean, I know exactly what you're doing. You're covering the conference of the North Atlantic Assembly."

"I'm impressed."

"See, I *do* read your articles." The expression on her face was proud, a combination of delight in her correct pronouncement and her determination not to be so coy. "In fact," she continued, "I'll even admit that I read this morning's international edition and your front-page story about the debate over the Strategic Defense Initiative."

The cynical journalistic-muse harbored in Robert was taken aback by her apparent knowledge. Nine out of every ten people he spoke with called the Initiative by its media-driven name—Star Wars.

"And what did you think?" he asked as his hand caressed the smooth silk jumpsuit and the finely toned muscles of her back.

"You're as good a writer as you are a dancer."

"I don't know how to take that."

"A compliment, like it was intended. But tell me, do you think they'll ever come to an agreement?"

"Who?"

"The allies." She placed her head softly against his chest, and Robert could smell the sweet combination of fragrances in her hair and perfume. "I mean, will they ever allow the system to be deployed?" she continued. "They all wanted American money for research and development, but can they afford to see the satellites in place? If nuclear war becomes obsolete, won't it be impossible for the Europeans to build up conventional defenses to match the Soviet Union?"

Robert Hamilton was bewildered. To the stirring jazz of Stan Getz on the dance floor, Diana Sillito had summarized three days of debate, the same debate that prolonged the military session of the conference this evening, backed up the plenary session by three hours, and threw the ambassador's reception off schedule. He could think only to answer.

"They'll have to come to an agreement," he said. "They've come too far."

"Too far?" she looked into his eyes.

"The Americans claim the Alliance has the upper hand. It certainly has the advanced technology," he said.

"But not the support of the people."

"Maybe not completely. But the Americans will be able to sell the idea."

"How?"

"Economics," Malibu answered.

"Economics?"

"Think about it." He gently brushed a wave of Diana's hair over her shoulder. "Nuclear deterrence is cheap, especially when compared to conventional defenses. But those in favor of the Initiative say the satellite defense will be cheaper in the long run—like nuclear missiles, a necessary evil to keep the peace at the lowest price possible.''

When he finished, Robert was proud that he had stated the situation so succinctly. He impressed even himself, doubted Diana would follow, and expected a simple nod.

"But there's still disagreement," she persisted.

"Some of it's propaganda by the East. Moscow's scared to death of the technology."

"But it's not all propaganda."

"I think a lot of it comes from the fact that the Americans seemed to make the decision unilaterally. When President Reagan announced the plan, back in '83, he took NATO by surprise. It was an insult to the allies, and it's taken them time to forget."

"Maybe they still haven't."

"It's getting better. All the Western countries have shared in the technology. Like you said, they all got research and development money. In fact, the question now is whether or not to deploy the system."

Diana leaned back and looked into his eyes. "You really believe we're that close?"

"Think about it. Since the eighties, we've had BMEWS in Alaska, Greenland, and—"

"BMEWS?" she asked.

"I'm sorry—Ballistic Missile and Early Warning Systems. We've got another in Fylingsdale, England. One under construction in Iceland, and maybe even covert, smaller stations elsewhere. And that's the first link in SDI technology—the systems for surveillance and tracking."

"But you need some kind of weapon, don't you?"

"That's where I have my own theories."

"And?"

"They're boring."

"No, really."

"I couldn't stand to watch your eyes glaze over."

"They won't glaze. I promise."

"Well," Robert began slowly, "you understand that Phase One in the SDI program was under way back in the eighties—and—" he grinned a doubtful grin. "Are you really interested in this?"

Diana nodded. "More than you'll ever know," she said. "Tell me about Phase One." She tightened her arms around his shoulders.

"It was a kinetic kill program, to use nonnuclear missiles to intercept incoming warheads. It required more than a hundred satellites and, consequently, would have been detected too easily, if deployed—something that our government didn't want, or couldn't afford, especially as Reagan and company made headway with the Soviets on arms control talks—" He paused to see her absorbing every word.

"And?" she said.

"Well, I've been watching through the years, and it's possible with the breakthroughs in laser technology—and remember superconductivity back in '88—that we were able to skip deployment of Phase One, except for the radar stations and surveillance satellites, and move right into Phases Two and Three."

"You mean deployment?"

"It's only a theory," Robert reassured. "But with lasers, you wouldn't need as many satellites. They could be smaller—especially with frictionless superconductors for energy—and maybe, just maybe, you could begin deployment without anyone knowing."

"That's—" she began with a dubious look.

"Like I said, it's only a theory." He backed down, then added, "Though I don't think I'm alone."

"But if we're that far along, why all the controversy?"

"First, because no one knows for sure. Speculation and uncertainty always breed controversy. Then there's the question of need. After the peaceful revolution in the Eastern Bloc—the democratization of Poland, Hungary, and others—some believe the system's useless, a waste of money. Especially with the improving relationship between the Soviet Union and the U.S."

"Maybe that it will threaten the progress."

"Exactly. But there's also real concern among the allies—"

"One more song," Diana interrupted as the saxophone trailed off "The Girl from Ipanema" and stated the theme for "Misty." She tightened her grip on Robert and then apologized for cutting him off. "There's concern among the allies?"

Malibu was enchanted, but continued without saying so. Her eyes were bewitching, even passionate while he spoke of subjects that often bored even him. "Concern that since most of the technology and money has been American, we'll see it as our program. We'll want to run it—use it according to our needs. The Europeans fear that the more it's developed and implemented, the more it will become buried in the U.S. government bureaucracy.''

Diana nodded complete comprehension, then again placed her head on his chest and through a stirring guitar solo said nothing. "But when President Reagan started the program fifteen years ago,'' she finally began without looking up, "he promised that America would not only share the technology with the allies, but with the East.''

"You've also followed this for some time,'' Robert said with a cocked head.

"So far we haven't offered the Soviet Union a thing, and if we do, and if your theory's correct, that would eliminate nuclear deterrence.''

"Mutually assured destruction.''

"With that gone, NATO would require stronger conventional forces. Wouldn't that be more money? And could the Socialist countries of Europe keep up with the Soviet Union's standing forces? Their money's already committed to domestic programs, not to the military.''

Robert laughed in disbelief.

"So tell me about the *The Agony and the Ecstasy*,'' he said, feeling a sense of guilt for the ignorant stereotype he attached to the Beautiful People, at least until tonight. From this moment on, he vowed to read the newsstand tabloids with greater respect.

"Don't make fun of me,'' Diana said as she dropped her head back onto his chest. Her voice was sweet. Again, her golden-brown hair fanned out on Robert's black tuxedo and fell gently onto the padded shoulders of her suit.

"I wouldn't—I'm not—I mean your insight impresses me,'' he said. "I generally don't find people who understand geopolitics—not as well as you, anyway.''

"These things are important to me. They should be important to everyone.'' She looked up and paused long enough to study Robert's expression. He was staring into her warm brown eyes. "Too many people think that if you're an actress, interested in anything more than a few good lines, you're a militant.'' She shook her head. "I'm hardly that way—not the protester type. Besides, I did graduate work in political science at USC.''

Robert's expression begged her to continue, but again she let the music sweep them silently across the dance floor before saying a word.

"Daddy's chairman of the department."

"Daddy?" he said. "Dwight Sillito's your father?" His surprise burst so suddenly that he worried he might have offended the woman.

"Do you know him?" She sounded flattered.

"Doesn't everyone?"

"He does get around," she said. "In fact, lately I think he's been on television more than I have. I'm not jealous or anything. I only wish he weren't so liberal."

The music stopped and the mellifluous "Misty" was replaced by the "One-Note Samba."

"You're the conservative?" he asked as they walked from the floor toward the bar.

"They say it comes with money," she answered and picked up a glass of white wine. Robert ordered straight orange juice. "God bless Daddy. He tried to raise me the best he could. His mistake was letting me drop out before my Ph.D. He said I'd have plenty of time for my dissertation when I'm old and wrinkled—that while people were still interested I should pursue my hobby—keep my day job—you know."

"I'm impress—" Robert began, suddenly challenged by the woman, only happy that she had not played the uppish game of asking where he had taken his degree. But before he could continue, he was interrupted by a small man sporting tie-dyed hair and wearing a silk jabot flowing over a burgundy velvet dinner jacket.

"Dear Diana," the man said, "where have you been? You're missing the most influential people and the most gorgeous foreign correspondent for CBS"—he stopped speaking long enough to take a sip of champagne—"people who would do wonders for your career. Remember, you're never at the top, dear. You're never at the top." The man glanced at Robert with the same expression he might give a longshoreman. It was apparent to the reporter that Diana was embarrassed by the intrusion, but for the sake of etiquette she remained pleasant.

"Mr. Malibu," she began, smiling uneasily.

"Hamilton," Robert corrected. When she had called him by his nickname earlier, he took it for granted that she knew his real name.

"Bob Hamilton." He extended his hand to the small man. "People just call me Malibu."

"This is my agent, Teddy Silverman."

"Where on earth did you get the moniker Malibu?" asked the agent. He took another sip of champagne. "Are you a surfer?"

Robert withdrew his hand and again steadied his orange juice. "Actually, I was raised by a sailor in Norfolk, Virginia. I've never seen Malibu."

"A seaman! And you a foundling," said the agent. "How quaint." He turned to Diana. "Listen, girl, I say we go over and check out the boy from CBS."

Robert could feel a prickle of heat flush his face. His first impulse was to squash the little man like a boll weevil, or, better yet, to burn him like a tick. *The power of the press*, he thought. He had never used it for spite, but there was always a first time. He could destroy this man's career. He knew he could, but he knew he would not. Instead, he looked away. He looked to Diana, and then to the crowded room. He examined his options for a face-saving escape. There was no one else he wanted to talk to. Leaving early would be a breach of etiquette, even for a journalist. But he could not stand alone, especially not after the derision by this cab chaser, and besides, he had run out of paintings to examine.

"Mr. Hamilton," a strong voice from behind caught Robert's attention. He turned to face a young Marine.

"Yes?"

"I'm sorry to interrupt, sir, but Senator Watenburg phoned from the Ambasciatori Hotel. He says he needs you there immediately. Says it's important, sir."

Hamilton looked from the officer to the actress and her agent, pleased that his exit would be so clean.

"We have an embassy limo and a police escort waiting out front," the Marine continued. "Please hurry, sir."

"Right now," said Robert, stepping to follow the young sergeant, but Diana's hand caught his elbow, and he glanced back at the beautiful woman.

"Thank you," she said and nodded a gesture of disapproval toward her agent. "I'm sorry."

"Don't be," Malibu answered. His voice was confident and his spirit lively after the ego-gratifying interruption. He was wanted by a United States senator, and without another word, he turned and followed the officer through the crowd and into the entrance hall, stopping only to shake the ambassador's hand and thank him for a wonderful evening.

"But you're leaving so soon," Markum objected. "It's only a little past one."

"Duty calls."

"At least tell me you had a good time."

"Great time."

"Did that actress, Miss Sillito, find you?" Markum asked as he held Robert's arm and accompanied him to the door.

"She did."

"Good. She asked about you the moment she came in. Said she couldn't remember your name, but knew you worked for the *Post*.

"She did call me Malibu?"

The ambassador laughed. "That's probably my fault," he said. "I should have told her your full name, but I've always known you as Malibu myself."

"That's fine," Robert said and walked out into the cold night. A stretch Cadillac was polished and idling. The Marine was talking to the chauffeur, who was standing with the rear door opened and waiting for the journalist.

"To the Ambasciatori. Immediately," said the sergeant. "Take security route three and return by the Via Pinciano to the Via Veneto. And, sir," he spoke to Robert, "the senator said to meet him in room four-eleven."

"Four-eleven?"

"Yes, sir." The guard snapped a salute.

Malibu walked past the chauffeur, around the car to the front door opposite the driver. The chauffeur slammed the back door and took his place behind the wheel, but before he could put the car in motion, a tap sounded on Robert's window, and the journalist looked up to see the smiling eyes of Diana. He opened the door.

"Great! You're coming with me," he said.

"I wish you could stay a little longer."

"You haven't consulted your agent on that one."

"Teddy's Teddy. I apologize. He probably has a crush on you." She looked away to a golden-lit fountain beneath the bell tower. "It seems as though we're always competing for the same men."

This time there was no mistaking. Robert knew it was an overture. A naked, almost anxious, proposition.

"Listen," she continued after an uncomfortable pause. "I know you have to rush, but I want to clear something up."

"Don't worry about Teddy." Robert smiled and took her hand.

"Not Teddy," she quickly corrected. "I just wanted to let you know that when I said you didn't know me yet—"

"Yes?" Robert could feel his stomach swelling, but he was not certain whether it was from embarrassment for what he had said earlier or from the anticipation for what he hoped she would say.

"It was portentous," she said quickly, kissed him on the cheek, and walked away.

Chapter Two

"European women marry prestige. They marry power and position long before they marry good looks or even personality," said Senator Grayson Watenburg. He extended his neck and twitched his head to the left, one of the many idiosyncrasies that Malibu had come to know over the eighteen-year friendship between the two men. "But after a year or two of marriage, power and position can't keep them home at night. They'll start to wander. Find a stud auto mechanic. Put the twinkle back in their eye." He rubbed his large nose. "That's why I'm not surprised she's out when her husband bites the big one."

Bites the big one? Robert thought. A United States Senator using the argot of the street surprised him, but he wrote the words in his notebook anyway. At the same time, he studied the eyes of the man he had known for so many years. They were cold.

Watenburg's apparent irreverence for death disturbed Hamilton. It disturbed him even more given the circumstances of the bloody scene that surrounded them.

Robert had arrived two minutes earlier to find the senator sitting on the edge of the hotel room bathtub with his chin resting on his hands, like a little boy waiting on the curb for the school bus. In front of the senator was a scene that bothered the reporter, even with his beat-calloused mind-set.

Malibu believed there were degrees of murder. The cause, the location, and the manner of death always determined the effect. To cover a story about a pimp riddled with bullet holes on Washington's Fourteenth Street was one thing, but to visit the scene of a grisly double-murder in a regal suite of the most exclusive hotel in Rome was quite another—especially when the dead included Hans Peterson, a conservative party leader and member of West Germany's Bundesrat, and another, unidentified man.

"Her side of the bed hasn't been touched. She probably hasn't slept with him since they got to Italy," Watenburg continued. "I doubt he cared. He was a great man. A good politician. Probably didn't even notice she's been gone. That's the way they live after a while."

"How do you know she didn't kill him," Robert asked, "if European couples are so estranged?"

"I didn't say they were estranged." The senator loosened the belt on his Burberry overcoat. "Statistics say marriages on this side of the Atlantic last longer than marriages on our side. There's just greater marital freedom—a morally casual attitude—a sense of acceptance."

"Gray, I think you're ethnocentric."

"Ethnocentric?"

"Ethnocentric." Malibu forced a smile so his words would not be offensive but his point taken. "And I'm going to do you a favor by not quoting your limited knowledge of matrimonial science."

"Preferential treatment?" Watenburg asked with a twisted smile.

"Just say we've been friends a long time."

"Could you have done that to your husband?" the senator asked. His smile faded into disgust as he pointed to the dead man on the bed. "Could you have cut his neck, watched the blood stain the front of the silk pajamas you gave him last Christmas, and then listen to him choke to death on his own blood and vomit?"

"Come on, Grayson," Malibu objected. "You can try, but you're not that hard." He wrote the word "vomit" in his notebook anyway and continued to look at the pale face of the dead German legislator. It was stiff and disfigured. The conflicting impulses he felt inside his conscience bothered him. At once he was both amazed and repulsed— amazed by the scene that was so bizarre it represented a once-in-a-lifetime opportunity for a political reporter, a scene he wanted to commit to memory—repulsed by its hideous reality. His confusion was only compounded by Watenburg's brazen attitude. For a very brief moment, while Malibu's analytical mind scurried unchecked by his professional discernment and personal knowledge, he went as far as suspecting the two-term senator. But just as quickly, he dismissed the thought.

"Believe me, she didn't kill him," Grayson continued. "She couldn't have killed both of them."

"Then did he?" Malibu pointed to the other body, a middle-aged man who lay spread-eagle on the bathroom floor, clutching a glass syringe with a two-inch needle. At the base of the man's skull, a pearl-handled stiletto protruded and was stained with blood made thick by mixing and coagulating with his long graying hair. The blade was buried deep into the cervical vertebrae, and reminded Robert of a matador's sword, placed with an experienced hand.

"Maybe," Watenburg answered. He craned his neck again and then loosened his tie. "You know more about murder than I do. Millions of motives. Millions of madmen."

"You seem so aloof, I'm not sure," said Robert. He noted the dark blond hair of the slain German and scribbled it in his slender note pad. "You're awfully collected. Do you know the other man?"

The senator shook his head no. "I owe it all to Saigon," Grayson said, "to Saigon and five years on the Council." He paused long enough to unbutton his collar. "Look, I'd better get you out of here. I gotta call security. You've seen enough. I've seen enough. You know this isn't going to help my career. I'm in my election cycle, and there will always be conspiracy nuts who'll think I had something to do with this."

"If you're worried about that, why did you call me? In a case like this, press could be your worst enemy."

"Or my best friend," Watenburg said. "That's why I called. It's speculation that kills political careers, not fact."

"I guess that depends on the politician." Malibu looked back at Peterson's body.

"There's a reason he was killed," the senator continued.

"Speculation?"

"Don't be an ass. At least until you know what I know."

"Sorry." Robert was embarrassed about his disrespectful quip.

"This evening, before they convened the full session of the Military Committee, Hans and I were collaborating on our testimony— expecting the debate on the Strategic Defense Initiative to heat up, especially with the Dutch Socialists. Ever since President Satterfield's budget for deployment made it past Congress, the European liberals have seen the writing on the wall. Too much has already been invested, and despite the thaw, SDI is the future. Now all the politicians who haven't supported it from the start are beginning to cry that it's going to kill a decade of diplomacy—that somehow the Soviet clemency toward Poland, Hungary, East Germany, and Czechoslovakia is based on newfound humanitarianism rather than economic necessity. It's asinine to believe the communist threat isn't real. Just look around you.''

"It's a little more complex than that," Robert said. His mind quickly recalled fragments of the conversation with Diana. The SDI question was a question of economics. It would make the East and the West dependent once again on conventional forces, and the Dutch, who had put so much of their money since World War II into social programs, would not be able to finance an army, especially without a political crisis. The people had come to enjoy the government as their caretaker. This was the controversy faced by many of the European nations.

"That's why Hans and I were meeting—to frame our arguments. We met downstairs in the restaurant to go over our notes. Twenty minutes later, he was complaining about a migraine. Said he had some pills in his room." Watenburg paused long enough to pull his shirt away from his chest. "He never came back. I figured he was sick and went on without him. When the session ended, I dressed for the ambassador's party. I was already downstairs in the car when I thought I'd check on him—see how he was feeling. That's the story.''

"Why call me?"

"Who else could I call, Malibu? You're the most objective man I know. Despite your profession. And that's what I need right now. I can't be associated with rumors about this. You understand. You've got to find out what happened here, especially before—"

"Before people start to speculate.''

"Damn right, before they jump to their own conclusions.''

Again Malibu looked back to the dead men. The blood was beginning to darken into crust. He was tired, and the scene was confusing. For a moment, he believed he would never be able to find the answers he needed. Then he dismissed the defeating thought and attributed it to the early morning hour. He would feel better with some sleep.

"Does anybody else know?" Robert asked.

"About Hans?"

"Yes."

Grayson shrugged his shoulders. "The killer."

"I mean anyone you spoke with."

"You're the first. The hotel's empty. Everyone's at the Villa."

"How did you get inside?"

"The room?"

Robert nodded his head.

"The door wasn't latched shut. When I knocked, it opened. I came in."

"You just walked in?"

"For a minute, I panicked. I wanted to leave. But I couldn't." Watenburg rubbed his eyes and then his nose. "I have to count on you, Malibu. You've got the story, and as far as I'm concerned, it's the most important damn story you'll ever have." He pointed to the dead German. "Somebody's wish came true tonight. I don't know whose it was, but I don't want to be next on his list. And least of all do I want this to ruin my career."

"You think this is related to SDI?"

"I don't know. I don't want to know." Suddenly, the senator's face dropped into the emotionless glaze that accompanies deep thought.

"What?" Robert asked.

"Nothing. I'm just thinking."

"About?"

"Nothing. I guess a guy could go crazy thinking about what happened here tonight."

"And why it happened."

Grayson nodded. "And why," he repeated.

"There are a lot of people who might want him dead. He was one of West Germany's leading parliamentarians. He was one of the most popular members of the Christian Democrats." Malibu wrote the word "Chancellor" in his notebook.

"You've got to promise me."

"I'll write whatever I find," said Robert. "You've got my word, but what did you say that drug was called? Sulfa—"

"Sulfazine. It's a pyrogenic. Easy to make—a form of sulfur suspended in peach oil. You can smell it." The senator inhaled deeply.

"Doctors used it sixty or seventy years ago to treat malaria. Some of our mental hospitals used it in the twenties to treat schizophrenia."

"And you know he was injected?" Malibu asked, looking at Peterson's body.

"You have the needle in that guy's hand." Grayson pointed to the man on the floor. "You can't mistake the odor. And look at Hans." He turned back to the German. "Look at his face. It's frozen in pain. His hands look arthritic, his fingers twisted. He was in terrible pain. That's sulfazine. It racks your body. You convulse. You vomit. Your temperature rises forty degrees. The pain is so intense you become disoriented. You lose voluntary movement of your muscles as they spasm against the chemicals and heat."

"Chemical interrogation?"

"Not really. It's just the pain is so intense, you can get anyone to say about anything you want."

"You know an awful lot about the drug." Malibu wrote an abbreviated version of the senator's description in his book.

"You worked for the National Security Council, too," Grayson said. "You should know about sulfazine. It was part of our training. It's used by the Soviet Ministry of Internal Affairs, in their psychiatric hospitals."

"Then this *could* be KGB," said Robert as he scribbled the acronym.

"Maybe," said Watenburg. He pulled his tie from his neck, snapped out the knot, and buried it in the left-hand pocket of his overcoat. "Maybe GRU. If it's related to SDI, Soviet military intelligence would be very involved." Again Grayson's face became void of expression. His stare was deep but hollow. Malibu was about to say something when the senator continued. "But I'm not sure." He took a deep breath. "I'm not sure of anything except that I drew the short straw coming here. I should have gone straight to the reception."

Malibu wanted to console the senator. The man's steely façade was wearing thin, and Robert wished he could tell him that everything would turn out fine. But he knew he couldn't. He knew that whatever motivated these murders still existed, whether it was one man or a group of men. Political executions, especially when carried out with such precision, are seldom random and never impulsive. A part of him actually feared for Grayson Watenburg, and because he feared he was going to let the senator's reference to the National Security Council drop without comment.

Otherwise, Malibu's association with the NSC was a taboo subject. Everyone knew better than to bring it up in front of the journalist, and Grayson was no exception, especially because no one understood the dynamics behind Robert's final days with the Council and his stormy resignation better than the senator. Because those same dynamics earned Watenburg a promotion within the NSC and eventually his office on Capitol Hill.

Hamilton was an undergraduate student at George Mason University in Fairfax, Virginia, when he first became involved with the National Security Council. He was studying journalism and earned a declassified internship with the organization in the basement of the Old Executive Office Building next to the White House. Eight months before graduation, he was offered a full-time position as a public affairs officer, and he accepted. Within four years, he climbed to the post of deputy assistant press secretary, where he spent most of his time preparing trial balloons—news stories to test public reaction before a decision became official or an action was taken.

One balloon he was asked to float concerned the Nicaraguan decision of 1978. Public opinion was divided over support for Anastasio Somoza, the man whose family had ruled the Central American country for forty-five years, and support for the Sandinistas, the revolutionaries who were seen by many as poetic liberators. Traditionally, America had been an ally of the Somozas, staunch anticommunists, but under the direction of Jimmy Carter, the United States began to question Anastasio, scold him, and finally cut him off from the economic aid and military assistance that had been his family's lifeblood.

Carter knew his Central American policy was popular with the Left but offensive to the Right, and the latter was raising its seldom-heard voice, and the President was quickly finding himself in a no-win position. His popularity waned and then fell to a record low in the opinion polls. Meanwhile, his secretary of state drew the ire of editorialists across the country, and rumors spread that the President's national security advisor would resign. While the Sandinistas were celebrating in the streets of Managua, there was a crisis on the National

Security Council in Washington, and into this conundrum Hamilton was thrust with his pen to discern the shifting winds of public opinion. A simple trial balloon would allow the White House to check the conscience of America, to determine how far the country would go to support the Ortega brothers and their revolution.

The majority of the information Malibu used for the press release was given to him by then Lt. Col. Grayson Watenburg from conditionally released National Security Council directives that came to the Executive Office Building by way of CIA headquarters in Langley, Virginia. From its primary source, the information was taken from Foreign Intelligence Reports—information gathered by field officers from paid agents, local politicians, scientists, economists and military leaders. It was also gathered by technical eavesdropping and photographic surveillance. But most of the information, eighty percent of it, was taken from overt sources like political and military journals, speeches by government leaders and other public documents. Despite the drama of Forsyth and Ludlum, and the do-or-die mentality of the spooks engaged in the business, the information that was passed back and forth under the red-stamped warning of "Top Secret" was the same information reported on page sixteen of the *Washington Post*, and NSC information was often two weeks behind and less accurate.

However, the National Security Council took its job seriously, as Robert Hamilton discovered when he prepared the trial balloon suggesting the Carter Administration was considering reversing its policy of support for the Sandinistas. As planned, information placed into the article, as well as the thesis, was leaked to the media before the President had supposedly approved the final draft. The public outcry forced the White House to issue a complete disclaimer, to vow "corrective measures against the perpetrators of such mendacious nonsense," and to call for the resignation of Robert Thomas Hamilton.

Grayson had carried out his directive with flying colors and eventually became the Central American field director. The Administration got what it wanted: information about how the public would respond to the reversal of policy without having to claim it as policy.

Malibu was the fall guy.

"Why did I have to find him?" Grayson asked.

The senator's façade was now gone completely and Malibu could see the torment and fear inside.

"The worst part is that he really was a friend."

Robert looked again at Peterson's body. Mutilated was not too strong a word for what he saw. The face of death was contorted with pain. The eyes were opened but disoriented and frozen in a gaze that reminded him of a blind man. For a very brief moment, he allowed himself to feel, and he was suddenly filled with the nausea of reality. The smell of sulfazine became overwhelming, and he felt himself growing light-headed. But just as quickly as the feeling came, he forced it to leave. He looked at the man on the floor. The face was not visible, and neither the senator nor the journalist dared disturb the scene.

Aside from the death around him, Malibu's next concern, whether it was born of his professional instincts or of his compassion for another human being, was for the woman, Peterson's wife. Where was she? Had she been taken? Did she already know? Was she involved? And how could she be contacted?

He gave little credit to Watenburg's suggestion that her life was disengaged from the dead man on the bed, and he was obsessed with questions, an occupational hazard of journalism. But this time he wanted to believe his obsession was not directed by a front-page byline, but by an emotion more humane. In a way, he wanted to believe that Grayson was right, that the woman was out all night, cheating, enjoying herself, and shellacking the emotions she was bound to feel when she identified the body of her husband. But something inside of him warned that that was not the case.

"What are you going to tell security—the police?

"What I told you. The truth."

"If they ask why you called a reporter first?"

"You're my friend."

"I can't sit on this story."

"I don't want you to. Better for me if you tell it." The senator took off his coat. It was apparent that he planned to stay for awhile. "You'd better get out of here." Grayson moved Robert toward the door. "I have to call security. I'd better call the Italian cops."

"You better let both embassies know." Robert slapped his notebook shut and placed it in the inside breast pocket of his tuxedo. "And you might want to call Senator Ashworth. In fact, you might want to call him first. He's president of the North Atlantic Assembly. He's got a right to know what happened at his conference."

Grayson took a deep breath. "It'll probably come as welcome news," he said as he exhaled. "Ashworth's been fighting SDI from day one. Hans was the European demon."

"Come on, Gray," said Robert. "Give Ashworth some credit." He looked deep into the senator's eyes. They were dark, and every wrinkle of his fifty years creased deep under the pressure he was feeling.

"Just watch him," Grayson said with a passing tone that told Malibu he did not want to answer any more questions. But the journalist could not let the statement drop.

"What do you mean?"

"Just what I said," Grayson answered. His voice was suddenly sharp.

"Watch him for what?"

"You'd better take off."

"Watch him for what?"

"It's late. I'll talk to you later."

"Watch him for what?" Robert demanded.

Grayson opened the door and pressed Malibu into the hall. "The roots on this one may be deeper than both of us understand, or even care to understand. Just do the best you can."

"Come straight with me, Grayson."

"I can't. Not now. I've told you what I can."

"But you—"

"I said something I shouldn't have. That's all."

"I'll hound you tomorrow."

"I'll answer tomorrow."

"Swear to me."

"I swear."

Robert turned his back and moved toward the elevator. The senator closed the door behind him. But before the journalist could get to the elevator Grayson opened the door again.

"Hey, Malibu," he whispered loud enough to get his friend's attention. Robert stopped and looked back at him. The senator's face was burdened with the events that were to come. "Thanks."

"For what?"

"For giving me time to think."

The door closed again.

Chapter Three

"To choose the victim, to prepare the strike with circumspection, to satisfy one's implacable revenge, and then to go to bed—there's nothing sweeter in this world." Joseph Stalin's words echoed in the mind of Sergio Castillo Armando as he sat at the corner table in the Cafe Giorgi. The small establishment was dark and crowded, warmed by the bodies of too many people. It was located in the Piazza Navona, across the way from a toy store that already had Nativity decorations in the picture window.

"Nothing sweeter in this world," Sergio's mind involuntarily repeated the thought over and over. At first, he had found the quote difficult to remember. The words came to him sound bite by sound bite, the phrases disjointed and awkward, as to a child learning the alphabet. As he moved furtively through the halls of the Ambasciatori Hotel, his mind struggled to remember what he had learned by rote over twenty-five years before, when he received advanced terrorist training at Doupov, the special camp run by the Soviet GRU in the deep forest thirty miles south of Karlovy Vary. But now, as he sat in the stuffy cafe, holding a demitasse, he could not shut the words out. Like a song carried through the day, they flooded his head in rhythmic aria, flowing from the mysterious memory banks that preserve this kind of information.

In the beginning, Sergio wanted to remember the words, because remembering made his action easier to understand—more conscionable. He tried to follow the philosophy of Nechayev, the nineteenth-century Russian nihilist. He tried to "stifle within himself all considerations of kinship, love, even honor, and know only the science of destruction.'' Still, he had to answer his conscience that often damned his atrocities, especially like the one he had just committed. He had to remind himself that Hans Peterson was the enemy, and he was taking revenge, not for himself, but for the people—the same mass of humanity that dictated all of his actions. His life was the people's tool, to do their will despite the consequences to his victims, to his associates, even to his spirit.

Sergio placed the cup of strong coffee to his lips to detect the heat before sipping. It was too hot, but he drank anyway. The taste was bitter and burned, the aroma was slightly noxious, but the liquid felt good going down, warming the inside of his body. Stalin's words still played in his head, now taunting him, challenging him, and keeping the scene in the German's room alive. For a moment he wished he had not coaxed the quote from its innocuous resting place in his mind, because with it came the malaise of too many memories and the lost and angry years of his youth spent in a French prison. Locked in a maximum security cell for fifteen years, he lapsed in and out of depression, keeping a daily journal on the walls around him and writing hostile poetry with a used wooden match on a bar of soap.

Prison was the result of indiscretion, of arrogant immaturity when impulse overrode reason. Under the sidewalk umbrellas of a popular night club on the Left Bank of the Seine, he bragged to a female acquaintance that he was Doblin, the commander of the Movimiento de Acción Revolucionaria.

A street mime dressed in black and a face painted white entertained the early-evening patrons as Sergio drank one cognac after another and watched the eagerness behind the blue eyes of the woman he had met only days earlier. He told her how he had been hand-picked by the KGB to attend Patrice Lumumba University for Foreigners. He told her how he had been taught the principles of Marxism, the need for violence in throwing off the shackles of Western imperialism. He explained that terrorists are really everyday people who do not kill in anger or haste, nor on impulse or improvisation. They kill only as a matter of course, since that is their sole reason for being.

The girl appeared impressed as Sergio quoted passages from his demented bible, Carlos Marighella's book, the *Mini Manual for Urban Guerrillas*. ''What matters is not the identity of the corpse but the total impact the murder has on the audience,'' he said. ''The purpose of terrorism is to terrorize, or as Lenin wrote, 'The use of violence is deliberate and dispassionate, carefully engineered for theatrical effect, and it takes a lot of doing.' ''

Even in his younger years, as he spoke these words to the girl, Sergio struggled with the conflicting emotions that infected his spirit. He was not raised to be a terrorist. He was raised to be a priest. France and Rome were a long way from the dry and dirty barrios of Mexico City, where he had grown up under a widowed mother and with a brother who wore the collar. Terrorism was the antithesis of what he had been trained for in the Seminario Primero, where he received his elementary education.

In those days, anticipation filled the Castillo home. Most mothers prayed to the Virgin for only one son to become a priest. Honor on earth and glory in heaven belonged to the *mujer* who bore a *cura*. But to bear two, that was exaltation, and to insure her destiny, Señora Castillo was a ruthless matron of her sons' time. She seldom allowed them to socialize in anything other than church activities, and even then, she was careful about selecting the children her boys were allowed to play with. Age and independence made little difference in her attitude. After the oldest son took his final vows, she cajoled him into living at home, an obligation that earned him the title of ''Slum Priest.''

To Sergio, however, his brother's curse was his blessing. Night after night, he was tutored by his elder, and the knowledge he gained opened the door to La Universidad de Teología, a prestigious and sacred school that had denied entrance to the lesser-educated Slum Priest. But Sergio had the opportunity, and he wanted the collar more than anything in life. He knew it would demand hard work, but hard work did not scare him. Love of God and family, social responsibility, and Christian ethics were ingrained in his mind. At the age of fourteen, he had read the complete works of Erasmus, and while they kept him with a headache, and he often did not understand everything, he adopted *The Handbook of the Militant Christian* as his guide. He believed in the Renaissance philosopher: he was more concerned with the practice of Christ's teachings than with dogmatic ceremony. He wanted to share feelings and values, to touch lives and return errant souls to God. The fourteenth rule of the handbook was one he committed to memory: "We should not make the mistake of assuming that if we practice most of the virtues, it will then be permissible to have one or two small vices. The enemy you ignore the most usually is the one who conquers."

Ironically, it was also the fourteenth rule that Sergio broke.

The woman with the black hair was called Gabriela. There was no last name, at least not any that Sergio knew of. She was taller than most women, narrow at the waist, and inviting—even to a would-be priest. Sergio believed she would cause even a prelate to look twice. Her clothes, unlike those of other women in the park, were tailored, usually melting over her attractive body like the statue of Isis, in a tasteful but seductive way. Another woman would not have cast such a spell over the single-minded youth, but Gabriela seemed to frequent the plaza as often as Sergio, and she never averted the gaze of her round brown eyes when he glanced at her. Rather, she smiled a warm, friendly smile and nodded a pleasant hello. Her appearance was innocent, unwitting, maybe a little vulnerable, but it reached out, across the plaza, and took hold of the young man like a mechanic's vice.

Still, Sergio never pursued. He only buried his nose deeper into the works of Eusebius, or Kempis, or whomever he was reading that afternoon—though his mind was numbed to the words. Thoughts of her stifled his concentration. Some of the thoughts made him ashamed. She sparked his vanity. Without looking up, he could feel her watching him, and he found himself governing his actions accordingly—sitting up straight, strategically positioning his body and tilting his head so his most favorable side faced her. And he always kept his eyes uncovered by the book.

Then one day she spoke. Only a hello. But the words shook the young man's frame and drained him of common sense. When he did not answer, she continued to introduce herself, a foreign exchange student from Uruguay who was studying political science at the University of Mexico.

"I'm Sergio," he finally found words. "I'm studying," he paused, "history."

"Of the Church?" she asked.

"Of—just history."

"But your books. They are always about the Church. No?"

"Sometimes." He closed the book he held in his hand and looked at the title, hoping it would appear more secular than it was. *Early Christian Writings*. No such luck. "My brother is a priest. He gives me these books."

"How honorable," said Gabriela. She smiled and Sergio felt himself growing weak with emotion. "Does he want you to become a priest?"

"Maybe a little. I don't know."

"For a while, I thought you were studying at the seminary. Your books are always religious."

"Mine?" Sergio filled his voice with surprise. He was flattered that she had taken an interest in his plaza activities, but shaken that he had no defensible excuse as to why he was always reading religious literature. "Well, I had better tell the truth," he finally conceded. "I am studying for the priesthood. I'm six months away from entering the University of Theology."

"I knew you were." She smiled again and touched his hand. The simple gesture caused a sensual feeling that he had never felt before. Immediately his mind rambled over a penance: "*Por mi culpa, por mi culpa, por mi muchísima culpa*. For my guilt, for my guilt . . ." His smile fluttered and his eyes looked away from the girl. "Why didn't you say so in the first place?" she asked.

"I—" Sergio struggled for an answer but could not find one worthy of admitting either to himself or to Gabriela. "I don't know," he said. He wondered why she was pressuring him to answer an embarrassing question.

"Your covenant is against marriage, not friendship," she said before he could continue. "It is against sex, not association."

Sergio could not believe she had uttered the word. Like a bolt, the caution of Erasmus flashed in his brain: "Let us first consider lust. This is the first evil that attacks us. Its temptations are the strongest of all; its influence is the greatest. Lust drags more individuals to hell than any other vice." Why had she given birth to the thought—if she had, in fact, been the one to give it birth? Again he felt guilty. *God free me*, he pleaded inside, *deliver me from the feelings I feel now*. At first, he tried to follow the counsel of his mentors, to think of how rotten, how unclean, how unworthy of human dignity lust is. "It puts the divine in us on the level with animals,'' Erasmus had written. Sergio groped even further for the words: ''We are destined to be with angels, to commune eternally with God. Remember how rotten and perverted, how momentary and fleeting, how pregnant with remorse and guilt lust is.''

Sergio tried to remember. He tried again and again, but he had never experienced the titillation of sexual attraction, and he was vulnerable. At first, the romance between the two was slow and deliberate, but soon Gabriela led him step by step into a relationship that ended in psychological as well as physical dependence. Guilt bubbled through his soul with the pain of heat and desire for passion. He loved the woman, and it had not taken long. Maybe a month. Maybe two. But it happened, and no more did he listen to the temper of his mother. No more did he sit under the once-inspiring voice of his brother. No more did he return to the plaza to study. His books were surrendered to the wiles of Satan, and the exchange held him captive.

Sergio took another sip of coffee and looked at his watch. It was 2:18 AM. The cafe crowd was beginning to thin out, and for the first time he felt a cold draft from the opened door. He looked at the faces of the people standing around the bar, at the smiles of the patrons who were leaving, and thought about the pain in his own life, about Gabriela and what she would be doing now if she were still alive. Would she still love him as much as he loved her? Would she still be involved with the revolutionary underground? Or would they have married and settled down, dismissed their political activity as a whim of youth? He would never know the answers to these questions, though he thought of them often. They were lost the day he received the cable announcing her death, that she was killed by a bank security guard in New York City, following a botched hold-up, three days before Christmas, 1978.

Only four days earlier, it had been their mutual decision that Sergio would travel alone to Stockholm, to the rump Refugee Council in Apelbergsgatan to get Libyan financial assistance from Qaddafi's representatives in the ''People's Bureau.'' He would be gone two weeks, traveling on a Chilean passport scheduled to expire on New Year's Day. Gabriela would stay in the United States until he returned.

She would live in the communal warehouse in the Bronx shared by the Movimiento de Acción Revolutionaria and its North American sister, the Black September Organization.

Their brief separation was the first in thirteen years. After Gabriela led Sergio out of the barrios of Mexico to Russia's Patrice Lumumba University, the two traveled together, from East Berlin to South Yemen to Algeria to Cuba. In each of these countries they worked out of Soviet embassies, teaching the elementary principles of armed insurrection to guerrilla leaders of the Third World. In Cuba, they were stationed at Camp Matanazas, just outside Havana, where they engaged in advanced training in political indoctrination, sabotage, explosives and weaponry. It was at Matanzas where Sergio was introduced to the Soviet-made Tokarev 7.62 pistol, his preferred firearm.

From Cuba, they were sent to a mountain camp thirty-five miles from Pyongyang, the capital of North Korea. There they engaged in advanced terrorist training, mastering the techniques of arson, martial arts, assassination, extortion, ambush, disguise, clandestine travel, recruitment and communications. They stayed in North Korea for two years, working eighteen hour days, learning, teaching and practicing. Then, in March of 1969, they were sent back to Mexico and placed in the hierarchy of El Movimiento. They worked under the direction of the KGB Referentura at the Soviet embassy and planned Operation Leo, a high-risk plot to overthrow the Mexican government.

In 1971, the operation was exposed by Mexican authorities working closely with the Central Intelligence Agency. Thirty members of El Movimiento were captured and jailed for robbery, murder and attempted insurrection. Sergio and Gabriela managed to escape the arrests and fled to Cuba, where they planned a counterattack to free their comrades. On May 5, 1973, they returned to Mexico City and successfully kidnapped the American consul. They demanded an exchange. The Mexican government complied immediately and El Movimiento was back in business. The group moved to Cuba for three years, and then in 1976, as the Black September began to establish a larger base of operation in New York, Sergio moved his cadre to the United States.

But after the winter of '78 he never returned to America. After Gabriela's death, the terrorist stayed in Europe, traveling from Stockholm to Brussels to Bonn and Paris. Without the girl, his spirit was broken. His vision faded from the utopian objective of terrorism to the mundane necessities of living from day to day. Rather than the large, elaborate and daring operations of his years with Gabriela, he began to engage in petty bank robberies, forgeries and burglaries. His criminal record grew from country to country, not with feats of which he could be proud but with embarrassing mistakes and minor altercations with the law—until Paris, where the woman from INTERPOL listened to his confession as they sat outside the night club on the Left Bank.

Now, as he warmed himself in the Italian cafe and looked out the window at the golden-lit fountain by Bernini that stands in the middle of the Piazza Navona, Sergio thought about how foolish he had been in those years. He looked from the statue to the church across the way, and he thought about his time in prison and the misery of seeing himself for who he really was, a disheartened revolutionary whose life had become the antithesis of what it was going to be. The memories of his youth were intensified by the rising dome of the Church of Borromini and the statue of Saint Agnes on the top of the façade with her hand covering her breast. A light was on in the top room to the right of the black dome, and for a moment he wanted to go into that room and talk to whoever occupied it. He wanted to confess, to return to who he once was. But he knew he never could. God would never forgive him for what he had done, and, besides, he still had work to do before dawn.

Chapter Four

President Delbert Satterfield rocked back in his leather chair and propped his right knee on the edge of the imposing desk. In his right hand, he held a paper clip that he had bent out of shape and was using to clean the underside of his fingernails. Satterfield was new to the office, inaugurated only eleven months earlier.

Prior to his election, he had served as secretary of defense under George Bush, who occupied the White House for eight years. Satterfield served for both terms as top man in the Pentagon. Before he was appointed to the Cabinet, he served two terms as a congressman from Wyoming where he made a name for himself as a proponent of a strong national defense.

His philosophy continued as secretary of defense, when he struggled against antinuclear groups, religious organizations, and the liberal media to build the MX missile system. Political analysts and even conservative consultants believed his pronuclear voice and aggressive personality would be his demise as a presidential candidate, even though he had the support of Bush—a President whose calm exterior, caution, and noncombative character made him popular with both parties. Three political consultants dropped him before the convention, and only a handful of political action committees publicly supported his candidacy. Consequently, most of his campaign contributions came from the hinterlands of the country, from the silent majority who still believed in a strong America. These people loved Delbert Satterfield, referring to him as "Dusty." Because of the tough politi-

cal battles he had fought in his life, and despite the abuse he suffered from the press and special interest groups, these people voted for
him.

Sitting directly across the desk from the President, and slouching in
an overstuffed office chair, the chief of staff, Tab Skillman, was
leafing through the National Security Council's evening report. Skillman was Satterfield's most trusted friend, a man who had been at the
politician's side since his freshman year on Capitol Hill, and the
President watched as Tab's head of thick white hair shook slowly as he
read.

The mantel clock chimed the half hour.

"This is incredible," Skillman said without looking up. He turned
the page. "You just received this?"

"Fifteen minutes ago," said Satterfield. He stopped scraping his
nails long enough to look at his friend. "The boys at the NSC asked
me to cancel my dinner with Secretary Stevens to receive it. Spencer's
staff must have been working on it all day."

"I can't believe it's finished." Skillman continued to read. "Have
you known we were this close? Does anybody know it's done?"

"I knew we were getting close. Most of the funding came through
the Defense Department. All told, we spent over a hundred and eighty
billion dollars the eight years when we were in charge. But Spence is a
good national security advisor. Only he and a few of his men knew
exactly when it would be finished."

"What he's done is magnificent," said Skillman.

"There's good reason George had me keep him. He's handled this
whole project with the secrecy F.D.R. had when he developed the
bomb."

"How about the Soviets?"

"Hell," Satterfield laughed, "outside of the dozen or so we
launched from the southern hemisphere—from Australia and
Antarctica—they've watched us launch every one of those satellites,
and they haven't been able to prove a thing. When private industry
came into our space program, it was the greatest thing that could have
happened to us. The Kremlin thinks that by and large the launches
represented nothing more than a bunch of capitalists trying to make a
buck in space." Satterfield dropped his knee from the desk and sat
forward. "They've been watching us all along."

"They have to know what kind of satellites they are," Skillman said. "Surely their sizes and shapes would give them away."

"Not necessarily," Satterfield answered. "First they'd have to be able to see them. This program's almost fifteen years old—longer than it took Kennedy and Johnson to put a man on the moon. We've had some brilliant military scientists and project managers working on superconductivity and particle beams. And when that technology exploded—as it improved—our satellites changed, and we were able to move straight from the drawing board, past kinetic energy, to beam technology."

"I see that," agreed Tab, looking back to the report.

Still the President continued. "It's unbelievable what superconductivity and particle beams alone can do—how small the satellites can be because of efficient energy and the complete absence of heat. Once we combined the space-based interceptors with the work the Army's been doing on the ERIS Project, with their Exo-atmospheric Reentry Vehicle Interceptor Systems, we were able to significantly minimize the number of our power-source satellites up there."

"Combine that with the space- and ground-based surveillance systems and you've got—" Skillman tried to begin, but Satterfield exercised presidential privilege and continued.

"We've got the Keyhole 20 series of surveillance satellites orbiting twenty-five thousand miles in space—up there scanning with synthetic aperture radar giving us twenty-four-hour monitoring even when Russia is clouded over. We've got our Magnum L40-E series picking up chatter over walkie-talkies. One furtive offensive move on their part, and we'll be able to launch the boxes. Their missiles will be knocked out in the boost and mid-course bus phase by our geo- and semisynchronous satellites in the northern hemisphere. And the ERIS boxes will get the remainder in the mid and terminal phases." Satterfield smiled. "The Soviets never should have rejected Eisenhower's 1955 Open Skies proposal for reciprocal aerial surveillance. Ever since then, our technology has exploded."

"Then they really have no idea?"

"None to hang their hat on. Right now, there are more than thirty-five hundred satellites orbiting out there. Two-thirds of them are for military purposes. Heaven only knows what the rest are for. We've been launching since 1957. Thirty-six more don't amount to a hill of beans.''

''Then who does know?''

''Well,'' the President shifted back in his seat and propped both feet on his desk, ''everybody knows we've been thinking about it.'' He tossed the paper clip in the wastebasket at his side. ''And everybody knows we've been doing some serious research and development. Ever since Khrushchev and his boys bragged about a missile capable of hitting a fly in space, we've been working like rabbits in heat against that missile. And frankly, you can't spend hundreds of billions of dollars on a defense program without people noticing, even if you do spread it out over fifteen years, four departments and nine agencies. Though we channeled part of the money through NASA and the Department of Energy, forty-eight percent went through the Air Force and another eighteen percent through other DOD programs. I'm sure the folks with access to the complete figures might have some idea we're getting close, but they'd still never know how close we are.''

''That we've actually deployed?''

''Exactly.''

''Then?''

''Then the only people who know everything are you and me, Dr. Steinbrenner, maybe five or six of his scientists and engineers, and Spencer—as well as Michael Kay.''

''General Kay?''

''Commander in chief of our Space Command out in Colorado Springs. Inevitably it will be his system to run under the Consolidated Space Operations and Control Station. I also imagine Secretary Bart at the Pentagon would have his briefing by now, maybe Secretary Parryman at State. Maybe a few other officers on Spencer's staff, but that's about it. Hell, even our deputy directors for technology and deployment out at SDIO don't know everything. It's all been compartmentalized through SCP. The scientists, the engineers and technicians, they've all received information piece by piece, and only the information that pertains to their individual jobs.''

''What about—'' Skillman began, but Satterfield cut him off.

''It's the same thing Roosevelt did. Rather than play around with the press and the opposing political and military brass—even the opponents in his own administration—he just went out and built the bomb, letting only certain people know certain facts. And, hell, he used government agencies, the military, university scientists and private industry."

Skillman shook his head.

"Reagan wanted this program pretty damn bad," Satterfield continued. "Never did it slip out of the control of the NSC. Hell, Sidey over at Langley doesn't know about it. Reagan and Bush didn't even trust the CIA."

"Can't blame them," offered Skillman.

"Hell, no," the President agreed. "We even about lost control on the NSC when Ollie North got caught in the Iran-Contra deal."

"Battlestar U.S.A." Skillman smiled approvingly.

"Please, Tab, Strategic Defense Initiative." The President corrected with a wry smile.

"Whatever." The chief of staff bobbed his head up and down in agreement. "Thirty-six antiballistic missile satellites protecting God's country, and the Reds have no idea. It's hard to believe. It's hard to believe it's finished."

"Don't say finished yet," corrected Satterfield. "It's not finished until we've staffed the BMCS and activated the HELs, and I'm not planning on doing that for some time yet."

"The BMCS? HELs?"

"Battle management and control stations, BMCS—and high-energy lasers, HELs. They're in the report you're holding, referring to the manned nodes and missile-killing components. In the event of war, once the national command authorities give the go-ahead, we've got one ground station per satellite—some of them automated and mobile. They take in the information from our space- and ground-based tracking stations and then retaliate, whether it's with laser or particle—or even a few of our Army interceptor missiles."

Satterfield paused and picked up his own briefing. "Anyway—" he continued as he opened it and found the page he was looking for. "Index tab J," he said. "Right now our satellites are dark and impossible to detect, but once we plug them into the communications network, and once we activate the HELs, the system will light up like a Christmas tree. Our secret will be out. Besides, we need to finish contruction of our last two phased-array radar installations first."

"Like the Soviets are doing in Krasnoyarsk?"

"We can't get a detailed and accurate picture of a missile attack until we make the Iceland installation operational and finish building the one in Spain."

"When will all this happen?"

"Maybe never."

"Never?" Skillman's tone was a mix of disbelief and protest.

"I'm in no hurry, at least not until after the February Summit in Luxembourg. Hell, it's a secret now. The Soviets still can't prove that those two radar installations are part of a more complex ABM system. They've guessed a couple of times, and we've denied it, explained they're for conventional missile detection. But once we finish them, and once we pull in the military personnel to staff the system—well, you figure it out. Outside of staffing the radar installations, which would take about five hundred men, each BMCS needs another dozen servicemen for round-the-clock monitoring. That's a lot of people who will have to know. You count it. Our secret would be as good as over. The Soviets would know as much about SDI as they do about our missile silos. So, right now, it's going to remain in the family. We can't risk a Soviet walkout on the Summit. We can't risk a reversal in Eastern Europe—not after all the work Reagan and Bush have done—especially. . ."

"Who cares about disarmament?" Skillman's voice was now completely filled with protest. "We've got SDI. We can thwart an attack. Who cares if they walk out?"

"It's not that easy," said Satterfield. "We have the capability, yes. We've got the damn know-how—God help us if we ever have to use it—but we've also got fifteen members of the North Atlantic Treaty Organization who think we're still in research and development. Not to mention the ABM clause we signed as part of the Salt I Treaty that outlaws the use of antimissile satellites, and the commitment President Reagan and Bush made to hold fast to that treaty when he negotiated the Disarmament Pact of '88, and then again at Malta."

"That restriction in SALT I was amended in 1974." Skillman sat straight in the chair. "Besides, it was applicable only to known technology. It didn't include lasers and particle beams and the ERIS technology. And how many times have the Soviets violated it. Their radar installation at Krasnoyarsk is only one example."

"But it only allows one ABM installation on each side of the Curtain. My hell, we've got thirty-six in various levels of orbit— dozens here on ground. And the argument about known technology isn't strong either. Four times the Soviets have tried to introduce a more sophisticated ABM treaty at the United Nations, and four times we've ignored them. Even now the allies are over in Italy arguing whether or not to move ahead with the development of the SDI. They have no idea that it's already up there. We've done it all on our own, and I don't have to explain the public-relations nightmare that's going to become a quick reality when they find out."

"We had to keep the deployment secret. Our allies will understand that."

"So you tell the West Germans we didn't trust them."

"We trusted them. It's their cousins to the east we worried about."

"Good luck."

"But we could use the system to bargain hard with the Soviets at Luxembourg, like Roosevelt and Churchill at Yalta. They had the bomb on the way, so they called the shots."

"I'm impressed. You remember your history," smiled Satterfield. "But you forgot one important point: Roosevelt and Churchill didn't let Stalin know they had the bomb. Just like I'm not going to let the Soviets know we have SDI."

"I think it's a mistake not to activate."

"My number one concern right now is the Alliance. We have to think about our allies. After Reagan and Gorbachev negotiated the Disarmament Pact of '88, we took the only security our allies had out of West Germany and Italy. With those medium-range missiles gone, they've had to spend a lot of money to build up their conventional forces, and now we're going to tell them they're on their own because the United States can no longer be held hostage to nuclear attack? Not on your life."

"But they can't be held hostage either."

"But they're in a rougher neighborhood than we are. The Soviets could launch such a quick conventional attack that Hitler's blitz on Poland would look as fast and efficient as a Model T. The conventional build-up of our allies is nothing compared to what it will have to be with SDI."

"But we could retaliate with nuclear weapons."

The President laughed. "Damn, I'm glad you're not sitting on this side of the desk."

"Come on, Dusty," Skillman argued, "by protecting ourselves and reducing the threat of nuclear attack, we can only make NATO stronger."

"You're talking about World War III. And, besides, the system is not activated. It's just in place. Right now we've never been so vulnerable."

"Vulnerable?"

"Tab, do you know the statistics?" The President's voice was incredulous. "Come on. Right now the Soviet Union has over nine thousand nuclear warheads, each with the power of seventy-five thousand tons of TNT. That's over two tons of TNT for every person on earth."

"We still have our arsenal."

"Seven thousand warheads with the average power not one-third the Soviets'."

"It's enough to deter a first strike."

The President shook his head. "You worry me."

"At least I'm not a yes-man."

"I'm glad something speaks in your favor." The President paused before continuing. "You and I both know that we can't sell the program to the allies overnight. I mean, hell, they're still hoping to get some more R&D money out of SDI. They're thinking that as it's researched and developed, they'll be calling the shots with us. The leftists think they can still kill the program. Now we come along and say, 'Hey, fellas, it's through. We went ahead without you.' " Satterfield shook his head. "No. Let's take our time and break it to them easy."

"I have to dis—" Skillman began again, but the President continued.

"You and I don't even know how our own congressmen are going to react. This program has been anathema for half of them since Reagan introduced it. Can you imagine what Senator Ashworth's going to say?"

"His usual diatribe about broken treaties and broken promises."

"He'll scream about how we've upset the balance of power and created a greater threat for war. What's that quote by Churchill he always uses? Something about survival being the twin child of annihilation?''

"Safety will be the sturdy child of terror and survival the twin brother of annihilation.''

"To a certain degree, Ashworth's right. Despite how much I disagree with him, and our bitter fights through the years, there was a sense of security in the threat of mutually assured destruction. There was a protective balance of power, and a real fear of the consequences to the world if nuclear war was unleashed. What we've done, Tab, is upset that balance—or prepared for it to be upset. The Soviets are scared to death about the militarization of space. Frankly, I'm scared, too. When we activate our ABM system, we'll be sending the arms race into its second stage of development. And I don't know if we can afford to do that right now. In some areas, the Soviets are just as advanced as we are. They already have operational antisatellite weapons. They've been disorienting and blinding our communications satellites since 1968. Hell, in 1977, things got so bad that President Carter tried to negotiate with the Kremlin to disarm them.''

"They never did.''

"Of course they didn't.''

"They've had no problem playing hardball with us. That's why I say we should activate now.''

"You know what my real fear is?''

"What?''

"That before long, war will be escalated to space. Before long, the USSR and all the developed nations of the world will have their own protective canopies. Then we'll begin to develop more sophisticated warheads and missile systems that will pierce and penetrate. Just as we've developed more sophisticated nuclear weapons. Remember, for a while, we, too, were the only ones with the bomb.''

"You make it sound like our Strategic Defense Initiative was a mistake,'' Skillman said. "I don't think I've ever heard you sound so liberal.''

"Oh, not at all, Tab. It's a very big step toward world peace if it's used effectively. That's the key.''

"And how's that?''

"To never use it.''

Skillman laughed. "To never use it," he repeated. "You mean we wasted hundreds of billions of the taxpayers' dollars on a system, just so it will never be used?"

"You surprise me." The President joined in the laughter. "You're a warmonger, I swear. We've spent hundreds and thousands of billions on our nuclear arsenal. Do you think we were ever really looking forward to using it?" he paused. "No thanks, Tab. If I want to see fireworks, I'll watch them over the Mall on the Fourth of July, along with the rest of Washington."

"We used it on Hiroshima."

"Come on, Tab, what we used then, compared to what we've developed since, is like the slingshot."

"The slingshot killed Goliath."

"That's not the analogy I'm referring to."

"You've got to admit, SDI would be a trump card at Luxembourg."

"But that's all it would be," the President said. "What I want—what all of NATO wants—is bilateral disarmament. We want to continue the work Reagan started, the work Bush advanced, and that's what I'm going after in February. It's nice knowing the system is ready to activate if, for some reason, we're unable to reach the agreement the world's been waiting for."

Skillman sat back in his chair. Delbert Satterfield could see that he had satisfied his friend's argument. "This Dr. Steinbrenner," Tab changed the subject, "isn't he getting too old to be involved in this sensitive of a national security issue?"

"There's nobody better." The President could feel himself relaxing after the friendly confrontation. He knew Skillman now wanted to shoot the bull. "He's the one who talked Einstein into writing Roosevelt about the destructive potential of the atom. He helped develop the bomb. Who else would be as qualified to oversee our ABM research and development? Despite his age, I've never seen anyone who works so hard. You'd be pressed to keep up with him." The President paused, taken by an insight. "Maybe he's driven by a moral thing. He saw the destruction his atom bomb caused. Now, before he dies, he wants to leave the world with the knowledge and potential to protect itself from such destruction."

"You're evading my question," Skillman said. "How old is he?"

"Seventy something," said Satterfield, looking away, "maybe eighty-six." He smiled.

"And you don't think it's dangerous to have a man that age in possession of our country's greatest secret?"

"He's a tough old man—a standard to all Americans."

"Come off the rhetoric," Skillman said.

"Have you ever met him?"

"Once. At a White House dinner. He was Bush's guest."

"Well," said Satterfield, standing, "you'll have another chance."

"When?"

"Sooner than you think. I'm calling a meeting of the Joint Chiefs."

"Why?"

"To introduce them to the news about SDI."

"But you just said secrecy is—"

"I know what I said," Satterfield cut in. "But the chiefs of staff are not security risks. Hell, they've forgotten more about ultra-secret projects than you or I will ever know."

"Tell them, and you're headed for a fight."

"Don't tell them, and I'm in a fight."

"Some are going to argue that the system should be activated immediately. Are you ready for that?"

"It won't be the first time."

"Are we going to tell the Joint Chiefs only?"

"Just the chiefs and the other members of the Security Council," Satterfield said as he turned and walked toward the door. "Except Sidey. Tell him and you might as well publish it in the *National Enquirer*. More people will know about it. And his running-mouths will leak a more sensationalized version." He placed his hand on the knob but then stopped and faced Skillman. "But of course, I'm going to have to invite Senator Ashworth. I wouldn't dare think of leaving the chairman of the Senate Armed Services Committee out of the circle."

"Are you crazy?" Skillman jumped to his feet. "That asshole's a communist."

"He's a liberal. Not a communist."

"He's a damn dove."

"And what more would he rather hear than that we have an antinuclear umbrella keeping him safe from foreign aggression."

"It's out of line," Tab said, and Delbert was taken aback by the harshness in his advisor's voice. "Besides, he's in Italy at the NATO conference."

"He has to know," Satterfield shot back. "He's got the security clearances. He's the most powerful member of Congress when it comes to defense issues, and we're only asking for trouble if we don't tell him—if we don't line him up on our side from the get-go. We'll call him home."

"The get-go's long gone—"

"Tab—"

"He's going to argue that we should have told him before. Here he is thinking he's going to kill the program in funding, and now you're going to tell him it's finished?"

"We didn't even know everything. How could we tell him?"

"He'll argue we should have told him what we knew."

"It was too sensitive and within the purview of the executive branch."

"He'll want to know where the money came from. Then he'll use it against us—politically."

"Listen, Tab," the President's voice silenced his friend. "I'm going to tell him. End story."

"I'm going to argue this one, Dusty," Skillman was calmer, but he was still insistent.

"Go ahead, Tab." The President smiled. "But I'm sorry I won't be around to hear you. I'm getting something to eat."

"Then I'll join you."

"Alone, Tab. I'm eating alone."

Chapter Five

When Malibu closed his hotel room door, he saw the red message light flashing on the telephone. He took his reporter's notebook from his breast pocket and tossed it on the bed, then he slipped the knot from his bow tie and slid the tie from under the collar of his formal white shirt. With one hand he picked up the receiver of the telephone, propped it between his shoulder and ear, and dialed the operator. With the other he unfastened his cummerbund, unbuttoned his shirt, and loosened his belt. The clock atop the Philips television flashed 2:48 AM, and Robert was surprised that he was not tired.

His morning had begun, like all his mornings, at 5:15 with a five-mile run and a shower of alternating hot and cold water. This particular morning, or twenty-two hours ago, he had run to the Piazza del Popolo, up the Viale del Muro to the Villa Medici, a heavily wooded plateau that overlooked the west side of the Eternal City. At dawn everything had been so peaceful. In the distance, on the opposite side of the Tiber River, he could see Vatican City and the bold dome of St. Peter's Basilica that reflected the rising sun. It was ironic to him that a day that began so beautifully could end so ugly.

"Hello," said the voice on the other end of the phone. Malibu smiled, entertained that the operator answered in English.

"Hello, I'm in room two-seventeen," he said. Then he thought how ridiculous it was to repeat the room number. *How else did she know to answer in English?* "I'm calling for my messages."

"Yes, Mr. Hamilton," said the operator. Her voice was pleasant, and Robert was enchanted by the strong accent. "You had very many

phone calls. Mr. Levin called from Washing-toon, about a feature
article. He said you would know how he means."

"Yes." Robert thought about the feature he had promised to do on
Senator Ashworth. He did tell Levin that it would be on the wire today,
but that was before the debate on SDI heated up. And, besides, he
thought, after the story he would file tonight, Levin would forget about
Ashworth.

"JoAnn Claiborne called. She would not leave a message, but said
you would be wise to call her tonight if you know what is good for
you." The operator paused. "You understand, no?"

"Yes." Robert smiled. He gave JoAnn an 'A' for effort. She was
the most persistent woman he had ever dated. In his five days in Rome,
he had been called by JoAnn three times. He reached for his notebook,
flipped it open to a blank page and penned: CALL J.C.

"Barbara Lewis called. She said she missed you. When will you be
at home?"

Barbara was the second most persistent. Robert added her name to
the list: CALL J.C. AND B.L.

"Go on," he said.

"One man named Jed-a-die-a More-house," the operator spoke the
name with great difficulty, "called from New York. He said the galley
proofs on the book are ready for you. Call him tomorrow—or I mean
today."

"Got it," Malibu said. He drew a large star and three exclamation
marks in his notebook. He had waited seven months for the galleys of
his first book, and suddenly his spirits were higher than they had been
all day. "Not bad at nine minutes to three in the morning," he
thought, and for the first time he realized he wouldn't be getting any
sleep tonight.

"A Cheryl Larson called also. She said the research is done. She
will wait for your phone call." The operator changed the tone of her
voice before she continued. "But I think it is far too late. She called at
two o'clock this afternoon."

"It probably is." Robert agreed. He did not need the research
before tomorrow anyway. It was on the President's budget figures for
defense, and Malibu would not be concentrating on his SDI wrap story
before he filed the piece on Hans Peterson. "Is that it?" he asked.

"Yes," said the woman, "except that a lady named Silly-toe called a few minutes ago and said if you would like to join her in the disco for a drink.''

"Diana?'' Robert said aloud. His voice sounded anxious and surprised, and for a moment he was embarrassed.

"There is no first name.''

"In the disco?'' he asked. "Where's the disco?''

"Take the elevator to level B.''

"How long ago did she call?''

"Maybe twenty minutes.''

He looked again at the clock. Then as quickly as he had become anxious, his emotions were tempered by reality. It was almost nine o'clock in Washington. His story on the Peterson murder would have to be filed by ten for the early morning edition. There was no time for Diana. He had to get to the bureau. "Is that everything?'' he asked.

"Yes, Mr. Hamilton.''

"Could you please connect me to the disco?''

"Yes, thank you.'' The line clicked twice and began to ring.

"Dee-sko,'' the voice of a man answered the phone. Music blasted in the background, and Robert thought about how out of place it sounded this early in the morning. The loud music he heard on the other end of the telephone contrasted sharply with his last hour in Peterson's room and with the silence in his own.

"Is Diana Sillito, there?'' he asked

"*Che*?'' the voice shouted.

"Diana Sillito. Is she there?'' Robert asked again. "SILLY-TOE.'' He repeated the pronunciation the operator had used, emphasizing the syllables. He knew the man would know who he was asking for. He imagined the attention of the entire disco focused on the actress. How often does an international star frequent the Ambasciatori discotheque at three o'clock in the morning? But the man did not answer. Instead, the line went dead. Robert clicked the receiver several times and then dialed "0'' again. Before the operator could answer, he hung up, tightened the belt around his trousers, placed the notebook in his back pocket, picked up his key from the nightstand, and left the room.

He took the elevator to the lobby and asked the concierge to call for a taxi. From the lobby, he could hear the music coming from the floor below, and he followed the steps next to the elevator to the red leather doors that opened to the smallest bar a.k.a. disco Robert had ever seen.

The lighted dance floor was no bigger than the area between the lines of an average parking space. Around the dance floor were tables covered with red cloths and topped by candles in round holders, the kind used by Pizza Hut. Behind the bar was a shelf of liquor that would not hold a sterno bum through a Saturday night. Robert was surprised that a magnificent hotel like the Ambasciatori would have such an aberrant night club. There were only two people in the place. Sitting at the table on the other side of the floor, opposite the door, were Diana Sillito and the man Robert believed he had talked to. The man was leaning close to the model, and Malibu could see she was uneasy, because as soon as he entered she stood and hurried to the door.

"I thought you'd never get here," she said. The same sweet smile that captivated Robert at the Villa Taverna flashed across her face.

"How long have you been waiting?"

"Half an hour." She took Robert by the arm and led him out of the noisy room. They walked up the stairs to the lobby.

"I just got the message."

"I always thought Don Juan was Spanish," she said and laughed.

"He gave you a hard time?"

"He set a record for the most lines dropped inside twenty minutes, and I don't even understand a word of Italian." She looked at Robert with adoring eyes that made the journalist nervous.

"I'm sorry."

"Everything's fine now," she said and squeezed Malibu's arm.

"Well," Robert began but paused.

"What?" she asked.

"There is one problem."

"You're married."

"Not that serious." He smiled. "It's just that I can't stay."

"I don't want to stay. Did you see that place?"

"I mean, I've got an appointment."

"It's three o'clock. Where on earth can you go at three o'clock? And don't give me the line about washing hair."

"I'm serious," Robert said.

"Really?" Her voice was filled with disbelief. "At three o'clock?" Suddenly, Diana's face filled with knowledge. "Oh, I'm embarrassed," she said. "I'm sorry. You have a date—I mean there's someone else." She pulled away from Robert and moved to the door. "I shouldn't have called."

"I've got to go to our bureau office and file a story." Robert laughed.

"Come on," she said. "At three o'clock?"

"It's only nine in Washington. They need the story by ten."

"Well, could I go with you? I mean if that's really where you're going, I'd like to go along. I've never seen a bureau office before."

"You're not missing anything."

"No. I'd really like to go."

"How about if I drop you off at your hotel, and we'll get together tomorrow?"

"You don't want me to tag along?" She frowned a dramatic frown. "There is someone else. I'm not dumb. I just hope she appreciates you."

"There's no one," Robert said. He was amused and flattered by the woman's antics. "It's just not the kind of story you'd like to hear, and I'm not going to be held accountable for ruining your night."

"I told you I like politics."

"This isn't what you meant, I'm sure."

"You sound like somebody died," Diana said with a laugh, and Robert let the comment drop.

The two walked to the revolving door. Malibu pushed her gently to the front of him. On the other side, a taxi waited with its green light shining in the night. Hamilton opened the door of the car and let the woman slide in. He sat next to her.

"Where are you staying?" he asked.

"You're really not going to let me go with you?"

"It's better that you don't."

"I won't beg."

"I don't think you'd know how."

"Albergo Cicerone on the Via Cicerone, number fifty-five," Diana said to the driver and then sat back in the seat and looked out the window opposite Robert.

"I'm sorry," said Malibu. "I've got one hour to file a story. I won't be any fun until after four. Besides, you'd be a distraction down at the bureau. Someone would want to interview you, and we'd never get out of there, and—"

"Let's just say it's strike one."

Robert chuckled. "Be careful, baseball's my sport."

"I'm surprised you ever score."

"What?" Robert's chuckle broke into full-blown laughter. The woman's remark seemed out of character.

"You heard me. I don't stutter." She looked at him out of the corner of her eye.

In the early morning hour, the car moved easily down the Via Vittorio Veneto to the Via del Tritone. The cobblestone streets were peaceful and dark, a sharp contrast to the lively narrow lanes crowded with a colorful throng of shoppers during the day. The lights in the tiny stores were off, and metal grates were pulled down over the windows. Every so often Robert caught a glimpse of a lighted fountain through the maze-like *vias* that connected with the main avenue. Street lanterns hanging high above the winter-thinned trees cast a hazy, haunted glow in the frosty air, and Robert thought that all the elements were present for a romantic evening, and the thought was heightened by the presence of the woman every man in the world dreamt about. But the story could not hold until tomorrow.

"I am sorry," he whispered.

"I'll probably forgive you." She took his hand. "But not for a day or two."

"Will it take that long?"

"My ego heals slowly."

"Then I should count myself lucky."

"Let's just say it's the Christmas spirit."

"Christmas is a month away."

"Don't push your luck." She smiled. "But I do hope for your sake that this is an important story. Teddy can get awfully nasty when his little girl has her heart broken."

"I don't doubt it." Robert gave her hand a squeeze. He found the imagery of the effeminate manager getting violent amusing. "But it is a very important story. See, Senator Watenburg—"

"No," Diana said quickly, "don't tell me. I'll read all about it in the morning. Besides, I'll only go to bed thinking, 'He put me on hold for that?' '' She looked out the window. "It would make for a miserable night."

"Le Albergo Cicerone," the cab driver said as he pulled the car into the hotel drive-through.

"*Molte grazie*," said Diana.

"*Prego.*" The driver brought the taxi to a halt and jumped out to open the woman's door.

"Can I walk you to your room?" Robert asked.

"You go to the bureau. Write your story. I'll be okay." Diana dramatically pouted and dropped her head.

"You are a good actress."

"Maybe it's not an act," she said quickly and gave Robert a kiss on the cheek. She stepped outside and hurried into the lobby.

"*Bella*," said the cabby once he was back in his seat.

"What?" Robert asked. His mind was still thinking about the sacrifice he was making for the story he was about to write.

"The woman—she is too beautiful."

"Very beautiful."

The driver smiled and pulled the car slowly onto the Via Cicerone. "You are no *italiano*."

"What?"

"You are no *italiano*. *Italiano* would stay with her. Make her smile. Now she is sad—*triste*. *Italiano* can see these things in woman."

"To the Via Padova, *per favore*," Robert said as he took a deep breath.

He pulled his notebook from his back pocket and held it high enough so he could read it by the light coming through the rear window.

HANS PETERSON—GRAYSON WATENBURG—KGB—CHRISTIAN DEMO-CRATS—BITES THE BIG ONE—WIFE GONE—NECK—BLOOD—WHITE SILK PAJAMAS—UNIDENTIFIED MAN—STILETTO—SDI DEBATE—COF-FEE SHOP—CHANCELLOR—SULFAZINE PYROGENIC (MALARIA/SCHIZO-PHRENIA).

He tried to make sense out of the notes, to read a story between the words, but his mind would not focus on a thesis. Instead, he thought about Diana, what she had said only moments ago and how she had left him. He thought about going back, asking the driver to turn the car around, and putting the story off until tomorrow. No one would know. He could say that he was detained getting to the bureau, that he knew it would be filed too late, so he decided to go after additional facts for a sidebar or two. Even if he waited, the *Post* would still have the story as quickly as the other papers. He shook his head and dismissed the rationalization. In his hands he held an exclusive, and that was the most important word in journalism.

He looked back at the notebook: WIFE GONE—WIFE GONE—WIFE GONE. He read no farther. He could not concentrate. He snapped the notebook shut and relaxed into the deep back seat.

The bureau was locked when Robert stepped from the taxi to the door. His light cotton shirt did little to thwart the cold night air, and he shivered until the night editor answered. It was a young man with an Ivy League look, hair perfectly trimmed and over the ears, pleated pants held up by solid blue suspenders, and Bass Weejun loafers. He even had a sharpened pencil tucked behind his right ear. Robert thought that a bit much in the age of word processors. But he also realized that this young man must be a bright reporter to have landed a plum foreign assignment before he was old enough to shave, even if he was the bureau editor from midnight to dawn.

"I'm Bob Hamilton," Malibu said after the man opened the door. He held up his notebook. "I've got to file a story."

The editor stepped aside to let Robert pass. He held out his hand. "My name's Brook Adams. We've never met, but I've heard all about you."

Robert shook the hand and walked farther into the hall. He was overcome by the sudden warmth in the building. "I'm glad you have the heat on."

"It's cold out there."

"Has there been much action tonight?"

"Nothing, except a Vatican press release reaffirming the Pope's stand against abortion and birth control."

"The news never changes," said Robert.

"Only the names," Brook added. He followed Malibu into the transmission room. "What do you have?"

"A murder story."

"Murder?" Brook shouted, then he lowered his voice. "You're political."

"A political murder."

"Who?"

"Hans Peterson."

"Peterson?"

"He's a German legislator. A senator."

"Murdered? In Rome?"

"Terrorists," said Robert as he picked up the telephone. He punched the speed-dial button, and before he could sit down, the call was answered.

"*Washington Post* switchboard," said the voice on the other end of the line.

"Simon Levin, please," said Robert as he sat in the chair.

"Thank you." The line rang again.

"Simon Levin's office."

"Gloria, this is Malibu. Is Simon in?"

"Do you have the Ashworth feature?"

"Come on, Gloria, let me talk to him."

"I'm supposed to ask. Do you have the Ashworth feature?"

"Not yet."

"Then he says he don't want to talk to you, baby."

"He's got to talk to me. I'm sitting on an exclusive."

"An exclusive?"

"Terrorist hit. Nobody's got it yet."

"Don't you be lyin' to me. He'll fire my butt if I put you through without the Ashworth story—unless you really got an *exclusive*," she stretched the final word for emphasis.

"I swear it."

"Hold on, sweetheart."

"Where in the hell's the Ashworth piece, Malibu?" Levin's voice was cranky, as always, but Robert knew he was not upset. He always knew the editor's mood from which of the four names he chose to address the reporter. If he used "Malibu," his anger was a harmless demonstration of editorial power. If he used 'Bob,' he was serious. "Robert," meant trouble. When he said "Hamilton," it would be time to clean out the desk drawers.

"Forget the Ashworth piece, Simon. I've got a terrorist attack."

"Bullshit."

"Seriously. Hans Peterson of the German Bundesrat. He was injected with pyro—, no, sulfer—, sulfazine—a pyrogenic. Then they cut his throat from ear to ear."

"Nobody in Washington gives a —" Levin paused. "Nobody cares about the Bundesrat. It's news for page twenty-three. I want the Ashworth story. The man's probably running for Senate majority leader, and you're in the same hotel with him for five days."

"Ashworth's for the Style section," Malibu argued. "This is terrorism. It involves the leader of the Christian Democrats—next in line for chancellor."

"You know my rule, Bob."

"I know," Robert said quickly, hoping to cut off the editor before he started to recite the morbid equation.

"One dead American is worth ten dead Europeans, who are worth two hundred dead Central Americans, who are worth a thousand dead Chinese, who are worth the entire continent of India. But this time, Bob, read one live politician—Boyd Ashworth. I want the story by ten."

"It's impossible. I haven't interviewed him."

"You what?"

"I haven't interviewed him. I was going to do it this evening, but the debate on SDI went long. By the time it was over, he had disappeared to the ambassador's reception."

"I hope you're learning Italian real good," Levin said. His voice was loud and angry. "You're not Bob Woodward. You're not even Carl Bernstein. I'll have you out of here so fast you'll have to pay your own way home."

"You've had a bad day." Mailibu tried to break the tension.

"Don't mess with my head, Robert, I'm serious. The trash you've been sending us the last three days is nothing that we can't get from the wire services. American Press International even had a better developed story on the allies and the defense initiative. Four of your facts were wrong. We had to print a correction this morning. The old lady upstairs is screaming. And I'll be damned if I'm going to eat your fallout."

"Management by menopause," said Malibu.

"That's it, Hamilton!"

"I'm fired?"

"After I get the damn Ashworth piece."

Robert laughed. "I'll get it in tomorrow. And sorry about the errors. It's difficult to double-check all the figures from this side of the

Atlantic. Maybe we should have held the story." He stopped speaking and waited for Levin to respond, but there was only silence, so he continued. "Look, this is a Page One story. I was in the German's hotel room no more than forty-five minutes ago. Senator Watenburg's involved, so there is a Washington angle. And there's no doubt about it being a terrorist attack."

"Has anyone claimed responsibility?" Levin was calm once again.

"Watenburg discovered the body around one—about two hours ago. He called me even before he called the police." As soon as Robert had spoken the word police, a chill ran down his back. His mind was suddenly a malaise of a thousand thoughts. "The police," he said again. "Dear God!" He dropped the telephone to the floor and shouted at Brook. "Do you have a car?"

"Out back."

"Hurry," he ordered as he ran out of the transmission room. Brook, unquestioning, moved to take his coat off the rack that stood by the front door of the bureau. "There's no time," Malibu screamed. His voice bit into the silent early morning air.

"Mr. Levin?" the young man protested.

"He can wait."

Brook ran to the back of the building and within a minute had a blue Volkswagen touring bus pulled to the curb out front. Robert jumped from the sidewalk to the seat. "The Ambasciatori. Fast."

"What's—" Brook began.

"There were no police when I left the hotel twenty minutes ago," Robert said. He was not talking directly to Brook, but organizing the thoughts in his head. "Grayson said he was calling the police. There weren't any—only the concierge, the taxi, and Diana." *Diana*, he thought. In the disco and in the lobby, he was so focused on Diana that he did not think that the police should have been there. "There's been nothing on the police radio tonight?" he asked Brook.

"Nothing like what you're talking about."

"Why?" Hamilton asked out loud.

"Why what?"

Robert did not answer. His mind recalled the face of Senator Watenburg. "Thanks," the man had said. "For what?" Robert asked. "For giving me time to think."

Brook slowed for a red light.

"Run it!" Robert demanded, and the young man obeyed.

Hamilton's mind returned to his final conversation with the senator. "It's better for me if you tell the story," Grayson had said. "It'll probably come as welcome news—Ashworth's been fighting SDI from Day One—Just watch him—The roots on this one may be deeper than both of us understand, or even care to understand."

"Can this go any faster?" Malibu asked. He was surprised by how angry his voice sounded.

"It's floored," Brook said. "Do you mind telling me what this is all about?"

"Senator Watenburg's dead."

"What?"

"He was preparing for a long stay," Robert said and closed his eyes.

Chapter Six

Sergio Castillo Armando walked slowly beneath the east colonnade of St. Peter's Square. In the predawn light, the crucifix atop the Egyptian obelisk in the center of the plaza looked like the flame of a shadowy candle. It was said that the cross contained a relic of the Holy Cross, and years ago Sergio had believed it did. Now he was not sure. As a young man, he had envisioned the square flooded with people, the faithful who gathered to recite the angelus together with the Pope. In his barrio over seven thousand miles away, he had listened to these prayers, attended the Navidad Mass through his radio, and even imagined himself one day standing in the magnificent square beneath the marble eyes of the statue saints that adorn the colonnade. But now the square was silent, and Sergio was alone, overcome by an ethereal feeling of being separated from humanity. The air was cold. His head was light. He looked at the towering dome high above the tomb of St. Peter. The bronze ball atop the basilica reflected the red of the rising sun.

"When you were young, you girded yourself and walked where you would; but when you are old, you stretch your hands, and another girds you and carries you where you do not wish to go." Sergio could not remember who had written those words. He memorized them in his childhood. Their meaning was different then, both sacred and foreboding. Why he remembered them now, he did not know, only that the original meaning was lost.

He glanced at his wristwatch. The time was 6:19, and by his

calculations, he had a thirty-minute walk to the train depot, Stazione Ostia Lido. That would give him time to eat a muffin and drink a cup of coffee before catching the train to Nice.

The route between the Ambasciatori Hotel and the station did not require that he walk by the Vatican, but Sergio's past drew him to the square, and the memories he recalled while sitting in the Piazza Navona returned with force. For a brief moment he wanted to walk to the doors of the mother of basilicas and pass inside. He wanted to kneel at the tomb of St. Peter and whisper a confession. He wanted to feel the faith he had felt as a youth, and more importantly, he wanted to feel the innocence. Instead, he stopped in the square long enough to study the statues of Peter and Paul that guard either side of the steps leading to the giant doors.

The face of St. Peter was long and drawn. Though it hid beneath a beard, it looked to Sergio like the face of a starving man. The eyes were hollow and shadowed, even blackened by the wear and erosion since it was completed by de Fabris in 1858. Sergio studied the nose. It was long and large. And then, suddenly, it was not the same nose, but belonged to the American senator—Watenburg. Sergio had left him dead, inside the German's room, where he had found him alone after searching the hotel. But this time, he had acted well and forced the American to talk before killing him.

It was genius, Sergio thought as he considered the method. But it was nothing more than the tradition of the matador, to cut off an ear to reward bravery. When the senator refused to talk, Sergio cut off first the left ear, and handed it to the American.

"No one will vote for a senator who cannot hear them," he told Watenburg as the victim winced in pain, his eyes filled with rage and disbelief. Still, he did not give Sergio the information he needed.

"I will not play with you, Senator," Sergio warned. "My people are not sympathetic to your people. Our struggle has little time for the likes of you. Look about you, see what I did to the Nazi earlier this evening. Do you like it?" He shook his head slowly. "No, it's not pretty. I thought the drug would make him talk. Unfortunately, it failed. He died before he spoke. My associate there"—Sergio pointed to the man laying on the bathroom floor—"he cut the German's neck much too soon. Much too deeply." Sergio paused, then continued. "That's why I had to kill him. He failed. I will not." He pressed the

side of the blade against Watenburg's temple above the the right ear.
"Now you speak to me. Who has charge of the Strategic Defense
Initiative?"

"I don't know what you're talking about." Watenburg's voice
trembled.

"The man at the top," Sergio demanded. "Is he military or political?"

"I—" as Watenburg began, Sergio pressed the steel blade harder
against the temple.

"You are about to lose your other ear."

"I really don't know what you mean." Sweat glossed Watenburg's
forehead. The stream of blood from the left side of his head soaked the
shoulder and breast of his white formal shirt. There was blood on the
ruffled cuff.

"The man," Sergio said. "Who is the man?"

"I don't have that kind of information."

"You and the German are the crusade leaders. Don't lie."

"There are dozens involved."

"The director!"

"It's not that easy."

"The man who speaks to the President."

"You can't kill a program by killing the—" Before Watenburg
could finish, Sergio sliced off the right ear. It fell into the senator's lap
and turned white as the blood ran out of it. "Steinbrenner—" Grayson's voice quivered. "It's—it's Steinbrenner. He briefs our Intelligence Committee."

A proud smile broke across the terrorist's lips. "You will be
famous, Senator," he said, and then, with a single, precise stroke,
ended the man's life with a slash across the larynx. He reached into
his pocket and withdrew a handkerchief. "This is for my success."
He wrapped the cloth around the ear and placed it in his coat
pocket.

Before the revolution, Peter and Paul were Sergio's heroes. Even now,
as he stared at their images, he was moved. In their hands they held
parchments, epistles that represented the law, the law that had once
meant so much to Sergio. "To share in their unity of purpose," he
thought, but then was startled by the sound of someone behind him.

There was a man in his late twenties who stood staring at the obelisk. Other than the Italian garbage men, dressed in their orange overalls, who gathered the refuse in the early morning hours, this was the first man that Sergio had seen since he left the hotel. That the man would be awake and touring this early in the morning was unusual, and Sergio's concern was compounded by the fact that the man was an American, well built and tall and wearing Levi jeans and Reebok shoes. A black canvas camera bag hung on the man's right shoulder, and with the deep red and blue colors cast by the rising sun, and the dramatic shadows filling the square, Sergio questioned why the man was not taking pictures. The world was fresh, the air clean, and the moisture of the morning stained the stone city. It was a perfect time for pictures.

Sergio approached the tourist. For a moment, his mind connected with the image of a man he saw earlier in the Piazza Navona, a man sitting at a table across the room in the tiny Cafe Giorgi, before Sergio had returned to the Ambasciatori to kill the American senator. He was not sure whether the memory was real or imagined, but he would find out. At first, the man only nodded as Sergio approached, and then he stepped backwards as Sergio came closer.

"You e-speak English?" Sergio asked.

The man nodded.

"I e-speak English, too." Sergio smiled and stepped even closer, violating what Americans call the comfort zone.

"Where you from?" the man asked with a nervous smile. He took another step backward.

"*España*," said Sergio as he stepped closer.

"Ah—what part?"

"Segovia."

The man looked at his feet and then to Sergio. He took another step backward, and Sergio knew that if he kept up the pressure the man would turn and leave. "Segovia?" the man said. "I've never been there, but I heard it's beautiful."

"It is. Very." Sergio reached out and touched the man's hand. He smiled and winked.

"Ah—listen," said the man, "I've gotta run."

"You just arrived." Sergio studied the man's eyes. He tried to remember if he *had* seen them hours before in the cafe. He believed he had. He believed this man had followed him to the Vatican. *What other reason does he have for being up so early*, Sergio wondered.

"I have to catch a bus to the Colosseum."

"*El Coliseo*," Sergio repeated in Spanish and nodded in understanding. "But the tour buses are not running." He reached into his pocket and gripped his stiletto.

"Not the tour buses," said the man. "I'm taking—I mean the regular buses."

"What is your name?"

"Duke." The man readjusted the strap of the camera bag on his shoulder. He stepped back again. "What's yours?"

"Andre," said Sergio. "Andre from Segovia." He whipped the stiletto from his pocket and clicked the blade into position. "And you're coming with me," he said and motioned toward the south colonnade.

"Listen, man," said the American, putting both hands where Sergio could see them, "I mean nobody no harm. Please."

"What do you have in the bag?" Sergio forced the man back between the stone pillars.

"Cameras. A passport. A little money." Duke's voice trembled. "You can have it. God—you can have it all."

"Don't profane on sacred ground," Sergio said and offered a wicked smile.

"Sorry—I—What did I say?"

"Thou shalt not take the Lord thy God's name in vain." Beneath the colonnade, Sergio pushed the man onto the ground. "Open the bag. Show me your camera."

The man quickly complied.

"Give me your passport."

"Come on, man. Don't take my passport. I'll give you money."

"Give me the passport!"

"Christ," said the man, and no sooner did he say that than Sergio came down on his left shoulder with the knife. The blade cut deep into the trapezius muscle. "Oh, God, no!"

"I told you," Sergio said, his eyes on fire, "never take God's name in vain."

Duke whimpered in pain. With a shaking right hand, he reached into his bag and withdrew his passport. He dropped it on the ground at

Sergio's feet and placed his hand over his wound. "Are you going to kill me?"

Sergio kicked the passport away from the American and then picked it up. "Duke Harrington," he read the name inside. "Nice picture." He snapped the blue booklet shut and placed it in the breast pocket of his leather jacket. "Duke," Sergio said, "are you a family man?"

"I've got two children."

"A wife?"

"Of course."

"Do you love her?"

"Of course."

"Is she in Rome with you, Duke Harrington?"

"She's at the hotel—the Ipponio."

"Can you prove that inside the next thirty seconds?"

"Of course I can't." Duke grimaced in pain.

"Then, Mr. Harrington, I will have have to kill you." Sergio leaned down and took the American under the left armpit and jerked him to his feet.

"Ahhh—" Harrington screamed. "Please, man."

"Walk to the trees," Sergio ordered as he motioned to a forested park across the street.

"Why?" Duke pleaded.

"I can't kill you in St. Peter's, beneath the eyes of men who mean so much to me."

"Please don't kill me. My wife and kids—they'd—"

"Walk to the trees," said Sergio.

"Please!"

Sergio brought the knife down again into the right shoulder.

"No—" the American screamed and tried to run, but fell to his knees. Sergio kicked him in the back with such force that the man fell face down on the cobblestone and his nose began to bleed.

"You have more blood than you know what to do with," Sergio said as he again lifted the man to his feet. "You may not die as easily as the other three." He paused long enough to look around and see that the two men were still alone. He pushed the American into the grove. "Look," he said, glancing at his watch. "I have to catch a train in twenty minutes. I think that gives us enough time."

"I won't tell anybody," Harrington pleaded. "I never saw you."

"Sure you did. My name is Sergio Castillo Armando. I am what you Americans call an international terrorist." Sergio walked the man farther into the park. "But you know all of this, don't you, Duke Harrington. You know it because you've been following me."

Harrington stumbled in front of Sergio and fell to the ground. "I haven't been following you." He held both shoulders with his hands. "I swear to—" he paused. "I haven't."

"Thou shalt not lie," Sergio said and brought his knife down a third and final time at the base of the man's neck. The body folded limp on the ground and Sergio walked away. He patted the passport inside his pocket, next to the ear of Grayson Watenburg. "I must start a collection," he said to himself as he pushed the blade of the knife back into the handle. But before it clicked into position. Sergio felt the sting and then the burn of a bullet entering his lower back. Then he heard the clack of the gun. His body collapsed in the dirt. His mind drifted in and out of consciousness, and he tried to keep himself awake, but it was becoming more and more difficult. He could not open his eyes and see who had fired the bullet. All he could think about was not dying. It was not time. His life was not in order. He remembered his brother.

Then he heard the voice. "Next time you kill me—kill me." It belonged to Duke Harrington, and it was the last voice Sergio heard.

Chapter Seven

The sun was breaking over the Washington skyline when Rubin David Steinbrenner, Ph.D., reached to his nightstand and turned down the volume on his clock radio. He awoke daily to the morning news on National Public Radio and habitually stayed in bed until the end of the broadcast.

Despite his pending appointment at the White House, this day was to begin no differently. As the newswoman reported on the United States' military involvement in Central America and the border struggles in the Middle East, and offered a summary of the NATO conference in Rome, Steinbrenner buried his face in his pillow and inhaled the fragrance of his dead wife's perfume. He was happy his life was coming to an end.

Ida had died in October, in the middle of the Strategic Defense Initiative's final phase. Only two more nodes needed to be tested and installed, along with the final radar stations, before America could man the system and have the capability of protecting itself against nuclear attack, and Rubin was on the testing site in Indian Springs, Nevada, when he received word she was dead.

His mind had been ridden with guilt as he sat silently through the five-hour flight back to Washington. Since the beginning of the Initiative, he had not spent much time with his ailing, but supportive, wife. He spent the weekends with her; together they attended the synagogue, but the kind of love and dedication she needed in her last years, he could not give. His obsession with completing the SDI project had numbed his senses and bruised his conscience.

71

Now, with the final, technical stage of his antiballistic missile system ready for activation—only the Iceland and Spain installations had to be completed—he had no way of celebrating his success with the woman he loved. Instead, he resigned himself to sleeping with a pillow splashed heavily with her simple perfume and held tight to his bosom.

The physicist had loved Ida from the day they met, and he had been a good husband. It was ironic that he now felt guilty. But guilt was an emotion that Steinbrenner knew well.

Rubin David, then a graduate student at the University of Krakow, was safely smuggled out of the country by a contingent of English schoolmates in September of 1939. He had studied under German chemists, Otto Hahn and Fritz Strassmann, and his knowledge of Einstein's Special Theory of Relativity and Ernest Rutherford's nuclear theory of the atom and his own successful work made him a valuable asset to the allied countries.

But his escape drew attention to the family that was left behind, and shortly thereafter, they were captured. His brother Viktor was one of the unfortunate Polish Jews who spent four years in a Nazi concentration camp during World War II. His mother and father met their fate in the gas chambers of Treblinka. His brothers and sisters, with the exception of Viktor, died from exposure and typhus. Viktor's own wife was butchered on the camp medical tables in an experiment that went too far. And Viktor, himself a renowned Polish surgeon, had been detailed to clean up the makeshift operating room when the experiment was over and his wife lay dead on the green metallic table.

The letter Rubin received from his brother was vivid, the source of countless nightmares through the years. The physicist believed he suffered more from not being there in Dachau with them, from not going through the pain and torture with the people he loved.

He, too, was a son of Israel. Why should fate determine that his family die while he be fortunate enough to escape to England and then to America?

Through the years, and the countless readings of Viktor's letter, Rubin had memorized each word and seared the images of his dying family in his mind. Viktor, now deceased after a life of medical service in Gdansk, had not been bitter about his camp experience, or about the torture and death that took his family. After the liberation, he, too, had been allowed to live, to return to Poland and bring meaning back into his life.

"I cannot paint in words nor on a canvas the pain and despair we knew in those years in Dachau," Viktor wrote after he was freed by the allies. "Stripped of our clothes, our jewelry and possessions, we were shorn like sheep and left totally naked, without identity. We were given a number and then separated, one from another. Some were picked to live; others were picked to die. Mother and Father were selected for the latter."

Viktor wrote of the labor detail, the six ounces of daily bread, and the watered pea soup. He wrote how he struggled to save the lives of those men who were dying of typhus—even their own brother, Marc. He wrote of the cruel Kapo and the illiterate guards who abused the educated prisoners. "These men knew nothing of Judaism, nothing of Zion. They spoke of their Christ, how we tortured and hanged him on a cross, and then they would strike us again. They knew nothing of their Christ, nothing of Christianity. They were calloused by the carnal nature of their environment. I kept imagining these men to be fathers of young children, husbands of loving wives. And I kept asking, did they think they were doing right?"

Each time Rubin read his brother's letter, he became disturbed by the imagery and by the guilt that he had escaped the plight of his family. But he knew Viktor's words were meant to console. "Thank you, Rubin, for giving us hope in those despairing years. We knew that what you were doing in America was of great importance. We knew the work you were doing for the free countries was significant, and that it was being done on our behalf. And this knowledge allowed us to be strong and maintain a positive attitude. Of all the Germans could strip from us, they could not take our attitude. And as long as we held the freedom to govern our attitudes, we held the freedom to hope and the freedom to believe. What mattered the most, Rubin, was the attitude we took toward our suffering, the attitude in which we took our suffering upon ourselves. We soon learned to turn our suffering and grief into sacrifice. And the very moment it found meaning, the very moment it became sacrifice, it ceased to be suffering. We learned that a man's main concern is not to gain pleasure or to avoid pain, but rather to find the meaning in his life.

"This is how we were able to survive.

"In you, and through you, our suffering was given meaning. We knew that whatever you were doing in America, it was right. And we were proud to suffer so you could be free, so you could work your projects and make the world better. Perhaps this is what Spinoza meant when he said, 'Emotion, which is suffering, ceases to be suffering as soon as we form a clear and precise picture of it.'

"I suffered greatly when my young wife, your sister-in-law, died at the hands of the Nazi surgeons. I suffered as, in anguish, I cleaned the room and she lay prone on the cold table. She was dead. She was empty of her organs, yet her eyes were still open and her face was without expression. The doctors had attempted to play God, and they failed—if they had really meant to succeed. I suffered as I held her limp and bloody body close to my own until the Kapo came and demanded that I transport her to the furnace before I clean the room. I wore her blood on my clothes until the day of our liberation. And I learned a powerful rule. I learned that even in death I could love my wife, and I could continue to live for her. Through loving contemplation of her I found happiness in desolation.

"Rubin, love goes far beyond the physical person of the beloved. It finds its deepest meaning in the spiritual being, the inner self. Whether or not the person loved is actually present, whether or not that person is still alive, ceases somehow to be important. Through my memory of her I continued to love, and like freedom of attitude, I found another emotion, another joy the Nazis could not take from me."

The letter was yellow and brittle now, but Rubin still kept it by the side of his bed, and on the nights when thoughts of his own wife kept him from sleeping, he read and reread his brother's words. He knew that he could not continue to suffer because of his destiny. He could not cease to live and work because his loved ones were all gone. Rather, he felt an obligation to them, to his wife and sisters and brothers, to his mother and father. He was obligated to bring even greater meaning to their suffering and death.

Rubin knew that when the impossibility of replacing a person is realized, it allows the responsibility which a man has for his own existence, and his responsibility to its continuance, to appear in all its magnitude. He understood that at this point in his life it did not matter what he expected from life, but what life expected from him. His destiny could not be compared to the destiny of those he loved. His purpose was solo. His life had a reason, and that reason allowed him to bear his guilt.

The newswoman finished her broadcast and a new commentator took the air with an editorial about President Satterfield's decision to move the American embassy in Jerusalem to Tel Aviv.

Steinbrenner lifted himself out of bed and moved to the bathroom. His feet shuffled on the carpet. He was old. His body was slow, and his mind, which had grown more agile with age, often became irritated with his reluctant muscles. As a young boy in Poland, he had little patience with the aged, and now he had little patience with himself.

The Strategic Defense Initiative, and the responsibility he felt to see the system built, had been his motivation, and now, with the project completed, he was ready to sit down and relax, to allow death to sweep him away as it had his family. He had been allowed to live, and in life he had completed his goal. He had met his destiny.

Dr. Steinbrenner's presence at the staff meeting heightened the speculation among the Joint Chiefs as they sat waiting for the President to arrive. They whispered about the old man and his Initiative. Each knew of the physicist's involvement in the 1942 Manhattan Project, where, under the direction of General Leslie Groves, he joined the scientific laboratory with Robert Oppenheimer, Enrico Fermi, Niels Bohr, and scientist-turned-spy Klaus Fuchs.

By 1943, these scientists, military personnel, engineers and support staff were living in a converted boys' school in a small town called Los Alamos. It was there that Dr. Steinbrenner met a perky young research assistant named Ida Goldfein. And it was there, on July 16, 1945, at exactly 5:25 AM, in an event that caused Oppenheimer, himself, to quote Vishnu from *Bhagavad-Gita*—"I am become Death, the destroyer of worlds"—these men changed the course of history.

From that very moment, Steinbrenner knew the future. He knew the time would come when all developed nations would possess the power of nuclear fission. His foresight became prophecy when the Soviets exploded their first bomb, and it was then he began to argue for the development of an antiballistic missile system.

With short and stout Ida at his side, he rarely made a public appearance where he did not endorse the ABM project. When the Soviet Union began to produce more powerful nuclear warheads in the sixties, with the capability of destroying U.S. missile silos, and thwarting the threat of retaliation, he began to speak about nuclear blackmail, and he warned of the Soviet weapons stockpiles and their advanced research and development of laser technology. For a time, in the early seventies, when the United States signed a treaty with the USSR banning the development of ABM systems, he fell silent.

But then, in 1976, when the Department of Defense uncovered information that Russia had been developing an antisatellite system, using lasers to blind American spacecraft, he began to speak out again. In 1977, when an American early-warning satellite and two other Air Force satellites were disoriented while in orbit over Russia, the Department of Defense declared the Soviet system functional and a serious threat to U.S. security. It was speculated that the communists had a number of antisatellite systems and that their systems could also be employed as ABM weapons in the event of war. This speculation led the United States to instigate three rounds of talks in 1978 and 1979, to ban the use of any space weapon. The USSR cited America's progress with the space shuttle development as a direct aggressive step toward the use of space for military purposes, and the negotiations ceased without resolution.

Suddenly, Steinbrenner found himself a media celebrity, a Nostradamus of the nuclear age. His face was on the cover of newspapers and magazines. Three of his books were published, one reaching the top of *The New York Times* nonfiction best-seller list. In it he documented Soviet superiority in the nuclear arms race and in space weapons technology, and he called on America to support ABM development. He provided evidence that the Soviets were spending three to five times the amount of money spent by the United States to develop laser technology for space war.

"Communism can only spread through the use of force," he told a reporter from the Associated Press on a flight from Kansas to Washington. "Peaceful co-existence is against communist doctrine. Nobody votes to be Red—Poland, Afghanistan, East Berlin, Czechoslovakia, these countries did not vote for communism. If the Kremlin begins now to honor its treaties, it will become impotent. Its government will wither and die. Only expansion is survival, and expansion includes nuclear blackmail—even nuclear aggression. We must learn to fight them using the rules they, not we, brought to the game."

Steinbrenner's philosophy caught the attention of Ronald Reagan, the governor who would become President. Reagan brought the scientist into his circle of advisors, and included the philosophy in his foreign policy. Steinbrenner assured the candidate that America could develop and deploy a fail-safe nuclear defense system with the same speed it took to develop the bomb. And while Reagan was careful not to be controversial about the issue, at least until after the election, he believed Steinbrenner's promise and made it known to his team that as President he would continue to move toward ABM development. Reagan appointed the physicist as his science advisor, and within a year he gave Steinbrenner the green light to begin the research conducted in the eighties.

Now, almost two decades after Reagan's election, except for the final two phased-array radars, the project was complete. The standing installations, at Thule AFB in Greenland, Clear AFB in Alaska and Fylingsdale, along with the Keyhole 20 surveillance satellites, could do the job until the more modern and accurate radars were operational. And as Steinbrenner waited with the Joint Chiefs for the arrival of the President, he knew his duty was done.

"Be seated," President Satterfield said as he rushed into the room. He looked agitated. Quickly he sat down at the head of the oblong table, then just as quickly he stood up. "Gentlemen," he continued. His breathing was not synchronized with the tempo of his speech. "I considered canceling this meeting. However, what we have to discuss is top priority, and Senator Ashworth is on his way from Andrews right now." He turned to Tab Skillman, who had remained standing at the door. "How much longer?"

"Maybe five," Skillman said, looking at his watch.

"He's been flying all night to get back. Until he gets here, let me begin with some bad news." He studied the faces on the men of his national security staff, especially that of General Doland Rheem, the Army chief. "Army Senate Liaison has just sent us word from Italy that Senator Grayson Watenburg has been killed."

Rheem dropped his head into his hands.

"We don't know everything," Satterfield continued. "But apparently, there was an attack in the room of Hans Peterson, a leader of the German Christian Democrats. Both men, and a third, unidentified man, are dead." The President glanced at General Rheem.

"Terrorists?" asked Jules Morrow, chief of naval operations.

"We don't know exactly. There were signs of torture. Watenburg's ears—they were—"

Rheem lifted his head slowly and had trouble getting to his feet. He looked at the President. "May I leave for a moment, sir?" he asked.

"Of course, Doland," said Satterfield.

The general brushed passed the President and exited through the door behind Skillman. "Give me a minute," Satterfield said to the others and followed Rheem out the door.

"I'm sorry, Doland," Satterfield said once they were standing alone in the hallway outside the Cabinet Room. "I know you and the senator were close friends."

"Who did this?"

"We don't know yet," the President answered. "No one's claimed responsibility."

Rheem did not speak, but stared at his feet. A single tear dropped on the toe of his glossy black shoe. Satterfield felt uneasy.

"I'm sorry, Doland. I'm sure I didn't know him as well as you did."

The soldier looked at the President, his eyes were red yet dry, and Satterfield wondered where the tear had come from. "His wife is seven weeks away from having their fourth child."

The President took a deep breath and shook his head in sympathy. "I don't think she even knows yet."

"I know she doesn't."

"How do you know?"

"Because she's my sister-in-law." Rheem barely got the words out before his eyes filled with tears. Still, he maintained his composure. He took a handkerchief from his pocket. "She's been staying with my wife and me for the last ten days, while Grayson's in Rome."

Suddenly, the President felt himself shaking inside. His limbs were cold and numb. He blamed himself for not knowing the family tie between Senator Watenburg and General Rheem, and he was embarrassed and angry that he had been so indiscreet with the news. "I'm sorry, Doland." He put his hand on the man's shoulder. "I didn't know. I—"

"I have to know who did this!"

"We'll find out. I swear it."

"His life has never gone as well as it has these last few years. He's moved from—"

"Good morning, Mr. President, General Rheem," said Senator Boyd Ashworth as he approached. Long strands of thinning gray hair were tousled and down on his forehead. His suit was wrinkled from the overnight flight, and he had forgotten to button the top of his shirt and cinch his tie. The lines around his eyes and mouth were well pronounced as he smiled. "I'm glad to see you haven't started without me."

"Boyd," said the President, shaking Ashworth's hand.

"Senator." Rheem followed without looking directly at the man.

"I hope you had a nice flight." Satterfield looked from the senator to the general and hoped the former would see that the two needed to talk. "Everybody's inside," he continued. "Take a seat, and we'll be right in."

"Good news, I hope."

"I believe it is, Boyd," the President answered, forcing a smile. "I can't wait to tell you all about it."

Ashworth opened the heavy door and stepped around Skillman to the table. Tab looked at the two men still in the hall, and the President motioned him to close the door.

"Mr. President," said Rheem, "I apologize for the—"

"Don't say it, Doland."

"But thinking about Vicky—her kids—I'll have to—"

"You don't have to tell her. We can send somebody over."

"No," Rheem said quickly. "I'll tell her."

"You don't have to come back inside."

"I'd better." The general tried to stiffen his brow.

"What if she hears before you get home? I imagine they'll contact his office this morning."

"Even his office doesn't know where she's staying. Few people know he's my brother-in-law."

"I wish I'd known."

"Nobody does."

"How about his kids?"

"What?"

"Where are they staying? What if they're contacted?"

"Two are away at school. One's at my place." Rheem paused and his face was overcome with a look of concentration. "The only way she would know is the *Post*."

The President shook his head. "The early edition is out, and the story's not in it."

Chapter Eight

"Sunny Italy," Malibu said to himself as he nursed a Diet Coke at the restaurant Girarrosto Toscano on the Via Campania. Outside, a torrential rain had cleared the streets, and Robert found refuge inside the Florentine restaurant. He could not remember ever seeing rain in Italy, and for a moment, he tried to remember if Rome boasted "year-around" sunshine in its tourism brochures. *Maybe that's Spain*, he thought, and took another sip of his drink. Though he was surprised by the rain, it was fitting that it should pour when it did.

Even heaven's pissing on me, he thought. He ordered a beefsteak to go with his Coke. The hour was 1:20 in the afternoon, and Robert had not eaten since the ambassador's party the night before. Still, he was not hungry.

Simon Levin had followed through on his threat, and Robert was now a free-lancer—a writer without a residence. "Jackass," he said and lifted his small glass in a toasting gesture to his former editor. "And to Brook," he thought as he placed the drink back on the table. "Good luck with my story. My story." He thought of the night before, the meeting with Watenburg. The look of concern on his friend's face. He thought of that same face only hours later, ghostly pale but calm.

Robert and Brook were the first to discover Grayson's body when they returned to the hotel. It had taken Malibu almost forty-five minutes to convince the concierge to open the door, and when the ornery Italian finally did, Robert wished he had not. His fear was realized. To think about something—to believe it—is one thing, but to

81

see it, that's quite another. Though he had prepared himself for the scene inside the German's hotel room, the sight of his dead friend caught him off guard anyway, and he could only stand and look. Nothing more. He could not move. He could not speak. He could not respond to the young Brook Adams, who moved directly to the bathroom, stumbled over the unidentified dead man, and collapsed on the floor in front of the toilet to vomit. The concierge phoned hotel security, and when he finished his call, Robert was surprised to see that Adams still had the presence of mind to dial Simon in Washington.

"To you, Brook," Malibu said silently as he looked into his drink. "You did a damn fine job with Levin." He took another drink. "But I can only blame myself."

"Excuse me?" said the restaurant proprietor as he stopped at Hamilton's table.

"What?"

"You say something?"

"No." Robert shook his head.

The Italian smiled. "Why you drinking Coca-Cola?" he asked. "This is *Italia—Roma*. I have good *vino sciolto*."

"Coke's fine. Thank you."

"Maybe a little," said the man as he motioned to pour the wine into a small glass on Robert's table.

"No—no!" The journalist's voice snapped, and he was suddenly embarrassed. But he could not touch it. He forced a smile. "You know—one's too many, ten's not enough."

The Italian did not answer, but walked away from the table.

"Get a hold of yourself," Malibu said, and his mind chastised. *He was only being a friendly host.* The journalist took a deep breath. "Damn, I could have used that wine." He tipped his glass and finished the last of his Coke with a gulp. From his pocket he took ten thousand lire and dropped it next to the plate with the cold steak. It was a generous tip from a man without a job, but he felt he had to apologize to the friendly owner.

In the street, the rain was still falling in sheets, and by the time Robert made it to the taxi stop, he was soaked, his clothes felt heavy and uncomfortable, and his wool blazer issued a faint stale smell. "Hotel Ambasciatori," he said and handed the driver two thousand

lire. The man smiled and put the cab in motion. "It's a beautiful day,"
Robert said and shook his head slowly, "a shit-ridden beautiful day."
   The driver stared into the rearview mirror and smiled in agreement.
   "I just lost my damn job," Robert said with a laugh.
   "Yes," said the driver with a more profound smile and nodding his
head.
   "My damn editor has no clue about news values."
   The driver was still in total agreement.
   "I'm sitting on the story of my life—does he care? Hell no. He
gives it to a baby-faced cub reporter. The kid even threw up. Imagine
that."
   The driver chuckled and shook his head in total disbelief.
   "The scumbucket," Hamilton said.
   "Scumbucket," the hack repeated.
   "Wanted me to follow some story about Senator Ashworth. Senator
Ashworth! Nobody gives a damn about Senator Ashworth."
   The driver shook his head no and turned the car onto the Via Vittorio
Veneto. Robert looked out the rain-swept window. The streets were
beautiful, clean and empty. The cobblestone glistened under the water,
and the beauty of the reddish-brown stone buildings was highlighted
under the stain of rain like mahogany under varnish. Black and green
tarps hung over the street-corner kiosks to protect the newspapers and
magazines. At the intersection of Veneto and del Tritone, a lone police
officer battled the rain, sheltered only by his dark blue kepi, and
directed traffic.
   "Who cares about Massachusetts, anyway? Do you?" he asked the
driver, who shook his head emphatically. "I sure don't." Robert
paused long enough to collect a thought that stormed over him with
greater force than the rain outside. "Grayson did, though," he
mumbled to himself. "Grayson cared about Massachusetts—about
Ashworth—about SDI." He pulled his notebook from the inside breast
pocket of his jacket and thumbed it open to the notes he had taken the
night before. His wet hands mixed with the ink on the pages and
smeared some of the words. He wiped his stained fingers on his blue
slacks and continued.
   HANS PETERSON—GRAYSON WATENBURG—CHRISTIAN DEMO-
CRATS—BITES THE BIG ONE—WIFE GONE—NECK—BLOOD—WHITE
SILK PAJAMAS—UNIDENTIFIED MAN—STILETTO—SDI DEBATE—

COFFEE SHOP—CHANCELLOR—SULFAZINE PYROGENIC (MALARIA/ SCHIZOPHRENIA).

It was not in his notebook, but Grayson had said something. Robert tried to remember. "Ashworth," he repeated and flipped through a few more pages, knowing nothing was there, but hoping that something would be. "Ashworth." He forced the image of Watenburg back into his head. At first, the image was that of the last time he saw the senator, lifeless and bloodstained. Then there he was in his tuxedo, the Burberry overcoat, and the open collar on the formal shirt. Robert had recommended that Grayson call Ashworth to report Peterson's death. "He's the President of the North Atlantic Assembly."

"It will probably come as welcome news," Grayson had said. Ashworth was no friend of SDI. "Hans was the European demon."

Malibu slowly closed his notebook and placed it back in his pocket. "Hans was the European demon," he repeated. "Watch him," Grayson had warned.

"What do you mean?'

"Just what I said," Grayson had been firm.

"Watch him for what? Watch him for what? Watch him for what?"

"I'll answer tomorrow."

That's today, Malibu thought as he relaxed back into the seat. That's today, and Grayson Watenburg is dead.

The cab turned into the semicircular driveway of the hotel and Robert reached into his back pocket, withdrew his wallet, and gave the driver another four thousand lire without remembering he had already paid. The driver said nothing, but smiled graciously, and Malibu went into the hotel.

Except for two men, the lobby was empty. At the front desk, a concierge studied the journalist as he made his way to the elevator. On the right side of the elevator bank stood the second man, a young police officer, a boy that Malibu guessed was still in his latter teens. He was dressed in a military-looking dark blue uniform with a beret and army boots. An Uzi was slung from his shoulder, and he, too, studied Robert's moves. He nodded a cocky, authoritative nod as Robert approached.

"Good aff-ter-noon," he said. "You are the American, Mr. Hamilton, no?"

Robert nodded.

"Please, Mr. Hamilton, go directly to your room. Some men are there waiting to speak to you."

"Me? Why?" Robert asked. "I answered questions all night."

"These things, I do not know," said the man, and Robert understood that the young officer was doing only what he was told.

"Well," he drew a deep breath and forced a smile, "I have no place else to go."

The young man pushed the up button, and the elevator door immediately to the left opened. Inside, another officer—this time a man in a poorly fitted gray suit—stood posed like a passenger. And Robert was unsure whether he should address the man as an officer or play the game of pretending not to know who he was. Either way, he realized, the police were going to make sure he did as they asked.

The door to his room was open, and two uniformed officers stood on either side. Hamilton nodded as he passed them and entered to see three more officers inside.

"Brought the whole precinct down, didn't you?" Robert said. His voice could not conceal his irritation.

"You did not sleep last night," said a short, stiff man dressed in a crisp knit suit. Robert guessed he was the detective assigned to the case, a different man than one of the regular officers who had questioned him in the predawn hours.

"Forget that," Robert said as he moved to the closet of his room. "Who's gone through my stuff?"

"You mean you do not live this way?" said the man as he made a sweeping gesture with his arms. The room was ransacked. The closet and drawers were emptied and the contents strewn about the floor.

"I'm not a suspect," said Hamilton. "So what in hell gives you the right to come into my room and tear the place apart?"

"Everybody is a suspect."

"I was with Brook Adams—Mr. Adams—our paper's bureau officer. I told your people last night."

"You were with him from about three o'clock this morning until you discovered the bodies," the man interrupted. "Before that?"

"Before that, I was with a friend."

"Yes," said the officer as he walked behind Robert and closed the door of the room. "This is where I have a problem with your story. A word such as 'friend' is not a good alibi in Italy. Maybe in New York, only.'' He motioned Robert to sit down. "In *Roma* it makes a man as intelligent as you appear suspicious.''

Robert sat on the side of his bed. "I realize that,'' he said. "I realized that when I chose the word.'' He looked on the floor at all the files that had been opened and scattered. It would take him days to put his life back in order.

"And words are your craft.''

"No,'' Robert said, looking back to the small man. "No, journalism is my craft. I know the media, and the friend I was with can't be identified. The press would have a field day.''

"Is this friend a woman? Maybe married?''

"I don't have to listen to this.''

"Is this friend any more famous than the two men butchered last night.''

"More famous?''

"Why are you protecting your friend?''

"Is that something you can't understand?''

"When murder is involved, no.''

"Because this someone is completely innocent.''

"And you know this for certain?''

"Of course.''

"How long have you known this"—the man paused—"this friend?''

Robert thought about Diana Sillito. "Long enough,'' he said.

"See, Mr. Hamilton, this is your problem: your answers are too vague. I asked you how long have you known this someone, and you answer me, 'Long enough.' This does not help me. It does not help you.''

"You know I didn't kill anyone.''

"But you are not forthright with the answers, are you?''

"I was at the ambassador's reception.''

"At the Villa Taverna.''

"You know that.''

"Of course,'' said the man. "I, too, did not sleep last night.'' He kicked away the pile of clothes that had been heaped on the floor in front of the chair opposite Malibu and sat down. "You were called from the reception by the senator. You met with him in the room of

Peterson. Tell me why you failed to call the police then—why you did not stay with Watenburg."

"I don't make the news," said Robert. "I only report it."

"A man was murdered, Mr. Hamilton. A man was tortured and then murdered. You did not report it, and so the senator was tortured and murdered."

"I thought," Robert began but then he stopped. It was the first time he had considered the idea that he might, in some way, be responsible for Grayson's death. "I couldn't call," he said. "I'm a journalist."

"And that somehow frees you from being a responsible citizen?"

"Of course not. But the senator—he was going to call."

"And you were going to write the story. Take the glory. Win the awards that are shared among your—what do they say—intellectual log-rolling society."

"I don't need to listen to this."

"I make the rules now, Mr. Hamilton, and you will listen."

"I know my rights."

"You have lost your rights."

"I want my attorney to—"

"No, no," said the detective as he shook his head. He made a clicking noise with this tongue. "We have new rules."

"I want to call the American embassy."

"Do not play with me." The Italian's voice was growing angry. "You are not under arrest. We are not coercing you. But you are withholding important information, and you cannot do this in Italy."

"Haven't you heard of freedom of the press? Protecting sources?"

"Of course, but we are a land of subsidized information. The government and the media work together and promote social responsibility. If the press steps from the rank, it loses the important subsidies it has grown to depend on. We work well together—a team."

For the first time in the last thirty hours, Robert felt the lack of sleep. His head was light and ached from fatigue, and he found it difficult to argue. Protecting Diana's identity was suddenly appearing to be less important. He imagined she was still at the Cicerone Hotel, still asleep with a calm and beautiful smile on her lips. He wanted to sink back in his own bed and throw the covers over his body, to wake up in eight hours and discover that the events of last night were only a bad dream—the grist for a novel he would write someday.

"Mr. Hamilton," said the detective, "I am going to ask you—"

"Listen to me," Robert stood up. "If you're going to arrest me, then you'd better arrest me. If you're not, then get the hell out of my room. You know I'm not a suspect. I can have one of a dozen people vouch for my character and whereabouts. I'm not giving you any information." He walked to the door and opened it with such force that both the men on the other side rushed into the room. Still, Robert paid them no attention. "I'm keeping the name to myself. Whether you can understand my reasons or not. Your rules may be different here in Italy. But then again, you elect porno queens to congress, and that doesn't say too much about who makes your damn laws in the first place."

The detective motioned the two uniformed officers out of the room. He then asked the other two men, who had been inside the room during the questioning, to leave. They complied, and the detective shifted his weight in the chair. "Sit down, Mr. Hamilton." He smiled and gestured Robert back to the bed. "We have gotten off to what you Americans call 'the wrong foot.' "

"On the wrong foot," Robert said.

"What?"

"*On* the wrong foot. Not *to* the wrong foot."

The Italian shook his head in agreement. "Oh, yes, forgive me. I learned my English from a textbook."

"Come on," said Hamilton, "you speak too well."

"A textbook at George Washington University."

"You lived in Washington, D.C.?" Malibu was surprised.

"Of course, Mr. Hamilton. I still do—at least six months of the year.

"I don't understand—" Robert began.

"I'm with counterterrorism, based at Langley."

Malibu collapsed on the bed. "Central Intelligence," he said matter-of-factly, embarrassed that he had not guessed it before. "You fooled me."

"Good," the man said with delight. "That's what I was trying to do. But it's time to drop back and punt." He extended his hand and Robert shook it. "My name's Aspanu."

"What's your first name?"

"That is my first name—Aspanu Niccolini." The man smiled.
"You'd think I take a lot of flak about my name, wouldn't you?" He
nodded. "I do. That's why I go by Andy."

"Close enough," Malibu said. "But tell me, Andy, why did your
people tear up my room?"

"I'm asking the same question."

"What?" Malibu sat up straight on the bed.

"I'm asking the same question, Mr. Hamilton. Who tore up your
room?"

"It wasn't you?"

"I didn't touch it."

Robert looked to the closet. "Housekeeping comes around about
eleven. It's almost two, now. That means someone had to—" Robert
paused "What time did you get here?"

"Noon."

Malibu cocked his head in bewilderment. Suddenly he was hungry,
and wished he had enjoyed the beefsteak when he had the chance. He
stood. "I haven't really eaten since yesterday. Do you mind?" He
motioned to the small refrigerator tucked under the desk cabinet next to
the television.

Andy nodded again. "Go ahead."

Robert opened the small door and studied the contents: two boxes of
mixed nuts, two tins of sardines, a jar of caviar, a box of crackers,
assorted sodas and miniature bottles of liquor. "Can I get you anything? A drink? Something to eat?"

"You have a beer in there?"

"No beer," said Robert. "There's some hard stuff."

"A Coke?"

Robert handed him the minisize red can. He took out both boxes of
mixed nuts and returned to the bed. "How do you open these damn
things?" he said as he struggled with the cellophane wrap that sealed
the nuts inside the box. Finally, he bit through the wrapper, tore the
box open and took a mouthful of nuts. "Who did go through my
room?"

"Knowing would be an important piece of the puzzle," said Andy
as he took a sip of Coke. "Maybe it was the person you were with last
night—the person you're trying to protect."

"Get off of that," Robert said.

"Think seriously about it. Who else knew what went on last night. Senator Watenburg, Hans Peterson, you, the police, hotel management. That's it. Now which of these would have the motive to pull your room apart?" He took another sip and then a deep breath. "Who were you with?"

"I was just getting to like you."

"Come on."

"There's no reason for concern," Robert reassured. He crumpled the cellophane and it crackled, and then he opened the second box. "The friend I was with last night has no idea about Grayson and the German. I didn't tell her a thing."

"Her?"

"What?"

"You said, 'Her.' You were with a woman."

"I wasn't with her that long. Maybe forty-five minutes. I had to file my story."

"But you didn't file it. Nothing's in today's *Post*."

"I got fired."

"They can't fire you," Andy protested. "You're a celebrity, like Woodward—Woodward and Bern—Bern—."

"Bernstein."

"Yeah, Bernstein. You're one of them."

"If only Simon Levin believed that."

"Simon Levin?"

"The editor who fired me."

"Then you really were?"

"I'm now among the unemployed."

Andy only shook his head.

Robert looked away and took a deep breath. "I guess I saw it coming." He thought about Simon Levin. The two men never got along, and Robert believed the editor wanted him off the staff from the beginning. Robert believed that Levin considered him to be nothing more than a political hack, a writer who emerged from journalism school and sold his objectivity and ethics for the higher pay and the security of a government public relations job rather than the challenge and ascetic life of a real journalist. More than once Levin had referred to the government leeches in the city, the men and women of Washington who "live off the honest taxpayers," and more than once Robert believed Simon was talking about him. Yet they worked together for fifteen years, and on many occasions enjoyed each other's company. Robert questioned whether his work *had* become lazy. He had dropped important information from some recent stories, and more than once he had not double-checked his sources but ran with his initial information. Consequently, more than once he had embarrassed the paper, and references to his stories were appearing with greater frequency in the corrections column. Inside, Robert knew that he was not a completely innocent victim of Simon Levin's fury.

"I'll miss your stories," Andy said, bringing Robert's mind back to the hotel room. "But if you are no longer with the paper, and you are not reporting on this Watenburg murder, then you don't have sources to protect. Why not just tell me who you were with last night, and I'll get out of here."

Robert stood up. "As I said, I was just getting to like you." He walked to the door and opened it. "But I'm going to have to ask you to leave. Suddenly, I'm very tired—maybe even a little irritable. You can take your Coke with you."

"I'll eventually get what I came for."

"I hope you do."

Andy looked about the room. "And you may get more than you want," he said.

"What do you mean?"

"I mean this." He gestured to the mess. "Someone knows you're involved. Someone knows about your relationship with Watenburg. They know where you were last night. And now it looks like they want to know more."

"I don't have any more."

"Who were you with last night?"

"Come on." Robert nodded his head toward the open door.

Andy stood up and moved into the hallway. "You know I'm going to find out."

"Not from me."

"But I will."

"Then good luck," Robert said and closed the door.

Chapter Nine

The light in the green room was dim. Cold shadows moved about, illuminated by the gray hue that filtered through a window on the far wall. Sergio heard voices, though he could not see who was speaking or what was said. His lower back was numb, and his shoulders and legs ached. Something burned in his left arm. His eyes could not focus well. Still, he could see there were other beds in the room, other beds occupied by patients, some of them breathing loudly, some of them coughing. He smelled the odor of sterilizing solvent, mixed with the odor of excrement and perspiration. His mouth was dry, and breathing through his nose was difficult. He tried to move, but could not. He tried to speak, but this, too, was impossible. Even lifting his head from the pillow was painful and exhausting. But his mind was completely awake, alert to all that moved about him. It was an unusual sensation, part of his body being completely out of synch, uncontrollable. He felt vulnerable, captive to his body, able to think clearly about what he wanted his arms and legs to do, but unable to execute his commands, and the feeling made him anxious. "Do not frustrate yourself," he tried to console himself. "Lie quiet. Rest."

The shadows continued to play, and Sergio remembered the last time he felt this helpless was after a morphine injection he received in France. The prison doctor had given him too much, and for three days his mind battled his body's painful lethargy. The memory of the pain and torment brought back a flood of images from prison, the fifteen years his soul screamed for freedom, and his mind grew black with emotion. He could not allow himself to be sent back to prison. He was not ready for death; he was not ready for prison. The anger and the vulnerability that racked his body made him ready only for revenge.

"How do you feel?" asked the voice of a woman. Sergio tried to see her, but could not get a clear image. She was dressed in white, this he could tell, and she reached for his wrist to check the pulse. "You are remarkably strong," she said as if she did not intend Sergio to answer her question. "Already they have declared your condition from critical to stable." Gently, she placed his hand back on the bed. "Everybody on this floor is talking about you, about your will to live." She readjusted the flow clip on the intravenous tube. "When you can speak, we all have questions. Even the police have come to see you. Not many people are shot in *Roma*. It is unusual. And they found you almost naked."

She pulled the covers off of Sergio and rolled him over in bed. His back felt as if it were going to explode. He wanted to cry out but could not. She untied the three strings that held his gown and took the soiled cloth from his body. "We have given you a name," she said as she ripped off the adhesive tape that held the dressing where the physician had removed the bullet. "We call you Achilles." With a cold sponge she cleaned around the wound and redressed it. "People ask me, how is Achilles? I feel like a celebrity." She moved the sponge over Sergio's buttocks and down his legs to his feet. For the first time since gaining consciousness, he felt pleasure. "Men like you are not often placed in the indigent ward," she said. "But the man who tried to kill you took your identification. We do not know who you are." She rolled Sergio to his back, and again the pain was intense. "We think you are not Roman." She bathed his chest and stomach and then moved the sponge to the genitalia. "Maybe Spanish. Maybe American."

"How is he?" asked another voice from across the room. This time it belonged to a man.

"Fine, doctor," said the woman. She quickly moved the sponge over the thighs and down to the feet.

Sergio tried again to speak. He wanted to ask how long he had been in the hospital, but his voice only squeaked.

"Shhh," the nurse whispered. "You are not that strong." She placed the sponge in the bowl of alcohol on the stand next to Sergio's bed, took another gown, still folded and crisp, placed Sergio's arms through it, tucked the cloth under both sides of his body, but did not tie it in the back. He was relieved that she had spared him the pain.

"I'll need your help on bed five," said the other voice.

"Yes, doctor." She gently stroked Sergio's forehead and brushed his black hair to the side. "Hurry and get well," she whispered. And then she was gone.

Chapter Ten

"As the President said," Dr. Steinbrenner began slowly. The Joint Chiefs were attentive. Anticipation filled the air. But the physicist had not been warned about Senator Ashworth's presence at the meeting, and the edge he would otherwise feel was lost. The other men were unmitigated supporters of his program. Ashworth was not. For six years, Steinbrenner had struggled in front of the senator's Armed Services Committee, been embarrassed by questions from the senator that at times became personal. It was Senator Ashworth who introduced the term Nuclear Guilt to describe the physicist and his drive to realize the Strategic Defense Initiative.

"This man," Ashworth told a press conference following a day of laborious testimony by Steinbrenner in front of Armed Services, "is driven by nuclear guilt. He gave us the bomb. He hasn't been able to live with himself for over half a century, and now he's driven to correct his mistake. But my opinion is that he is doing nothing but thrusting us farther into the nuclear abyss, leading us one more step toward annihilation."

Steinbrenner tried not to look at Ashworth as he spoke. "As the President said, it is finished. The most important phase of the Strategic Defense Initiative is completed. Today, we have thirty-six anti-ballistic-missile satellites in semi- and geosynchronous orbit. Each protects a zone of equal proportion to the others. One-third are equipped with a ten megawatt laser mechanism, powerful enough to destroy the guidance system of an attacking missile, powerful enough to put the missile into eternal orbit. The others are equipped with

95

particle beams that are capable of total destruction.'' Steinbrenner stopped speaking and picked up ten red-and-white striped folders. On the front of the folders was written: EYES ONLY. "I have the briefing books with me," said the physicist, "and I am happy to hand them out. But please leave the books on the table when this meeting is completed."

Ashworth took his folder from Steinbrenner but did not open it. He placed it beneath his briefcase on the table and sat back in the chair. His mouth was drawn tight. His eyes were angry. Steinbrenner could see an attack was imminent.

"You all know that the Strategic Defense Initiative is nothing more than the natural progression of a philosophy that began in the 1950s, when the Cold War forced us to build a formidable strategic air defense,'' Steinbrenner continued in an effort to extinguish the fire of Ashworth's rebuttal before it began. "At one time, we had Nike rings around our major cities and an air defense command with more than twenty-five hundred fighter-interceptors. Unfortunately, the Soviet intercontinental ballistic missiles forced us out of using such a defense as our major form of deterrence. In the 1960s, we began to move toward the development of an ABM system. Secretary of Defense McNamara first emphasized the ABM role in protecting our territory against Third World powers such as China, as well as against accidental missile launches. Later, the Nixon Administration put forward a more defined concept of the defense philosophy to protect key military installations such as our own ICBM fields. We had to insure the survivability of our retaliatory nuclear forces."

Steinbrenner finished handing out the folders and walked back to the head of the table. He glanced at Ashworth. "However, because of certain political maneuvers, we were unable to implement one simultaneous, and might I mention cost-effective, effort. The on again, off again, somewhat capricious, nature of Congress, forced us to close shop more than once. As you know, in the early 1970s, we did not even deploy the one ABM site allowed under the ABM treaty of 1972."

"Dr. Steinbrenner," interrupted Senator Ashworth.

"One minute, Senator," said President Satterfield. "There will be time for questions.

"However, new leadership under President Reagan restored—or should I say re-emphasized—the program. When we returned to our shelf technology, we discovered our space program had provided us with the capability to make the program a reality. This was fortunate because the Soviet Union never stopped developing an ABM system of its own. Unlike the free world, the Soviet Union has never accepted the concept of Mutually Assured Destruction. Almost thirty years ago, at the Glassboro Summit, when President Johnson attempted to interest Premier Kosygin in an ABM ban, the Soviet leader told him that his country could not abandon projects which held the prospect of protecting its people.''

"Dr. Steinbrenner," Ashworth began again.

"Wait, Boyd," said Satterfield. Tab Skillman shifted uncomfortably.

"Soviet work on strategic defense against our missiles has been going on as long as Moscow has been developing its own missiles. For the last fifteen years, the Kremlin has actually spent more on strategic defense than on its offense. Despite the Reagan-Gorbachev meeting in 1987, despite the agreement both sides made to keep their development in the laboratory. In fact, we know that the Soviets have virtually thrown the ABM treaty aside, and they have begun to install a nationwide defense system.''

"This is preposterous," said Ashworth.

"Hold on, Senator," the President ordered.

"You hold on, Mr. President. I'm not going to sit here and listen that our country has broken a signed treaty and deployed killer satellites.''

"There will be time for comments," said Satterfield.

"We know the Soviets have spent three to five times as much as the United States for research on directed energy weapons such as lasers,'' said Steinbrenner, trying to intervene.

"Three times as much as our *published expenditures*," corrected Ashworth.

"Let Dr. Steinbrenner finish," Satterfield demanded.

"To a certain degree, they are actually farther ahead in most areas of neutral particle beam research, and we all know of their antisatellite capability.''

"This is absurd, Mr. President." Ashworth's voice indicated that he would wait no longer to be heard. "We have violated a treaty. I'm sitting here, and you're telling me that we have violated a treaty. And the good scientist, here, is trying to justify and condone our action.''

"It's finished, Boyd," said the President.

"Finished? Are you kidding? We've just begun." The senator stood up and grabbed the briefing file and gestured in the direction of the Capitol. "Every damn senator on that hill thinks we're just researching and developing. They think this is a damn hobby of the Republican Party. Wait until they get the news!"

"It's finished, Boyd," the President repeated. "Now sit down. You can't grandstand in here."

"Where did the money come from?"

"Sit down."

"Where did the money come from?"

"I said," the President began, but before he could finish, Tab Skillman jumped into the fray.

"Sit the fuck down, Senator," said Skillman, emphasizing each syllable.

"This is outrageous," Ashworth continued, undaunted. "How could the deployment be so secret that my committee wouldn't know about it."

"We trusted no one," said Steinbrenner.

"Especially your committee," said Skillman, and Satterfield looked at him with surprise.

"That," Ashworth pointed his finger at the President, "was your mistake—your fatal flaw."

"You know damn well we've been developing this project," said Satterfield.

"Like hell! That was the Global Ballistic Missile Defense. We were researching a system to share with the world, not to put three dozen satellites up there to throw the balance of power out of whack. And no one—no one—talked about the actual deployment." Ashworth finally sat down, and Skillman followed his example. "Have you even considered our allies?"

"Of course we have," said Satterfield.

"They're going to revolt." The senator shook his head. "You've destroyed NATO—that's what you've done—destroyed NATO. They'll never trust us again."

"We've destroyed nothing," said Steinbrenner. His voice was finally angry. "NATO will understand the need for secrecy. They all assisted in the research and development. Their defense contractors were well paid. Their economies benefitted. But we had to begin the deployment somewhere—sometime."

"And this is a good start," said the President.

Steinbrenner looked from Satterfield to the other men in the room. They were tense, embarrassed by Ashworth's bold outburst against their commander in chief. Secretary Wilford Parryman of the State Department and Rich Spencer of the National Security Council already knew of the deployment. The others were surprised by the announcement. General Dan White from Air Force, Chief of Naval Operations Jules Morrow, and Marine Commandant Raymond Bradford had spoken quietly to each other during the outburst. General Rheem remained silent.

"It's a breach of public trust," said Ashworth, "a damn breach of trust."

"Senator Ashworth," Steinbrenner began, "it is for the protection of the American people, nothing else. There has been no lie. There has been no deceit. We have provided for our own."

"Some things have to be done without taking opinion polls," said Satterfield. "Roosevelt didn't go to the American people to ask if he could build a bomb capable of blowing up the world."

"We'd be better off if he had," said Ashworth.

Satterfield let the comment pass.

"The question remains," the senator continued, "where did the money come from?"

"It's been appropriated from several areas within the defense budget," said Skillman.

"My best recollection is that Congress has appropriated money for research and development," Ashworth said. "We never appropriated money for deployment."

"There were emergency appropriations," said the president.

"You mean you stole from other budgets."

"My—" Skillman jumped to his feet again, but before he could say anything else, Steinbrenner interrupted him.

"We stole nothing," said the physicist.

"Then where did the damn money come from?" Ashworth looked at the President.

"There was nothing illegal," said Steinbrenner, "nothing unethical."

"This from the man who gave us the bomb."

Ashworth's comment brought General Rheem to his feet. "One more word from you, and so help me—" said Rheem. His face was red, and blue-green blood veins bulged below his jaw. Skillman sat down, yielding the floor to the general. Steinbrenner was surprised to see a general stand up to the senator. At once, he was grateful and concerned. He guessed that Rheem knew the same frustration of testifying before the politician's committee, of watching the senior senator posture in front of the national media with loaded questions and caustic remarks.

"Come on," said Satterfield. "I'm not about to let a National Security Committee meeting start World War III. "Sit down, Doland." His voice was in command. He looked from the general to the senator to his chief of staff. Skillman smiled and rolled his eyes. "Please," he said, once the room was calm, "please continue, doctor."

"I believe," Steinbrenner said deliberately, "the system we have in place is the most advantageous at this time. It does not give us a great superiority over the Soviets. But it is a step toward a nuclear-free world. It allows us to once again speak to Moscow from a posture of strength equal to theirs."

Ashworth grunted and shifted in his chair. Steinbrenner continued: "The Soviets have maintained a five-year lead in space-based laser technology. It could very well be that they have their own network of protective satellites. We're not sure. Since 1981, we have believed their Kosmos 1267, frequently docked at their space station, Salyut 6, is a defensive weapon—capable of destroying multiple spacecraft. What we've done is evened the odds."

"It sounds a little more than evened odds," said Jules Morrow.

"I say evened because we have yet to activate the technology. And we must still complete our two phased-array radar stations before the system is fully functional."

General White rocked forward in his chair. His snow-white hair and well-lined jaw made him the most distinguished looking man at the table. He spoke with a deep voice. His eyes were cold. "They're not activated?"

"That's right," said Satterfield. "This is something we have to discuss."

"Had we activated them already," said Steinbrenner, "surely you men would know about the program."

"Had we activated them already," the President continued, "the whole world would know about it."

Ashworth sat straight in his chair, poised to re-enter the conversation.

"But can't we assume the Soviets already know?" Morrow asked. "They have seen us launch them."

"Seen us, yes," said Satterfield, "at least some of them. But there's no way of being certain which kinds of satellites they are. The launch gap created by the Challenger disaster played in our favor here. Moscow was not alarmed by our frequent launches, knowing how much we had to make up. Other satellites we launched from the Southern Hemisphere—out of sight. And you have to remember that these boxes have been launched over the past thirteen years. As far as the Soviets are concerned, they could be weather satellites, network machines, you name it."

"Actually, it's quite difficult to determine the function of a satellite," said Steinbrenner. "Had the Soviets not prematurely disoriented three of our satellites in the early eighties, we still wouldn't know about their Kosmos 1267."

"Getting back to the point," said White, "when will they be activated?"

President Satterfield sat back and looked at Skillman. "Well," he began, "this is where we run into a game of chance."

"A game of chance?" said Ashworth. "How many hundreds of billions of dollars out there orbiting in space, and you're saying it's a game of chance?"

"What we want, Boyd—gentlemen—is bilateral disarmament. We want the progress in the Eastern Bloc to continue. Reagan and Bush opened the doors, and now it's our job to finish—to complete the process, both with the remaining ICBMs and reduction in conventional arms." He paused long enough to look at the scientist. "When Dr. Steinbrenner began this project, it was a secondary defense philosophy only, a secondary strategy that would be used if disarmament failed. It was serious enough that my predecessors refused to bargain it away. It was serious enough that despite all the deficits and political grab-assing that went on, we continued with the program. To this end, I compliment Dr. Steinbrenner. Ironically, however, as the project matured so did relations between the superpowers. No one could have foretold this thaw in the Cold War. Right now, we're closer to mutual disarmament and real progress for peace than ever before, and I'm not going to gamble that away.

"I know it's what we want, and I believe it's what the Soviets want. What we do not want is an escalated space war. Let's not underestimate the Soviets. Sure, they've had economic problems of their own, and those problems have forced them to make concessions for peace that they otherwise would not have made, but they are still more than capable of mounting a fast and furious space defense system of their own. And it's more than clear that they're capable of developing a series of missiles that will penetrate our shield. To activate the system now would be wrong. It would be to our disadvantage.

"Too many people would have to know about it, and the possibility of a leak—especially months before our Luxembourg Summit—would be devastating to the progress we've made over the past decade. It would also be dangerous. Like a bear against the wall, the Kremlin could panic and decide its only recourse is to attack before the system is fully operational. It would also"—the President looked at Ashworth—"it would also send a panic through NATO. And we don't need that, either."

Morrow cleared his throat, then spoke. "In the event that the Soviets did discover our system—"

"Again," said Satterfield, "we don't know how they would react, but the possibility exists that—"

"They might mount an attack—a nuclear attack," said Ashworth. "And how would the system fare against submarine-launched missiles?"

"It wouldn't," said Steinbrenner. He believed the time had come to outline the deficiencies of the system. "And at present, it is only able to strike intercontinental ballistic missiles, and then only in their boost and mid-course range of trajectory. This limitation allows a projected ratio of eighty percent."

"We do have ERIS for the terminal and re-entry stages," Satterfield began to add, but Ashworth interrupted him.

"Eighty percent?" he yelled. "And on ICBMs only? That's asinine."

"It's what we have now, senator," said the scientist. "Eventually, we will have total capability. In order to be one hundred percent effective, it's required that we have the beam potential to hit offensive nuclear missiles in all four stages of their trajectory—boost, post-boost, mid-course, and terminal. Currently, the Army technology for terminal and re-entry, as the President said, is still kinetic—ballistic.

"We also need the earliest possible warning systems," he continued. "These are provided by the phased-array system, and two are not yet complete. Ultimately, our system will be able to destroy missiles before they deploy their multiple warheads. This is the secret to success. As it is now, some of the warheads are dummies. The others are real. Our system cannot distinguish between the two, and as it fires on some of the dummies, the others will break through the canopy."

"Why don't we have the capability to hit the missiles in the pre-boost phase?" asked General White.

"And why don't we have the capability to hit other targets on earth—targets like munitions plants and missile silos?" Morrow added.

"Because to provide a satellite with a laser or particle beam powerful enough to reach that far would require too large of a power source. In such a case, the Soviets would easily determine the satellite's function, and because it would have to be so large, its survivability would be in question."

"Even at eighty percent, the odds seem appropriate to me," said Morrow. "I recommend that we activate the system."

President Satterfield looked at his national security advisor. Rich Spencer had been silent so far. "No," said the President. "The recommendation is that we wait to activate. We're not going to risk a walkout on the Summit."

"We've never been this close," said Secretary Perryman. "I agree with the President."

"Dr. Steinbrenner," Ashworth began, his tone indicating a difficult question, "how long is it going to take us to access these satellites? To make them fully operable."

Steinbrenner looked at the President. "Selection of the military staff will take sixty days. Training will take another ninety."

"Then the Summit will be over anyway," said Morrow.

"Wouldn't the potential discovery of the system by the Soviets raise the threat of an immediate attack?" asked the senator.

"I think we've talked about that already, Boyd," said the President.

Undeterred, the senator continued, "Wouldn't they strike before the system is activated? If they knew activation were imminent, and they would be vulnerable, wouldn't they be provoked to strike first?"

"That's more than possible," said the President.

"Let's just hope they hit Massachusetts first," Morrow said, and then laughed alone at his joke.

Ashworth continued unmoved: "So what we have in effect done is established an unworkable ABM network—a network of presently useless satellites—that once discovered by the Soviets could possibly be destabilizing enough to scare them into a first strike before the system is even operational. We've spent heaven knows how much money—or where it came from—to deploy a strategically dangerous system, and we are five months away from accessing it." Ashworth laughed sarcastically. "I sure as hell hope your little secret doesn't leave this room," he said to the President.

"Respectfully, Senator, you're an asshole," said Morrow, and then he looked at Satterfield. "Mr. President, I think we should move immediately to activate the system. I believe we can keep it secret." He looked at Steinbrenner. "And those hundred and fifty days, they can be cut, can't they?"

"I agree," said Marine Commandant Bradford. He leaned forward at the table to engage in the discussion. "It's an acceptable risk."

"Not if we adhere to security needs," said Steinbrenner. "We need those five months."

"And not if we want to see further democratic progress behind the Iron Curtain," Perryman added.

"It appears to me that the system needs to be activated," said White without acknowledging the secretary of state. "And, frankly, I think the sooner the better."

"Again," the President re-emphasized, "we're not going to initiate the final phase of the program when we're so close to the bargaining table."

Spencer slid his chair closer to the table and cleared his throat. "Very few people know what's happening," he said. "We've held national security secrets for years, letting three times as many people in on the scoop. Presently, there is no need to worry about a security leak. Still, the President's decision must stand."

"The only reason we would need to activate the strategic defense system now would be in the event of a security leak," Satterfield said. "If someone who knows of the system were to talk out of class, we would have a race on our hands to activate before the Kremlin made a dangerous move."

"Before they launched a first strike," added Ashworth. "Say what you mean, Mr. President. Personally, I think we're past that point. Surely there are enough people who already know of the system. As far as we know, the information may already be on the streets."

"Like Spencer said," Steinbrenner corrected, "you would be surprised by the small number of people who actually know the details of the operation. Only men with the most sensitive security clearances have all the pieces of the puzzle—men who have worked on projects of equal national importance."

"Gentlemen," President Satterfield stood up, "the decision not to involve additional military personnel has been made. After the Summit, and based on the Soviet's decision to negotiate on ICBMs and further reductions in conventional forces, we will reconvene and determine the future of the Initiative. This meeting, however, was to inform you of the capability, that we have the satellites in place, and to let you ask technical questions of the good doctor here." Satterfield looked at Ashworth. "Some men might try to play like they've never heard of the program. If it's good for their politics, then so be it. But we've all known of the research and development. Nobody can play naive enough to make us believe they did not suspect the gradual deployment. I would say that if they were, in fact, that ignorant about the project—well, it'll be their fatal flaw and not mine. But the fact that we've gone ahead over the last thirteen years and completed the actual deployment should not surprise anybody. And there's nothing to fear. Believe me. We are still holding a full nuclear arsenal. In firepower, we do not have the parity we might want with the Soviets—I, for one, believe our stick ought to be bigger than theirs—but we have enough to deter any immediate threat. Now, if you have any final questions for Dr. Steinbrenner."

"Professor," Bradford asked, "the wandering missiles that go into orbit after they've been disoriented by our lasers, won't they pose some kind of threat of their own, nuclear warheads orbiting in space?"

"That's exactly what they will do, orbit. If they are struck by another spacecraft or missile then, yes, they might explode, but they will explode outside our atmosphere."

"Then there's no chance of a nuclear missile falling to earth?" asked Ashworth.

"The laws of probability and chance say no."

"And what do you say, Dr. Steinbrenner?" the senator prodded.

"I agree with the laws."

"But those that do explode in space," General White said, "being outside our atmosphere will carry the threat of electromagnetic pulse."

"That's right," said Steinbrenner. "We have included these facts in your briefing books. But you're right, the threat of electromagnetic pulse is very real. This is another reason we are discouraging activation at this time."

"Electromagnetic pulse?" Ashworth asked.

"A high-altitude nuclear explosion that produces electrons that are caught by the earth's magnetic field and converts the energy into radio waves. The effect, per nuclear explosion, would produce a microsecond burst of intense, broad-frequency radio-wave energy."

"This is harmful?" questioned the senator.

"Not to life, but it disrupts, or destroys, unprotected solid state electronics, including those used in radio and telephone services, computer systems, aircraft instrumentation and flight controls. It would have an effect on ignition and control modules in automobiles, electric distribution in the United States, and even our satellites and their ground stations."

"Then our entire defense network would be vulnerable," said Ashworth.

"Not everything," Steinbrenner answered. "Since 1982, we have hardened our strategic circuitry. We have made it immune to the threat of EMP. However, there are still necessary links that have not been upgraded."

"More than three-quarters of our arsenal was deployed before 1982." Ashworth's voice was on the rise. "And you're telling me it will be useless by one shock—by one EMP."

"Possibly." Steinbrenner's voice was flat.

"What a comedy." Ashworth shook his head.

"How real is the threat of this EMP?" Morrow asked.

"It's very real. I won't paint it any other way. One nuclear explosion over one hundred and fifty miles above the geographic center of our country is far too distant to threaten life on earth, but at that altitude the expanding gamma radiation would excite a lens-shaped segment of the upper atmosphere several thousand square miles, creating large-scale blackouts—"

"At least we wouldn't have to worry about conventional bombings," Ashworth interjected, but was ignored.

"—triggering fault sensors and forcing power plants to automatically shut down. The resulting power distribution grid would then be imbalanced causing more generating facilities to shut down in response to surges and overloads."

"How long would these plants be down?" asked Bradford.

"Without additional EMPs, power distribution could be restored in a matter of hours or a day. But the more serious problem would be destruction of electronic circuitry. On-line equipment would receive the EMP through electrical service connections. New equipment— even that not on-line—could receive a shock through wire leads."

"The main effects of this electromagnetic pulse are only temporary," Spencer added.

"Temporary enough for the Soviets to launch an effective retaliation," Ashworth said.

"To be honest," Steinbrenner said, "the senator is correct. There would be some danger. The system is not without its bugs."

"But remember, Senator," Spencer added, "our ABM system that would cause this pulse would only be used in case of Soviet aggression. Moscow would not be in a position for retaliation, but for a first strike attack—an attack that would be thwarted by our SDI."

"What we would have to worry about," Satterfield said, "is the safety of our allies. NORAD and our communications with NATO would be damaged. The Soviets could follow a nuclear attack with conventional forces through Eastern Europe."

"This EMP would damage our fleet operations and surface transportation systems," Parryman added.

"So our conventional forces would be disrupted, maybe even rendered defenseless," Bradford said.

"Hell, Commandant," Senator Ashworth offered a caustic laugh, "we're talking about a mobile nuclear strike. There would be no need for conventional forces. There would be no need for Europe. In fact, I'd venture to say there would be no Europe fifteen minutes into the attack.''

"Gentlemen," Satterfield began with a voice that said the meeting was over, "you understand the need for complete secrecy. One thing this Initiative does is make nuclear war an all-or-nothing proposal."

"Nuclear war has always been an all-or-nothing proposal," Ashworth corrected.

"You're right, Senator," Satterfield agreed. "But the idea of a limited nuclear war is now a part of history."

Chapter Eleven

Robert Hamilton was in deep sleep when the phone rang. His room was dark and he was disoriented. It rang again. He pressed himself to remember where he was, and why his mood was wrapped in malaise. He looked at his watch. The dial was barely lighted by the fluorescent green that marked the numbers, and he could not make out the time. It rang again.

"Malibu," Robert said. His voice was hoarse and he cleared his throat.

"Mee-ster Ham-ill-toon." The voice on the other end belonged to a woman. It was both foreign and weak.

"Yes." Robert shook his head, hoping to wake up.

"I am sorry to call you."

"What time is it?"

"Six o'clock."

"Morning or night?"

"Morning."

Robert looked at his watch again. Still he could not make out the time. He rolled over and turned on the nightstand lamp. "Who is this?" he asked.

"I must speak to you."

"Okay." He sat up in bed. He was still in his clothes, and began to remember where he was and the events of the last forty-eight hours—*Hotel Ambasciatori, Grayson Watenburg, Simon Levin.* The images and memories suddenly flooded back into his mind. It was more than a bad dream, and he understood the reason for his depression. "But who is this?'' He looked at his wrinkled shirt and remembered lying down for a few minutes after Andy Niccolini left. Those few minutes must have turned into all afternoon and all night, he thought, and at once he was both relieved and upset. He was relieved that he had compensated for his lack of sleep in the last two days, but upset that he had squandered valuable time.

"My name is Julie—Julia.''

"Why do you want to—''

"Julia Peterson,'' her voice cracked. "You saw my husband, and I—'' She could not talk.

"That's okay,'' said Hamilton. "I understand.'' Suddenly he was wide awake. "When and where do you want to meet.''

The woman tried to control her sobs. "I am not—I am not in Rome.''

Robert understood why her voice sounded so weak. She was calling over an international line. "Germany?'' he asked.

"Spain.''

"Spain?''

"In Alm—Almería. Do you know where it is?''

"I'll find it.''

"It is important.'' She was regaining control over her emotions and voice.

"You can't come to Rome?''

"I cannot leave. You will understand when we speak. Please hurry.''

"But where,'' Robert asked. He reached to the nightstand for his pen and notebook.

"A little bar called the Casa Blanca. The Casa Blanca.''

"The White House,'' Robert repeated.

"Yes,'' said Julia, "the White House.''

"How will I know you?''

"I will find you,'' she assured. "It will be easier that way. But please hurry. And tell no one.''

"Sure,'' Robert said. He placed the notebook back on the nightstand. "Tell me, though, why call me?''

"You are the last man who saw my husband.''

"How do you know?''

"The police. They told me."

"But your husband was already dead."

"I can trust you."

"How do you know?"

"You are a journalist."

"Are all journalists trustworthy?"

"No, but they have only one loyalty."

"One loyalty? To what?"

"To themselves, Mr. Hamilton. They serve no one else, and right now that is very important to me."

"I think I understand," Robert said. He was surprised that the woman who began the conversation sounding vulnerable would make such a bold statement.

"Can you come now?" Julia asked.

"I can probably catch a plane today."

"You must come through Madrid. There is no direct flight. From Madrid, Iberia Airlines flies to Almería."

"I'll be there," Robert said, "at the White House. What time?"

"Six o'clock tomorrow night."

"At six," he confirmed.

"Thank you, Mr. Hamilton."

"Tell me, though—" Robert began, but she cut him off.

"Thank you, Mr. Hamilton. And please hurry." Julia hung up first, and Robert placed the receiver back in the cradle. For the first time since waking, he noticed the message light was flashing. Hotel management was courteous enough to stop the calls throughout the night, Robert thought, but then accepted the fact that he could have been tired enough to sleep through the rings. He picked up the phone and dialed the hotel operator.

"Good morning, Mr. Hamilton," a woman said. Her words dripped with an Italian accent. Again, Robert was impressed that she knew to answer in English.

"I'm calling for my messages."

"One minute, please."

"Sure."

"Thank you for waiting. You received a call from Mr. Morehouse. He said, why have not you called him?"

"Oh, that's right." He took his notebook and scribbled JED. The literary agent was now more important to Robert than anyone else. He represented the closest thing to a job that Robert had.

"JoAnn Claiborne called to say do not bother to call her. She is getting married on Friday."

I should have called her, Robert thought. He wrote J.C. under JED. *She's so sensitive about being ignored. But she did have a sense of humor. Married on Friday*, he thought and laughed.

"And Barbara Lewis called to say she met JoAnn at a reception at the National Gallery of Art, and she cannot wait until you get home."

Amusement turned to chill. He crossed out J.C. and did not enter B.L.

"Julia Peterson called more than once, but would not leave her number."

"Is that it?"

"Gloria Nelson called. She wants to know where you would like your final check sent."

"Did she tell you how much it would be?" Robert asked. Suddenly he was angry. He knew that Simon Levin was behind the call.

"Oh," said the operator, "we did not ask."

"No—no," said Robert. "I'm not upset with you."

"I am sorry."

"No, I'm sorry." He was embarrassed he had offended the operator. "Are there any other messages?"

"Miss Sillito called three times." The operator paused, and Malibu could tell she was organizing the messages. "She wanted to know if you want to have breakfast. She wanted to know if you want to have lunch. She wanted to know if you want to have dinner."

"Thank you," said Robert. His mood rushed from anger with his former editor to delight. "Thank you very much."

"Our pleasure."

Could you please connect me with the airport da Vinci. I think it's Fiumicino."

"Yes, of course." There were five or six clicks, and then the line was ringing.

"*Aeroporti Leonardo da Vinci.*"

"Iberia Airlines, please."

"*Che?*"

"Iberia—Iberia Airlines."

There were several more clicks and rings.

"Ee-bear-ee-a."

"I need to check your flight schedules."

"One minute please." There was a pause, and a new voice took the line. "Hello."

"Yes, I need to check your flight schedules to Spain. To Almería, Spain."

"A flight leaves at 10:05 AM."

Robert looked at his watch. The time was half past six. "Are there any others, later in the day?"

"Only 10:05 if you want to get to Almería. You must connect in Madrid.

"Please reserve a seat for me. Hamilton, Robert Hamilton."

"Will this be a return trip?"

"I don't think so. I will be returning to the United States, but I'm not sure when."

"Will you be flying alone?"

"Yes."

"Mr. Hamilton, I have you booked on Iberia flight 443, departing Fiumicino da Vinci at 10:05 AM, arriving Madrid International at 2:15. You will transfer to Iberia flight 121, departing Madrid International at 2:45 PM, arriving at Almería National at 3:28. I can pre-check you if you would like to pay now with a credit card."

"Sure." Robert took his wallet from his back pocket and pulled out the green American Express card that had been issued to him by the *Post*. But a pang of guilt forced him to put it back and take out his personal gold card. He read the number and the expiration date to the agent.

"We will look forward to having you fly Iberia."

"Thank you," said Robert. He hung up the telephone and moved from his bed to the bathroom. He turned on the shower and began to undress. But before he could take off his trousers, the phone rang. He slipped them off as he walked across the room and answered the call in his boxer shorts. "Malibu."

"I might as well be interested in President Reagan," said the enticing voice of Diana Sillito. "He'd be easier to get in touch with."

"He's dead."

"See what I mean?"

Robert laughed. "How are you?"

"Quite driven, thank you."

"Driven."

"You're enough to give a girl a complex."

"Not you."

"Yes, me. But I warn you, I don't play the hard to get game."

"I can tell."

"I'm serious, Robert."

He loved the way she said his name. *Robert*, he repeated it in his mind. "I'm not playing hard to get."

"Then not returning phone calls is your modus operandi?"

"I thought you were filming *The Agony and the Ecstacy*, not a police show."

"I've been in enough crime dramas to know the phrase 'modus operandi.' And don't change the subject. Why haven't you returned my calls?"

"Diana, one day we're going to sit down together, and I am going to tell you a story you won't believe. In fact, maybe I'll take a crack at turning it into a screenplay. You can star. No kidding. It could be your big break!"

"Don't patronize me. Besides, haven't you heard the phrase, 'Everyone's a writer'?"

"But I *am* a writer."

"See what I mean."

"And I wouldn't dare patronize you."

"Why haven't you returned my calls?"

"You're something else."

"Robert!"

"Diana, I can't tell you right now. But I *will* tell you later. I promise."

"I'm not used to being the hunter. I don't like the game. And to be honest, I'm not going to keep at it long."

"I can't wait to get together," Malibu said.

"I was thinking that maybe we could have—"

"Breakfast?"

"Yeah—breakfast—how did you know?" She paused. "You *have* been getting my messages."

"I wish we could," said Robert.

"What do you mean, we can't?"

"I have to leave Rome."

"Leave Rome?"

"I have to go to Spain—to Almería."

"Damn you, Robert."

"What?" he laughed. In only two days, this woman had charmed him unlike any other, and he had yet to get to know her.

"I said damn you. And I mean it. You're proving fatal to my career."

"To your career?"

"An actress has to be confident. Don't you read the tabloids? We're supposed to have the upper hand."

Robert was laughing even harder. "I'm sorry," he said. "I really should know better—shouldn't I?"

"Star-crossed love, that's all I've ever known."

"Yeah, I'm sure it's been a real problem in your life."

"I'm serious."

"I promise," Robert said, "when we get back to the States, you and I will have a whirlwind romance that will make Bogart and Bacall blush."

"Tracy and Hepburn?"

"They'll look like amateurs."

"Promise?"

"I promise."

"Wait a minute," Diana's voice suddenly filled with awareness. "I'm not going to be done filming for three weeks."

"Great things are worth waiting for."

"You do talk like you write," Diana said, and then she added, "Please take care of yourself. I have a feeling these will be the longest weeks of my life."

For the first time since meeting Diana, Robert was at a loss for words. *How do you respond to that*? he wondered. It seemed appropriate to say I love you, but that would be much too premature. He settled for the most ill-suited, uncreative phrase he could grasp: "I'll see you then."

Diana hung up without saying another word, and Robert could not stop thinking about her until his plane landed in Almería.

Chapter Twelve

"Qué pasa, amigo?" Robert said as he ducked into the taxi. His command of Spanish left much to be desired, but his mood was light, and he was taunted into using it.

"No-thing," the *taxista* answered as he looked into the rearview mirror. He did not return Hamilton's smile. His eyes were sharp.

Robert was surprised. Like all American visitors, he expected the Spanish people to be warm and friendly, especially in the Andalusian region. But in the eyes and short response of the dark Spaniard, there was hostility. The man would not even entertain Robert's attempt to speak Spanish.

"Do you know where the Casa Blanca is?"

"Qué?"

"The Casa Blanca," Robert repeated. "Do you know where it is?"

"Qué?"

"The White House?" His voice grew sharp. *"Sabe donde está?"*

"La Casa Blanca?"

"Sí."

"Washing-toon, D.C."

"No. No," Robert was irritated. "Here in Almería—*en* Almería."

"The *Americano* bar?"

"Do Americans go there?"

"Yes. Many."

"That must be the place then."

There was a lengthy pause as the driver continued to study Robert's reflection in the mirror. "What, Smith, we go to the White House, or what?"

"Of course," Robert answered, though he was a day early. He was not to meet the Peterson woman until tomorrow night, but journalism had taught him to avoid surprises. He wanted to see the bar, to get a feel for where he would meet Julia. He sat back in silence and looked out the window. The car passed along fifteen minutes of coastal highway before it found its way through the twisting cobblestone streets of the ancient city. "Why do Americans go to the Casa Blanca?" he asked.

"*Porqué no?*" asked the driver, "Why not?"

Robert wondered why Julia wanted to meet him at that particular bar. "Are there that many Americans in Almería?"

"They make many movies in this city. Many movies. That is the bar they like."

Hamilton nodded and looked out the window again. The city was beautiful. The stone fronts of the buildings reached to the streets and created a mazelike effect. The walls were washed white and contrasted sharply with the black dresses of the old Spanish widows who moved along the narrow sidewalks to the *carnecerías*, the *lecherías*, and the *panaderías* to buy meat, milk and bread for tomorrow. Robert looked at his watch. The time was half past four. The city was built on a hill, and every few streets he could glimpse the massive walls of the castles that once protected Almería from the Moors across the Mediterranean. The taxi turned from rustic Almería, where the people lived, onto the main avenue, and in the course of the turn Robert found himself back in the twentieth century. On the avenue, the department stores, supermarkets, restaurants and hotels were out of place in a city that otherwise appeared unaltered by steel and electricity. The car moved quickly down the avenue and turned left into a rundown barrio where children played naked and dusty.

Another minute passed and the cab stopped.

"*Aquí está,*" said the driver.

"What?" Robert looked out the window at nothing more than a door leading through a large wall.

"This is Casa Blanca."

"Casa Blanca?" Robert craned his neck to read the name of the bar posted on a small Aquila beer sign that hung over the door. "This is it?" From outside, the bar looked dirty and in disrepair.

"*Claro*," said the driver. "Of course."

"Movie stars come here?" he said aloud, though he did not intend for the driver to answer.

"All of them."

It was not the glamorous establishment Robert had imagined. His colorful illusions faded to black and white, and he wondered if Julia Peterson had not meant another bar. He wondered if the Americans that were supposed to frequent the place were bothered by the posters that hung on either side of the weathered door. They announced a demonstration by the Spanish Communist Party to oust the remaining American military bases in Spain. A red neon light flashed the name of the bar above the door.

"You going to get out, or what?" said the driver. Robert believed the man delighted in his disillusionment and the affront presented by the two posters.

"How much do I owe you?"

"*Tres mil pesetas*. Tree-tousand."

"Come on," said Robert. "This isn't New York."

"*Quatro cientos veinticinco*."

"Four twenty-five is a lot less than three thousand. How could you miscalculate?"

"You have baggage."

"I have a briefcase and one carry-on, and you haven't touched either."

"Just give me five hundred."

"I'll give you four twenty-five." Robert said. "You should've thought about the tip before you became an asshole."

"Ass-hole?"

"Look it up," Robert said and tossed four bills and a twenty-five peseta coin into the front seat. He grabbed his hanging bag and stepped out of the taxi.

"Julia," Robert muttered to himself as he walked to the door, "I hope you know what you're doing. More importantly, Malibu, I hope you know what you're doing."

He opened the heavy wooden-frame door. The paint was green and blistered. The sudden ray of light drew the attention of the early-evening patrons, and they stared at Robert as he entered. At first, he could see nothing. Except for a flashing yellow and red neon light over the bar, the room was black and filled with the bitter aroma of cheap tobacco. Robert felt vulnerable that he could see no one, but they could see him. He placed his bag on the floor and waited for his eyes to adjust to the darkness. An American song played on tin speakers. It was something by the Bee Gees, a disco song that had been popular so many decades ago that Robert had forgotten the name. *Americans come here?* he thought, and strained his eyes to see in the darkness. Finally, he could see the bar across the room. It ran from wall to wall, and behind it wooden shelves held the liquor, and the bottles reflected in a mirror. Crowded at the bar were Spanish men wearing tight American designer jeans and knit shirts. They all looked alike, but apparently that did not bother the painted ladies, who reminded Robert of the whores on 14th Street back in Washington, D.C. He was surprised the bar was so crowded this early in the day.

Two dozen tables were randomly placed on the floor, and each table was controlled by a party of two or more. Robert had seen enough. He looked at his watch and thought about finding a place to stay. He needed a shower, and there were several hotels on the avenue two blocks away. He grabbed his bag and turned to leave.

"*Usted es americano, no?*" A pleasant-looking woman startled Robert when he turned around. He was surprised at how close she was. He had neither heard nor felt anyone walk up behind him, nor had he seen the light flash into the bar that would have happened had she come in through the door. "You are American, no?" Her accent was strong, and she rolled her r's.

"Yes, very American," he answered with a smile. "You are not, no?"

"*Sí*, I mean, no," she laughed. "I mean yes, I am no *americana*."

"Let me guess," he said taking a step backward. "You must be *española*."

"*Qué listo*." She smiled a high-cheekbone smile. Her eyes were pure; her skin, smooth. "You are smart."

"Thank you." Robert attempted to be inconspicuous as he studied her. She appeared out of place in the bar. Her straight dark hair and slender, carefully groomed features looked more appropriate for a university library. She wore a loose-fitting white cotton top with an embroidered yoke and a drawstring around the collar. It gathered at the waist. "You speak English well."

"Oh, no," she laughed, "very bad. I learned in school many years ago."

"Do you spend a lot of your time sneaking up behind American men?" As soon as Robert asked the question, he felt foolish for being so bold, but he was enchanted with her willing answer.

"As much as I can," she said with a delicate laugh. "*Claro.*"

"Not that I mind," he laughed along. "You can sneak up on me whenever you'd like." He stepped to the side and turned slightly so she could pass into the room.

"*Gracias,*" she said and walked on.

Robert watched as she moved. The fit of her denim jeans was flattering. Her gait, like that of many sensual Spanish women, was well practiced. As she walked past the table closest to the bar, she won the attention of all four men sitting there. Robert shook his head and studied the adoring look in the eyes of the faces he could see. *This is what is meant by 'undressing with the eyes,'* he thought and turned again to leave. But suddenly he was overcome by a sense of recognition. He knew the face of one of the men. At least, he thought he knew the face. It belonged to Bower Thompson, a man Robert had known briefly but well. He turned and looked again. This time he could not see the face, and he thought he might be mistaken. *Maybe Americans do come to this bar, after all,* he thought and walked out the door.

It was dusk and the children still played in the streets. They stopped long enough to watch him. One shouted, "What time is it?"

"*A las cinco,*" Robert said. He knew the children did not care so much about the time as they did about knowing what nationality he was. How he answered the question would determine, and Robert only confused the boy by understanding the question in English and answering in Spanish. The children laughed. Robert smiled and walked on. By the time he arrived at the hotel—Los Libereros—the bars along the avenue were beginning to put up their umbrellas and canopies for the evening crowd. Lights were coming on and Robert was taken by an air of celebration, *the land of fiesta*! When he checked in, the desk manager, a friendly Spaniard, offered a larger room with a window that faced the avenue and overlooked the Mediterranean for the price of a smaller room with a less beautiful view. "This is the Andalusia

I've read about," he said, but the manager only smiled and nodded, and Robert went to his room.

After his shower, he turned on the Vanguard television and tuned it to one of the three national channels. He found a rerun of "This Week in the Plaza de Toros" that highlighted the summer bullfights. He understood only about forty percent of what was said, but the visuals made the program enjoyable. Each of the highlights was accompanied by an American rock song, and Robert found it amusing that the words of the songs fit so closely with the theme of the film clips. Without turning off the television, he lay on one of the double beds in the room and picked up the telephone. Still he had not dressed, and he did not think he would for the rest of the evening. He could not remember the last time he felt as comfortable as he did at the present.

"*Operadora.*"

"Yes, operator," he spoke slowly. "Can I dial directly to the United States."

"*Los Estados Unidos,*" she paused, "yes."

"What is the international number?"

"Dial one, the area code and the number."

"*Gracias,*" Robert said and was about to hang up when he asked, "And what is the country code for Italy?"

"Italy?"

"Yes. Rome."

"The number is three-nine-six."

Robert jotted it next to the number of the Hotel Cicerone. "Thank you," he said and hung up. For a moment, he stared at the phone, uncertain of whom to call first. He needed to speak with Jed, but he wanted to hear Diana's voice. He dialed three digits, and when he received the dial tone, he dialed the digits in his notebook. The line clicked twice and began to ring.

"*Albergo Cicerone.*"

"Is this the Hotel Cicerone?" Robert shouted because the voice sounded so far away.

"Yes. The Cicerone."

"Will you please ring the room of Diana Sillito?"

"Miss Sillito has left for the evening, sir. May I take a message?"

"She's left?" Robert asked. He felt a twinge of jealousy, but realized he had no reason to feel that way.

"Yes, sir. May I take a message?"

"Tell her Malibu called."

"*Ché?*"

"Robert Hamilton. Tell her Robert called. I'm staying at the Hotel Los Libereros in Almería, Spain. She can reach me at—" he looked at the hotel number on the base of the telephone. "She can reach me at seven-five-seven-two-one-one."

"Seven-five-seven-two-one-one," the Cicerone operator repeated. "Yes, sir."

Robert allowed an uncomfortable pause to swell. There seemed to be something else he should say. "If I'm not at the hotel, she can reach me at the White House Bar. The Casa Blanca."

"Yes, sir, the Casa Blanca."

"I don't know the number, but I'll probably be spending some time there." He realized he did not need to explain the details, and he wondered if he should have given the information in the first place.

"I understand."

"Well," Robert said, "I guess that's all. Tell her hello." He hung up and waited for the sinking feeling to settle in his stomach before he dialed the number of Jed Morehouse. It took a minute to make the connection, and the line began to ring.

"Morehouse-Johnson-Morehouse and Associates, good afternoon."

"Jed Morehouse, please." Robert wanted to call the receptionist by her first name, but the agency was large enough that he could never keep track of who answered the phone. He believed there had to be at least half a dozen girls in the front office alone.

"Mr. Morehouse's office."

"This is Bob Hamilton returning Mr. Morehouse's call."

"One minute please." Robert was put on hold, but the woman quickly returned. "He will be right with you." The phrase "right with you" meant four or five minutes, by Robert's unofficial calculations. But the time gave him the opportunity to take his notebook, from where it rested next to the television on the dresser, and go over the notations he had made concerning the murders. His mind cornered him on Senator Ashworth; over and over, he could not free his thoughts that locked on the senior senator from Massachusetts. Watenburg's warning seemed like the McGuffin of a Hitchcock movie, the line that portends the climax. He wrote the name Bower Thompson on the page next to Ashworth's. It did seem more than coincidental that the senator's administrative assistant would be sitting in the same bar that Robert had been summoned to by a woman he had never met. For a moment, he considered a setup, then, just as quickly, he dismissed the thought. "But what is Bo Thompson doing in Almería?" he asked. "Vacationing with three men in dark suits and white shirts? Highly unlikely." He wrote "Three men—Almería—Casa Blanca" under Thompson's name. "What is so damn important about Almería?"

"Bob?"

"Jed."

"Where the hell are you?"

"Spain."

"Spain?" Morehouse's voice was fatherly, a commanding voice that both frightened and reassured.

"Almería—chasing a story."

"The story's here, boy, and I suggest you get yourself back home." Morehouse paused, and Robert could hear him puffing on the five-dollar-Cuban that was as constant a fixture on his face as his nose. "Publisher's talking about cutting your first print run in half."

"Come on, Jed, you can take care of that." Robert suddenly felt empty. "I'm counting on the full advance on royalties."

"They'll cut that, too, if you don't get your ass home."

"This story's important."

"Bob, I'm not going to argue with you. This is your first book. You have no foundation to stand on with these people. They're as nervous as stalked coons that when the book is hot off the press, you're going to be in Sri Lanka, or some gosh-awful place like that, and your book will end up remaindered before it sees the inside of a bookstore. You come home, and they plan to put your face all over hell—the Carson Show, Letterman—damn, maybe even an interview in *Playboy*."

"How much time do I have?"

"The proofs are ready. We've waited over a year. You have got to be here."

Robert took a deep breath. "I promised someone that I would meet them here tomorrow night."

"That's too late."

"Come on, Jed. One day's not going to hurt."

"You're not going to get the second half of your royalty advance."

"You can stall for one more day."

"I can't stall another minute, Bob. I've got three dozen clients I handle personally, and I'm not going to jeopardize my relationship with a major publishing house over one unpublished author. The decision's yours."

Robert could feel the prickle of heat move up his chest to his forehead. His arms were suddenly cold and weak. "Jed, what I'm on to is huge. There's a terrorist running around Europe who has just killed two major politicians, a German and Senator Watenburg."

"We got the press." Morehouse barked, his voice was not the sympathetic tone Robert was shooting for. "It's all over the front page of the *Times*. I got a copy of the *Post*, too, and I noticed your name wasn't on the byline. Somebody named Brook. I wrote it down to ask you about him. Thought we might get the boy to write a book."

"Don't play with me."

"Then get your ass home."

"This is my story," Robert said. "I was the last man who saw Watenburg alive."

"You killed him?"

"You know what I mean. I was the last man who saw him alive. I have an idea what these murders are all about. Now I'm meeting—" Robert paused. He felt uncomfortable naming his sources, and he was never sure if this reluctance was out of concern for the sources or out of concern that he was giving away a lead.

"Who?"

"I'm meeting Peterson's wife."

"Peterson?"

"The German politician who was murdered in the same room."

"Dammit, Hamilton." The strength of Morehouse's voice broke to a sympathetic tone. "It's writers like you who tempt me to get out of this business."

"You can stall them?"

"I'll see what I can do."

"Tell them we'll give them the first option on this new book."

"Book?"

"The way this is shaping up, we're talking a best-seller."

Morehouse laughed. "You're cocky for an author with only one book under his belt."

"Isn't that the way you want me?"

"Of course," Morehouse answered. "Look, you said something about needing the second half of the royalty."

"I was canned at the *Post.*"

"Fired?"

"Fired."

"Shit, Hamilton. You amaze the piss out of me. You really do."

Robert felt his arms grow cold again. He wondered if his status with the *Post* would affect his value to Jed and the publishing house. "That's why my name was not on the byline. But it's my story."

"Your being a reputable journalist is important for this book."

"I understand," said Robert. "But getting the ax at the *Post* doesn't put me in disrepute."

"But it takes away your credentials."

"Screw the credentials."

"It's not that easy." Morehouse paused to puff. "It's not that easy, dammit."

"There's nothing we can do about it now."

"Leave those kinds of statements to me. I'll decide. Damnit." There was an uncomfortable pause. Robert did not know what to say. "We're just not going to tell them—that's all. The publisher doesn't need to know the book he spent so much money on was written by an unemployed journalist."

"Come on, Jed," Robert said. He was surprised the agent was so blatant with his insult.

"Listen to me, Hamilton. You get your story, and you get your ass home. Do you understand?"

"Sure," Robert answered. "Sure—I understand."

"Now," Morehouse took a deep breath, "how much money do you need?"

"You said the advance—"

"How much money do you need?"

"If someone could place five grand in my account—"

"Three thousand, and it will be there tomorrow."

"Thank you, Jed."

"My old man—God rest his soul—would kick me to Tijuana if he were here right now, so don't you say another word."

"Thank you, Jed." The line went dead.

Robert reclined into the two small pillows on his bed. His body and mind felt renewed, optimistic. It was a good phone call. Morehouse was an honorable man, something that Robert believed was becoming rare in business, where the ever-increasing motive was profit. He looked at the notebook again, particularly at the name of Bo Thompson. What could he remember about the man? He thumbed the book to a blank page and forced his mind into the uncomfortable mode of digging up names and dates.

Robert easily remembered his own ninety-day prison sentence, which he served in Petersburg, Virginia, for contempt of Congress, when he refused to name Bower Quincy Thompson as his source on the three-part series he wrote about the MX missile. Those were days never to be forgotten—days of endless hours and sleepless nights when he would lie awake in the dormitory cubicle that served as his cell and stare at the bunk above him. They were days of uncertainty, when Robert did not know if his incarceration would last a week or years. The special counsel for the Senate Intelligence Committee, who acted more like a hot-shot prosecutor bent on browbeating a confession from a drug lord, wanted to break him down.

"We want a name, Mr. Hamilton."

"I can't give it to you."

"One name."

"No."

"Do you know what you face?"

"No."

"Prison, Mr. Hamilton. You face a charge of contempt, and it is possible that you'll grow old in prison until you come forward with a name."

"I'll have to trust the First Amendment, thank you."

"Not on matters of national security."

"I don't recall the Framers including that condition."

"When did you become a constitutional lawyer?"

"I'm not."

"Then you'll have to believe me that the Framers, Mr. Hamilton, did not have to deal with subversive journalists."

"I object to that."

"You can't object in here. This committee has been empowered by Congress with exclusive rights necessary to promote and protect national security." The prosecutor paused and opened one of a dozen large black binders on the table in front of him. "So tell us, who tipped you about the MX tracking system, more particularly, about the tracts of land that you write—and please turn with me to page 232 in exhibit book seven—you write: 'A highly placed Capitol Hill source confirmed Wednesday that seventeen of the forty-six tracts of land purchased by the Department of Defense for placement of the MX track were purchased from Wortman International. The added cost of diverting the tracking system through Wortman property is estimated at $19.3 million dollars. The property, which runs between Lovelock and Elko, Nevada, was obtained by Wortman only six months earlier at one-third the price paid by the U.S. government.' " The prosecutor stopped reading and looked at Robert. "Mr. Hamilton, for reasons of national security, those figures, as well as that transaction, and all information concerning the MX, and the MX tracking system, have been closely guarded. Never were they intended for publication. So why don't you simply tell us who told you. That's all we need to know."

"Again, sir, I cannot."

"Who explained to you Mr. Wortman's relationship with the chairman of the House Appropriations Committee?"

"Again—"

"Mr. Hamilton," the prosecutor yelled, "you are moments away from contempt. This is the third day you have refused to cooperate, and it will be the final day. Our patience has worn thin with you."

"I wish I could say I'm sorry."

Robert was told he would remain in Petersburg until he agreed to name names, but the first week into the third month, the issue surrounding the MX missile blew away like desert dust and he was released. He had never spoken with Thompson since. But here he was in Spain. In Almería. In the Casa Blanca—the same bar where Robert was to meet Julia. He placed the notebook in the nightstand. He was disturbed by the seeming coincidence, but not disturbed enough to stop fatigue from overtaking him, and within minutes he was fast asleep.

Chapter Thirteen

Sergio's arms exploded with energy, but he could not use them. The muscles were tense and needed to be moved, but they would not react to his will. It was night, and only an electric light illuminated the room. He could see well, and the bed next to him was empty. In another bed someone screamed. He felt surrounded by death, and wondered why God spared him, kept him alive, rather than let him drift off to sleep in the park. The bullet did not hurt. It was warm, and for a moment, the pain of life was gone, vanished after thirty years of torment and despair. "Why did you not let me die?" he mumbled. His mind was filled with darkness. "Let me die now." He took a strong breath and tried to let go of life and sink into the unknown chasm. "Dear God, let me die." Then he remembered the barrio and his youth. He remembered his mother and the slum priest. It was thoughts of them, and his ideals of youth that refused to let him die in the park. He remembered that he could not die now. Christ would not atone for him if he died now. Of this he was sure. But the pain, it was overwhelming, and he did not care anymore. "Let go," he said silently. "Let go."

"I am sorry." It was the same woman's voice.

"What?" Sergio mumbled in Italian.

"I was holding your hand too tightly."

"You were holding it?"

"Much too tightly."

"But I could not feel— Am I paralyzed?"

"Shhh," the woman protested. "No. Not paralyzed."

"But I cannot move." Sergio tried to roll his head on the pillow to see the woman, but his effort was in vain. She let go of his hand and gently took his head and moved it so he could face her. "You have the face of an angel," he whispered.

"You were attacked in the park outside the Vatican. Do you remember?"

"No," he answered.

"You were left for dead."

"Do they know—"

"Who attacked you? No. You were robbed. They took even your clothes."

"I feel nothing but pain."

"The doctors cannot let you move."

"But the pain."

"There is little else that can be done."

"Will I walk?"

"They say you can walk now, but until the surgical wound heals, you must not."

"How long have I been here?"

"What is your name?"

"Juan."

"Juan?"

"Juan Pedro Sánchez Ruiz."

"From Spain?"

"Spain. Yes. How long have I been here?"

"Two days. We must notify your relations. We are surprised no one has reported you missing."

"I have no relations."

"Everyone has relations."

"I have no one."

The woman took his hand again. This time he could see her holding it. With her other hand, she brushed the hair off his forehead. "Until you heal, you have me."

Sergio closed his eyes and tried to smile, but the muscles in his face hurt.

"There is a police officer in the hall. He has been waiting to speak with you." She placed her hand on his chest. "Shall I tell him not yet?"

"No."

"You will see him?"

"Yes. But before you go, what is your name?"

"Agnes di Vincente." She smiled.

"Thank you, Agnes."

She stood and walked out of the ward. Moments later, Sergio opened his eyes to see two men standing above him. "Do you speak Italian?" asked the man closest to Sergio's head. He was dressed in a gray three-button suit and wore a burgundy tie on a blue-striped shirt, much too expensive for a detective.

"Yes."

"When did you learn?"

"I have vacationed in Italy many times. I also studied for the collar."

"You are a priest?"

"No. I never took my vows."

"But you are a man of God."

"Yes. A man of God."

The man in gray sat in a wooden chair next to the bed. The other man, much younger, and dressed in baggy trousers and a safari shirt with a slender black leather tie, remained standing. "Perhaps it is because you are a religious man that you were able to withstand the assassin's bullet." He nodded to the young man who took out a notebook. "I have to ask you a few questions."

"Fine."

"They say your name is Juan Sánchez."

"Yes."

"You are from Spain. What part of Spain?"

"Málaga, in the south."

"How long have you been here?"

"I came three days ago."

"You stayed?"

"The Hotel Majoli on the Via Nevio."

Before the man said another word, the young officer left the room. "Do you know who shot you?"

"No."

"Did you see this person?"

"No."

"What were you doing in the Gianicolo?"

"Gianicolo?"

"The park."

"I was waiting to enter St. Peter's."

"But you were walking the other way. And you did not see the man who shot you."

"I was wandering in the park until the basilica opened."

"It was not yet seven o'clock."

"I did not know what time it opened. I was enjoying the early morning peace. I have had many things on my mind."

"What do you do for a living?"

"I am an associate owner of a small *bodega*—a wine booth in the market at Málaga. Vino San Cristóbal." Sergio took a deep breath and grimaced from the accompanying pain. "I need to rest for a minute."

The officer did not reply but stood and walked out of the ward. Sergio was proud of his performance. He had been trained well for inquisitions, and despite the pain and narcotics his mind responded naturally. But he was tired, and he slipped from consciousness enough to lose track of time. The next thing he remembered was being awakened by the men.

"How much money were you carrying when you were robbed?"

"Four or five hundred thousand lire."

"That is a lot of money."

"Not enough. They say he took my clothes, too."

"Still, it is a lot of money to carry at once."

"I could not leave it in the hotel room."

"The hotel manager confirmed your story. We apologize for any inconvenience we have caused you. This has been a terrible week for the city, and we must be careful. I promise that we will do everything in our power to find this man. We have reason to believe he has killed others."

"Thank you."

"Please, before you leave Rome, however, please call us to let us know."

"Certainly."

Chapter Fourteen

"Dr. Steinbrenner," shouted a young man standing in the back of the crowded auditorium.

The physicist had been warned by the White House Communications Office not to accept questions. Opinion polls showed contempt for nuclear armaments, and "all related issues," at sixty-two percent, higher than any other time in eighteen years. But Steinbrenner did not know how one could call a lecture series a lecture series without entertaining the students' questions, and he stopped speaking to let the young man continue.

"My name is Drew Hiatt. I'm with the *American Daily* here at the university, and I want to know how, or what, do you personally believe are the chances of a nuclear holocaust in our lifetime?"

"I guess that would depend on whether you are speaking of your lifetime or mine." Steinbrenner smiled, and there was scattered laughter in the crowd.

"In this decade," said Hiatt without emotion.

"Actually, that is a very good question," said Steinbrenner. His voice trailed into a pause, and he mentally outlined his answer. "There are many factors—very complex factors—that must be considered in the answer."

"With all due respect to the factors, doctor, what is your personal opinion?"

Steinbrenner knew that whatever his answer was it would be in the headlines next morning. "Without considering these *important* factors, I would have to say the chances are fifty-fifty."

The hall stirred with whispers.

Another student jumped to her feet. "What are these factors?"

"The strengths of the conventional standing forces of the two superpowers and their allies, global economics, the continued democratization of former communist nations, the policies of expansion endorsed by either the Soviet Union or America, the likelihood of a radical Third World leader obtaining nuclear technology, the likelihood of a nuclear accident, the Strategic Defense Initiative—these are all very important."

"The size of our stockpiles?" asked the student.

"Yes. The size of our stockpiles—both our active and passive defenses."

"Active and passive?"

"Simply put, it means how carefully we deploy—or augment and disperse—our potential targets. If we add to the number of areas the Soviet Union has targeted for attack, even the most successful offensive on its part will be less destructive on our part. We will be less vulnerable, because hitting all the targets will be made more difficult. This is called augmentation, and it represented our basic strategy from the mid-sixties to the early-eighties. In the early-eighties and early-nineties, our strategy was dispersion—to spread the targets over a wider area so that fewer could be damaged by a Soviet attack. Of course, the mobility of our missiles, how those missiles are concealed, and the defensive fortifications we build around them are also major factors in limiting, or avoiding, a nuclear confrontation. Nobody wants to start a war he cannot win."

Hiatt stood up again and said: "But these are only defense strategies. How will they postpone a nuclear war?"

"Like I said, nobody wants to start a war he cannot win."

"This is called passive defense?"

"Passive defense, yes. The more difficult we make it for the Soviets to mount a successful attack, the less likely they will attempt one."

"But—"

"And," Steinbrenner continued without acknowledging the interruption, "the better prepared we are to launch an effective counterattack, the less risk there will be of a Soviet first strike."

"And it is this counterattack that we call active defense?" asked a short, plump woman sitting in the front row.

Steinbrenner looked into her eyes, and for a moment he saw Ida. She had a soft but stern presence, filled with intelligence. He paused for a moment to absorb the total memory. When the pause became uncomfortable, he answered. "No. Not exactly. Active defense is the destruction of incoming weapons. Most of you have heard of ballistic-missile defense, I'm sure. As early as the forties, when the Soviet Union built its first atomic bomb and began to work on its first bomber fleet, the United States and Canada worked together to construct an effective defensive system that included three lines of radar stretching across North America, up to the Arctic Circle and out to sea. We maintained thousands of alerted fighter-bombers, armed with their own nuclear missiles, and our major cities were surrounded by Nike sites with antiaircraft nuclear missiles. This entire defensive structure was operated by NORAD, or our North American Defense Headquarters in Wyoming. Of course, this was only the beginning. As time passed, this system became obsolete. Technical innovations introduced new ways to circumvent the system, and new ways to strengthen the system. The Soviets abandoned their bombers for intercontinental ballistic missiles, missiles which our fighters could do little to destroy."

"So now we have no protection?" asked the woman.

"We have been researching a more sophisticated ballistic-missile defense system for many years now, and we have come up with some wonderful concepts. Interestingly enough, one of the final tasks of the Rosenburg spy ring was to transfer some of our early ballistic-missile defense research to the Soviet Union."

"But we have only concepts?" asked Hiatt.

"Dr. Steinbrenner," said an older man, interrupting the student journalist's question. "We have all heard about the space initiative, or the attempt to militarize the heavens. While your history is amusing, doesn't it skirt the real issue? What is being done with our modern technology to guard against nuclear aggression, and won't our efforts escalate the arms race and send us into a star wars?"

The man had a gray beard and heavy black glasses, and Steinbrenner figured he was either a professor or a Soviet agent, one of hundreds who openly roam Washington, taking in public meetings and gathering information wherever they can find it. But he could not tell which. For a moment, he recalled the morning meeting in the White House. He recalled the confrontation with Senator Ashworth. *Why can't these people understand*, he thought. *America has always been the country of explorers and risk-takers. The Strategic Defense Initiative represented only one more step—one more venture into the unknown—and it would be made by either America or the Soviet Union.*

"It is true that defending against incoming nuclear missiles with antiballistic missiles is often perceived as being as difficult as hitting a bullet with a bullet," Steinbrenner began slowly, organizing his thoughts carefully. "To a certain degree, it is difficult. Consequently, an effective missile defense system must be built in four phases: first, the system must detect incoming missiles; second, it must determine if the incoming objects are missiles or decoys sent to confuse the system; third, our technology must be able to intercept them; and fourth, it must be powerful enough to destroy, deflect, or disarm the weapons." He paused and studied the face of the man to see if his answer had been accepted.

There was positive indication, so Steinbrenner continued. "To successfully thwart an attack, two systems have been conceived. The first is an exo-atmospheric system that can intercept an incoming missile in the early trajectory phase, or when the missile is at its highest altitude, and destroy it. This is the system that can be based in space and armed with laser or particle beams that are not only accurate, but powerful enough to defend a large area of space against multiple missiles. The second system that has been considered is endo-atmospheric, or one that would operate within our atmosphere and offer us late kill capabilities. Of course, at low altitudes it is more difficult to insure accuracy, but the endo-atmospheric system would add another blanket of protection. There is also the advantage that only real missiles will stay on course once they have re-entered the earth's atmosphere. Decoy missiles, if they do not burn away on re-entry, will fall off course, and the endo-atmospheric system will be less confused than the exo-atmospheric system. I hope this is not too confusing."

"You're evading the real issue, Dr. Steinbrenner," the man said. "I think we have the right to know what exactly is being done. You're only talking about concepts. My question is, have we deployed an anti-ballistic missile defense yet? If not, how close are we to doing so? And if we have, will these deployments lead to an escalated arms race? To a space war?"

"To answer your question, sir, I am certain that if we have, in fact, deployed such a system—antiballistic missile weaponry—whether it be in space or on the ground, our press would have let us know by now. In America, we have the most awful damned time keeping secrets. Next, I believe your term, 'arms race,' is misleading. Logically, an arms race would be a race to build arms—or weapons of death and destruction. The program called Strategic Defense Initiative would do none of that. It is not a race to destroy, but a precaution taken against destruction. If you can call this a race, then I would suggest it is a race worth running. Perhaps you mean it is a race in the financial sense of the word—an economic race to develop and deploy more powerful defense systems that would make it impossible for the Soviet Union to compete because it does not have the money to keep apace.

"Again, I suggest that this would serve our country well. One very dark geopolitical fact is that a permanent peace between the superpowers will be achieved in one of two ways: either through financial limitations that make war too costly—historically human life has not been valuable enough, maybe money, though—or through the total destruction of life on earth—at least as we know it. I only hope, for our generation and the generations yet to come, that war becomes too costly. An effective defense on our side will make it more difficult, cost the Soviet Union too much, to wage a successful all-destructive attack. In academic circles we call it the cost-exchange ratio, and once that ratio weighs in our favor, and the burden on communist countries is too great, Soviet expansionism will end—something we witnessed the beginning of 1989 and the early nineties. President Reagan's policies made it too difficult for the struggling Eastern economies to keep up with the West—either militarily, publicly or privately. Therefore, when the satellite countries began to march for democratic reforms there was very little the communist hierarchy could do but allow concessions.

"Someday, and I hope to God it's soon, this tide of freedom and human rights will be complete—all nations will be open and free. But until then, America must be strong and keep the peace through strength. Because if one thing is certain, it's that in dealing with totalitarian regimes each step forward can be followed by two steps back—just as we saw in China with the massacre at Tiananmen Square."

Polite applause passed through the audience.

"I do not mean to inveigh against what was a very good question," said Steinbrenner.

Four students rose to their feet to ask questions, but the man engaging the physicist refused to yield.

"That's quite all right," said the man in the audience, "but let me clarify what you're saying: that by making it more costly for the Soviets to penetrate our defense, we will lessen the threat of an attack?"

"That is close enough," Steinbrenner said. "If a three hundred-billion-dollar shield costs a trillion dollars to penetrate, then the cost-exchange ratio is too high, and the fight is over."

"Over?"

"Let's say it will assume a different character."

"Maybe guerrilla warfare. Maybe terrorism."

"Maybe."

"And still, the possibility of nuclear attack."

"We must always fear an attack—never be caught off guard. How true it is, as Demosthenes told his fellow citizens twenty-four centuries ago, that we must be careful of those who criticize the men who advise us to defend ourselves by saying these men press for war. In his vain effort to incite Athenian resistance to Philip of Macedon's drive for hegemony, he described with precision some of the eternal springs of what can be called the psychology of advance surrender. He said, 'As soon as Philip is mentioned among you, one of his agents immediately rises to tell you how sweet it is to live in peace, how costly to maintain an army. They are out to ruin you,' he said. 'Thus they persuade you to put everything off and give your enemy the time and means to achieve his ends undisturbed. You win a brief respite, but someday you will have to admit how much this respite has cost you. The agents beguile you—and earn the pay they were promised.'"

Steinbrenner felt uneasy after quoting Demosthenes. *Maybe it was too erudite*, he thought. *However, the point is good*.

"But the cost to America—the vital social programs that will need to be cut—what about that?" asked a student undeterred by the older man in the audience, who still refused to sit down. "I mean, who is going to benefit from the peace dividend?"

"I am a scientist," Steinbrenner answered. "Your Department of

Health and Human Services, your President and his Cabinet, your Congress, they are ones who must make those decisions. However, I will say that the most inexpensive defense is a strategic, high-technological defense. The cost of maintaining conventional forces to match the Soviet Union's conscripted army is overwhelming by comparison, especially given its proximity to Europe. Fortunately, however, we are still Americans, and we still have the right to vote for the candidates of our choice—at least those candidates who make it out of Iowa and New Hampshire alive—'' Steinbrenner's remark dropped without laughter and he continued. "Consequently, if we do not like the way our money is being spent, it is our right to be heard. Unfortunately, the millions of people living in the Soviet Union who are not represented by the twelve percent of their country that is communist—they cannot be heard. They cannot decide how their money is to be spent. So they go without bread and shoes while their leaders build more powerful warheads. But they go without bread and shoes in silence.''

"But taking war to space," asked another student, "isn't that a question of ethics? Like we can't do enough damage here on earth, we've got to have the heavens, too?"

"War went to space when the Germans invented the V-2 ballistic missile in 1944," said Steinbrenner. "Besides, I believe we *would* rather see a confrontation in space, where no one gets hurt, then here on earth, where billions of lives are involved. Ethically speaking, what policy is more moral than one that saves billions of lives?"

"Then our purpose is to scare the Russians from mounting an attack," said the man in front, "to reassure Americans and our allies that we are safe from communist aggression, to beat the Russians economically. Is that an effective way to deal with foreign policy?"

"Let me first say there is a tremendous difference between Russians and Soviets—and as a man from Poland, I believe I can make a clear distinction. The Russians pose no threat to America, they are a good and peace-loving people living under repression. Gorbachev has given them some hope—something they can smile about, but they are still seeking freedom. The handful of Soviets who run the country, they are our concern. And to answer your question, I am only a scientist. I leave global political strategies to the experts."

"Come on, Dr. Steinbrenner, you have taken a very active role in foreign policy."

"Only in a micro sense."

"Your bomb has affected foreign policy more than anything else in history."

"It was not my bomb." Steinbrenner felt heat flush his face.

"But it *has* affected foreign policy."

"It has. Certainly. But it has preserved the peace for half a century. No one, here—I would venture to say, even you—" he looked directly at the man, "has seen a great world war. To that end, I am proud of my work."

"But we live in fear," said the man, and he sat down.

"I know who you are," said Steinbrenner, and he stepped back from the podium. He shook hands with the university president and waved modestly to the students. The applause was scattered. Reporters rushed to the edge of the stage and hurled questions like over-ripened vegetables. Camera lights that had been confined to the back of the auditorium were now blinding Steinbrenner, and he was growing nervous in the confusion. He tried to listen to the verbal onslaught, but knew it would be impossible to answer one of the newsmen without staying to answer them all. He turned to leave.

The voices peaked and declined, and when there was silence among the reporters, the man from the audience shouted: "If we want to eliminate the threat of ballistic missiles, Doctor, we better eliminate ballistic missiles."

For a moment, Steinbrenner wanted to stop and answer the man. He wanted to tell him that our allies are not equipped to handle conventional forces, that the Soviets outnumber us two-to-one and maintain more conventional hardware, but he stayed silent. He heard several reporters ask the man to identify himself, but before he heard an answer, he moved off the stage and was ushered out the back door to the dark blue Lincoln Continental. His two escorts helped him into the back seat. One got in next to him, and the other took the wheel.

From American University, the driver navigated the automobile southwest rather than southeast, and Steinbrenner was concerned by the change.

"Where are we going?" he asked the man sitting next to him. "I'm to have lunch at the Press Club."

"Yes, sir, but there's a demonstration on 16th Street, in front of the White House. We're catching 495 to George Washington Parkway and coming in from behind."

"I've seen demonstrations before."

"It will be safer this way."

"They are burning me in effigy, or what? Why can't we take the short route?"

"No," the Secret Service agent laughed, "they're not burning you in effigy. But it is an antinuke demonstration."

"At Lafayette Park?"

"Yes, sir. Lafayette, and then they're moving down Constitution to the Capitol."

"The Soviets are stirring."

"Sir?"

"The Soviets are stirring. They are affecting public opinion before the Luxembourg Summit. Putting pressure on the President."

"But at the Capitol they're going to listen to some folk singers and a speech by Senator Ashworth."

"See what I mean."

Both men laughed and Steinbrenner leaned forward and tapped the driver on the shoulder. "Turn this car around," he said, "I want to see this demonstration."

"I can't do that. I'm sorry, sir."

"Hockey, you can't," said Steinbrenner. His use of the word "hockey" was awkward. "You do as I say, or I will report how I caught you sleeping when I came out of the auditorium."

"I wasn't sleeping."

"Yes," Steinbrenner sat back in the seat, "that is what they will expect you to say."

"I really don't think it's a good idea," said the agent sitting next to the physicist.

"I want to hear what Ashworth has to say."

"But he's not speaking until they get to the Capitol."

"That could take an hour," said the man in the front seat. "Maybe two."

"And you have a luncheon in twenty minutes."

Steinbrenner tapped the driver's shoulder again. "Go ahead to the Press Club," he said. "Some luncheon this is going to be. No reporter will be within miles. News is made in the streets."

"I'll take your word for it," said the man next to him.

"The Press Club will be empty. This sensational distraction was undoubtedly planned."

"I couldn't say. But you did make a commitment to be at the Press Club."

"I did at that." The physicist was silent for a moment, then he tapped the driver again. "But after lunch we go to the Capitol."

Both escorts nodded in agreement.

The freeway traffic was light before noon, and except for some construction on the Chain Bridge and a stalled cement truck on 14th Street, there was no delay in getting to the Press Club. The car pulled to the side door, where a gaggle of reporters greeted Steinbrenner with the questions he had not answered at the university. The physicist was not certain if the reporters were the same, but the questions always were.

Dr. Steinbrenner believed the Washington press corps was different from any other in the world. It was more professional. More accurate. But in the most powerful city in the world, the city of monumental decisions, it had to be more ruthless than its counterparts in the hinterlands. The game was recognition, and to earn a good beat or an anchor spot on any of the networks, reporters had to work like hungry junkyard dogs, their eyes always open, their teeth ready, and their attack fatal, because their careers fed on their prey. The more disturbing their questions, the more critical their analysis, the more dogged their pursuit, the more popular they were with their audience. Consequently, to those in power, they were bastards. To those out of power, they were heroes, godsends that protected the integrity of American politics.

Despite how he felt about the media, Steinbrenner appreciated their efforts. He had come from the old country, and he knew the social paralysis that exists without them. He remembered the words of the philosopher Heraclitus: "Through strife, all things arise and pass away. The mixture which is not shaken decomposes." *They are self-serving men,* he thought, *but they serve their purpose. Without them, America would offer no greater freedom than any other country. Freedom of the press, in the truest sense of the word, sets America apart. It is the most important freedom, because, in a way, it monitors all others.*

"Professor Steinbrenner," shouted a young reporter, a charismatic fellow with stiff hair, "only yesterday, your former colleague and most recent critic, Dr. Robert Garvey, said there is no possible way to realize an effective satellite-based antiballistic missile system. Do you have a reply?"

"Yes," said Steinbrenner as he stepped from the car. "There is only one way to find out, and God help us if we ever have to—especially if that system is not in place."

"Dr. Steinbrenner," a woman called out, "there is some speculation that the incredible effort you are making to promote the ABM system, to allegedly protect America from nuclear attack, is out of guilt for your participation in the Manhattan Project. Is this true?"

"Is it true that there is speculation? Yes. It is true."

"Is it true that you feel guilty for the Bomb?"

"I feel no guilt about what we did in Los Alamos."

"But with the force of destruction that you have brought into the world, how can you say that?"

"I say it in English—not in Japanese, nor in Russian."

"Then there are no regrets?"

"Of course not." Steinbrenner's brow grew taut. "The power of the atom bomb existed since the sixth day of God's creation. It needed to be harnessed—to be controlled—before it could be used as a weapon. Somebody, sometime in history, was destined to harness it. And I thank God it was us."

"Dr. Steinbrenner—" another journalist began, but before he could continue, the physicist cut him off.

"I will be happy to answer all the questions you have. But right now, I'm hungry. I say we eat first and talk later. How about that?" He started to move through the sparse crowd toward the glass double-doors.

"But Dr. Steinbrenner," the journalist continued, "we have an antinuclear demonstration to cover, and we'd like your response."

Steinbrenner stopped and turned to face the reporter.

"You want my response before the demonstration?"

"If you could."

"How can I respond to something that has not already happened?"

"Just a general response."

"A general response?"

"Yes. Something like how you feel about so many people gathering to protest against a cause you stand for—a cause you feel so strongly about."

Steinbrenner paused. Took a deep breath. "I will say this. I understand Senator Ashworth is speaking. Is this correct?"

"Yes, sir."

"Well, then, I would suggest you all go listen to the good senator, instead of lunching with me. He is so much more colorful. Very emotional."

"But Dr. Steinbrenner, won't you go on record with your feelings about the increasing number of antinuclear demonstrations all over the world. Two people were killed yesterday in a West German rally where more than one hundred and twenty-five thousand turned out."

"Call me after the demonstration, after I have a chance to hear our good senator. My response will be more educated."

Steinbrenner entered the building and only two members of the press followed him inside. The others left for Lafayette Park, and as the physicist had predicted, the luncheon crowd was not more than thirty journalists scattered around forty tables. Each table was set for eight. Steinbrenner sat at the head table, and even it was not full. The president of the club sat next to him, and for a moment he thought about how much fun it would be to spill the details about the Strategic Defense Initiative, how much fun it would be to tell the few journalists who bothered to attend that the Initiative they thought was only on the blackboard was really overhead, ready to be turned on. *Flip a switch,* he thought. *Presto. Star Wars. But the damn journalists are too busy out there making the news rather than reporting it. The only ones here,* he thought, *are either hungry or just too damn lazy to walk to Lafayette. Why does the White House communications staff do this to me,* he wondered. *I should put an end to it. I should tell these feckless bastards what the President and his advisors are really doing.*

He laughed at the mental image he conjured of these few laggard journalists running out of the Press Club, like school kids on their last day of class, to tell the more respected reporters that Steinbrenner just broke down and admitted that America secretly deployed its ABM network. *The White House would never send me out again,* he thought, *That's certain. But then again, maybe these journalists wouldn't share their information—their scoop. Maybe while the New York television networks were running their stock film of another Washington demonstration, the Buckwall County Examiner would be breaking the most important story of the decade.* The physicist chuckled again. In the next twenty minutes, one small slip on his part, and the world could be introduced to another Bob Woodward. *It would be fun,* he thought, and then he finished his sandwich.

The Secret Service escorts sat at either end of the head table, attacking potato salad and peach cobbler. Steinbrenner stood up and the agent on the right rose to meet him.

"Sit down, son," said the scientist. "I'm not defecting—just going to the restroom."

The man sat and glanced at his partner. With his lips he silently formed R-E-S-T-R-O-O-M, and his partner turned back to his plate.

Steinbrenner looked at the journalists in the large hall, and not one of them looked back at him. He walked out the opened door and turned left in the oak-paneled corridor. A crystal and brass chandelier hung overhead and the ceiling was mirrored. Someone in this club has class, he thought, as he walked through the door marked MEN.

The old scientist had a small problem with continence and liked to make a practice of visiting the restroom after each meal, especially when he was scheduled to speak. He was happy his minor health problems had been delayed, at least until after Ida died. He loved her too much to ever have her think of him as a sick and frail old man. She was a strong woman, even when she was ill. Her Old World values prohibited her from showing weakness and pain, and because of them, her death took Steinbrenner by complete surprise. He had never even known she was sick.

He passed by the mirrors in the large room and stopped to study his reflection. As a youth he had been vain, masculine, tall and intelligent, worthy of respect and admiration. Now he was glad that Ida could not see the broken man he was. His eyes were permanently red, bloodshot and heavy. The skin hung low over his cheekbones and his nose was more angular and boney. Dark blotches of age spots covered his forehead and his white hair was thin and untrimmed. "Hurry, Ida," he said but then jumped as the bathroom door burst open, and a man he assumed was one of the journalists from lunch entered. The professor was embarrassed that he had been caught gazing at his reflection. He rubbed his face with his right hand, tried to bring deeper color back into his skin and convince the journalist that he was looking in the mirror for a reason.

"Good afternoon, Dr. Steinbrenner," said the man as he passed the urinals.

"Good afternoon," Steinbrenner answered and moved toward the stalls.

"I'm Chuck Hendricks of the *Fort Worth Telegram.*"

"Fort Worth?" Steinbrenner questioned. "You don't have a Texas accent." He pushed open the stall door and stepped inside.

The man at the urinal turned and faced the scientist.

"Well, I wasn't born there." He took a step toward the scientist. "You know Americans. We're so itinerant."

The way he said *itinerant* disturbed Steinbrenner. It did not sound natural, relaxed the way a journalist, a man who crafts words, would say it.

"I understand," Steinbrenner said and backed deeper into the stall. The man made him nervous. He stepped closer.

"How about you, Doctor. Where were you born?"

"Poland."

"Poland!"

Steinbrenner felt the backside of his legs touch the toilet. He placed his right hand on the top of the stall door and began to close it, slowly at first. The man continued to come forward. He had a pleasant smile on his face. For a moment, Steinbrenner thought he might be a homosexual. He hated how awkward he felt. Uncomfortable. Vulnerable.

"And you," Steinbrenner asked as he shut the door completely and began to slide the latch. "Where are you from?"

"Moscow," said the man as he broke the door open and pushed the physicist onto the commode. He slapped the side of a straight razor against Steinbrenner's neck. He placed his other hand over the mouth and shoved the head against the tiled wall. "Stay quiet, professor, or I'll cut you open."

The physicist heard the restroom door open again. Another man had entered, and Steinbrenner thought it was one of the agents. He estimated that he had been gone long enough. Maybe not long enough, but surely one would come looking.

"Not a word," the man warned.

But Steinbrenner believed he had nothing to lose. He bit into the man's hand until he felt blood squirt into the corner of his mouth, then he yelled.

The man who had entered the restroom moved to the stall and opened the door. Steinbrenner recognized him as the bearded man from the university, and it was the last image he saw. His attacker jerked his head forward, and then slammed it into the wall. There was a light smear of blood on the smooth ceramic white tile as the scientist slumped forward into the arms of his captors.

Chapter Fifteen

Malibu wanted to take in as much of the port city as he could before his meeting with Julia Peterson at the Casa Blanca. He left the Hotel Los Libereros at 11:15 AM, after a late breakfast of *galletas, café*, and the international edition of the *Post*. There was a small follow-up story, on the murders of Peterson and Watenburg, buried in the international section. Robert was sure that the Washington edition was filled with stories about Grayson, eulogizing him as a hero now, after they had spent a decade shuffling through his dirty laundry. But the international edition was not complete. The thesis of the little story was that no terrorist group had yet claimed the attack.

Brook, Robert thought, *you're sitting on the story of your career, and you're not scratching the surface.*

But at least he has a job.

Shut up, Robert told the squishy right side of his brain. He tucked the paper beneath his arm and walked up La Avenida Andalu to La Calle de los Gitanos—the Street of the Gypsies. Immediately, he understood why they called it Street of the Gypsies. Battered tents and aluminum and pasteboard lean-tos were spread over a distance of about a quarter mile, ending at the swell of a mountain that protected the backside of the city. The mountain also belonged to the gypsies. Hundreds of caves were bored into it, and each cave was a home. The doors were blankets, and the rock around them was whitewashed to reflect the heavy Spanish sun and keep the caves as cool as possible.

Not a city on a hill, Robert thought, *but a city in a hill*. He walked the quarter mile, through the twisting pathways that ran between the tents and lean-tos. Old wet clothes hung on wooden poles, drying in the Mediterranean air. Despite the fall month, it was hot, and Robert could feel his shirt sticking to his chest. He wanted to climb to the top of the mountain, above the cave dwellings, and look out on the city. He walked on, and no one paid attention to him as he passed through the gypsy territory. Old ladies still screamed at their children, and the children still laughed. Somewhere a cheap tape recorder played flamenco guitar music. The sound was hollow but still beautiful, especially amid the squalor that surrounded him. He wanted to stop and listen for a minute, but he did not.

Once he cleared the barrio of tents, he came to a dirt area about the size of a football field. On the other side of it were the caves of more *gitanos*, dressed in rags and nothing like the seductive paintings of gypsy women dressed in colorful costume with scooping décolletage and tanned cleavage. In front of the primitive dwellings, real gypsy women worked their fires. Some had hair, tangled and thick, hanging about their shoulders. Others bound their heads in handkerchiefs. But all of them had the same eyes, hungry and tired, and the air was filled with the smoke of open fires and burning fat. Little girls, no older than twelve or thirteen, held crying babies, and a skinny woman without teeth held a child to her bosom. The child must have been four, yet it still sucked at its mother's limp breasts. Robert was overcome with a feeling of helplessness, the vulnerable feeling when emotions demand that something be done and resources will not allow it. At least a hundred children played in the dirt, some together and some alone, but all of them only partially clad and dusty. None had shoes, and the first thing Robert noticed about the children, after their scant dress, was that they were happy, content in their simple games. One boy, about eight years old, stopped playing, stared at Robert, unzipped his pants and urinated in the dust. The other children played on, and then the boy zipped up his ragged brown pants and rejoined them. Robert realized that the boy was the oldest of the males in the poverty-stricken village. There were no men, only women.

He continued to walk toward the caves and to the mountain, and passed through the children and within feet of the women. Still, they did not speak. *Where are the men?* he asked himself, and imagined they were in town either drinking or whoring or pandering. He climbed above the caves. It took him twenty-five minutes, and when he finally stopped, he was at the edge of the mountain's crown and winded. He bent over and took two deep breaths, and when he stood back up, he noticed for the first time a giant earthen gray pillbox sitting on the plateau. It was another half mile above Robert, but was plainly visible against the brown rock and low brush and surrounded by a tall chain-link and barbed wire fence.

Its size was startling, and three large buildings around it were in various stages of construction. The military installation seemed out of place, a concession to modern technology next to the gypsies' primitive living conditions. It puzzled him why a race that could build sophisticated machinery to track and communicate with satellites could not solve poverty.

He was above the women and caves and tents now, and he turned to look at the city. The view was worth the hike. To the right of where he stood, and about a mile away, was a massive stone castle, and Robert imagined it defending the ancient city against the Moors. Below the castle, the city spread along the coastline, tall buildings like huge sandcastles grew uncontrollably out of the beach. Beyond the city was the dark and jutting Cabo del Gato land mass that cut into the Mediterranean. The sea itself was beautiful, a perfect blue and clean and calm. It reflected the bright sun and clear sky and was speckled with colorful fishing boats. Malibu sat down on a rock and tried to soak in the beauty. He knew he would have to go away, and probably never see Almería again, and he wanted to remember not only the sights he saw, but the feelings he felt. That is what is wonderful about being a writer, he thought, and he took his notebook from his back pocket, you can give words to the emotions. He wrote about the tents, the lean-tos, the gypsies, the brown stone buildings, the castle, and the sea. And he considered the irony that the gypsies had the best real estate in the city.

A minute later, he slid down off the rock into the dust. It was cool, and he leaned against the stone. His mind wandered from the beauty before him into thoughts about what he was going to do when he returned to Washington, thoughts about Diana, about meeting Julia Peterson. He thought about Grayson, and for the first time since finding the senator dead, Robert felt sorrow. He would miss him. He thought about the terrorist who was probably still in Rome or maybe gone. He did not know. He thought of Senator Ashworth. Was he involved? He opened his notebook to Ashworth's name. "Who the hell are you?" he asked aloud.

Ashworth had been in the United States Senate as long as Robert could remember. He recalled seeing the man, more slender and with darker hair, on television when he was still a boy. The old man, his hair gray now, was as much a part of American culture—American politics—as President Kennedy, or Reagan, or any President whose image and influence outlive his own time. "You're an institution. That's who you are."

"It will probably come as welcome news," Grayson had said of Senator Ashworth when he spoke of Peterson's murder. "He's been fighting SDI from day one. Hans was the European demon." Bob scribbled the dead senator's words in his notebook next to Ashworth's name. "It will probably come as welcome news . . . Just watch him." He looked at the other words he had written on the page: BOWER THOMPSON—THREE MEN—ALMERíA—CASA BLANCA.

Strategic Defense, Robert thought, and suddenly he felt uneasy. His body shuddered, and he turned around to stare at the four-sided satellite-tracking station

"Why Almería?" he asked. The mild shudders turned to chills as he remembered the face of Bower Quincy Thompson in the Casa Blanca. "It *was* Bo," he said. "It *was* Ashworth's administrative assistant." Suddenly he was excited. Journalist Jitters began to torment him, those uncontrollable nerves suffered by journalists when they know they are uncovering an important story and they do not want to be scooped. Something was happening in Almería—something either wonderful or horrible—and Robert Hamilton was determined to find out what it was. He wanted to walk up to the military installation and speak to one of the officers on duty at the control station.

But what would he tell me? he questioned. Besides, it was getting late. The air was cooler, and Robert realized he had lost track of time. His face was dry and a little burnt. He stood up and dusted off his pants. The smoke rising from the gypsy village was dark now, the fires were burning brighter and the smell of burning meat drifted up the mountain. Robert was hungry. He looked at the sun. It was off far to the west. He looked at his watch. It was four o'clock, and the boats were gone from the sea.

Evening begins, Robert thought and tucked the notebook into his back pocket and started to walk down toward the gypsies. The closer he came to the village, the stronger the smell of meat grew. It was not a smell he was familiar with, only that it was meat, and it teased his hunger.

When he passed by the caves and through the pasteboard barrio, he noticed the men were back, slumbering in the aluminum chairs that were kept outside the dwelling doors.

Tough day at the office, dear, he thought and smiled and walked on. It would take forty-five minutes to get back to the hotel, another twenty to shower, and he could be at the bar by six. He would not have time to get anything to eat, but was sure he could get a *bocadillo* and a Fanta at the Casa Blanca.

"Even the best-laid plans," he said as he arrived at the bar thirty minutes late. The water heater in the hotel was not working. The gas was not igniting the flame enough to heat the coils before the water passed through them. Malibu would not have minded taking a cold shower. He took alternating hot and cold showers every morning— something he had read about Soviet athletes and how they maintained their competitive edge—after his regular shower he would turn the cold on for thirty seconds, then the hot for a minute, then the cold for another thirty, the hot again for a minute, and then the cold one last time. It was invigorating. The skin tightened and expanded, tightened and expanded, and then tightened again. And drying off with the towel was like a massage. The skin was tender and turned red even under the softest cloth.

Malibu, however, made the mistake of calling hotel maintenance, and they would not allow him to shower until *"todo está bien"*—all is well. *Sometimes the Andalusians are too hospitable*, he thought as he walked into the depressing bar.

His eyes did not take as long to adjust this time, as it was darker outside, and the bar was not as crowded as it was the day before. Malibu had not forgotten his hunger. He walked directly to the bar.

"Buenas noches," said the barkeeper as he dried a shot glass and placed it on the shelf behind him.

"Buenas noches," Malibu answered.

"You are American."

"Is my accent so bad?"

"No. No." The barman picked another, larger glass off the bar and wiped it. Robert noticed that he was not washing them first. "But you do have an accent. And you are tall, like many Americans."

"You had some Americans in here yesterday."

"Yesterday, *sí*. But I get many Americans. They like this bar. They say it is very like bars in *los Estados Unidos.*" He picked up a third glass, wiped it dry, and placed it with the others. "What I can do for you?"

"*Bocadillo?*"

"I have best sandwiches in Spain." The man smiled and pulled a loaf of bread from the large paper bag propped against the bar. With one stroke, he sliced it down the middle. "*Jamón y queso?*"

"What kind of ham and cheese?"

"*Serrano y Suiza.*"

"Great."

The Spaniard sliced three thick slabs of ham off the smoked hind leg that hung crusted and red and brown above the bar. He laid the slices on the bread and took a wedge of Swiss cheese from a tin-lined drawer. Again, he cut large slices and put them on top of the smoked ham. He smiled at Robert.

"What you want to drink?"

"Fanta."

"Fanta?" The barman looked surprised. He placed the top piece of bread on the sandwich and slid it to Robert without a plate. "Fanta no is a drink for man. Only for boys." He pulled a bottle of Aquila beer from beneath the bar and popped the top. "Only for boys and priests. Are you a priest?"

"No," Robert said. "I'm a journalist—a writer." He realized that in a country like Spain, drinking anything other than beer and hard liquor somehow emasculated a man. However, he did not dare flirt with disaster. "But I still want the Fanta."

"Fanta?"

"Orange—please."

"*Bueno.*" The Spaniard took a long swallow from the bottle of beer, made a toasting gesture to Robert, and then placed the bottle on the bar. He reached beneath and took a Fanta orange from a separate cooler. "You sure you don't want a Bitter Kas at least?"

"I'm sure."

The man popped the top and poured the orange into a glass he had just dried and placed it in front of the journalist. Robert paused before he took a drink. He was certain the alcohol from the previous drink killed any germs that might otherwise be on the unwashed glass. Besides, he was thirsty. The sweet orange felt wonderful flowing down his parched throat. Before he could stop, he emptied the glass and asked for another.

"*Hombre*, you can hold your drink," said the barman with a smile. He opened another bottle of soda and poured it into the same glass.

Robert laughed and took a bite from the sandwich. He could not remember tasting anything so delicious. The ham had a salty and rugged taste. The cheese was moist, unrefrigerated, full and sharp. The sandwich was not polluted with mayonnaise and mustard and all the other condiments Americans use to hide the flavor of processed cold cuts. *If I could patent this sandwich and sell it in Washington*, Robert thought, *I'd never have to write another story as long as I live.* The bread was soft and chewy inside and crisp on the crust. He took a drink of orange. *Maybe I'm just hungry*, he thought and took another large bite.

"Here come more Americans," said the Spaniard. He pointed to the door.

Robert turned to look. Suddenly he stopped chewing. It was Bower Thompson with two men, each of them in a dark suit and already looking out of place in the informal bar atmosphere. There were only about a dozen patrons scattered among the tables. Robert was the only man at the bar, and he watched as Thompson and his associates took a table in the far corner. He did not recognize the other men, but he guessed that they, too, were Senate staff members. *Maybe a congressional delegation. But I would have heard about it*, Robert thought. *Besides, Ashworth would be here.* He took another bite. *Unless, of course, Ashworth had an emergency back in Washington.* "There's one way to find out," he said aloud and placed the sandwich on the bar. The floor was littered with torn lottery tickets and several stuck to Malibu's shoes as he walked across the room to the table where Thompson sat.

The administrative assistant saw the journalist approach, and he stood to greet him. Robert extended his hand.

"Mr. Thompson, I'm—"

"Robert Hamilton," Bower said before Robert could finish. "Of course, we all know who you are. Have a seat." Thompson pointed to an empty chair opposite him on the table.

"Do you mind if I join you?"

"Hell, no. Americans have to stick together." He motioned to the

Spaniards sitting sedately around the establishment. "Especially in such a hostile environment."

Robert smiled. "I've got a sandwich at the bar. Can I get anything for you men?"

Thompson looked at his associates and nodded his head. Turning back to Robert, he said: "Sure. Ask the bartender to bring us six beers."

"Any special brand?"

"Just six beers." Thompson sat down and Robert returned to the bar. He would have liked to study the expressions on the faces of the other men to see how his intrusion was being accepted, but he did not turn around.

"They would like six beers."

"*Seis*?"

"Six, yes." Robert looked at his sandwich and Fanta on the bar. "By the way," he asked, "do you know a woman named Julia? Julia Peterson?"

"Pete-ur-soon?" asked the barman as he opened six bottles of Aquila.

"Julia Peterson. She's *alemana*, or at least married to one."

"I am sorry."

"No problem. She was supposed to be here a little while ago, at six o'clock."

"At six o'clock?"

"Yes."

"La María was here."

"Maria?"

"Yes. A woman who spends much time here. Maria. She asked if an American had been here. I thought she meant the men there." He pointed at Thompson.

"She left?"

"About twenty minutes later."

"Thank you," Robert said.

"Be careful with la María."

"What?"

"Be careful. She looks innocent."

"Innocent?"

"*Sí. Pero cuidado.* Be very careful."

Robert gathered the six beers on a tray and returned to the table. He was surprised he did not feel defeated that he had missed the woman. But then he was not sure she was the woman. The bartender said Maria. He wanted Julia. Besides, if Maria were Julia, she would return, and right now Robert was interested in pumping Bower Thompson for information.

"Don't forget to leave your tips," Robert said as he placed the beers on the table. "I work hard for my money." He returned to the bar for glasses and his sandwich and soda. He wondered if these had been washed or, like his, merely dried.

"What do you mean be careful?" he asked the bartender.

"*Prostituta.*"

"Prostitute?"

"*Sí.* And in e-Spain this is no good thing."

"Thank you," Robert said and gathered his food and drink and returned to the table.

"What's an ace reporter like you doing in Almería?" Bo asked as Malibu sat down.

Robert was caught off guard. For a moment he panicked, and then he felt foolish for not having preconstructed an excuse. "Basque terrorists," he said without much thought.

"Basque terrorists?" Bo laughed. "Hell, you're about five hundred miles too far south."

"I'm on my way to Bilbao."

"By Almería?"

"I love this city." Robert smiled and took an uneasy sip of orange soda.

"You know Almería, Mr. Hamilton?" asked the man sitting immediately to the right of Robert.

Malibu knew he could not lie. Surely his knowledge of the Mediterranean city would not be enough to support him. In fact, he doubted he knew enough about the city to fill a five-minute conversation.

"A little bit," Robert said anyway and took another sip.

"Mr. Hamilton—" Thompson began but Malibu cut him off.

"Call me Bob, or Malibu. Everyone calls me Malibu."

"Why Malibu?" asked the man to his right.

"My stepfather was a sailor in Norfolk. I guess he had something for the other coast."

"Malibu," Thompson said with a smile. "It's a nice nickname. Anyway, this," he pointed at the man on the right, "is Byron Brown from Washington."

Robert shook the man's hand.

"I have heard good things about you, Mr. Hamilton."

"Thank you."

"And this," said Thompson, pointing to the other man, "is Nathan Block."

"Nathan," Robert said as he extended his hand.

Something about the second man seemed strange to Malibu. Nathan had the altered form of a dwarf, yet he was not short. *His body must stand at least six feet*, Robert thought. But he looked compressed, no neck and stubby, powerful arms, short fat fingers. To compound his unusual appearance,.the man wore a crew cut, and Robert could see that his suit was ill-fitting.

"Are you from Washington, too?"

"He works on Embassy Row," said Thompson.

"What embassy?"

"He doesn't work for an embassy, exactly," said Bower. "He works for the Foreign Broadcast Information Service."

"You're a journalist?"

"Of sorts," said Bo.

Robert wondered why the strange man could not speak for himself, and his wonder compounded the suspicion that was mounting in his brain about Bower Thompson, Senator Ashworth, and these two new men. He wanted to jump right into the questions that were flooding his head: *What are you doing here? Does it involve the Strategic Defense Initiative? Do you know Julia Peterson? Do you know about the terrorist attacks in Rome? What is the satellite-tracking compound for on the hill outside the city?* But questions were the hazard of his profession. People liked talking until you started to ask questions. In his years at the *Post*, he had learned to be more prudent, more circuitous in his conversations. He would get the information he needed, but it would take time. He learned to save the incriminating questions until the end of the interview, and then ask them with one hand on his coat and the other on his notebook. Sometimes his tactics took too long, to the displeasure of his editors. He remembered a limerick Simon Levin offered when Robert was first assigned to his staff:

> There once was a writer from Treadline
> Who interviewed drunks in a breadline;
> They chewed on his legs,
> Reduced him to dregs,
> But his story came in right on deadline.

Those were the days when Simon still tolerated me, Robert thought, *but the lesson remains.* There was a story involving the three men around this table, and he had to get it. He also realized that if he did not ask some of the questions, he, too, would be suspect.

"What are you doing in Spain?" *That is a normal question*, he thought.

"Bullfights," said Bo.

"In an official capacity?" Malibu asked, and the men laughed.

"Just as friends on vacation."

"America's sending a lot of heavy artillery to the *corrida*," Robert said, but he knew it was not true. That was a costly error. *Why are you lying to me, Thompson?* he wondered. *The bullfight season ended months ago.* He was not sure if he should point out the mistake to the men. To do so might shut them up, put them on the defensive. But to say nothing might be just as dangerous, especially if Thompson said it with the intention to explore Malibu's motives, knowing that if the journalist let the erroneous answer drop without comment he would be after other information. It was a game. But Robert had played it for years, and he was very good.

"What matadors have you seen?"

"El Niño," said Bower. "El Cordobés."

Come on Bo, Robert said to himself. *El Cordobés hasn't fought in years.*

"El Migelito," Bo continued.

"Here in Almería?"

"All over. We've been in Madrid, Seville, Málaga."

"Have you seen a bullfight here in Almería?"

Thompson suddenly looked nervous, and Robert realized that he was not intentionally lying, that he really wanted the journalist to believe that he and his associates were in Spain for the bullfight season.

"We haven't—" Bo began, but Robert interrupted.

"Were you in Rome with Ashworth?"

"No. I sent our legislative assistant for defense policy, and three members of the committee staff. They can keep the senator company."

"That's right, this is vacation time for most of the Senate," Robert said. Now he wanted to help Thompson fortify his story.

"We won't convene officially until after the first of the New Year, after the President's State of the Union." Bo smiled.

Robert could see tension leave the man's face.

"Where do you work?" he asked Byron.

The man had a large head with thick brown hair and deep-set green eyes. His complexion was dark, and though he was clean shaven, his beard was heavy. He looked like the strongman in a gangster film, a contrast to the frail-looking Bower Thompson with his wisps of thinning hair pulled unattractively over his head and his pale, sickly skin. There were rumors in Washington that Thompson was gay, but then there were rumors that everyone on Capitol Hill was gay, even the conservatives and moral coalition.

"I work for the International Council on Global Economics, a think tank in Georgetown."

"You're an economist?"

"Professor of political philosophy."

"Then you teach?"

"As much as I can. The pay is horrible. I spend most of my time in research and writing."

A real liberal, Robert thought. The pay is horrible, he repeated to himself. I'll act sympathetic toward humanity—just make sure the pay's good. "And you're with the Foreign Broadcast Information Service," he said to the third man, the man who had remained silent. He could not believe how easy they were making his job. He knew with certainty that he was sitting at a table in Almería, Spain, with three left-wingers—radical left-wingers—maybe even Soviet spies. Even Bower Thompson was showing himself to be a sellout. The bullfights. Hell, Bo, you're no fun at all.

The man only nodded.

For the first time Robert noticed there was something wrong with his right eye. The socket was larger than the left. The eye bulged like a bug's, and the flesh of the lid clung to it dry and colorless. It was disoriented when compared to the other eye, which fluttered and jerked and studied every movement in the bar. *He isn't even going to speak to me,* Robert thought. *He knows he can't cover his Slavic accent. What have you gotten yourself into, Bo, and why?* He looked back to Ashworth's aide. As an administrative assistant on Capitol Hill, the man made over one-hundred thousand dollars a year. *Why sell out?* Anyone could live well on that kind of money. But maybe it was not greed. Maybe it was philosophical. Maybe Bo had been swallowed by the socialist wave that washed through the universities in the late sixties. But philosophy is one thing, Robert thought. Surely Bo is familiar with the endless procession of Russian dissidents—Vladimir Bukovsky, Mikhail Makarenko, Natan Shcharansky—who seemed like permanent witnesses before Congress. Surely he had read the books of Sakharov and Solzhenitsyn. The stories of these men were depressing with tragedy and abuse, corruption in government, religious persecution, families torn apart, and human bondage.

Robert's mood grew black. He looked at Bower Thompson. *You're a damn fool,* he thought, and then he realized he had been quiet much too long.

"So when are you going home?" he asked Bo.

"Thursday. It will give me the weekend to rest before I have to get back to the office. How about you?"

"When I get finished with the Bilbao story, I guess. I'd like to take a few days and see the country."

"This is your first time in Spain?"

"I came when I was in college. Stayed three weeks. Had the goal of reading every Hemingway book published at the time. I remember *Islands in the Stream* came out while I was here, but I read everything else."

"Hemingway!" the man with the wicked eyes smiled and bobbed his head up and down. It was the first word he had uttered.

It figures you would relate to Hemingway, you communist bastard, Malibu thought. In the Soviet Union, Hemingway was considered the voice of America, a man who became an expatriate, a part of America's "lost generation," who glorified the communist-dominated loyalists in *For Whom the Bell Tolls*, and wrote for the communist pulp magazine, *The Masses*, in America.

"I was enamored with him once," Robert continued. "But I still haven't read *The Garden of Eden*, and it's been out over ten years now. It's the only book of his I haven't read. I've even read anthologies of his old byline material.

"Then you *are* incomplete," said Bower with a nervous laugh. He took a swallow of beer.

"Hemingway did move my world—once."

"And who moves your world now?" asked Byron Brown.

"I don't know. Maybe I've become cynical."

"Reporting in Washington will do that to you," Bo added.

"Hemingway was cynical," said Nathan Block, and Robert detected an Eastern European accent.

"Yes, he was." Robert took a drink of Fanta. His bottle was almost empty, and the soda left at the bottom was much too sweet. He lifted it in the air and caught the bartender's attention.

The barman waved and smiled and lifted another bottle of Fanta orange above his head. Robert nodded his approval. The man wiped off the bottle with a rag, pried the top off, poured half the drink into a glass, and brought it to Malibu's table.

Out of habit, the journalist stood up to greet the bartender and introduce him to the other three men. The barkeep smiled and shook hands and then asked Robert to step away from the table for a moment.

"La María, she is here," whispered the barman.

Robert laughed, "But I thought you told me to stay away from her." He lowered his voice to a half-mocking whisper. "She's a prostitute."

"I know. This is what I said, but—"

"Now you want me to meet her?" A condescending grin spread over Malibu's face—the kind of grin a student gets from a teacher who has caught him in an act that is both shameful and amusing. Robert was certain the Spaniard was working on a commission basis. It would not be unusual for the proprietor to receive fifteen or twenty percent of the whores' evening take when they worked out of his establishment, especially if he set up the tricks.

"No. You should stay away. She is no good for you. But she tell me she needs to talk to you."

"Needs to talk to me?"

"*Sí*. She say to me, you know journalist *Americano, no*? I say yes. She say, I must talk to him."

"Did you tell her I was here?"

"Not yet. I wait to see what you say."

Was Maria really Julia? Robert wondered. *How would a prostitute know to ask for the American journalist*? He was almost certain she was. "Sure," he answered. "Sure, I'll meet with her."

"She is at the table in back. Over there." The man pointed to the far right corner of the bar.

Robert could see the woman's back, but that was all. Her face was hidden from view, however, he could see the long dark-brown, almost black, hair that flowed over her shoulders and down until it became hidden by the back of the chair.

"Tell her I'll be there in a minute." He took a note for five-hundred pesetas from his pocket and gave it to the barman. It was four times the cost of the drink, but Robert believed he had gotten his money's worth from the man.

"A friend of yours?" asked Bo, once Robert had taken his seat.

"Everybody's my friend." The journalist gestured a toast with his soda. Bo and Byron returned his salute, but Nathan sat motionless, watching Malibu with his lifeless eye. "I do have to meet someone. How long will you be here?"

"Maybe another thirty minutes," Thompson answered. "Maybe an hour."

"Perhaps we can get together a little later, then."

"Fine." Bo looked at the other men. His face showed no emotion. Nathan appeared angry.

Robert stood up. He felt uneasy and tried to think of something amusing to say to leave the men laughing, but his mind was overloaded with questions about the woman Maria, and he could think of nothing to say. There was a clumsy pause. Maybe he was leaving the men too abruptly, but there was no other way to do it.

"Sorry to drink and run." He grasped at the most cliche exit line his mind would permit.

"That's okay," said Bo. "We understand."

Robert turned toward the back of the bar, but before he took a step, Nathan Block spoke.

"Mr. Hamilton."

Robert turned around.

"We will see you again." His voice was flat. *Was it a warning? Or a parting gesture of friendship?* He lifted his bottle of beer, and Robert only smiles.

"I'll look forward to that."

Hamilton walked across the bar. The woman's table was not far from where the three men sat, and he was certain they were watching him. Did they know who Maria was? Did they know who Julia was? He reached the point directly behind the woman and stopped. She was wearing a red silk blouse and black leather pants. At once, her clothes were elegant and sexy. Expensive. Robert saw that the pants were soft, maybe lamb skin, and the blouse was real silk, not nylon or a polyester imitation. The woman made a good living, whoever she was.

"Maria?" Robert spoke loudly enough that only she could hear. She turned slowly to face him, and Robert was taken by surprise. The woman's cheekbones were unmistakable. Her features were too elegant for a prostitute. Her skin was dark and smooth, and her eyes were as clear and deep as the sea he had seen earlier that morning when he was on the mountain. This was the same woman he had met in the bar yesterday.

"*Hola, qué tal?*" she said with a smile. Her teeth were white and perfectly lined, and as she smiled her eyes sparkled even brighter.

You're not a prostitute, Robert thought. *You're someone's daughter, or wife, or sister, or girlfriend. What are you doing here?*

"May I sit down?"

"Please."

"You are Maria?"

"Yes."

Robert noticed her drink was a finger from empty. "Can I get you another?"

"Thank you. I am drinking *vino blanco.*"

White wine? In this dive? It was no more unusual than a full-grown man drinking orange Fanta. Robert walked to the bar and ordered the drink.

"Did she say American journalist?" he asked the barman.

"Yes—American journalist."

"How did she know?"

"What?"

"Nothing. I'm thinking out loud—that's all." He walked back to the table.

"Thank you," she said and took a soft sip from the new glass.

"The barman said you wanted to talk to me."

"We met yesterday afternoon."

"You think I'd forget."

"We only talked for a moment."

Robert nodded and took a drink of Fanta. *It's not the talk I remember*, he thought. "What can I say. You made a great first impression."

"Are you married?"

Robert laughed suddenly. "You don't let any grass grow under your feet, do you?"

"What?"

"Nothing." He placed his drink on the table. "It's just a Yankee expression."

"Are you?"

"What?"

"Married?"

Maybe she is a hooker. Robert was aware of the possibility. Until now, he had doubted. "No. I'm not married."

"You were, though?"

"I've never been married."

"Why?"

"I don't understand all the questions."

"I just want to know you."

"Inside five minutes?"

"Why not?"

"Because you'll find out how boring I am. Real fast."

"Do you love another woman?"

"Now come on!" Robert smiled, unsure whether he should be angry or flattered. "I've never taken a standardized test in a bar."

"Standardized test?"

"Nothing," Robert said. He realized what it felt like to be on the other side of the questions. *That's it*, he thought. *Let's turn the tables.* "But how about you? Are you married?"

"Me. No." She made a clicking sound with her lips and shook her head.

"Yesterday, you said you learned English in school. You speak very well for having learned in school."

"Thank you."

"Where?"

"What?"

"Where did you go to school?"

"Here in España."

"But you've traveled in America."

"Why do you say that?"

"You don't dress like a Spanish woman. Your clothes are too expensive—out of place here in Almería."

"Maybe I bought them in Madrid or Málaga."

"To come back and work in a cheap neighborhood bar? I doubt it."

"You don't know."

"And you speak English too well. In fact, you don't speak English at all. You speak American." Robert paused for a moment and then continued. "Yesterday you were convincing. The white cotton top and jeans."

"I don't know what you're talking about."

" *'Don't? You're?'* Be careful. Now you're using contractions." Robert could see she was getting frustrated. Her face was flushing. She was breathing heavier. "Who are you?" he pressed.

"Do not insult me." She stood up, and before Robert could say anything, she was gone, out the front door and into the night. He bolted after her, but she had disappeared down one of the many side streets that ran into the plaza. He took a deep breath. The air was fresh and a little cold. He did not have a jacket.

Chapter Sixteen

Robert turned the corner onto the main avenue. The bright lights and music, the sidewalk tables cluttering the street, the men and women walking arm in arm, filled the air with fiesta. But it was only Thursday.

No other people in the world celebrate life more than those who live in Iberia, he thought, and turned his attention back to the bar, to Maria and Bo and the other men. He should not have pressed the girl with his questions, at least not so quickly. He knew better, but the game he was playing was wearing on him. Getting information quickly somehow seemed like a matter of life and death, and he did not have time to waste. Things were happening too fast. Even while he talked to the woman, Bo and his associates had left the bar. Robert did not notice them leave, but found them gone after Maria had fled and he returned into the bar. The barman said he did not notice them leave either. Robert settled his bill, paid for Maria's two drinks, and left.

Now he was walking down a crowded evening street, admiring the form of a young Spanish woman walking in front of him. She wore a yellow cotton dress, tied at the waist with a red belt. Her legs were bare, beautifully tanned, toned, and smooth. She wore white sandals on her feet and yellow silk ribbons in her flowing dark hair. Beneath the thin dress that set off her deep brown skin, her body was slender and graceful, full of life. She was young, maybe eighteen, and for a moment, Robert coveted her age and the years that awaited her. He remembered when he was that age. Girls so beautiful, so perfectly formed, were out of the question. He was not their "type"! At least that was the excuse they used when he gathered the courage to ask them for dates.

They wanted football players; he was a writer. They wanted boys who partied; he studied. They wanted flighty relationships; he was intense and committed. They wanted drinkers; he was sober—at least then.

Harper, the closest thing Robert had to a father, told him not to worry about it. Harper had never married and claimed that he never worried about it.

"Women wouldn't have me," he would say, and Robert would stare across the dinner table at the food stains in the old man's grizzled beard and believe him. "Man doesn't need a woman in the way a woman needs a man. Man's got to roam the land and sea. He's an explorer. Can't tie him down to some gosh-damn-awful home with flowers and a mortgage. He doesn't breed well in captivity."

"Traditional family is important," Robert would argue.

"For nothing more than laws and paperwork and lawyers."

"Children are better off with two parents."

"Whale shit! Look at all the great men. They were bastards, a lot of them."

"Who?" Robert always asked.

"Alexander Hamilton, for instance," Harper always answered.

"I see what you mean."

"You'll grow out of this stage. Women'll follow you all over the world. They'll be at every port. But damn you if you ever settle down."

"That's fine if I were going to be a sailor."

"You're going to be a sailor."

"We've gone over this a thousand times."

"Don't start talking about writing. Damn journalists are cutthroats, the kind of people who come down from the mountains after the battle and kill all the wounded. I raised you to be a sailor."

"I'm going to college."

"To what?"

"College. You know, higher education."

"You don't need college to be a sailor."

"That's my point."

"You're serious about this."

"I've already applied."

"We got little money."

"I know. I've applied for a scholarship, and I'll work as a stringer for a newspaper, maybe even the campus daily."

"You're really going to leave me?"

"Not far. I'll be in Fairfax. George Mason University."

"He was a good man."

"What?"

"George Mason. He wouldn't ratify the gosh-damn Constitution because it didn't have the bill of rights."

"I'll come home once or twice a month," Robert said and counted himself fortunate to have such a father-figure in his life. Harper was one of the wisest men he knew, a self-educated sailor with a love of books that filled the four walls in the library of their little Norfolk home.

"I'll be here." The man's eyes grew red with emotion. "And I'll come visit you. I'm not sailing much anymore, anyways."

It always happened that way, Robert thought as he walked down the avenue, no matter how their conversations began, they always ended with a discussion about his future and an emotional old man who knew Robert would leave one day. For not wanting to be tied down, the sailor made a mistake the day he assumed responsibility for the baby child.

Robert always referred to it as assuming responsibility because to this day he was not certain how he came to live with Harper, or whether he was officially adopted. His imagination had provided wonderful stories about what might have happened, about how Harper rescued him from an island after the cannibals had killed his parents or they had died from some tropical disease. He dreamed of sinking ships and being afloat, alone for days, in a lifeboat, of being discovered by Harper and his crew of merchant mariners. In Robert's dream, Harper loved the baby immediately and made his men sign a blood oath that they would go to their graves without speaking a word about the infant boy to the authorities. They must have honored that oath, because the authorities never came, and Robert grew up with the old man.

The girl stopped to talk to a teenage boy who sat nursing a beer beneath a red and white umbrella that advertised Cinzano. The romance of night was everywhere, and Robert was not ready to return to the hotel. He was not tired, and the prospect of watching one of the three national television channels, alone in his room, was not appealing. He walked to the end of the long avenue, which sloped downward to the ocean, and out onto the large pier. Enjoying a flowing feeling of calm, for the first time in days, he looked at the red and white lights of the small fishing boats that speckled the black sea. The men and their boats would stay out until dawn, and then return to sell their catch in the open-air market.

Maybe Harper was right, Robert thought. There is something powerful about the sea. Something inviting. Melville knew that, and Robert knew Melville:

I thought I would sail about a little and see the watery part of the world. Whenever I find myself growing grim about the mouth; whenever it is damp, drizzly November in my soul; whenever I find myself involuntarily pausing before coffin warehouses, and bringing up the rear of every funeral I meet; and especially whenever my hypos get such an upper hand of me, that it requires a strong moral principle to prevent me from deliberately stepping into the street, and methodically knocking people's hats off—then, I account it high time to get to sea as soon as I can. This is my substitute for pistol and ball. With a philosophical flourish Cato throws himself upon his sword; I quietly take to the ship. There is nothing surprising in this. If they but knew it, almost all men in their degree, some time or other, cherish very nearly the same feelings towards the ocean with me.

At the edge of the pier, on the wooden benches, sat two lovers locked in an erotic embrace, the girl straddling the boy, her legs wrapped around him and her body pressed closely to his. They were oblivious to the people strolling by. There was little shame in this land of romance. Robert smiled and thought about Diana. In three short days, she had captivated him. He wondered what she was doing at this moment. Once this assignment was over, he could return to her.

But it's not an assignment, his mind objected.

Then why is it so important?

Because you're a thorough journalist, with or without a paper.

But isn't Diana more important than chasing this silly story?

That's your decision.
What's all this talk about Diana? You don't even know the woman.
That's what makes her desirable.
Concentrate on the story. Diana will come in time.
What story? The only reason I'm in Almería is because Julia
Peterson asked me to meet with her. Now she's gone.
If Maria is Julia Peterson in the first place.
She's Julia. I can feel it.
Who made you so instinctive?
It comes with the profession.
Then why did you send the woman running away?
I'm not always a hundred percent.
You might as well go back to Rome. You're having better luck with
Diana.
Shut up.

Without breaking from her lover's grasp, the young woman on the edge of the pier looked at Robert. He returned her glance and soon they were staring at each other. She did not turn away like coy American girls. While she kissed her boy, and he stroked her backside and caressed her hips, she gazed at Robert. He grew uncomfortable but flattered, believing she was attracted to him because he did not look Spanish. He was taller, much taller, than the average Spanish man— six foot, two inches. His eyes were a clear blue, and women— especially dark-eyed foreign women—found them his most attractive feature. One time, while he was working the Middle East, a liberated Arab woman asked him to father a child with blue eyes. His skin was fair, but darkened easily under the sun. His neck was long and joined his head at a rugged jawline. His cheekbones were high—almost Polynesian—and when he smiled a creased dimple showed vertically on the left side of his face. His nose was straight, unaltered by contact sports, and his beard was light, but his eyebrows thick. Now, as he stood on the pier, he was dressed in a white polo shirt with khaki pants and Bass Weejuns.

The girl did not turn away, and Robert could stare no longer. He stepped back, off the pier, crossed in front of cars waiting at a stoplight, and faded into the shadows of the oceanfront boulevard. The palm trees were tall and narrowly spaced, and the light from the yellow street lamps fell on the broad sidewalk like the spokes of a wheel, light where it shone through the trees and dark where the trees blocked the light. There were fewer people on this side of the street. Most walked along the other side, the ocean side. Robert enjoyed the solitude, but still looked for the image of Maria or Julia or whatever her name really was. He chastised himself for being so quick in the bar. He could have waited and let the conversation develop naturally.

Maybe I was worried about losing Bo, he reasoned. *But then I lost them both.*

With that thought, his mind was struck by the possibility that Bo and Julia were together. He had not considered it before, but it appeared more than coincidence that Thompson was in Almería the same time as Julia. And Thompson had clearly lied about his reasons for being there. Robert's heart began to beat faster and he felt cold, the Journalist's Jitters.

They can't be together, he tried to convince himself. *But does Bo know who she is? Does she know who Bo is? Who tracked whom to Almería?*

Robert jogged across the boulevard to the ocean side and walked until he found a patch of beach. The sand was white and cold. The waves broke softly on the shore. He sat down, opened his notebook, and tried to design a graph that capsulized the situation.

First, he wrote the name "Hans Peterson" on the top of the page. Directly beneath it he wrote "Grayson W." He circled both names and wrote "Dead." To the right of Peterson's name, he wrote "Julia Peterson," and beneath that, "Bo Thompson." Under Bo's name, Robert scribbled the names "Nathan Block" and "Byron Brown." Those were not their real names, he was sure of that. In small letters next to each, he wrote a.k.a. and drew a circle around the group, leaving out Julia's name. Though it was still possible, his instincts told him that she was not involved with the men. To the left of the circle, he wrote the word "Terrorist." He thought it might be overly dramatic linking a terrorist to a congressional staff member, especially someone as prominent as Bower Quincy Thompson, but it was the most logical assumption so far. Then he made the next connection. If Thompson were involved—he wrote the name "Senator Ashworth" beneath the three men and connected it to the circle above.

He looked at what he had so far:

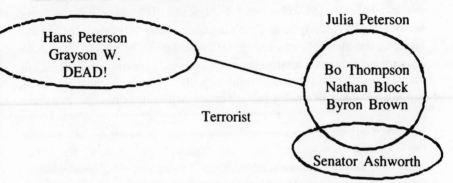

Above the model in large letters he wrote "S.D.I." This is how things were coming together. He looked at the word "Terrorist." *Who was it?* He shook his head when he considered Bower. The man was too sickly and effeminate. Nathan looked like a terrorist. *No problem killing his own mother*, Robert thought. His mind pictured the man's lifeless, hanging eye, and a chill shot up his spine. Byron seemed like a nice-enough man, the kind of foreigner popular with Washington's party crowd. Senator Ashworth was out of the question. Robert was certain his involvement was purely ideological. He drew a line under the word "Terrorist," and he considered the possibility that the man— or woman—could be someone else entirely, someone Robert did not know. At least not yet.

He closed his notebook, stood up, and brushed the sand off the seat of his pants. The time was 9:53. In twenty-four hours, he had gone from a state of being fatigued to his present state in which he knew he could not sleep if he tried. The hotel was three blocks away. It would take him ten minutes if he walked at a leisurely pace.

That would put me in past ten, he thought. *I could get something at the hotel bar, settle into my room.*

He slipped the notebook into his back pocket and within ten minutes found himself inside the clean and tranquil bar, having overestimated the time it took him to walk from the beach. Now there was more time to kill, but that was okay. He enjoyed the ambiance of the small establishment, a sharp contrast to the noisy and dirty Casa Blanca. Well-dressed patrons—many of them Americans—were scattered throughout the large room. A Spanish crooner stood in the corner, next to a grove of miniature palms, and moaned his songs to recorded music. He reminded Robert of Julio Iglesias. His voice was far from the quality of Iglesias's, but his size and mannerisms were the same. Holding the microphone in his right hand, he stiffly imitated Iglesias, moving his left hand around his body—under his suit coat, behind his back, beneath the pit of his right arm. He closed his eyes while he sang, and when he had a bar of music without words, he hummed along.

Robert sipped a club soda and orange juice. In his mind he replayed the conversations of the day. The Spanish girl, Maria, he found beautiful, and her beauty was enhanced by her sweet voice—unusual, foreign and throaty—at odds with her delicate, almost innocent appearance. Malibu thought of her pronunciation of vowels, her short sentences, and her attempted misuse of modifiers. She knew English too well, and had given herself away using contractions. The more he thought about her, the more he believed she was Julia Peterson. It was unusual for a Spanish whore to command English as a second language, but it was not unusual for the well-bred wife of an international political figure. A woman like Julia Peterson would spend months out of the year in England or the United States. She would entertain officials of the English-speaking countries on a regular basis, and cultivate transatlantic relationships. Often foreigners spoke English better than Americans, especially the well-educated foreigners who mastered the grammar and locution in school rather than on the street.

The prerecorded music changed from nightclub blues to swing-era jazz.

You must take the "A" Train ·
to go to Sugar Hill way up in Harlem. If you miss the "A" Train,
you'll find you've missed the quickest way to Harlem.

Duke Ellington in Almería, thought Robert. *Some things never fade away. They never die. Instead they become immortal and are adopted by the world, no longer to be claimed by any one nation. It was like that with Shakespeare and Tolstoy and Bob Hope. It's like that with Bob Hope.* Malibu smiled. *Nobody ever remembers that Bob Hope was not born American.*

Four couples moved to a ceramic-tiled dance floor.

Hurry get on now it's coming.
Listen to those rails a drumming.

Duke Ellington was international, too. Robert moved his mind back to the Casa Blanca—to the short conversation he had with Bo and his associates. They were not so international. Robert easily detected their accents and formal use of English. It was not wise for Thompson to associate with the foreigners, even if the association was innocent—which he was certain was not the case—especially if those foreigners were from Eastern Bloc nations.

Robert was thinking something about security clearances, and about how Bower's would be jerked by the FBI, when suddenly his mind recognized what had happened in the Casa Blanca.

He had been set up by Julia Peterson. The reason Maria did not admit to being Julia was because that was not important. In fact, it was safer for Julia to remain as far removed as she possibly could, but she wanted Robert to find Bower Thompson and Byron Brown and Nathan Block. That is why she had lured him into the Casa Blanca. And Bo and his friends were up to no good, or they would not be meeting in the seedy neighborhood bar—even if it used to be a watering hole for Americans who came to Almería to make movies. It was old and run-down now, and the Spanish patrons were laborers and hookers and the air stank of perspiration. Regular tourists, in town for the bullfights or the beach or any other reason, would stay at the hotel bar, or at least a bar on the main avenue where the ambiance was clean and entertaining.

Robert felt himself getting nervous again. His instincts were acute, and he knew he was getting close. He stood up, threw five hundred pesetas onto the table, and took one last, long drink of his soda and juice. His mind was racing. He had to move.

But where? Who could he see at this hour, and where would he find them?

Start with the Casa Blanca, he told himself and looked at his watch. It was almost 10:30. The bar would still be open. Spaniards were up all night. *Cena*—or dinner—did not even start until 11:00 for many of them.

Bo's not there anymore, objected the logical part of his brain. *Don't waste your time. You need sleep. Do this tomorrow morning.*

I couldn't sleep now, even if I tried. I'll pump the bartender for information. We're friends, now.

Friendship ends where questions begin.

We'll see.

Robert left the bar and walked through the lobby to the revolving door.

Get your jacket at least. It's getting chilly out there.

Don't have time.

Why are you so rushed? People will still be alive in five minutes. You've got plenty of time. You don't even have deadlines anymore.

He turned around and walked to the elevators, then to his room, but no sooner had he stepped inside when the door slammed shut and he was hurled to the floor by two men who had been waiting inside. One was a burly man, taller than Robert, with a dark brown nevus covering the left side of his face. The other man, Malibu was not surprised to see, was Nathan Block.

"Stay on the floor, Mr. Hamilton. And do not move." Block pointed a Makarov at Robert's forehead, suppressing any desire the journalist might have to fight back.

"I'm not moving." Robert raised his hands to his head very slowly. "Just don't do anything foolish."

"Like shoot you?" Block had a devious smile. His dead eye seemed to pulsate in its socket.

"Exactly."

"But why would I want to kill you?"

"I'm asking myself the same question." Malibu began to sit up. Nathan snapped the slide on the pistol and loaded a bullet into the chamber.

"I said not to move."

Malibu slid back onto the floor. "KGB?" he ventured a calculated guess.

"Don't be silly." Bower Thompson's voice came from the dark bathroom. He stepped into the larger room that was lighted by one nightstand lamp. "You think I'd be foolish enough to join the KGB?" He shook his head. "Too well known."

"Your friend, here, isn't holding a Smith and Wesson."

"The KGB is for paperback novels. No one sells out America for the KGB anymore."

"Something more practical then?"

"Exactly."

"GRU?"

"You're very good, for a journalist."

Robert did not know much about the GRU, except for the formal information he received working at the NSC. The initials stood for the Russian translation of Chief Intelligence Directorate of the General Staff, and the organization concentrated on military intelligence specifically. He knew it ran spy networks out of Soviet embassies, buying and stealing secrets, and it was sometimes linked to assassinations of military and political leaders. He also knew that it rivaled the KGB as the most vicious and effective intelligence organization in the world. And he remembered reading an article in *Foreign Affairs* about the rash of GRU activity in Spain. In the last decade, almost a dozen suspected officers had been expelled by the Spanish. Two of them were directors of Aeroflot in Madrid. But that was the limit of his knowledge.

"Don't flatter, me," said Malibu.

"But you *are* good. In fact, too good."

"I don't know what you're talking about."

"This charade."

"Charade?"

"You posing as a journalist who chances into Almería. Nobody comes to Almería anymore."

"You're here. For the bullfights, isn't it?"

"You know damn well there are no bullfights, and you didn't correct me."

"It wouldn't be polite."

"Screw polite. What are you doing in Almería?"

"I'm on my way to Bilbao."

"By way of Almería? From Rome? Don't play with us. Your alibi is as foolish as my bullfight story."

Robert looked into the bug-eye of Nathan Block. The man appeared half crazed. The gun was weighing a little heavy and his hand was slightly shaking.

"It's the truth," he said to Thompson.

"Bullshit! The woman? Who is she?"

"Woman?"

"The woman in the bar."

"Some hooker. She wanted to meet me, that's all."

"Let me kill him," said Block, and Robert winced. Suddenly he realized Bower Thompson would have to kill him. The decision had already been made, otherwise Thompson would never have dropped his cover.

"Not here. Our work in Almería isn't finished, yet, and a dead American journalist would attract too much attention, especially this journalist." Thompson looked at Malibu. "Besides, he's not the only one who knows what we're up to. Someone sent him here. Who was it?" He barked the question.

"I don't know what you're talking about." Robert calmed down. He felt he had been granted a reprieve—a stay of execution.

"Who in the Council sent you over here?"

"The Council?"

"The National Security Council. Whose direction are you working under?"

"I was a press officer, and that was over fifteen years ago."

"Hurt him."

Suddenly the man with the birthmark kicked Robert in the ribs. The foot felt like a horse's hoof. A snap shot through the room, and Robert lost his breath. He buckled in pain.

"Next time in the balls," said Thompson.

"I'm not," said Robert in a burst of breath, "working," he inhaled, "for the NSC."

The pain in his ribs was nothing compared to the agony that racked his body, from his groin, through his stomach, into the roof of his mouth when Birthmark kicked him the second time on Bower's command.

"Come on, Hamilton. Don't jerk me around." Bower paused. His eyes met Malibu's. "Have you ever read Sun Tzu?"

Malibu shook his head.

"Too bad. It's a little late to have you read it now, so here's a crash course." Bower moved to the bed and sat down. "Sun Tzu says all war is deception. That's what you're doing now, and I can see through your deception. Do you know why?"

Malibu shook his head. Perspiration was breaking on his brow. His body hurt so much he thought he was going to pass out.

"Because I'm a living agent. A living agent. I return with information. I fill all of Sun Tzu's criteria: I'm clever, talented, wise, and able to gain access to those of the enemy who are intimate with the sovereign and members of the nobility. I'm able to observe the enemy's movements and to learn of his doings and his plans. I've learned the true state of affairs, and I return and tell my comrades. This is all Sun Tzu, Hamilton. You should have read him. You'd be a lot smarter than you are. You'd understand the game better. He talks a lot about us, about you and me. As living spies, we're intelligent but appear to be stupid. We seem to be dull, but we're strong in heart. We're agile, vigorous, hardy, and brave. We're well versed in lowly matters and able to endure hunger, cold, filth and humiliation."

The pain in Robert's stomach was abating into a dull nausea. "Why are you telling me this?" he gasped.

"Because I can see right through you. I know who you are."

"I'm"— Robert took a deep breath— "I'm a journalist."

"And I'm Amelia Earhart."

Malibu closed his eyes. A sudden shock of pain thrust from his stomach up the small of his back. No one had touched him, and he was certain something was rupturing inside his body.

"Look," said Thompson. "If you'll just tell me who you are, we might be able to make arrangements—a deal. But you've got to give in. Sun Tzu says it's by means of the double agent that native and inside agents can be recruited and used. Get the picture? He says it's essential to seek out enemy agents who have come to conduct espionage against you and to bribe them to serve you. Give them instructions and care for them."

Malibu took another deep breath and opened his eyes. Consciously, he forced the pain out of his body. He looked at Thompson. "What kind of deal?"

"Now we're talking." Bower smiled. He reached to the wall and turned on the lights. "Pick him up," he said to the other men.

Nathan kept his pistol leveled as Birthmark helped Robert to his feet and directed him toward the bed. Once standing, Malibu felt the pain flush down through his stomach and out of his body. He straightened, and that eased it even more. The man helped Robert walk past the window. Only the sheer drapes were pulled. For the first time since entering the room, Hamilton noticed that the place had been ransacked. The contents of his briefcase were spilled onto the floor. His hanging bag was out of the closet and open on the dresser.

"Find anything?" he asked as he sat on the bed next to Bower.

"Informal notes on SDI. That's all."

"Those are from Rome."

"The good agent never carries his information. He memorizes it."

"Sun Tzu?"

"No." Thompson smiled a flattered smile. "Bower Thompson." Malibu nodded.

"Let's talk about what you've memorized?" Bo continued. "How long have you been following me?"

"Four days," Malibu lied.

"You know what we're after, then?"

"I know you killed the German and Senator Watenburg."

"I didn't kill them."

"You mean personally."

"That's right. Besides, the revolutionary who did kill them has met his maker."

"He's dead?"

"Very."

"You play for keeps, don't you?"

"He was old, a has-been. That's why we used him. He was of no worth any longer.

"But you're a team player. You killed those men by association."

"I don't make the rules."

"They were proponents of SDI."

"You know this is about SDI?"

"Watenburg knew that before you killed him."

"What do you know about it?"

"I know you're interested in the radar installation being built above the gypsy camp on the mountain."

"That's more than a simple installation. It's part of a phased-array radar network. The most powerful tracking and communications system the West will have. You must know about the atmospheric conditions of Almería.

"It never rains here."

"The skies are always blue. The air is clearer than any other place in the world. The particle count is way below normal. The troposphere is unusually high, and the ionosphere is thin.''

Robert only nodded.

''That installation is the beginning of a phased-array system that can track anything over Europe, especially a missile out of the Soviet Union. Because of the position of the ionosphere, its ability to communicate is almost limitless. These significant details lead us to believe that the United States is deploying its SDI technology in complete violation of treaties.''

''Nothing more than what the Soviet Union has been doing for decades.''

''Perhaps,'' said Thompson, ''but when America violates treaties it's hypocritical, a double standard. Nobody expects such mindless and moral ethics from communists. We're more pragmatic.''

''Anything for the cause,'' said Robert.

''Yes,'' Bo agreed, ''anything for the . . . ''

A knock from the door silenced Thompson. He drew a 9-millimeter Browning from his shoulder holster and snapped a round into the chamber.

''Answer it,'' he ordered Hamilton and waved Nathan and the other man into the bathroom.

The knock sounded again.

''One mistake and I'll kill you.''

Robert stood up. Thompson moved to the far corner of the room, where he would be hidden behind the opened door. Malibu studied his position as he moved to answer. He could feel the gun pointed at the back of his head. A chill ran up his spine.

''*Quién es?*'' Robert asked. ''Who is it?'' His body was cold with nerves, but his legs felt lethargic and heavy. He did not want to move. ''Who is it?'' he repeated.

''*Soy prostituta.*''

''Prostitute?''

''*You called me.*''

Robert unlocked the bolt and opened the door to see Maria. With the peril inside the room and the pain inside his body, he was calloused to the depression that otherwise would have overcome him on finding that Maria really was a Spanish whore.

"I don't want you," he said. His tone was harsh.

"You called me, *hombre*. You owe me hundred dollars."

Robert turned and looked at Bo. He looked at the door of the bathroom. The other two men were out of sight.

"I don't owe a thing."

"The bartender said you were interested in me."

"I asked about you."

"One hundred dollars!" Maria held out her left hand. Her right reached into her purse.

"Go away." Robert could not believe his nightmare. Three men in the room ready to kill him and a crazy woman in the hall. *"No debo nada.* I owe you nothing. Nothing!"

"The bartender said . . ."

"I asked about you. That's all."

"Cerdo!" she shouted and spit in his face. "Pig!"

Robert closed his eyes and tried to clear his mind.

"La policía," Maria shouted. "I call *la policía."* As she spoke, she drew her hand from the purse. Robert's heart jumped when he saw the Ruger .38.

A Ruger! This *was* Julia Peterson. He looked from the gun to the woman's eyes, and was surprised to see her expression change from wrath to understanding.

"Okay," Robert said, "I'll give you the money. Just go away." He withdrew his wallet and took two fifty-dollars bills. Slowly, he handed the money to the woman, and she handed him the pistol in return. The door blocked the careful transaction from Thompson's view.

"You Americans are all the same. You think you are great lovers and deserve something for nothing. Lovers of self." She stepped back.

The door covered Robert's right arm, hand and gun. He looked again at Bo, who was holding his gun with both hands and aiming at Malibu's head. At this point he could think no more. Instincts took over and he jerked the Ruger past the door at hip level and fired twice. Thompson fell to the floor and fired back, but Robert had rushed into the hall, slamming the door behind him. He grabbed the woman's hand and bolted to the stairs at the far end of the corridor. Three bullets burst the plaster above his head as he pushed her down the stairs and stepped behind the wall. A flood of adrenaline and he looked around the corner at the three men rushing from behind. He fired again, hitting the third man in the center of his birthmark. The man's face caved in and Robert realized Julia had loaded the gun with soft-tipped hollow-points. Thompson and Block jumped to the floor and returned a fusillade that tore the walls surrounding Robert into a frenzy of plaster and dust.

"How many did you kill?" the woman asked as they ran down the stairs.

"One," said Robert.

"Only one?"

"I'm a journalist, not a sharpshooter."

"Only one? she repeated. "You have three more rounds."

"Take the gun if you can do any better."

Julia accepted the offer, took the Ruger, crouched in the corner of the landing and motioned Robert to the floor below. The sound of steps on the stairs above allowed her the timing to aim and shoot accurately. As Block turned the corner, two white-hot bursts from the Ruger opened his chest like a grenade. The force threw him against the wall, then he crashed to the ground.

"How many are there?" Julia asked.

"One more."

"Bower Thompson?"

"Yes."

She placed the gun in her purse, and was calm. "He won't come after us."

"How do you know."

"He's too valuable." She walked to the landing below, where Robert was standing. "Besides, he's already left the hotel."

Robert could hear the commotion on the floor above. Doors were opening. Women were screaming. He took the woman's arm and left the hotel through a service entrance into the alley.

Chapter Seventeen

The sound of sirens filled the night as Malibu and Julia ran in the shadows of the streets. His side ached, his groin was stiff, and every step felt like it cost him a bit of life. In his mind he tried to run away from the pain, to leave it dead on the ground behind him. But he could not. It kept up with him, even ahead of him. And every step racked his body like rolling thunder, each shock stronger than the one before, as if the pain were waiting for him. Impressed by the woman's stamina, he bore his misery in silence and followed her lead as she moved quickly through the night. She seemed to know the city, the narrow and hidden passageways that grew darker and darker as the two moved deeper into the ancient heart, the oldest section, high on a hill, where some of the wall-front homes were still lit by oil lamps. Robert realized his fatigue was not only from the pain, but that the two had been running uphill for a long time. He was tired and thirsty and found it hard to breathe. The air was filled with the smoke of burning coal.

"Run faster," the woman ordered, and Robert stumbled. He gripped his side to reinforce his broken ribs.

"Where?"

"The castle."

"How far?"

"Another mile. Maybe two."

"Why the castle?"

"Do you have a better idea?"

"Your place."

"Too many people know where I live." She grabbed his hand to pull him along. "The castle is safe."

"Safe?"

"No one will look there. If you're gone by morning, before the tourists come, no one will find you."

Robert closed his eyes and let out a long breath. The pain was making him light-headed.

"You have the story now," she said. "You know who Bower Thompson is?"

"A communist."

"He works for Senator Ashworth."

"He's GRU," Robert added.

"I know he's GRU, the most highly-placed spy in America. He works for Senator—"

"Most highly placed?"

"With Senator Ashworth chairman of your Armed Services Committee and sitting on Intelligence, Thompson has access to information so sensitive and noncompartmentalized that he is very dangerous."

"Noncompartmentalized?" Robert slowed his pace. He needed to concentrate on what the woman was saying, and with the pace and pain it was impossible.

Julia allowed him to slow down and soon they were walking. "Most spies have access only to certain information, small, technical bits and pieces—components that without additional information make little sense. They get information this way because they work in one specific agency. For example, if they're placed in the military organization of another country, such as the navy, they might know something about a specific technology in submarines that they are responsible for, but they will know little else. Bower Thompson is different. Bower Thompson gets information from all branches as they report to his senator's committee. He is very dangerous. He is an expert not only on technologies but strategies."

"Who are you?"

"Me?"

"You said you were Julia Peterson, the German's wife."

"And so I am—or was," her voice trailed off.

"Don't play with me." Robert's stomach tensed and he could feel the pain from his ribs move to his spine. "You know too much."

"You mean more than who to seat with whom at dinner parties."

"You know what I mean."

"I stay very involved in my husband's work."

"It's more than that."

"You don't believe me?"

"Wives of American politicians stay very involved in their husbands' work. But few of them can open a man's chest with two hollow-points at fifteen yards."

"It wasn't fifteen yards."

"Answer me." Robert gripped his side.

"Hans and I were married seven years ago. He was serving his third term in the Bundesrat. I was in the Bundesnachrichtendienst, the Federal Intelligence Service."

"You're a spy?"

"I was." Julia stopped and looked at Robert. The ordeal in the hotel and the miles they had run made her look vibrant. Her coal hair was tossed, and a strand clung to the perspiration on her cheek just above a beauty mark. "When I met Hans, I was a field operative, mostly here in the Mediterranean, Spain, Italy, Turkey. When we married, he asked me to give it up. He believed it would be too dangerous for both of us, difficult for me to keep my cover." She looked away. "I agreed, but I couldn't leave the Service. With his help, I was assigned to a bureau desk, in charge of Mediterranean affairs."

"You fit well in the Mediterranean."

"My parents are Malagueños."

"Then you *are* Spanish."

"They moved to Munich three years before I was born." Julia started to walk. "We'd better keep moving."

Robert stepped to follow, but the pain was overpowering. He stopped and bent over. "We *should* have kept moving." He took a deep breath and coughed. "My muscles are stiff now."

"Let me help." Julia placed a shoulder under his right arm and eased him forward. "Go slowly."

"I'll be okay."

"What did they do to you?"

"I think they broke a rib." He tried to stand straight and coughed again. This time he could taste the blood in his mouth. Now he was certain something had ruptured. For a moment he was frightened, but then resigned himself to that fact that nothing could be done about it, not now anyway. It was late, and going to a hospital would attract the police.

But why couldn't we go to the police, Robert thought. He wanted to ask the woman, but believed the question would reveal a flaw in his character, a demonstration of cowardice. Besides, he still did not have the full story. What was the woman doing in Almería, following Bower Thompson, especially only days after her husband's murder? Instead of asking the question, he determined she knew what she was doing in eluding the police, and resigned himself to the excuse that since Spain had threatened to withdraw from NATO, and was beginning to assert its neutrality, he would be held for trial, or worse yet, extradited to the Soviet Union to stand trial there.

Spain and NATO. Robert had not considered the implications of Spain's discontent with the Alliance. If the country was pulling out of the organization, why was it permitting the radar station to be built in Almería. Unless, he reasoned, America and its allies had been deploying the Strategic Defense Initiative for so many years that they secured the leases on the land when Spain was still faithful to the Alliance. Without further warning, his mind exploded with the logical sequence of facts and information he was looking for—the answers to his questions concerning the radar station and the deadly interest Bower Thompson had in the SDI project.

"Since 1986?" he said aloud.

"What?" asked Julia.

"There's a radar station being constructed outside the city."

"You know of it?"

"I stumbled onto it this morning." He tried to remember what Thompson had called it. "Phased-array station," he said.

"What do you know about phased-array radar?"

"I'm supposed to be asking the questions." Robert pressed his hand against his side and took a deep breath.

"Too many questions are dangerous."

"You mean the answers are dangerous," Robert corrected. "What do you know?"

"Nothing, really."

"Don't lie to me, Julia." Robert stopped and faced the woman. She brushed the hair from her face.

"I can't tell you anything."

"Tell me anything?"

"No."

"You have to trust me."

"You're a journalist."

"You called me because I'm a journalist."

"You know Bower Thompson is a spy. That's why I called you. He killed my husband, and now you know."

"You didn't need to call me. You could have killed him yourself."

"That's cold."

"But it's the truth." Robert looked away. The rush of information had turned to impatience. "How do you know he killed your husband?"

Julia did not answer.

"How do you know he killed your husband?" his voice mounted in anger.

The woman looked away.

"I'll tell you," he continued. "This whole nightmare has to do with the Strategic Defense Initiative. Your husband was involved. Grayson Watenburg was involved. They were killed. You and I might be next, and you're still refusing to answer my questions."

"I can't," Julia snapped. "I can't. Damn you. I'm not supposed to know. Don't you understand."

"Your husband broke silence," Robert said. "He broke his oath and told you all about it, and now you're trying to play dumb."

"You don't understand," her voice fluttered.

"I understand that something is happening that involves national security."

"Global security," Julia corrected. "It involves global security."

"And your husband broke silence with you."

"I have all the security clearances. I—"

"He told you SDI was being deployed."

"My husband was a great man." Julia's eyes glistened with tears.

"He violated his covenant of silence."

"He was a great man," Julia began to cry. Robert had stripped away the veneer of professional composure to reveal a woman in love.

"I know he was," Robert said, his voice calming down. "But, damn, this is important."

"Why? Why is it so important?"

"It's the most important story of my career."

"Is that all you think about?"

"Two days ago, when you called me, that's all you were thinking about. There were no conditions attached to my coming here. Now I want the whole story."

"So you can bask in professional glory?"

"Maybe so I can get my damn job back."

The woman's eyes were ablaze with emotion, and Robert was not sure whether they were filled with anger or sadness. Nor was he sure how far he should press her tonight.

"I called you to help," Julia said, and Robert determined it was sadness.

You're an asshole, Malibu, he thought. *You should never have criticized her husband. When did you become so damned calloused to human feelings?*

But she was holding up so well, so distant from the death, he argued—*at least until now.*

Because she's a professional. But even professionals have their breaking point.

"And I came," he said. "But we both know this story is bigger than life, and now I need *your* help." Robert took his hand from his side to see if the pain had diminished. It had not. "Look, I'm sorry for some of the things I said. They were out of line. It's so confusing, but you don't have to say anything. With time I can put the pieces together. I saw the phased-array installation this morning, and Thompson told me about it tonight—that it can track any missile coming out of the Soviet Union. I figure since it's still under construction, even though Spain is pulling out of NATO, the agreement to build the station must have been finalized years ago, probably in the mid-eighties."

Julia nodded. It was the first encouraging gesture of the conversation.

Robert placed his hand on her elbow and gently pushed her forward until the two of them were walking. The pain was intense, but his concentration was elsewhere.

"Then America has been violating the antiballistic-missile treaty."

Julia nodded again. "You could see it that way." she whispered, and the words were covered with sadness.

"I see it no other way," Robert returned with a sympathetic whisper.

"How well do you understand the treaty?"

"I've written about it. Better than the average man."

"In 1987, Reagan and Gorbachev signed the INF Treaty at the Washington Summit. Your President refused to gamble away the Strategic Defense Initiative, and America committed that through 1994 it would not deploy operational strategic defenses. But it also reserved the right to withdraw from the commitment for reasons of supreme national interests or material breach of the ABM or START treaties."

"And?"

"There is no doubt that the Soviet Union has violated both treaties, and the progress it has made with its own ABM systems clearly affects the national interests of America and its allies."

"Then you condone the breach?"

"The West has not breached the treaties. We have only responded to the Soviet's breach. When one side refuses to live up to a commitment, it becomes suicide for the other side not to respond. That's all the West has done, responded to the Soviet threat."

"To what degree?"

"Excuse me?"

"To what degree has the West responded?"

Julia shrugged her shoulders, but Robert could tell in her expression that she knew the answer to his question. If the Soviets were so concerned about the Strategic Defense Initiative that they were willing to kill two prominent political supporters, then deployment must be further along than the simple construction of a radar station on the Iberian Peninsula.

"Do you know anything about—" Robert began, but stopped suddenly.

A faint blue light flashed on the cobblestone street of the narrow intersection in front of them. The woman noticed it first and stopped cold. She grabbed Robert's arm and pulled him back. His torso twisted and he groaned under the strain.

"Police!" she whispered.

Robert saw the cast of the flashing light, and though the car was not in view, he estimated it was close to the intersection, maybe a hundred yards, no more. The light grew stronger, then came the sound of the engine, and finally the squawk of the radio. The car was moving slowly, then it stopped in the intersection. Robert and Julia backed into the shadow of a door frame.

"Go on," Julia whispered as if her voice could command the automobile. "Don't—

The car turned down their street. Immediately, the woman threw herself in front of Robert, pressing him against the door, and passionately kissed his lips. She caressed his back, ran her hands beneath his shirt.

"Undo my blouse."

"What?"

"My blouse," she said, and before Robert could respond, she ripped it open. "Kiss me hard."

Robert pressed himself against her tight body, still wet with perspiration. His hand rubbed against the curve of her back. Out of the corner of his eye he watched the police car approach. The pain in his rib cage, especially with the pressure of the woman's body, made his breathing irregular and difficult. The emotions of the sexual moment, the approaching car, and the pain collided in his brain. He could not follow any one of them, but the most overpowering was fear. The car stopped in the street directly in front of them.

"*Alto ahí,*" ordered the driver. "Stop there."

The command made the woman more passionate. She forced her tongue into Robert, then kissed his cheek, his neck, his chest.

"*Alto!*"

Julia continued to concentrate on Robert until the car door opened.

"What do you want?" she demanded finally, the rolling sound of her flawless Andalusian accent filled the street. She turned around, her blouse open, and the policeman did not get out of the car.

"We are looking for an American."

"I am Malagueña."

"An American man."

"I have seen no one, but I am not looking. I am engaged." She laughed and stepped toward the car, making sure that the shadow of Robert remained behind her. She gathered her blouse together and tucked it inside her pants.

"We are sorry," said the police officer opposite the driver and gestured to him to put the car in motion.

Julia turned back to Robert. "Juan, have you seen an American?"

"No," Robert answered quickly.

"Sorry," said the driver and waved Julia back to her man. He put the car in gear and continued down the street.

"Good luck," Julia said under her voice and returned to the shadow of the doorway. "You speak Spanish very well," she laughed.

"That's four years of college."

"It probably just saved your life." She reached up and kissed Robert on the cheek.

He wanted to ask her what it was for, but decided to the let the gesture stand in silence.

When Malibu opened his eyes, late the next morning, he was embarrassed by a group of Oriental tourists standing around him as he lay on the ground in the spacious banquet room of the ancient Santiago Cristóbal Castle. Half a dozen men in the group were taking pictures of the bruised and dirty American with their complex Canons and Minoltas, and two Spanish girls, castle guides, giggled and pointed at Robert as he tried to remember where he was and the events of the preceding night. His eyes were stiff and swollen. His head ached. His mind recalled the emotion of the events in his hotel room, but it was still not clear enough to remember the details. He sat up on the cold stone floor, and the pain in his ribs rushed bits and pieces of reality and all its vivid detail to the front of his memory. With a start, he looked around the stone room for the woman, Maria—or Julia—Peterson's wife. She had been at his side as he moved cautiously through the maze of streets and plazas to the castle on the hill, but now he could not see her. His sensitive eyes fought against the offensive sunlight striking through the large window cut in the stone wall above. She was nowhere to be seen.

When did she leave? Why did she leave? Robert tried to recall how long she had stayed with him. He tried to remember what they had talked about. She must have waited until he was asleep before leaving.

Why wouldn't she? he reasoned. She did not want him to follow her back to her place. He was dangerous. Bower Thompson wanted him dead. But she had risked her life once, and wasn't she just as dangerous, if not more, to the secret organization for which Bo worked.

Maybe she was dead. The thought shook the cobwebs from his heavy head.

With a start, he struggled awkwardly to his feet, holding his ribs under constant pressure. He looked at his wrist for the time, but his watch was gone, and he could not remember if he had left it at the hotel, or if someone had taken if off him during the night. He needed to find the woman. He needed to remember something, anything, from the previous night that would lead him to her. *What had she said? Where did she live?* What clues did she leave that he could use to find her again? He could not recall their conversation, or if they had talked once inside the castle.

He remembered the pain—the pain and the kiss. She had kissed him.

The police! She kissed me after the police left, he remembered.

"What time is it?" he asked and stumbled toward the crowd. "The time!" he hit his wrist with his hand.

"Almost noon." A balding Japanese man with a soft voice ventured from the pack. "You okay?"

Robert took a deep breath and grimaced from the pain in his ribs. He coughed, and again he could taste blood, deep and stale. The taste connected with memories of the pain he felt running through the streets. Then he remembered the brief conversation with the woman. She worked for the German sister of the Central Intelligence Agency.

"You're a spy?"

"I was. When I met Hans, I was a field operative, mostly here in the Mediterranean, Spain, Italy, Turkey. When we married, he asked me to give it up. He believed it would be too dangerous for both of us, difficult for me to keep my cover. I agreed, but I couldn't leave the Service. With his help, I was assigned to a bureau desk, in charge of Mediterranean affairs."

But there must be more, Robert grappled to open the part of his brain that stores short-term memory.

"You hurt?" asked the small man.

"I'm fine, thanks."

"Your stomach hurts." The tourist handed his camera to his wife and walked to Robert.

"I broke a few ribs last night."

"We thought you were homeless, maybe drunk."

"No," Malibu forced a smile, but even that made his ribs bite. "I'm no drunkard."

"You fall?"

"No. No, I," Robert began but stopped. He knew he could not explain what really happened. "There were some muggers, and I," he tripped through his words.

"You were attacked?" The man reached out and took the American by both arms and helped him back to a stone bench. He spoke a few words of Japanese to the others, and they burst into conversation. "Sit here. We find a doctor."

"No, really, I'm fine," Robert lied, but broadened his smile to look convincing. He took another deep breath. *The pain.* He collapsed onto the bench and closed his eyes. "No problem," he said and leaned back against the wall.

The wall. The window. He remembered scaling the wall, the panic of walking along the narrow ledge on the other side and the pain of dropping about ten feet from the window to the floor.

But that wasn't all. Think!

There was a tree. The woman knew what she was doing. Robert had commented that she must have used this escape route before.

"I plan ahead," she said.

They climbed the tree at the west corner of the castle. There was about a three-foot jump from the limb to the castle wall. *The fear.*

"Go ahead," the woman ordered. "Jump."

"What's on the other side of the wall?"

"A forty-foot drop. But you have about two feet of wall. You'll make it."

He jumped. It was easier than expected. But the motion racked his body with pain. The woman followed with the grace of a cat, one flowing motion from the limb to the wall.

"Follow me." She moved past Robert and walked along the stone for about twenty yards.

Malibu looked down only once. The distance to the ground made the two-foot ridge seem like a tightrope. As they moved farther away from the west corner, the wall became the extension of a steep cliff that dropped another two hundred feet below the stone fortress.

Suddenly, the woman stopped, sat down on the rock, swung her feet to the outside of the wall, turned, and dropped down to a narrow opening where defending archers of the castle once stood and slung their arrows at the attacking Moors. She looked up at Robert.

"You have a three-foot drop to this guard window," she said. I'll help you."

Robert imitated the woman, sitting down, swinging his legs over the side. But the pain of holding on to the top of the wall caused him to drop early. His right foot slipped from the base of the opening, his left foot followed, and soon he was hanging two hundred and fifty feet in the air, holding on to the base of the cold stone window.

The woman grabbed his wrists.

"It's okay," she said.

"The pai—" Robert groaned, and then everything was black.

There had been no conversation in the castle, he suddenly realized. He had lost consciousness. Somehow the woman had managed to pull him from the wall and carry him to the banquet room.

"You are American?" asked the Japanese man.

"Yes."

"From Cincinnati?"

"No," Robert chuckled only slightly, and his insides flared. "Wash—ington. The capital."

"Washington, D.C.," the man nodded. "I have brother in Cincinnati."

"How about that." Robert stood up slowly and walked forward. His ribs hurt with every move. "I have to find someone."

His mind now replayed the conversation about the Strategic Defense Initiative and treaties and the grief Robert had caused the woman when he insulted her husband.

"A doctor?"

"That's right, a doctor." He stepped around the tourists and walked through the crowd that parted as he passed to the huge doorway. The room was dusty, and waves of motion danced in the sunlight as he moved out the door. Behind him was the sound of a dozen clicking cameras.

At twelve o'clock, the bright streets of Almería were silent and empty. Small stores were closed and metal grates were pulled down over their doors and windows. The silence was broken only by the infrequent sound of a car racing along another street. The Spanish men were home, eating hearty meals of seafood, rice and pasta. Then they would sleep, and the streets would be empty until two o'clock, when they would force themselves back to their offices, stores and factories for three more hours.

In the lethargy of this *mediodía*, Robert moved to his hotel. He tried to stand straight as he went, without showing his pain, but it was impossible. He imagined he looked pathetic, shuffling along like a lame man, his khaki pants and white shirt now gray and dirty. He could taste his breath and tried to comb through his hair with his fingers. It was better that Julia had abandoned him, he thought. He probably stank, though he could not tell. The air was filled with the aroma of saffron and shellfish, and he realized he was hungry.

"Where are you, Julia?" he whispered and was grateful to the woman. She had taken a risk coming to his room, giving him the gun, taking the gun back, and fighting his battle.

My battle? he thought. *Not my battle. I just stumbled into it.*

But you'd be dead had she not come.

My battle, he conceded, and again felt guilty for his conduct in the street. *That was no way to thank her.*

"Who are you, Maria?" Her persona fit the image of German spy as awkwardly as it fit that of Spanish prostitute. She looked soft and vulnerable. But soft and vulnerable could not pull him from the castle wall and carry him down the narrow stone steps on the backside to the banquet room. Soft and vulnerable could not blow open a man's chest and then elude police throughout the night.

"My guardian angel," he said silently, and then grinned. *Damn the pain.*

From thoughts of Julia, his mind reviewed the words and actions of Bower Thompson and his comrades. The image of the man with the ugly birthmark lying dead in the hotel corridor made Robert tense. He had never killed before. As a journalist, he had seen the thousand faces of death, but he had always managed to disassociate himself from it, a third party, omnipresent yet unattached. This time it was not so simple. He had pulled the trigger. For a moment he thought he could remember the man's face exploding around the hollow-point bullet, and everything seemed in slow motion, the bullet entering the skin, the tearing and melting and then the explosion as bits of the face sizzled into the wallpaper and blood stained the carpet.

Robert shook his head to clear the thought. *Don't feel guilty for saving your own life*, he demanded. *You've been one step away from death all night.*

Chapter Eighteen

Spotlight number seven was too close to Diana Sillito. The heat was breaking her concentration, and she could see the bold yellow glare on her forearms. Under what felt like a pound of greasepaint, she believed she was melting away like the Wicked Witch of the West, slowly and painfully—but this time from heat and not water. At first, she wanted to say something about the heat, about the light, about the fact they would have to shoot the scene over again. But she did not want to complain. Her reputation was unsullied by ego and bad attitude. She was known in Hollywood circles as an actress easy to work with, something that in her world was as rare as birthdays.

Instead of breaking the scene with her complaint, Diana tried not to think about the heat and the yellow hue. If the cinematographer did not catch the jaundice before her part began, he would certainly catch it in the dailies—the film developed on location and previewed by the director and technicians. But he was a good cinematographer with more than one award from the Academy on his office shelf, and the woman believed he would stop the scene before her part began. She forced her mind back to her lines:

Why do you think he wanted to show the ceiling? She repeated: *Why do you think he wanted to show the ceiling?*

She looked up, at the ceiling. It was beautiful. Michelangelo was a genius, a genius borne by his work and his overpowering drive. He had said, *Lord, grant that I may always desire more than I can accomplish.* Diana had discovered the quote her freshman year of college. The sculptor from Florence had uttered the words almost five hundred years ago, yet they still moved her, and she wrote them on a postcard and carried them with her for nearly ten years. *Lord, grant that I may always desire more than I can accomplish.* She looked at the hand of God, the fingertip stretching to the hand of Adam, and the spark of life. From that dried paint, history unfolded on the ceiling above her in the Sistine Chapel—the expulsion from the garden, the flood, Moses—it was all there, except that half the ceiling was covered with gray-brown paper. The film crew had covered it to make it look, on camera, as if Michelangelo were only half finished with the fresco.

"Reload!" shouted the cameraman sitting atop the crane.

"Cut!" shouted the director.

The set best boy scrambled up the crane with another reel of film.

"We're going to shoot straight through from Raphael to the Contessa," said the director. He smiled at Diana. "Are you ready?"

She looked at her forearms. The light was awful. "I am concerned about the lighting," she said. "I think it's too close."

"Move number seven back," he ordered.

"Hang on," interrupted the cinematographer. He looked through the light meter around his neck. "About two feet," he said. "Can she stand a little to the left of the table?"

"Left?" asked the director, then he turned to Diana. "Move a little left," he said. "Yeah. That's fine." He turned to face the actor who played Michelangelo. "When you leave Raphael and his companion and walk to Diana, keep about six inches right of the toe-line mark."

"Should I move the mark?" asked the best boy as he jumped off the neck of the crane.

"Do you need him to move the mark?"

"That's fine," answered the actor. "I can stay six inches left."

"Right," shouted the director. "Six inches right." He looked back to the best boy. "Move the toe-line."

"We're loaded!" said the cameraman.

"Okay, listen up," said the director. "We're going to shoot straight through. Remember the emotion of the scene, and play it from your hearts. Pope Julius has just gone off to fight the French and Germans. His army is grossly outnumbered, and the Vatican is in a crisis. And now Michelangelo, who has been reluctant to paint the ceiling and working laboriously slow, has had his commission jerked. He believes he'll never finish the work." He turned to face Diana. "Contessa, you have to convince him to do it. Now let's make Mama proud."

RAPHAEL'S COMPANION: Michelangelo, the chapel has been crowded all day.

RAPHAEL: Master Buonarroti, you claim not to be a painter, but you have sent us all back to school. But we are wondering when you are going to decide to finish the work?

MICHAELANGELO: Ask yourself that question, the Pope will want the ceiling finished, and who else would he choose but you? You've mastered my style already.

RAPHAEL: It is true I wanted your commission. I admit it freely. But today I came here in good faith to tell you of my admiration for your work. I don't want to finish your ceiling now, and I doubt if I could.

MICHELANGELO: Right. Still, I mean it—I hope you will finish the chapel. I'll never go in it again.

COMPANION: He should apologize.

MICHELANGELO: Popes don't apologize.

RAPHAEL: Excuse me, but I think you should apologize to him.

MICHELANGELO (angrily): For being beaten by him like a disobedient servant? (shakes his head no)

RAPHAEL: But what is an artist in this world but a servant, a lackey for the rich and powerful? Before we even begin to work to feed this craving of ours, we must find a patron—a rich man of affairs, or a merchant, or a prince—

COMPANION: Or a Pope.

RAPHAEL: We must bow, fawn, kiss hands to be able to do the things we must do. Or we must die. We are harlots, always peddling beauty at the doorsteps of the mighty.

MICHELANGELO: If it comes to that, I won't be an artist.

RAPHAEL: You will always be an artist. You have no choice.

Michelangelo turns away from the men and walks to area left. There standing at a table overlooking his sketches is the Contessa de' Medici.

CONTESSA: Are you really so blind? Why do you think he wanted to show the ceiling, because he was ashamed of it?

MICHELANGELO: Ashamed of it? Of course not. What a stupid thing to say. He was proud of it.

CONTESSA: So he insulted you by showing it to the world.

MICHELANGELO: Half finished.

CONTESSA: Half finished, yes. But think, Michelangelo, he rode off in an almost hopeless cause, knowing that he might never live to see the fresco finished. Are you the only one in Rome who doesn't know that?

MICHELANGELO: Maybe. I don't pay attention to these—

CONTESSA: Is it a crime that he wants the world to see it and to share in his pride—this—this fresco that he has forced you to paint—come day and night to watch—defended against its critics—the work of art which to him has become a work of love.

MICHELANGELO: Of love?

CONTESSA: Yes—love. We always come back to that, don't we Michelangelo? That's one emotion that you seem unable to comprehend.

MICHELANGELO: Was it love that made him break his stick across my back?

CONTESSA: Love takes us in strange ways. It is the language of the blood. It is neither cold nor indifferent. It is either agony or ecstasy—sometimes both at once.

MICHELANGELO: Everything you say may be true. But it's come too late. He's withdrawn the commission.

CONTESSA: Then can you think of no conditions under which he might restore it—even if it means swallowing that mighty pride of yours?

MICHELANGELO: Tessina!

CONTESSA: Michelangelo, make up your mind once and for all. Do you want to finish that ceiling?

MICHELANGELO: More than my life.

CONTESSA: Then finish it!

"Brilliant! Cut!" shouted the director. "Diana, you were brilliant. I've got chills. A beautiful woman who can act!" He walked over and gave her a hug. "And you—" he turned to Michelangelo. "Keep this up and you'll be more famous than Charlton Heston ever dreamed of being. There's a chemistry here. I can feel it." He turned to the cinematographer. "This is going to work. We've waited five years for the Vatican to let us do this remake, and it's going to work." He looked up. "God bless you, Michelangelo. God bless you, too, Irving Stone."

"And God bless everybody," said Teddy Silverman as he stepped over a bundle of cables outside the parameter of cameras.

"Teddy!" Diana smiled and kissed her agent on his check.

"I tried to get in earlier, to see your scene, but that fat script girl wouldn't let me in."

"Glad she was doing her job," said the director before he walked away.

"I hate that man."

"You don't hate him," Diana corrected. "You just don't get along with him." She took the silver choker from her neck and handed it to Teddy. "I can't stand having things around my neck. I must have been strangled in a previous life."

"I hate him."

"My afternoon's free. What do you say we get a late lunch and go see the Villa Giulia. They have the archaeological exhibit—seventh century B.C."

"I hate museums."

"Do you have a bee in your britches?" Diana smiled. The best boy took the choker from Teddy and left the agent with a contemptuous glare.

"I just don't like being treated like a second-class citizen."

"You are a second-class citizen." Diana winked and offered her agent a hug.

"And I need to talk to you."

"We are talking."

"That dress is a horrible blue on you. Had I been allowed in to watch the scene, I would have objected to that dress."

"That's probably why they didn't let you in." Diana wiped the perspiration from her cheeks, taking care not to smear her heavy eye liner. "What do you want to talk about?"

"We can't talk here."

Suddenly, Diana was serious. She stepped away from Silverman and untied the sash around her waist. "I told you I'm finished."

"We can't talk about it here."

"I'm not going to talk about it. Period."

"Diana. You have no choice."

"Don't you dare talk to me like that," Diana exploded, and the technicians breaking down the set stopped working to listen. Teddy grabbed her arm.

"Don't get menopausal, dear."

"Don't touch me, you bastard. You swore to me it was over." She turned to face the technicians. "What in the hell do you think you're looking at?" The crew hustled back to work.

"Let's go into your trailer."

Diana turned and quickly walked away. "You come near my trailer and I'll have you arrested."

"For what, Diana? Keeping your father alive all these years?"

"Shut up."

The crew came to a standstill.

"Shut up," she screamed. She rushed out of the chapel and into her trailer. Teddy followed and slammed the trailer door behind him. "Get out of here. I'm warning you."

"You can't have me arrested. You're just as involved as I am. And what are you trying to prove talking like that in front of the crew?"

"I've done nothing."

"You've been an accessory."

"I haven't done a thing."

"Don't be so naïve, dear. How many years have you known about your father and done nothing?"

"I can't be held accountable for my father's sins."

"You can't atone for them either."

"What do you know about atonement?" Diana scoffed. "A Jewish faggot!"

"Don't taunt me, Diana. I swear, I'll—"

"You'll what? What will you do? You faggot. You say you've kept my father alive all these years. I've kept you alive. I've fed you and clothed you, and put you in the damn pink palace you live in with all your queer boyfriends."

"I said, shut up." Teddy rushed forward and threw Diana onto her sofa. "Shut up." He put his hands around her neck. "Shut up or you're going to be choked to death in this life."

"Don't touch my neck!" Diana shouted and kicked her agent in the groin. Teddy buckled in pain. Diana stood up to get out of the trailer.

Teddy tripped her. She kicked him in the face, but he held her ankle anyway. "Let go," she shouted. "Let go." She began to cry. "Why are you doing this to me? Why, Teddy?" her voice deteriorated into sobs. "Why are you hurting me like this. Let me go. Let my father go."

Silverman let loose of her ankle and stood up gasping for breath. He moved over and helped Diana to her feet. "Call me a faggot again and I won't choke you. I'll *break* your fucking neck."

"You're killing me already." Diana was weakened by the trauma. Her legs felt like they were going to collapse. She let Teddy help her back to the sofa.

"You don't know death," Teddy said. His voice was hard. "Your father's friends—my friends—they're dead."

"They deserved it." Diana's eyes grew cold.

"Then your father deserves to die."

"Don't talk about my father."

"It's true. Isn't it? If our friends deserved to die, we deserve to die. And you, Diana—you, too, deserve to die."

"I was forced."

"Nobody forced you."

"I had to protect my father."

"Bullshit!"

"What do you know, Teddy? What do you know about the relationship between a father and daughter? You're nothing but a—"

Silverman raised his hand to strike Diana, but withheld the blow. Instead, his face grew calm and his voice dropped low. "You don't understand, and it's not your fault. You can't understand those years and what they did to us. They were turbulent and ugly, but they were exciting and alive. We were a nation at war with ourselves. We were all young and into revolution—the Black Panthers, the Chicago Eight. Some were more dedicated than others. Eldridge Cleaver was in Algeria getting aid from Chairman Mao. He would have gotten it too—guns and supplies to bring the war to America—but Kissinger and Nixon fucked it up."

Teddy dropped to the sofa beside Diana. "They opened relations with China, and Mao, the man who would sponsor our revolution, closed his embassies to our revolutionaries. We were learning at his knee. We were studying in classrooms inside his embassies the art of revolution—how to overthrow old governments and make the new, revolutionary government, appear indigenous. That's what it's all about, you know, patriotism. You make the people salute the new as fervently as they saluted the old. You rewrite history. That's what we were going to do in America. We were going to do to Nixon and his henchmen what Mao Tse-Tung did to Chiang Kai-shek. We were going to pull the gold out of their teeth, strip them of their power and wealth. We were going to build a people's party. Imagine that—the greatest country on earth was going to care for the people. It was a beautiful vision. And your father was one of the most dedicated philosophers of our movement. He could write like nobody else. His words were powerful—moving and potent. Finally, we had our Thomas Paine. But this time he was on the right side of reason, and that's what we needed, someone who could inspire the masses, someone who could incite them to join with us in our fight against discrimination and poverty and the economic vampire that drains the blood from the worker.''

Teddy paused and fell into the pillows on the sofa. He looked at Diana, who was calm now. The black eyeliner had stained her cheeks and run into the corner of her mouth.

"But it's only a memory now," Teddy continued. "Today Cleaver's even got religion. *Zeitgeist* has been reborn."

"It's more than a memory for you."

"Maybe, yes. Your father and I got too involved. We found out too much. Got to know too many people."

"You were trapped by your overzealousness." Diana rubbed the eyeliner into her cheeks. "Even Eldridge Cleaver is free from his past."

"He didn't know what we did. The revolution people saw on television was nothing compared to the economic revolution taking place in corporate boardrooms and even in Congress. People watched the news at nights, and thought, 'How horrible, those kids being clubbed with nightsticks in Chicago. How horrible, Kent State.' That was nothing, Diana. Nothing compared to what was happening on Wall Street. Who do you think financed *Ramparts*? Who do you think financed the war in Oakland? That's where your daddy and I were involved. We were involved with the elite leftists, the revolutionary gentry. We saw the breast that fed the revolution, and that breast still gives suck."

"Will it ever end?"

"I hope not."

"My father doesn't feel the same."

"You don't know what your father feels. All you know is that those who tried to pull away have met their untimely demise, and that scares you."

"It scares my father, too."

"And so you must continue to help us."

Diana stood and walked past the kitchenette to the dressing room. She closed the door but spoke loud enough to be heard. "I loath the very day my father introduced you to me."

"But I'm your manager. I've made you who you are."

"Let's talk about who made whom." Diana opened the door and stared at Teddy. "The only thing you managed until I came along were a few feminist writers and a singer in Las Vegas who made more money on her back."

"Your daddy spun this web, and I believe you have no other choice but to go along."

Diana emerged from the dressing room wrapped in a scarlet terry-cloth bathrobe. "I told you, I'm finished. Now if you'll find your way out, I'm going to take a shower. It was a long day on the set, and—"

"You're not finished, Diana." Teddy stood up and grabbed her by the wrists.

"Let go. You're hurting—"

"You will be finished when I say. Not a moment before." He threw her arms down to her side. A smile creased his lips. "If I didn't know better, I would say you have actually been taken by this Malibu character."

"Three times—three times, I have given you information on his whereabouts. Now I'm finished."

"You *have* fallen for him. Haven't you?"

"Get out of my trailer."

"That's it. Evade my question." Teddy turned his back to Diana. "But it's true. You've fallen for him, perhaps because he's the only one who has refused your advances."

"Get out—"

"Perhaps because your beauty and charm haven't worked on him."

"I'm warning you."

"Perhaps because he'd be more interested in me." He turned to face her. "Is that it? Is he gay?"

"He's busy."

"Too busy for you?" Teddy shook his head. "Come, come, dear. How could any red-blooded American male be too busy for you?"

"I don't even understand why it's so damn important that you know where he is."

"Those are my orders."

"Don't you ever question your orders?"

"I value my life, Diana. I don't question. Neither should you."

"There must be a story—something that your people don't want written—something that's happened here in Italy—" Diana stopped. Her face filled with understanding. "The murders. The politician. Senator Watenburg. The German. Your people killed them. They killed them. You know about that."

"I don't know about any such thing."

"They killed them."

"Don't be so dramatic."

"You're responsible for their deaths. You didn't want Robert to get the story. I was supposed to distract him. But he got it anyway." Diana's shoulders dropped as if she was suddenly exhausted. "How could I have been so stupid?"

"What you're saying is stupid."

"How could I have failed to see? I was supposed to take out the journalist—the man who could link the murders to your people."

"We don't know what Watenburg told him." Teddy sat back in the sofa.

"Watenburg was one of your people?"

"Not exactly." The agent sounded defeated. "But he was a member of the Senate Select Committee on Intelligence. He knew that we exist. He knew what we were after."

"And what are you after, Teddy?"

"You don't have to know that."

"I want to know."

"It would only put you in greater danger."

"Does my father know?"

Teddy nodded. "He does," he said softly.

Tears began to appear in the corners of Diana's eyes. For a moment she tried to fight them back, to deaden the pain by her professional training to control emotions. But she could not stop them. Her father was responsible for the deaths of two men, maybe even more, and she suddenly felt the pain of betrayal, the pain of discovering that the person you have known and loved your whole life is a counterfeit, a fraud, a murderer.

"What's involved that could be so important?" she whispered beneath her tears.

"I really can't tell you."

"How long has my father been so involved?"

"Since our innocent days in the sixties."

"Not so innocent," corrected Diana.

"They were when we started."

"And now?"

"We're in too deep to turn back."

"Damn you." The emotional pain broke out and Diana began to cry aloud. "Damn you."

"You have to contact Robert Hamilton."

"I can't deceive him anymore."

"But isn't that what you do best? You're an actress."

Diana did not answer. She put her hand to her mouth and tried to calm her sobs.

"Call him and it will be all over."

"So you can kill him?"

"It's him or your father. The choice is yours."

It appeared to Diana that the agent was enjoying her misery as he sat on the sofa with a distorted smile and his head nodding up and down like a reggae musician, half stoned and half attentive to the pleasure and tempo of his music. At the moment, she hated him and his attitude, and her impulse was to take a knife from the drawer in her kitchenette and end his amusement. But she knew the moment would pass, just as it had many times before. She looked at the purple tint in his hair and the frown lines that creased his face even when he smiled, and as strong as her feelings of contempt, so, too, was her sense of pity. It was this way each time they fought; something deep inside of her, while it could not condone the actions of her agent and her father, allowed her to accept them. Often, they had persuaded her to join their activity. At times she had, but never had their actions resulted in murder. Until now, it had seemed more like a game, nothing any more real than Spy versus Spy, and she believed she could withhold her participation at any given moment. But now the game was real, people were dying, and Teddy Silverman was not going to give her the latitude to leave.

And what had he said about Malibu—about Robert Hamilton? That she loved him? Was it true? She did not know. She was tickled by the journalist, amused by his wit and impressed by his depth of knowledge. But love him? Maybe he was prey in more ways than one. Certainly, she should know. But she did not, and now, if she followed Teddy's order, she never would. They wanted to find where he was, and then they were going to kill him.

"I haven't heard from him since he got to Spain," she said, and her agent sat up straight.

"Then will you help us find him?"

"It's either him or my father. You already said."

"A wise decision." Teddy motioned for her to sit by him and she responded. "We know he's still in Spain, but he had an—" he paused. "He had an encounter with a few of my colleagues. He fled, and we don't know where he is."

"You've already tried to kill him, haven't you."

"I haven't tried, no—"

"Your butchers have." Diana spat the word "butchers."

"Doing what they must."

"If you don't know where he is, how will I find him?"

"Sooner or later, he'll have to get back to his hotel room. I'm sure if you leave a message, he'll return it."

"But if he left the hotel?"

"He left suddenly. There was a shootout. Two of our men were killed."

"How many more have to die before you people stop?"

"It's not death that counts, Diana. It's the objective."

"You're sick."

"Will you do it?" Teddy let the insult drop. "Will you place the call?"

Diana took a deep breath. Her stomach was filled with butterflies. She sifted through a pile of scrap paper on the side table next to the sofa. She found what she was looking for and read it: "Hotel Los Libereros. Almería, Spain, Seven-five-seven-two-one-one. White House Bar—Casa Blanca."

"We already have a man at the bar. Call the hotel." Teddy picked up the phone on his side of the sofa. "What's the national number for Spain?"

"Thirty-four."

He dialed the number and handed the receiver to Diana. She brushed the hair away from her ear.

Chapter Nineteen

Helicopter Marine One was lifting off the South Lawn of the White House when Tab Skillman ran onto the green waving his arms in the air. The decoy chopper had taken off thirty seconds earlier and was already over the Potomac River and bound for Andrews Air Force Base. The pilot of the command craft, Colonel Mark Gillespie, was the first to see the chief of staff and motioned to President Satterfield, who was sitting at the rear of the copter in the seat the crew referred to as the throne. Satterfield picked his headphones off the seat beside him and placed the cup over his ear without messing his hair under the headband. He adjusted the mouthpiece and spoke.

"Take her down," he said and Gillespie nodded. The helicopter made a broad swing over the Ellipse, around the Washington Monument, and returned to settle on the South Lawn. Before the engines were tamed, Skillman hunched over and bolted to the aircraft. Sargeant Major Cliff Rogers moved from his jumpseat to open the reinforced door and lower the steps. He got the portal opened, but before he could turn the gears on the steps, Skillman jumped the three feet and caught his balance on the officer's elbow.

"Welcome aboard." Satterfield smiled. Rogers abandoned the task of lowering the steps and returned to his seat. He looked at his superior, Captain David Crane, the Marine responsible for the "doomsday football," the black briefcase that holds the daily command codes for America's nuclear arsenal. The case was handcuffed to Crane's wrist and was positioned on the floor between the throne and the captain's seat. The two Secret Service men in black suits and white shirts sitting opposite the President looked at each other through their dark glasses. One shrugged his shoulders.

"Mr. President," Skillman was formal in front of the Marines, "we have a serious problem."

"More serious than me getting to Andrews before my flight leaves?" Satterfield was in a good mood and tried to play with his chief, but gathered by the expression on Skillman's face that he was not of like mind. "What's the problem?"

"Can we speak outside, please." Skillman looked to Rogers to lower the steps. The Marine moved to stand, but Satterfield stopped him.

"No. If Tab can jump up, I can jump down."

"I'm sorry, sir, but I'd rather carry you from the helicopter myself than let you jump. I don't want your broken leg on my service record." Rogers lowered the stairs and stepped onto the grass to help the President. Satterfield unfastened his seatbelt and moved to the door. He nodded to Captain Crane to follow, but before the Marine could move, both Secret Service agents blocked his way and followed the Commander in Chief out of the craft. Satterfield walked to the bottom of the stairs, paused and turned to Rogers. "Thanks for helping me save face."

The officer only smiled.

"Tell the captain to wait here. I'll be right back."

Skillman allowed Crane to precede him down the stairs, but quickly caught up with the President and walked him thirty yards in front of the whirling bird, until they were comfortably outside the storm of air. Crane remained five yards away with the briefcase, though the agents stayed on the President's back.

"What's so important?" Satterfield asked once he came to a stop.

"We need to speak alone." Skillman nodded to the two men in dark glasses.

"See what the captain's up to," the President ordered and both men retreated a distance equal to Crane's. He turned back to Skillman. "Talk to me."

"You may have to cancel your trip."

"Nothing's more important than my trip. We already postponed it for Senator Watenburg's funeral yesterday."

"We may have to postpone it again."

"Hell, do you know how much it costs the taxpayer to send four C-141s to Tokyo? And my poor wife's been waiting at the air base for over an hour."

"Dr. Steinbrenner has been kidnapped."

"What!"

"Steinbrenner has been taken. We don't know who. We don't know why. He just disappeared."

The President stepped back and closed his eyes. He hated to ask the next question, but he knew it would make the difference as to whether or not he followed through with his trip to Tokyo. "Was he taken alive?" he asked.

"We don't know."

"What do you mean, you don't know?"

"We don't know. He was by himself. We don't have witnesses, but there was blood on the wall and—"

"Wait!" Satterfield snapped. "Blood on what wall?"

"The men's room at the National Press Club. He was scheduled to speak—"

"What was he doing unattended in the men's room?"

"Delbert, I don't know what he was doing unattended in the men's room. Given the circumstances we face with his abduction, somehow those details escaped me."

"Circumstances?" the President yelled. "It's a son-of-bitchin' crisis!" He looked at the security men staring at him. He knew they could not hear him over the whistledown of the engine and swish of the rotor, but he could see that his countenance disturbed them, and he calmed down.

"I'll find out why he was unattended. But for now, we have a problem to deal with, and I don't think you'd better go to Japan. After all, you were going to brief Prime Minister Karamada about the upcoming summit in Luxembourg, and frankly if our worst nightmare's realized, there will be no summit."

"Nuclear war?"

"My nightmares aren't that dark," said Skillman. "I'm thinking more about the Soviets learning from Dr. Steinbrenner that we've got the satellites in orbit."

"Nuclear war," said the President in a matter-of-fact tone.

"We don't know that they'll launch missiles just because of the satellites."

"It's their only preemptive move," said Satterfield. He looked back at the Marines. "We went over this with the Joint Chiefs. Especially if Steinbrenner tells them the system isn't manned."

"That's if he tells them about the system."

"What do you think?"

"About whether he'll talk?" Skillman shook his head slowly. "I don't know. He's old, and—"

"They have ways of making him talk."

The chief of staff did not respond, but Satterfield could see from Skillman's eyes that he was worried.

"It pains the hell out of me to say it, but if we just knew he was dead."

"But we don't," Tab said. His tone was rather harsh.

The President let out a sharp breath. He looked at his wristwatch then back to the Marines.

"You have to make a decision," said Skillman.

"What's my excuse for not going to Tokyo?"

"We'll let the press office handle that."

"I can't go," the President said. His eyes squinted as he looked away from the helicopter and across the Ellipse to the white marble obelisk that stands between the Capitol and Lincoln Memorial on the Mall. The nobility of the monument represented well the nobility of the man it honored. For a moment, President Satterfield wanted to trade places with that man—General Washington. Put me six feet under, and he can handle this crisis, Satterfield thought. "Is the—"

"The Situation Room is set up," Skillman answered before the President could finish his question. "I've already called for the secretary of state and the rest of the National Security Council."

"Twice in one week. The media are going to put the pieces together on this puzzle."

"They don't have to know."

"They always know." The President paused in thought and then asked the next logical question. "Did you call Senator Ashworth?"

"No," Tab said quickly.

"Why not?"

"You know how I feel. We already have a crisis. I'm looking for solutions, not to compound our problems."

"I don't know whether to be angry or grateful."

"Let's see how it goes." Skillman tugged gently on the President's arm and tried to direct him back to the White House. At first, Satterfield took a step, then he quickly turned and jogged to the helicopter. Both Secret Service men and Crane fell in behind. Rogers stood by the door and saluted. The President only nodded.

"Go to Andrews," he ordered. "Tell Mrs. Satterfield the trip's been cancelled. She's not going to like it, but she'll have to understand. Tell her it was her fault for wanting to meet me at the airport rather than coming back to the house to leave together."

"Sir?"

"Nothing," said the President. His voice fell to a whisper. "Just tell her I miss her and to get home."

The Marine saluted and shut the door. The President returned the salute, and Gillespie took the helicopter straight up and over the Ellipse. Then, for the first time since he left the craft, Satterfield noticed the crowd of people gathered on the other side of the south wrought-iron fence. Without breaking his salute, he turned to them. They cheered, and he thought about how simple their lives were. None of them knew the pressure he was about to face in the Situation Room.

"Let's get some heat down here," Satterfield said as he walked into the bunkerlike room in the basement of the West Wing. "This place is always too damn cold."

A member of the watch staff in his army greens rose from the communications desk he manned and moved to the north wall where the thermostat was located next to the door and turned the heat to seventy. The President walked into the adjoining conference room. Only four of the dozen chairs that lined the twenty-foot by fifteen-foot room were filled. Secretary of State Parryman fumbled with the manuscript of a speech inside a blue folder, and the President could see his lips, and the gestures on his face, as if he were already in front of his audience. On Parryman's left sat Air Force Chief of Staff White, and next to him sat Rich Spencer, doodling on his ever-present list of things to do.

Spencer was the most organized member of the Satterfield Administration. The national security advisor's full head of black hair peppered with gray, and his deep brown eyes, set narrow on his dark face, provided all the charisma a man needed to be a good politician, and it was ironic that he had never entered the fray. Instead, he was an academic, a professor of Strategic International Studies at George Washington University. Satterfield would have liked to boast the professor as his find, but President Bush had appointed him head of the council in his second term. Once Satterfield secured the nomination, he tried to convince the Republican leadership that Spencer would strengthen the ticket as his running mate, but the pollsters warned the election would come down to California, and the Golden State's governor, Arlen Meyers, was forced on Satterfield instead. As a subtle gesture of revenge, after the election, the President restructured the Emergency Management Team, which historically came under the direction of the Vice President, and gave Spencer that position as well. And Meyers spent most of his time doing what he was selected to do, staying in California and keeping the big state happy.

All the men dropped what they were doing and stood to greet Satterfield as he entered the room. He nodded to the three men together and walked to the end of the row of chairs and shook General Rheem's hand first.

"How are you, Doland?"

"Fine, Mr. President," the distinguished-looking army chief answered with a forced smile.

"How's," Satterfield paused and sifted through his mind for the name of Watenburg's widow. "How's Vicky?"

"She'll be fine, sir."

"It was a beautiful service."

"Thank you."

"If there's anything Mrs. Satterfield and I can do."

"Thank you. Everything will be fine now."

The President squeezed the general's hand and then turned to the other men. "Has Tab told you what this is about?"

Spencer responded affirmatively and then nodded at two members of the army watch staff who still stood at attention on their raised platform in front of a lighted wall map of the world.

"At ease, men." Satterfield smiled. He was still not used to the protocol and the strict attention from subordinates that came with the office. "Would the two of you mind joining your officer at the communications desk?"

Without another word, both staff members stepped off the platform and walked into the L-shaped communications room. In the conference room, the five men were now alone.

"I imagine Tab will be here shortly," said the President.

"He's been here already," answered Spencer, now apparently feeling freer to speak with the two watch staff in the other room. "He left with Jules and Raymond. They went to get the SDI briefing books."

"All three of them?"

"You know our rules about 'EYES ONLY' material."

"Why do we need the books anyway?"

Before Spencer could answer, Skillman entered the room, flanked by Chief of Naval Operations Morrow and Marine Commandant Bradford. He held the red-striped folders in his hands. His brow was taut, and the expression on his face was even more grave than the expression that troubled the President when the two of them spoke minutes earlier on the South Lawn.

"I'm afraid we have a problem that compounds our crisis," Skillman said as he laid the folders on the end of the table.

"What?" asked Satterfield.

"The folders are numbered one through ten."

"Okay," the President said, waiting for the conclusion.

"We're missing folder number three."

Satterfield walked to the end of the conference table and spread the folders in front of him. "Who had number three? Dr. Steinbrenner?"

"We don't know," said Skillman. "They've only been distributed once. In our Council meeting three days ago."

"Did we have all ten?"

Rich Spencer stepped next to the President and answered. "Yes, we did. Tab and I delivered them personally to the meeting and gave them to Dr. Steinbrenner."

"Who gathered them after the meeting?"

"Dr. Steinbrenner," Skillman answered. "He gave them to me."

"And me," said Spencer. "Tab and I secured them in the crypt in the Council office."

"Well?" Satterfield asked, begging for the next logical response. When it did not come, he asked, "Did you count them?" He sounded agitated. Both men looked at each other. "Did you count them, Tab?"

"Mr. President," said Spencer. "Neither Tab nor I thought to count them. The meeting was tight. We didn't think that someone would walk out with a book."

Satterfield pulled a chair away from the wall and sat down at the table. He counted the briefs again. And then again. There were only nine. Number three *was* missing. "Are you sure it wasn't left in the crypt?" he asked Skillman, but Commandant Bradford answered.

"It's not there."

Satterfield turned around to the other men in the room. "Did any of you mistakenly take the folder?"

Rheem and White shook their heads slowly. The President turned back to Spencer. "Was there any method to giving them out the other day?"

"If there was," answered Bradford, "only Dr. Steinbrenner would know. He handed them out."

The President slumped back into his chair. *Nothing was ever easy,* he thought. *First, Dr. Steinbrenner was missing. Now, a folder.* Satterfield was sinking into the malaise that often tormented him when he believed he faced an impossible situation. He took a deep breath and tried to force the dark emotions from his mind. *Approach it logically,* he ordered. *Don't be governed by your emotions. They betray you. Analysis. Analyze the situation.* "Dr. Steinbrenner is the key," he said aloud. "He may have taken number three." *He was absent-minded enough,* the President thought. *Maybe he was a security risk.* "Or he may know who he gave number three to. Either way, he's our key."

"You know what this means, Mr. President," Skillman began, but a glare in Satterfield's eye stifled the comment.

"We'd better get on with this meeting," said the President. "Please, gentlemen," he motioned toward the chairs around him, "take a seat." Skillman did not have to finish his comment. Satterfield knew exactly what was on the mind of his chief of staff. Everyone present at the Council meeting was present now. Everyone who had received a folder about the Strategic Defense Initiative was sitting at the conference table in the Situation Room. Everyone except Steinbrenner and Senator Boyd Ashworth. "As you've heard," said the President, "Dr. Steinbrenner has been abducted—taken from the National Press Club where he was scheduled to be the luncheon speaker." He looked at Tab. "Why in the hell we think he should be out and about, speaking to the media, at his age and with his sensitive role in national security, is beyond me—as is how the hell those two jackass Secret Service men allowed him to go in the men's room alone."

Skillman shrugged his shoulders and flipped open a leather folder that held a yellow pad of paper.

"I think our first move is to contact Langley and have Central Intelligence and the Bureau comb every known Soviet safehouse in the city, Maryland and Virginia," Satterfield continued.

"We have to be careful," said Skillman. "One of our concerns is appearance. We can't look nervous just because our science advisor has been kidnapped. But then, of course, we have to deal with the question, why on God's earth would anyone want to take him in the first place?"

"I think it's a matter of time before people start to speculate," said General White, and his colleagues nodded. "Everyone knows the professor has been involved with SDI. I'm sure that's what he was scheduled to speak on at the Press Club."

"He was," said Skillman.

"Where are the two Secret Service men?" asked Spencer. "Have they been debriefed."

"They know nothing," answered Skillman. "They didn't see anyone in the halls. Hell, they didn't even check the bathroom for fifteen minutes."

"Fifteen minutes!" the President shouted.

"They said they figured he was old, slow and—how did they put it—methodically lethargic."

"I want them out of the Service by tomorrow morning," ordered Satterfield.

"They've already been suspended."

"Forget suspended. I want them fired. I want them ground up and fed to the sharks. They're never going to work again—do you understand—not even selling soft pretzels at RFK."

"I'll take care of it," said Skillman, and he wrote in his notebook.

"Right now our problem is the good doctor." Spencer stopped the conversation he had started about the agents. He was the cool head, the man Satterfield could depend on as the eye of the hurricane, the competent and unflappable voice of wisdom whatever the circumstances. "It is possible that Dr. Steinbrenner is already dead. If that's the case, then our concern is the briefing book. If it was in his possession, it's possible that the abductors have it now." Spencer looked at Satterfield. "It might be wise, Mr. President, to have someone search Steinbrenner's home and office."

"I don't think he's got the book," Satterfield answered. Out of the corner of his eye he could see Skillman staring at him. "I'll have Tab take care of finding the book."

"How are you so certain he doesn't have it?" asked Morrow. His large, tanned hands played with his white hat with scrambled eggs on the black visor, and then he wiped his brow.

"Good Lord," said Spencer before the President could answer. "You think Ashworth took the book."

"I don't know," Satterfield fumbled with his Mont Blanc. "But I'm going to find out."

"Gentlemen," said Rheem. His voice was unnaturally deep and commanding. "I believe our crisis has come full circle."

"What do you mean, Doland?" Satterfield asked.

"I believe a strong case can be made that Dr. Steinbrenner's kidnapping is tied to the murder of Senator Grayson Watenburg. And now, with the briefing book missing, and the possibility of Senator Ashworth's involvement, I'm almost certain of it."

All eyes focused on the general.

"Senator Watenburg and Hans Peterson, the German who was killed in the same hotel room, were leading proponents of the Strategic Defense Initiative. In fact, they were debating the issue at the North Atlantic conference the very day they were murdered."

"Are we talking terrorists?" asked the President with an incredulous tone. "In Washington?"

"There's something more profound at work here than any of us realizes," said Rheem. "That's all I'm saying. I'm not accusing anyone of terrorism—not Ashworth—not anyone. But is it coincidence that within one week three important players in the Strategic Defense Initiative are murdered?"

"But we don't know if Steinbrenner's dead," said Spencer.

"The point remains," answered Rheem. "There is a deliberate and systematic attempt under way to either stop the Initiative or get information."

"Killing Senator Watenburg wouldn't stop the Initiative," said Satterfield.

"But it might lead to Steinbrenner," Skillman added. "And who more would you want if you were after information?"

"Remember, Mr. President," Rheem said, "Senator Watenburg was tortured. And Senator Watenburg knew of the professor's involvement—I mean, beyond his simply being a proponent."

"Steinbrenner briefed the Senate Intelligence Committee on a regular basis." Spencer's voice was filled with sudden understanding. "But those briefings are so top secret, the senators are under strict orders not to mention either the subject or the witness."

"But I'm sure the professor never told the senators how close we actually were," said Satterfield. "Ashworth acted like he didn't know." Mentioning the senator's name made him think about the briefing book again. *Ashworth must have the book*, he conceded the thought that until now he had cautiously refused to accept. *Why would Steinbrenner want it? He already knew the project inside and out.*

"But if there's a leak somewhere on the committee," said Spencer, "and if that leak ever knew how close we were getting, or that we had the technology that would make the Initiative operable, then any means of getting that information would be worth it to the Soviets."

Rheem shook his head in disagreement. "If the leak were on the Intelligence Committee, then why kill Senator Watenburg? He was tortured for a reason, and I think that reason was to find out who held the deck of cards on SDI."

"Then you think Grayson talked?" asked the President. He knew his question was bold considering the relationship between the two men. Suddenly he regretted using the senator's first name. It dawned on him that Rheem was trying to emphasize the formality of office rather than reveal the family tie.

"They cut off his ears," the general said sharply. "One at a time. They even took one of them as some sort of gross souvenir. Under those circumstances, I imagine anyone would talk."

General White, the most openly sympathetic of the military men, nodded in agreement. "And there was no way that Senator Watenburg would know why they wanted the professor's name. Certainly he wouldn't know they were planning to kidnap him."

"I agree with General Rheem. The mole has to be second generation," said Spencer, unattentive to what White said. He was the first one to suggest that the informant was more than someone simply speaking out of class—a political leak—but someone spilling military secrets to the Soviet Union. "It couldn't be Senator Ashworth," he continued, boldly suggesting what everyone else was thinking. "If Ashworth was talking, then there would have been no need to kill Senator Watenburg. "The man talking must be someone who knows enough about the Intelligence Committee to be informed about its agenda, but not enough to know the details of who is testifying when and about what."

"A member of a congressional staff," said the President as if it were the only right answer.

"Capitol Hill is a beehive," said Skillman. "There are fifty thousand staff members up there—"

The President raised his hand to stop Skillman. "This would have to be someone close to the Intelligence Committee."

"That narrows it to ten thousand," Tab said sarcastically.

"Mr. President," Spencer filled in the uneasiness left by Skillman's sarcasm, "I'll have my team look into the staff of the senators who sit on the Intelligence Committee. I think that's a good idea, but I think we're getting away from the crisis at hand. No matter who is responsible, or whether or not there is a mole, we have to make a decision about how we're going to respond to Dr. Steinbrenner. What do we tell the media, and how do we prepare for a possible confrontation with the Kremlin?"

The President drew a deep breath and looked at the ceiling. He was disturbed by the delicacy of the crisis. Respond too aggressively and everyone from the Potomac to the Volga would know that Steinbrenner was more than an academic who advised the White House on scientific matters. Respond too passively and risk that the old man might still be alive and would talk. Satterfield closed his eyes and exhaled. *If Steinbrenner is alive*, he thought, *and if he talks, his information will draw the superpowers to a nuclear confrontation.* The President did not want to wish anyone dead, but it would certainly solve one factor in the critical equation. He looked at Skillman. "We have to find out who's talking on Capitol Hill. But first, we have to determine whether Dr. Steinbrenner is dead or alive. I imagine that until I get a call on the red line, we can assume he hasn't talked. We can also assume that wherever the briefing book is, it isn't in Soviet hands. But we've got to find the book, Tab, do you understand?"

Skillman nodded and jotted.

"And frankly, it may not be a good idea to involve Langley right now—or the FBI. You help him, Rich."

The security advisor looked at the chief of staff.

"But Mr. President," Commandant Bradford said, "we have to find Steinbrenner, and if the communists have him, they're keeping him in one of their safehouses. That's Central Intelligence."

"No covert operation in our government is monitored like the CIA. Those boys have more books and articles written about them than the rest of the federal government combined. Half of the books are written by turncoat jackasses like Agee. In fact, there are so many leaks out at Langley, we don't need a director, what we need is a urologist. No, I'm turning over the responsibility of finding the professor to Spencer and his staff. His boys are the most informed about the Initiative, about the need for secrecy, and about the doctor's status in this administration. You've got twenty-four hours, Rich, and I would like an update every hour on the hour."

"Yes, Mr. President," said Spencer, "but I will have to bring more men into the circle."

"Do what you have to do. But I want the most trusted sons-of-bitches you've got."

"Yes, sir."

"We've mixed a big stew this afternoon." The President looked from one man to the next. In their eyes he saw a little uncertainty, a lot of determination and a hint of fear. "What we've discussed, to a great degree, is speculation. All the ingredients seem to fit into the stew, all right. But, hell, maybe our recipe is so far off with stew that what we should have been making is ice cream." He offered an uneasy smile. His analogy wasn't working. All faces were still drawn and intense.

His voice became more solemn. "I'll be in my private office for the next twenty-four hours. If any of you have new ideas, or information, dial on the direct secured line. Don't use the switchboard. But give me thirty minutes. I'm going to call Senator Ashworth personally. We're going to find that book, and then—if our stew's right—we're going to find the man whose been spilling his guts to the Soviets—we're going to find him, and we're going to fry him."

Chapter Twenty

Robert Hamilton stood across the street from his hotel looking at two members of the Guardia Civil posted on either side of the front entrance. Both men stood at attention in green wool uniforms, their black leather triangular hats propped squarely on their heads. To their left, parked at the curb of the U-shaped driveway leading to the door of the hotel, was a gray van. A man in a suit and tie rested on the left rear fender of the van, and the license plates were diplomatic. Directly behind the van, with the driver still in the front seat, was a black limosine. Jutting skyward about two feet above the left side of the front bumper and waving gently in the breeze was the Soviet flag.

The journalist felt foolish for believing that he would be able to simply walk back into his hotel, ask for his messages, gather his belongings and catch the next plane to the States. His mind recalled the countless James Bond movies he had seen, and he wondered how 007 had been allowed to return time and again to his hotel after he and others had murdered and left stiff, cold corpses behind. Nobody ever questioned the British agent. Bond was never harassed, never sought by neutral local officials. *To have a license to kill*, Malibu thought. *Hell, I don't even have my passport to get home.*

Not only did the officials have his passport, they had his briefcase filled with information: address book, notes on other news stories, checkbook, airline tickets, paycheck stubs, apartment keys, even his late income tax return was buried in one of the case compartments. They had a photograph of him, his social security number, even his fingerprints. *By the balls*, he thought and winced at the mental image.

223

The rush of anxiety prompted Robert to step from the sunlight, back into the shadowed entrance of a dirty bar. Two young boys were playing pinball next to the door, and four old Spaniards, dressed in black, two with berets, huddled around the edge of the bar. Malibu kept his eyes on the hotel door, on the two men in green, on the automobiles. The *guardias* held stubby automatic rifles that hung from their necks on taut black-leather straps. He could not see what kind of guns they were, but their power was accentuated by the broad black leather, clip-filled bandoleers each man wore with armed authority.

I should have stayed in Rome. Nobody gave a damn who I was in Rome.

Because you hadn't killed anybody, asshole.

Robert turned briefly and caught his image in the mirror behind the bar. He was filthy. His shirt and trousers looked like they belonged to a *gitano*. His hair was tossed and matted to his forehead with perspiration. Soiled streams of sweat flowed unevenly from his temples. He had not eaten in more than a day, and his hunger added to the depression welling inside. For the first time in his life, he felt helpless, cornered in a country with nowhere to turn. For a minute he thought of the stories, recounted so many times with detail in the buzzing newsroom, of the scores of American newsmen who never returned from their assignments. Many of them were killed or kidnapped—or both— in foreign countries while they covered politics and revolution. Most often misfortune occurred in the Third World. He remembered the televised footage of the network reporter shot in cold blood after Salvadoran officers demanded he lie face down on the ground. The cameraman kept his camera rolling, but it bobbled and lost focus as the newsman's head jumped violently when the officer pulled the trigger of his forty-five.

Spain was not a part of the Third World, and for this Malibu was grateful. He found comfort in the fact that the nation had remained a stable parliamentary monarchy since its transition from the authoritarian regime under the late Generalissimo Franco. But his comfort was checked by the fact that since the late seventies, the Spanish Socialist Workers Party and the Spanish Communist Party had moved the country to the center in the East-West conflict. As an ever-growing neutral country, unattached in its political ideology, Spain would demonstrate no undue favoritism in the gunfight at the hotel. One side would not be exonerated because it was democratic and the other guilty because it was communist. Spain was its own country, led by its own people—unattached and without favor.

In the hotel, men were dead, and the authorities found them, one lying in the hall outside Robert's room, the other crashed in a heap on the stairway. Robert figured that if Bower Thompson had done his job, the dead would be stripped of their weapons and any identification that associated them with the Soviet government. He had little doubt that the Soviet authorities currently inside the hotel knew the official capacities of the dead men. More than likely, Thompson personally contacted the embassy, and like good Russians, they would do everything in their power to convince the *Guardia* that an unprovoked homicide, capable of international repercussions if not solved, had stained their southern resort paradise. As far as the Soviets would tell it, the dead men were nothing but innocent tourists, victims of Western violence.

Robert was thirsty. His lips were dry and stiff. He wanted to move toward the bar and order a drink, but he was nervous his unkempt appearance would attract attention, especially in light of the activities across the street. Instead, he turned and asked the two boys at pinball if they knew the time.

"*No sé, señor,*" said the *chico* concentrating on the metal ball in play. The boy did not look up.

The other turned to Robert, studied the American's face, and looked out the door at the *guardia* standing on the other side of the street before he turned and looked at an old brown electric clock on the wall above the mirror. "The time, it is there, mister," he said in English, and then turned back to admire his friend's skill.

Robert glanced at the clock. Directly below it was a shelf running the length of the bar and lined with spirits from different countries. He recognized some of them. Beneath the shelf and propped on a cabinet in front of the mirror was a television, turned off at *mediodía*, and surrounded by wooden casks of wine. Above the bar hung more than a dozen smoked hams, and their aroma filled the air. The men below the hams did not acknowledge the American, but continued to speak among themselves. The time was 1:15.

"I've got five hundred pesetas for the boy who gets me a Bitter

Kas,'' Malibu said as he dug into his pocket and withdrew a thousand-peseta note. Both boys jumped at the offer. The metal ball hit the base of the board as the boy who had ignored Malibu earlier for a run on the scoreboard was the first to catch the money out of the journalist's hand.

Both ran to the bar, shouting at the tender to give them a cold Kas. The *chico* without the money argued that they should split the reward evenly, and Malibu moved to the pinball machine and cautiously turned his back to the men at the bar. Smoothly, he flipped a steel ball into play. It dinged a bell or two and then dropped through the middle of the flippers on its first roll down the board. He clicked the second ball into the launch position, but the boys returned with his drink before he pulled the pin.

"*Gano! Gano!*" shouted the boy who had jumped for the money. "I win! I win, mister!" He waved the Bitter Kas triumphantly in the air.

"*Muy bien,*" Robert forced a smile. He took the drink and change from the boy and returned five hundred pesetas. Then without turning to look at the reaction from the men at the bar, he walked directly out the door into the sunlight. Turning right, he stooped forward, slouched his shoulders, and held the drink tightly in both hands until he came to the first street corner where he could escape, out of sight of the standing *guardia*.

The soda felt good on his parched lips and dry throat. His taste buds were extremely sensitive to the sour kick, but the tiny bottle of Kas only teased his thirst and provoked him to look for another bar.

He continued to walk south on the long street. Life was beginning to return to the *calles*, as the men bid their wives goodbye and returned to work for their final shift of the day. The gradual crowding of the streets made Malibu feel more comfortable as he faded into the scene of men, many of them laborers and in soiled clothes. Though he was much taller than the average Spaniard, he could compensate with a stoop. His clothes, as well as his Bass Weejuns, did not fit into the image he was trying to project, but his filth and perspiration did, and he was grateful for that.

The street ran straight down the hill upon which Almería was built, and Robert could see far below where it ran out onto the large dock he had visited the night before. Beyond the pier, the Mediterranean was a heavenly blue, and from the horizon a dim trail of smoke rose vertically and faded into the sky. Shadows of smaller boats speckled the water between the point where the smoke rose and the shoreline, but it was not the visible boats that interested Robert. Rather, he was thinking of the ship large enough to make such a stream of smoke. It was headed for Africa, for Morocco, and suddenly his spirits lifted. He remembered the advertisement on top of the television in his hotel room: "Explore the Dark Continent. See Morocco within four short hours. Round trip cruises leave the Port of Almería every two hours."

Four hours from Almería to Melilla, he thought. Once there, he could contact Jed, or even Diana, and explain the whole story—the terrorist attack in Rome, the mysterious Mrs. Peterson in Almería, the traitor Bower Thompson and his gang of spies. Jed and Diana hobnobbed in powerful circles, and certainly one of their influential friends could get him back to D.C. *What about Ashworth himself?* Robert stopped dead in his tracks. *If Ashworth knew that Bo was a spy—and certainly if I dropped the hint—the senator would move heaven and earth to get me home.*

Or would he talk to Thompson first? In that case, the Soviets would be on your scent again. Stick with Jed and Diana. Right now they're the only people in the world you can trust.

You're a shit, Simon Levin.

Robert continued to walk toward the sea. His mind tempted him to surrender to the Spanish authorities and tell his story, or better yet, to get to the nearest American consulate. But one way or the other, he would be detained and lose the time he needed to finish his story. Besides, the nearest consulate was in Málaga, and Robert was certain the bus and train station would be drowning in *federales*. There would be more gray and green uniforms than business suits, and worse than surrendering would be getting caught.

Where are you Julia? You got me into this mess. You must have the contacts we need right here in Spain, and now you've freak'n abandoned me. Save your own ass and hang mine out to blow in the Iberian wind.

She saved your worthless life less than twenty-four hours ago.

For what? To run like a convict? To get my teeth kicked in by the Reds?

Call Diana the next chance you get. Tell her you're on your way to Morocco. You'll call her from there. You need her help.

Sounds like a damn movie—"Hello, Diana? Can't talk now, but listen good. I need your help. Trouble? No, not trouble. Let's just say it's a matter of life and death with the security of America at stake. But you've got to agree to whatever I ask of you, and you can tell no one. Understand?" Robert smiled. He got all the clichés he could remember. Except that he had to call at midnight, with a storm raging outside, and Diana had to let the phone ring three times.

His feet kept moving while he pulled his wallet from his back pocket. His notebook was stuck to the leather by perspiration. He was thankful for the small favor that in light of all his possessions, which had by now been confiscated, he still had the notebook, and he pressed it back into his pocket while he held onto the wallet. Without a passport and looking the way he did, Robert knew he would have to bribe a crewman to smuggle him aboard the ship. That alone could cost four to five times the fare, which he estimated to be about fifty, maybe seventy-five dollars. In cash he carried a little over two hundred dollars in Spanish currency. In traveler's checks he had another four hundred and fifty.

That's it, bribe the sailor with freak'n traveler's checks. They'd never find you then, asshole.

Stop beating yourself. You gotta get out of the malaise.

Malaise? Malaise? Are you kidding? It's a nightmare.

He put the wallet back in his pocket.

Turn yourself in. Hell, a day or two in the slammer while they iron this thing out and you'll be on your way.

A day or two and there goes the story.

We're talking life, here.

I'm talking a Pulitzer.

Pulitzer?

Hell, yes, then every paper in the world will be begging for me to sign their front page.

Pulitzer?

Why else would this nightmare be worth the time?

You got a point there.

Hell, yes, I do, and do you think they'd let me out of the clink to chase a Pulitzer? You think that once the commies know I'm on to their man in Washington they'll even let me live to write the story?

Another point well taken.

And what about Diana?

Diana?

Sure, you think she'll go for some flyweight who turns himself in rather than hangs around to be the hero in the final scene.

Diana?

Maybe I shouldn't be thinking of Diana, but—

Hell, no, you shouldn't be thinking of Diana. Think about getting us out of here, and if you want to save face while your at it, well, that's all right with this side of the brain. We'll even accept the Pulitzer idea.

"But leads don't win Pulitzers," Robert whispered, and a passing Spaniard in blue jean overalls and carrying a black rubber bucket filled with mortar looked at him. "Neither do chicken-shit reporters," he said loud enough so the man could hear him, then he quickened his pace. He knew the information he had at the moment was enough for a yellow story, perhaps more than a lead, but for nothing more than a supermarket tabloid. It was not as deep as he needed to go. The journalistic muse gripped his stomach. He could not lose this story; his future depended on it. Twice the *Post* had put him in a de-tox program at the Bethesda Alcohol Rehabilitation Center. Twice they had patiently waited for him to return. Simon was patient no longer. The ax had fallen, and Robert wondered if maybe Simon did not suspect that he was sucking the joy juice again. His only chance was the story—a story so explosive it would rock not only America but the allies as well.

The Strategic Defense Initiative was being deployed despite the treaties. Julia knew this. She did not deny it. Robert looked toward the sky. *Maybe the satellites are up there already.*

With his next step, Robert forced himself to understand that he could not leave Almería. Though the creative, emotional side of his brain protested the logic, Robert knew he could not leave without Julia. *She is the link I need to tie everything together. She knows what I need to know. In fact, Julia is the story.*

But what about Morocco?

I'll take you there on vacation.

At the next corner, he turned off the main street and walked in the direction of the Casa Blanca. The bar was the only link the journalist had to the woman, other than the fact that she had mentioned an apartment in the city. *But where?*

Across the street stood a telephone booth, and Robert took the opportunity to check the phone book for her listing. Nothing under Julia Peterson. He looked to see if the Germans had a consulate in the city. Again nothing. His last chance was the bartender, the man who put Robert onto her in the first place. Maybe he knew something about the woman that would put Malibu back on track.

Within fifteen minutes, he stood outside the decaying wooden door. The neon red light still flashed above the entrance in the bright afternoon, and nothing had changed since the night before, except the posters announcing the communist demonstration were now hidden behind a plastered line of new notices advertising a baptismal exposition for the Mormon Church: "Join family and friends at the chapel of the Church of Jesus Christ of Latter-day Saints, located at 141 Calle Maestro, in Almería." Malibu found the new posters, with pictures of two Mormon missionaries walking side by side, with hair cropped above the ears, their dark suits and ties and white shirts, more pleasant than the posters they hid. And he was not sure whether his preference was influenced by the change in color and design of the posters, or the fact that the political left had been plastered over by the religious right. As a journalist craving professional respect, it would not serve him well to favor one over the other ideologically. Frankly, it would not be ethical. He remembered a comment one of his university journalism professors offered once in private.

"I've been a journalist so long," she said, "that I don't have an opinion anymore. I don't know what I think. I'm not right. I'm not left. I'm not a flag waver, and I'm not a flag burner. I guess I've been calloused by the facts."

Something inside Malibu made him admire the woman's objectivity, but he believed he could never feel the same. To be without an opinion, to be calloused by the facts, Robert believed would make a man like a kite in the wind, shifting with the changing breeze and anchored to reality by a thin line capable of breaking at any moment. Unlike his professor, Robert believed he needed something to stand for, something outside of his professional comfort zone that demanded complete objectivity. He needed something larger than himself or his byline to believe in. He did not mind if his opinions changed from year to year. Sometimes they changed from minute to minute. What he did mind was calloused objectivity, the cold, uncaring, facts-oriented abyss into which his professor had fallen. What he admired, he loathed. And he felt good about that.

Inside the nightclub, Robert was overcome with a delightful ease. The room was dark as always, and when his eyes adjusted, he was even more comforted to find that it was almost empty in the early afternoon. Only the corner table farthest away from the bar was occupied, by a man and a woman who sipped their drinks and laughed and talked in hushed tones.

Behind the bar was the friendly face Robert wanted to see. The bartender was carefully taking his bottles, one by one, from the long shelves and wiping them with a white towel. Absent the dust, their reflection in the mirror was more brilliant, and the journalist felt an impulse, one that would have to settle for another Bitter Kas.

"*Hola,*" he greeted with a smile and tipped his head toward the bottles on the wall. He expected to be met with familiarity, but the bartender only stared at the bottle he was wiping. Malibu wondered if the man had heard him, and he repeated his greeting. "*Hola,*" he said, "I would like a Bitter Kas, *por favor.*"

Again, without speaking, the proprietor reached into his metal cooler under the bar and withdrew a small bottle of the sour red drink with the yellow label. He popped the top with an opener mounted to the bar and poured half a glass. The rest of the drink he placed to the side.

"Here's to friendship," Robert said softly and then took a deep swallow that burned his throat.

The barman turned his back on his patron and replaced the bottle on the shelf.

"Things will pick up later?" Robert asked, but the man did not acknowledge. He took another long drink and then carefully set the glass on the bar. "Look," he began again, lowering his voice to warn the man that he was serious about getting his attention. "I don't know who you've talked to, and I don't know what you've been told, but I need your help. You're the only—"

Before he could finish, the man from the table stood, approached the bar, and ordered two more Camparis with soda. He studied the face of the American as he waited for his drinks. Robert nodded, but the man remained emotionless. His eyes were angry beneath his protruding forehead and his nose looked like that of a boxer, pressed wide into his face. He wore dungarees and continued to stare. Then, with the sweating glasses in his large hands, he turned and walked back to his woman.

Maybe it's the way I look, Robert thought and watched the man as he walked away. In the dim light, he could not make out the details of the woman's features, but by the play of shadows and light, he could see her expression as the man sat next to her. Suddenly, she looked at Robert, and he turned away and jumped back into his conversation with the bartender.

"You're the only man in Almería who can help me. You know who I am, don't you?"

The Spaniard turned back and stared at his bottles. Robert saw him take a deep breath and grip the white towel in his hands.

"I don't know what you've been told," the journalist continued in whispered tones and through his teeth, "but I'm in trouble. You know that, too, don't you?"

The man did not move.

"Someone has come back to talk to you. The woman? One of the men I sat with at the table last night? Who spoke to you? What did they say?"

"They said nothing," the man answered in exasperation. He looked at the bottles resting on the top shelf below the ceiling.

"Who said nothing?"

"*No sé nada.*"

"Don't lie to me. I'm in too much trouble. You were so damn friendly last night. Someone spoke with you. Who?"

"*Nadie habló conmigo. No hé hablado con nadie.*"

"Speak English."

"I have spoken with no one."

"Then why the chill?"

"Chill?"

"Why so unfriendly?"

The man shrugged his shoulders.

"Look, I want you to answer one question—no more." Robert looked at the thin line of Bitter Kas left in his glass. "Last night, you told me the woman—Julia—or *la María*, rather, was a whore. You said she was a prostitute—that she often worked this bar. I need to find her. It's very important, and I don't care what you've been told, but I am the innocent man. I'm a journalist from America, and I need to find her. Please—you've got to help me. Do you know where she is? Where she lives?''

The man's head dropped.

"Please, help me.''

Slowly the head began to move up and down.

"Thank you,'' Robert seized on the gesture in gratitude.

"People I talk to, people who know *la María*, say she live on *la Calle Santo Domingo*,'' the man said as he turned around, then suddenly his eyes opened wide in terror.

"Hello, Mr. Hamilton.'' A strong Russian accent sent chills up Robert's spine, and the pain in his ribs flared, as he felt the barrel of a gun thrust into the small of his back. "Do not turn around suddenly. I have two associates waiting for us outside.''

"How do you know me?'' Robert asked as he looked into the frightened eyes of the bartender.

"We work for Mr. Thompson.''

"I figured he'd be out of the country by now.''

"He is safe, but he is waiting for you. He says you are very dangerous. But that is the way Americans think—that the press is so powerful—so dangerous.''

"Where is he?''

"You are not the one to ask the questions.'' The man stuck the gun deeper into the muscles, and Robert winced. "Now, please turn slowly. Walk toward the door. And stay close to me. I would rather not have anyone see my weapon. I do not like to kill innocent people.''

"You think the barman doesn't see what's going on?''

"Is he innocent?''

Robert obeyed and turned toward the door. He heard the bartender whisper *suerte*, but he was not sure whether the wish was to him or the Russian. He gazed out of the corner of his eye and saw the boxer sitting next to his woman. They had grown quiet, but simply because the man had spread a collage of family photographs across the table, and the woman was studying them as he explained the stories behind each one.

"Where is Bower?'' Robert asked once the two men were outside. He squinted in the bright afternoon sun.

Like the man promised, two colleagues were standing on either side of the door. One ground out a cigarette as the bar door slowly shut. He looked at the other man, who wore sunglasses and was the most casually dressed of the three.

"Do not talk until we get to the car," ordered the man with the gun. The other two fell in behind as they moved up the side street to the main avenue.

"Is the bartender on your payroll?" Robert asked, hoping that if he was not he would be calling the police about now.

Again, the gun jammed into muscle and he took that as his answer.

Mediodía was completely over now. The Spaniards had returned to the factories, the women were shut in their small *pisos*, and the streets were dead, except for an occasional passing car and six old men gathered around a table at a small cafe, playing dominos in their mourning clothes. Parked in front of the cafe was a late model Mercedes, and Robert was sure the car belonged to the Soviets. If he was going to escape, he had only seventy-five yards left before the car. But the empty streets and the pressure of the gun forced him to realize that any attempt would be fruitless.

Chicken shit, he listened to his mind protect his decision not to run. *You've been nothing but a coward since this adventure began.*

Adventure? You call this an adventure?

Do you feel alive?

Well, yes a little bit.

It's an adventure. Now you gotta get the hell outta here. This side of your brain doesn't want to die, either.

I can't just run.

There's only one gun.

Only one that I see.

Right. Well, disarm the man.

Now?

You got what, maybe twenty yards more before the car?

In one motion, Robert slammed across the hand with the gun, hitting the man's wrist with the elbow. Then he kicked back at his knee, but missed. The gun had not fallen from the hand, and Robert could think only to run. He heard the first shot as he dived behind the other side of the Mercedes. The two colleagues were running after him. The six old men stood under their table umbrella and began to shout. Across the street a woman with a baby carriage screamed and ducked into a storefront. Before either man could reach the car, Robert dived in front of a speeding bus, and the driver slammed on the brakes as the journalist rolled to the other side of the street. He opened his eyes. He was still alive. The driver put the bus in gear and drove on, and Robert caught his first glimpse of the tiny car, a red Seát 600, the smallest made in Spain. It was directly behind the bus, almost at its bumper.

The driver's face was familiar, tough and unsettling. It was the boxer in the bar. The woman sat on the passenger side, and the car pulled forward enough to provide the shield Robert needed to break again into a run. But before he could bolt, the man opened his door, reached out, and grabbed him by the collar, almost choking him. The woman opened her door, put one foot on the ground and fired a fusillade at the three men running across the avenue. Under the umbrella, the old men hit the cobblestones, and glass from stray bullets shattered around them. Two of the Soviets, the man in the sunglasses and the man with the cigarette, were dead with the first burst. The man with the gun rolled under his Mercedes, and the woman, her eyes fixed on the rear of the car, pulled the trigger and sent a roaring hot round into the gas tank. The car exploded, and the Seát sped down the street.

Chapter Twenty-One

Basalobre left me to die. Basalobre set me up to die. Sergio tried to remember the face of his comrade, Basalobre. It was round and fleshy and red. The eyes were blue and set deep into the skull. Too blue for a South American. At once the face could be both angelic and devilish, from the highest throne of heaven to the deepest chasm of hell. With a laugh, the face would glow like the brightest *fogarada* whose flames touched the midnight sky as they burned in the plazas of Mexico City during *fiesta*. Angry, it became the face of death. Basalobre's last name was Libertad, at least this is what the *viejo* revolutionary claimed his last name to be. It was the only name Sergio knew, the name the old man used when Sergio first met him outside Havana in Matanzas over twenty years earlier. He was a crusty and pleasant man then, a man much admired by the young Mexican, a man Sergio adopted as his mentor. Basalobre insisted he was from Bahía Blanca, Argentina, but Sergio believed otherwise. In his world of deception, Sergio knew a man could, and most often did, claim any country as home and show the passports and birth certificates to authenticate his story, but he believed that unless you were the mother who bore the child, you could never trust the story. And even if you were the mother, there was reason for doubt.

Sergio's mind was alert. He had been awakened by the crush of a crisis in the bed across the aisle from where he lay, still feeling the dull ache from the hole in his back. The man in the bed died as two doctors beat on the pale chest.

"Now," one doctor shouted, and the other hammered the motionless sternum. "Again," and another thud. Sergio awoke and was surprised that he could lift his head from the gray-striped pillow. He was surprised that he felt alert, and that except for the constant pain in his back, his body was no longer suffering from the dull ache of lethargy that tormented even the parts of the body untouched by the surgeon.

Finally awake, quenching thirst was his first priority, and though he was unmoved by the scene of the dying man in the other bed, he did not want to interrupt the doctors in their crisis. In fact, he found pleasure in the action. For the first time since awakening in the indigent ward he felt alive. The panic and fury of the physicians' fight to save the old man's life, the fact that another unfortunate soul, and not himself, had been claimed by God, made Sergio smile, if only a little. He dropped his head back on his pillow and thought of Basalobre, a man who had cheated death for too long.

"I trusted you, my friend," he whispered under his breath. "I placed my life in your hands and you sent me here to die. But this time, I cheated death, and you will cheat no more."

Sergio drew a deep breath until the covers felt tight around his chest. A bare lightbulb burned in the ceiling above him, and he guessed the time to be somewhere between midnight and sunrise. Outside the high window, the sky was black. Everyone, except the dead man and the doctors, was sleeping soundly, and even considering the frenzy that awoke him, Sergio was filled with the serenity that softens predawn hours.

Two orderlies entered the ward to wheel the bed down the wide aisle that separated the rows of beds lining either wall in the long room. One of the orderlies, a heavyset man dressed in a light-blue uniform, took a handful of shortbread cookies from the stand next to the dead man.

"He will never miss these," the fat man laughed and shoved two cookies into his mouth.

"Give me one," the other ordered. He was much older and weathered, but the fat man handed him one, and again Sergio smiled. As the orderlies maneuvered the bed out of position and into the aisle, Sergio asked the fat man for some water.

"Right there." The man pointed to the tiny metal nightstand where a small pitcher of water and an empty glass with watermarks sat next to a plate stacked with cookies.

The bed rolled out of the room and Sergio moved his arm toward the nightstand. It moved freely, and the motion felt good. It released the tension that had swelled in his muscles. He moved his legs. They, too, responded easily to his command.

The pitcher was shaky in his left hand. Sergio steadied it with his right as well and did not bother pouring into the glass. Rather, he lifted his head up and swallowed anxiously until the stale water began to spill over the corners of his mouth, down his neck, and onto his gown and bedding. A quick gasp for air and then the water again.

"Not so fast," said the curt voice of a woman. "You must drink slowly. Do you want vapors?" She reached over and took the pitcher from Sergio's hands. "You have not taken liquid orally for almost a week."

"A week?"

"Since they operated."

"I feel better."

"You should. You were fortunate. Dr. Picano was in surgery the day they brought you here. He is our best, our chief surgeon, and he operated on you. Very fortunate for a man in this ward to have Dr. Picano."

"I am grateful," Sergio said sincerely.

"Agnes says you are not like most of the men here."

"Agnes?"

"The morning attendant." The nurse tightened the sheets around Sergio by tucking them under the mattress. "She says you have charisma."

"She does," Sergio said matter-of-factly but with a smile.

"I tell her to be careful."

"Of me?"

"*Che?*"

"Why do you say that?" Sergio rolled his head on the pillow to follow her form as she walked around the bed and tucked the sheets on the other side.

"We do not know who you are, and she is a foolish young woman."

"Of course you know who I am. I am—" Sergio shuffled quickly through his mind "—I am Juan Pedro Sánchez Ruiz."

"Yes, of Málaga." The woman straightened the pillow under his head. "You told the police you own a *bodega* in the market."

"We sell the best *vino* on the Costa del Sol."

"The police say no one there knows you." The woman stepped back and looked at the patient sternly. Her eyes were as bleak and uninviting as the room she attended.

Sergio felt suddenly stranded. His assumed identity was only as good as the shadow team verified it to be, and now they were balking. *Curse you, Basalobre.* He could not wear his emotions on his face, and so he smiled innocently. "You should not joke about such a thing."

"There is no joke," the woman said flatly. "The police have returned three, maybe four times, and always have been unable to question you. *Le voci* fill the halls of this hospital."

"What rumors?" Sergio could feel his smile stretching, but he was afraid to let it drop.

"That you are not who you say you are." The woman walked to where the dead man's bed had rested against the wall and kicked the dust balls out of the corner. "That you are hiding your identity."

"Hiding from what?"

"Only you would know that."

"I am Juan Pedro Sánchez Ruiz. That is what I know."

"I am happy that at least you are not suffering from amnesia."

"That is for certain." Sergio dropped his head deep into the pillow. "What time is it?"

"Almost four minus a quarter."

"The police checked with the Hotel Majoli. There was no problem."

"According to the rumors, they also contacted the *bodega* you noted with the registration desk as your domicile in Málaga, and the people there said they knew nothing of you."

Your mother was a whore, Basalobre Libertad. Even in the sanctuary of his mind, Sergio spit out the words. *And your father did not care.* "Everything seems so quiet tonight," his voice remained calm. "What time does Agnes come to the ward?"

"Leave Agnes alone." The woman's eyes spoke with fire, and she walked to Sergio to make her point more poignant.

The reaction warned Sergio that *le voci*, the rumors whispering through the halls of the hospital, were more than simple conjecture. *What did you tell them, Basalobre. I should have known I was too old and beaten to help your cause, but I needed to be needed. After France, I needed to live again, and you welcomed me back because I was expendable. I was expendable just as Estaban was expendable when I followed your orders and killed him in the German's room. He, too, was past his prime, a burden on the organization. Well, I will show you how expendable, how old and beaten I really am.*

"Of course," Sergio smiled again, "but I think she is very nice. She has treated me well."

"Too well." The nurse shook a bony white finger. Her wrinkled cotton smock vibrated with the movement.

For the first time, Sergio noticed the name tag: Pitti. No Miss. No Mrs. No first name. Simply Pitti.

"Do people call you Pitti?" he asked.

The nurse glanced at her tag. "Yes, they do."

"Is that the name of your husband?"

"I am not married."

"Neither am I."

"They say you have no family."

"None to speak of." Sergio sat up slightly. He looked at the water glass on the edge of the nightstand, then back to the woman. "I remember telling Agnes I had no relations."

"Do not even mention her name."

"You are too sensitive," Sergio said with a smirk. His plan was falling neatly into place.

"They have moved her to another floor."

"Why?"

"She was paying too much attention to you—you who are hardly worth it."

"I am surprised you feel that way," Sergio studied the distance to the nightstand out of the corner of his eye. "For one who does not know me, your judgment is very bold."

"Accurate." The nurse moved to the bed on Sergio's left and pulled the gray blanket up to the sleeping patient's neck. "I have seen many come and go in this ward, and—"

"You treat me like a criminal, and I am not."

"I treat you as you deserve."

"Agnes never treated me this way."

The woman jerked around and thrust her face within inches of Sergio's. "I said never mention her name."

The man felt the words fly from her mouth as he focused on her eyes and reached for the glass with his left hand, then raised it to break the mouth on the nightstand. His heart beat faster, and he tried consciously to control his breathing. The pain in his back vanished, and energy surged through his limbs. Though he had killed dozens of times in his life, still, each death provided the euphoric rush of adrenaline, and he did not want Pitti to sense the emotion. But before he could strike, the excitement of the kill vanished as quickly as it arrived when he heard the two men enter the room with the empty bed. On top of the blanket and sheets was a black canvas bag.

"*Miseria*," said the older, sinewy orderly. "Another burden on the taxpayer gone the way of the earth."

The fat man laughed and added, "But the poor taxpayer must pay for the burial."

"*Madre di fortuna, amico*. He will be thrown in the beggars' grave with the other *vagabondi*."

"To rot in hell." The fat man continued to laugh.

"They should burn him," said Pitti as she turned away from Sergio and smoothed out her smock. She helped the two place the empty bed in its position against the wall. "That would save even more money." She threw the black bag on the floor, and in one motion stripped the blanket and sheets off the bed and piled them next to the bag. "The money they get from the sale of the clothes," she nodded to the bag, "could pay for the flame."

"You will see to it that they are given to the priest?" asked the fat man.

Pitti nodded.

Sergio placed the glass back on the nightstand, grateful that he had not killed the woman—at least not yet.

Guard against your impulses. Every action is to have a reason. But I must get out of here immediately. Time is against me.

Were you going to run in your hospital gown? Now you have clothes. Wait until the orderlies leave and then kill the cagna.

To think and it was so. The tall fellow slapped his chubby associate on the back and gestured toward the door. "My stomach speaks, and I imagine yours must be screaming."

Pitti chuckled, and Sergio was surprised by how pleasant it sounded. He looked at her, expecting to see that her countenance brightened with her laughter, but it did not. Even as she smiled, her face still appeared angry, wrinkled and unnatural. Her silver, twisting hair shook up and down, bobbing violently on her head. Suddenly the laugh was tormenting.

Control your impulses.

I have good reason to kill her.

Only if you have to.

I must. She has the clothes.

"Go and eat," Pitti said. "I will make up the bed."

"Let me get you the sheets and blanket," offered the fat man.

"I will get them from the linen room." She pushed both men toward the door.

"My stomach thanks you," said the senior orderly.

"My stomach will give you its first born," said the other.

"And that should be sooner than we think." The senior man patted his friend's stomach and then flipped him on the chin.

Sergio caught a glimpse of the canvas bag on the floor.

"No need," said Pitti. "I must go to the first floor anyway. I promised Dr. Nerini that I would check in on his mother-in-law every hour." Pitti whispered, "She had a tummy-tuck, but do not tell anyone that I told you."

Both men laughed.

"There is still hope for you, then," the skinny one teased as the three walked out of the door.

After their voices faded down the hall, and Sergio looked around the room to see that every patient was still asleep, he slowly lifted his head from the pillow and then his back from the bed and braced himself on his elbows. A skeleton of a man sleeping next to the door had been stirred by the loud talk and laughter. He turned to his side with his back toward Sergio, and the latter continued to move. At first his head felt light, and he drew a deep breath, trying to force oxygen into his brain. He pushed the covers off and swung his feet over the side of the bed, surprised that the motion did not hurt the wound more than it did. For a moment, he wondered if he was on drugs, and that when the effects wore off the pain would return full force. Then he dismissed the thought, concentrated on the black bag, and resigned himself to the fact that, pain or no pain, he had to get out of the hospital.

Pitti had been vague about the rumors. Sergio wished she had been more specific. In the back of his mind, he hoped that she would return to the ward so he could kill her. That would increase the chances of getting caught, of course, but what pleasure it would give him. He wouldn't even use the glass. He would break her neck with his hands—feel the snap.

A demented crease broke in the corners of his mouth, and he slid off the bed and put weight on his feet for the first time in a week. When the bed recoiled from under his pressure, an aluminum bedpan that Pitti had placed at the foot flipped onto the floor with a loud clatter. Someone coughed, and when Sergio turned around, he came eye to eye with the emaciated man in the first bed. Sharp ridges of cheekbone protruded grotesquely beneath the black sunken eyes. The nose was spindly and white and red. Splotches of gray whiskers, where an orderly had hastily shaven the old man, made the face look discolored and diseased. Sergio put his finger to his lips and the man shook his head slowly and then dropped it back onto his bed. Within thirty seconds, his eyes were closed.

Now get the bag. Sergio took his first step and was overcome with dizziness as his head rushed from light to heavy and his neck strained under the weight. *No time to waste.* He gripped the iron footboard of his bed and took the next step. The numbness in his lower back gave way to painful stiffness. With his right hand, he reached across the aisle and took hold of the dead man's footboard. *Steady yourself.* He shuffled his feet until he stood next to the black canvas, and keeping his back straight, bending only his knees, he reached down slowly and grasped the rough fabric.

The bag was not heavy. Sergio placed it on top of the dead man's bed and pulled open the drawstring. At first it appeared there was another bag—a heavy burlap bag—inside. He pulled it out and a dark brown leather boot fell to the floor. The other boot remained inside the canvas, but there were no clothes. Sergio fumbled to open the burlap bag, but discovered it was not a bag at all, but a burnoose, a hooded cloak that tied with a belt.

Qué mierda. What shit. I cannot wear this.

What else do you have?

This is the robe of an Arab. And it smells of death.

He pulled the boot from the bag and estimated its size. As he turned it over, a cloth bag fell to the floor and the sound it made was the clink of coins. Slowly he retrieved it and the other boot and placed them next to the bag.

You have no choice, and you are losing time.

Without taking off his hospital gown, Sergio placed the burnoose over his head and cinched the belt. Against his back that was exposed under the gown, the robe was heavy and irritating. *A robe of remorse*, he thought, and remembered the sinners during Semana Santa who wore the flax and hemp robes and paraded in the procession of Christ with their ankles locked in shackles. Some crawled, but all were bleeding by the end of the procession and forgiven of their sins. The right boot was missing its laces, and he placed it on his foot first. It hurt him to lean over, and he was thankful the laces were gone. The other boot he did not tie. Both were uncomfortable but did not cause pain.

The notes in the money bag totaled one hundred thousand lire, and then there was the change, maybe another five thousand. But more important than the money was a green-covered passport—issued in Abu Dhabi. He was grateful the hospital had not yet taken the contents, and he tied the bag tightly to his belt.

I was brought in naked. Now I leave as a dead Arab.

Sergio looked around the room to find a weapon, something he could carry easily. It was the first rule of an offensive life, to have a more powerful weapon than your opponent. Knives against fists, guns against knives. Cowardly, some might call it, but he had been in the business long enough to know it was a matter of survival.

His eyes returned to the stained and empty glass on the nightstand. *That will have to do.*

He tapped the rim against the edge of the stand until, chip by chip, the smoothness gave way to a jagged edge. His finger touched it lightly to inspect the work, and it made him smile.

I am not on the first floor, he thought, remembering that Pitti said she had to go to the first floor to check on the other patient. Sergio looked at the window. It was too high on the wall for him to see which floor he was on, and for the first time in the early morning hour, he realized it was raining outside—a good omen in his business. Rain meant people were less attentive to their surroundings. Rather than pay attention, they were too busy running and hiding from the wet skies, from the harmless rain, to notice a stranger acting in strange ways. And in the rain, the dead man's clothes would not attract undue attention. The burnoose would be seen simply as another interesting hooded raincoat.

God has been kind to me, Basalobre. He was growing more confident with each discovery—Pitti's warning, the Arab's death, the bag of clothes, the passport and money, and now the rain. There was little doubt in his mind that he would make it out of the hospital. It was sometime around four o'clock, and the graveyard shift was half over, beginning to tire. The orderlies spoke of eating. Many would be taking lunch. *May God now be as kind to you, my old friend.*

Sergio looked for a pocket to bury the broken glass in. There was none, but the sleeves on the burnoose were long and baggy enough to hide his hand if he slightly crooked his elbow. This he did and moved toward the door.

Think not of the pain, and it will go away. The first two steps were the most difficult. The stiff body moved only with effort, and Sergio had to consciously place his feet. The muscles were weak and even the glass began to feel heavy in his hand. He was surprised what a bedridden week could do to the body. *Maybe it was not an entire week,* he thought. *The old woman said almost a week.* Either way, he walked slowly and not by choice. *If the orderlies return from eating, I am in trouble.* He squeezed the glass in his hand. *Never would I be able to defeat two of them at once. But if the cagna returns alone, she will not stand a chance, and the pleasure will be mine.*

Sergio placed his empty hand on an iron footboard. He was impressed that someone was watching him. He looked to the bed and discovered it belonged to the man who had awakened—the frail, gray-skinned indigent who watched Sergio from across the room. Now the man, without lifting his head, was still watching. His eyes were frightening, deep and disturbed. His head was shaved and sunken around the temples. Blue-gray veins bulged on the sides of his forehead, and he shivered.

"Can you speak?" Sergio whispered in Italian, but the man did not respond.

"*Español?*"

Still nothing.

"English?"

Only a stare.

Sergio let go of the footboard and took another step. Then he stopped. *You must kill him*, his mind warned.

He is a dying man.

He is not dead. He has seen your face, the way you are dressed. Maybe he knows who you are.

You are frightened. Old and frightened. In your youth you never thought of killing such a weak innocent.

Kill him. Do not think about the ethics.

Sergio took another step toward the door.

Obey your instincts, his mind ordered and he stopped and looked back at the man.

Maybe you will be doing the viejo a favor. How much longer can he live like that?

Do it now!

Sergio turned around and took a step back toward the bed. His hand came out from beneath the sleeve of the burnoose. He turned the glass to expose the most jagged edge to the old man's Adam's apple, and pausing he looked into the black eyes. There was no emotion.

He is dead already.

But he still breathes, now kill him.

Sergio turned the glass again and then slid it beneath the shelter of his long sleeve. *I will not*, he whispered and walked out the door.

The corridor was dark and sterile and empty. Green-tiled walls were lined with wheelchairs and metal gurneys, like cars parked along a crowded sidewalk. Sergio discovered himself holding his breath. *Out of fear?* he wondered ashamedly, and then he exhaled, relieved to find himself alone.

At the far end of the hall stood two elevator doors; beside them, painted white on the green wall, was the number two. The floor numbers above both doors showed the elevators to be docked on the first floor. Little movement in the early morning hour.

The hospital was old. This Sergio could tell by the ancient dial that pointed to the floor numbers. Rather than the modern elevators, with lights that flash as the elevators move from floor to floor, this had the old black metal wand that spun like the hands on a wristwatch. The numbers reached as high as six, not tall enough to be a modern hospital, but one that was built even before elevators, when buildings rarely were taller than a person's ability to walk the stairs.

After another step, he detected the faint smell of wintergreen. The scent became more pronounced as he moved closer to the elevators. His empty stomach began to churn as he realized he had not eaten anything as far as he could remember and that the smell of wintergreen was coming from the cadavers of indigents that were being preserved in some room on the floor for donation to medical schools. He guessed the room to be the one on the right of the elevators. Two double doors with dented bump plates where countless gurneys had been rolled in and out closed off the room, but the smell of wintergreen was most pungent.

One more step and he reached to a wheelchair on his right to steady himself, but a loud cry erupted down the quiet hall and distracted Sergio to the extent that he lost his balance and crashed to the floor on his back. The pain begged for a scream, but he held his lips tight and closed. Again the loud shrill echoed through the hall. It was coming from behind him. He cocked his head and looked back at the door of the ward. Again the cry. It was the old man. He stood like a specter, clothed in rags, pointing and screaming and pointing and screaming. Sergio had dropped the glass and it shattered on the floor around him. The pain shot from his lower back to his shoulders to his arms as he reached out for the largest piece of glass he could see on the floor. It was no more than four inches long, but it would suffice. His bare hand sliced open across the palm as he grabbed the jagged edge with undue force and turned toward the man. *The pain. The back. The shoulders. The hand.* He moved to his knees and began to crawl, but stopped as the power of the old man's scream mesmerized him, a scream that seemed surreal, to have come from another world, through the oracle of the *viejo*, to swirl like demons through the hall and alert the world to Sergio Castillo Armando.

Sergio moved again. This time he was stopped by the sound of the elevator. He looked back at the iron dial. It was moving. *Roll into the room*, he commanded, and his body responded. The double doors burst open, then closed behind him as he scrambled under a metal table draped with white sheets. The smell of wintergreen was nauseating. He heard the voice of Pitti in the hall as he peeked out from under the sheets and saw the room full of tables.

"*Signore Giovanni*," she shouted in anger. "Back into the room. Look at what you have done."

The man screamed again and a chill raced up Sergio's spine.

"Do you hear me," Pitti yelled.

Again he screamed.

"*Signore*, I will call the orderlies and they will bring the gun. Now back into your room."

Sergio expected to hear another scream, but it never came. He crawled from under the table and pulled himself off the dark green tile with the one hand that did not clutch the glass. As he stood, he was surprised to see the death face of an attractive woman. Her hair was blond and waved and pulled back tight against her skull. Her lips were blue and her face a pasty blue-white. Blood veins beneath her nose had exploded and left startling red streaks like a mustache.

He would have liked to study the dead girl more, but the sound of Pitti running toward the elevators and pounding on the buttons turned his attention to the window located in the same place on the wall as the window in the indigent ward. Between him and the window were a dozen or more tables with cadavers buried beneath white sheets. Under the night light falling through the window they seemed to float in the darkness, suspended like the beautiful woman in a magic show.

He took a deep breath and straightened his back in an attempt to relieve the constant pressure of pain. In the hall, Pitti was frantically hitting the buttons, and it sounded to Sergio as if the elevators were not responding. Within a moment, she began to scream for help, and he stumbled toward the window, tumbling onto tables, redirecting his course and moving again. Near the wall, he knocked the cadaver of a middle-aged man to the floor. The nude body spilled out of the sheets and sprawled open in the darkness.

That is good, Sergio thought, and he slid the now-vacant gurney next to the wall. His first attempt to mount it met with failure. He could not do it with one hand, and reluctantly he surrendered the broken glass. Both hands freed, he leveraged himself into position and brought his legs up under him. Blood smeared the white sheet that remained on the table. Standing, he could reach the window.

He heard the elevator doors open and Pitti stopped screaming. They closed and she was gone. With a sudden blow, he used his already wounded hand, broke the pane of glass, and chipped away the fragments left wedged in the frame. His hand grew numb from the pain, and when the frame was smooth, he placed both arms through and lifted himself off the table until he straddled the bottom edge of the window under his armpits. The weight of his body pulling against the wound in his back made him light-headed. He wanted to groan in pain, but his discipline forbade it.

Driving rain quickly soaked his hair and glossed his already perspiring forehead. For a brief moment it felt good, comforting and cool. The drop beneath him was more than twenty feet. Fortunately, it was into a garden, and even if it had not been, he had no other choice. Like a snake, he redistributed his weight until he teetered on his waist on the base of the window seal, and with a rolling motion he flipped out of the opening and tried to get his feet beneath him before he hit the ground.

They did not make it, and he landed on his buttocks in the muddy earth. The burnoose protected him from the thorns of the overgrown rose bushes, but the pain in his back from the shock of the landing drove him from his senses until it abated.

Chapter Twenty-Two

Dr. Rubin David Steinbrenner smelled the gas first, and the odor shifted his dream back to his youth in Krakow. He was surrounded by his parents, Abrham and Pani Steinbrenner, his brothers, Viktor and Marc. They were sitting around the dark dining-room table distinguished by its thick, round, smoothly lathed legs that grew like tree trunks from the hardwood floor in their working-class flat. Pani was serving coffee after dinner, and young Rubin could not avoid watching her breasts, heavy inside the faded gray print cotton dress. She was a stout woman, and the fullness of her breasts was comforting to the young man, though he was a decade beyond weaning.

Viktor was arguing with Abrham, the soft-spoken patriarch who worked hard in the machine shop to pull his small family out of the ghetto in which he was raised, to send his boys to school, then to the university, to educate them as doctors and lawyers and scientists. Viktor was of age to enter the university. His grades in secondary school were good, but now he argued that rather than continue his education, the time had come for him to marry and move into the machinist trade with his father.

Viktor loved Jadwika, the dark-eyed girl from the river. Rubin called her a gypsy to tease Viktor, but he knew she was not, and he coveted his brother's luck to find such a pleasing woman. He knew of Viktor's fear that she might not wait for him while he attended university, though Rubin believed she would. Rubin, eight years younger than Viktor, believed any woman would wait for his older brother, his idol whose rugged looks and athletic ability and intelligence placed him in an upper-class neighborhood. Viktor never looked good on Zamosc Street, but should have lived out where the chalets were spaced on wide lots in the Buko district.

Rubin smiled and nodded his support as he listened to Viktor's arguments for not attending the university.

"I know my marks are good, but the money I earn in the machine shop could go toward a larger home, and Jadwika, as my wife, could live with us and help Mother, and we could send Rube to the best schools in all of Europe, and you and I, Father, we could eventually buy our own shop and work together, and that would allow us to move from the neighborhood to the homes across the river."

Abrham blew black smoke from his dark tobacco cigarettes into the air and laughed. "Listen to you, an idiot in life. Listen to the man who scored almost perfect on his placement exams, a man born with the hands of a surgeon. God does not want you to be a machinist."

"How do you speak for God?"

"Because I am the man of this house."

"Viktor would be a good machinist," Rubin offered respectfully.

"Viktor would be a great machinist," corrected Abrham, "but he was raised to be something more. That is our family way. My grandfather was a peasant farmer, liked well enough by his landlord that he was endowed with his land and his freedom. My father moved as a free man to this city and began life in the ghetto as an unskilled laborer in the machine shop. I was blessed to learn the trade from my father's employers and offer my services during the war. I gained respect, and I have provided well for my family—"

"You have provided very well," said Pani as she poured her husband's coffee and kissed him on his soiled forehead.

"Now why should our progress stop?" Abrham finished.

"It will not stop." Pani moved to Viktor and poured his cup next, and then on to Marc, and finally Rubin.

"But Rubin is the most intelligent," Viktor pressed.

"All my sons are intelligent," said Abrham as he tousled Marc's hair. Marc was the silent one, wise but unspoken. He only smiled. "We are men of royal blood but common backs."

"You have said that before," said Rubin.

"Now it is time to follow the blood." He crunched out his cigarette in a tin ashtray next to his plate of carrot and potato scraps and meat fat. He took a shallow sip of coffee, and Rubin could see by his expression that it was still too hot. "You will be a great surgeon, and you will thank me for my stubbornness."

All three boys laughed, and with a smile Pani placed the coffee back on the gas stove.

Then the dream changed again, and Steinbrenner remembered Treblinka, at least the literary portrait of the camp Viktor painted in his letters. His father was choking in a windowless room and cradling Pani's head in his hands. Men and women were clawing their way on top of each other, believing that fresh air was only another breath away. But it was not. And then came the screaming.

Rubin's eyes opened in shock and he looked around the small room, an efficiency apartment with a bed, a bookshelf, a reclining chair in the corner, and a gas stove with a teapot turning the screams of his dream into the whistle of steaming water.

A thin black man, dressed nicely in a three-piece suit, slid out of the recliner and moved to the kitchen. "I thought you was dead," said the man as he pulled the teapot off the flame and poured it over the instant coffee crystals at the bottom of his cup.

"Excuse me," said Dr. Steinbrenner. His voice was hoarse and the back of his head hurt. Then he remembered the restroom at the Press Club and the face of the man from the university.

"We thought you was in a coma or something. You want coffee?"

"Please." Steinbrenner slowly lifted his hand to head. His captors had been thoughtful enough to wrap it in gauze. They had also taken off his suit coat, but he still remained in the same clothes he wore the day he was abducted, and he knew it was not recently, because of the faint smell of urine. He was not wet, but he must have been before it dried.

The man handed Steinbrenner a white Styrofoam cup. "It's got caffeine."

"Fine," he said reaching for it. His movement rattled a chain and he saw that it was locked around his ankle and anchored to a radiator next to the bed. He breathed the bittersweet aroma before sipping, and it, alone, stimulated his throbbing head. "How long have I been here?"

"Almost a day now." The man answered and took a drink.

"Would it do any good if I asked where I am?"

"You're on 16th Street, right above Malcolm X Park."

"Malcolm X?"

"Yeah, by Howard University. You know, a part of the woods you probably never get to."

"I know where it is."

The man nodded and took another drink.

"KGB?" Steinbrenner guessed unoffensively.

"GRU."

The professor's brow questioned the response, and the man continued. "Surprise you that the GRU would want a black man?"

"Should it?" the scientist took his first sip.

"We're all fighting for the same thing—freedom—whether it's from apartheid or economic slavery or imperialist expansion. It's all the same. Those who got the money shittin' on those who don't."

"I see, and what class do you fit into."

The man laughed, "Me? I'm Donald Trump, Jr."

Steinbrenner nodded his head and closed his eyes. *This is it*, he thought. *My life boils down to the GRU, this efficiency, and whatever they are after—information, ransom, whatever.*

Not ransom, he corrected. *They want information. So it doesn't boil down to this. You still have control, because you still have the information.*

Of all the Germans could strip from us, they could not take our attitude, he remembered Viktor's letter. He loved Viktor. *And as long as we held the freedom to govern our attitude, we held the freedom to hope and the freedom to believe. What mattered the most, Rubin, was the attitude we took toward our suffering, the attitude in which we took our suffering upon ourselves. We soon learned to turn our suffering and grief into sacrifice. And the very moment it found meaning, the very moment it became sacrifice, it ceased to be suffering. We learned that a man's main concern is not to gain pleasure or to avoid pain, but rather to find the meaning in his life.*

Steinbrenner knew that the GRU, as the military branch of Soviet espionage activity, was interested in the Strategic Defense technology. He was certain they wanted to know how far along the Americans had progressed with the Initiative. The professor had that information. He controlled that information.

*So it all does not come down to this. You are still in control here.
They need you, and you will decide who gets what and when.* He
opened his eyes and looked at the man, who had lighted a cigarette.
"Do you smoke?"

"No," Steinbrenner's voice cracked as he answered and took another sip of coffee. The small of his back and his buttocks ached from lack
of movement. "I would like to walk around, though, if that's okay."

"Be my guest." The man took a lengthy drag on the Winston and
gestured with both arms that the room belonged to the scientist.

"Thank you— What's your name?"

"Call me Mohammed."

"Islamic." Steinbrenner said matter-of-factly.

"Like I said, you're above Malcolm X Park."

The professor slid off the bed and stood up very slowly. His back
cried out against the weight, and his legs were heavy and awkward. He
tried to shake his feet, but they were reluctant to obey his command.
"This body is getting old," he said. "And I am growing frustrated."

"You're in great shape, old man," said Mohammed as he dropped
into the recliner. "Took two of our strongest to bring you in."

"It's not easy growing old. Your mind remembers how strong you
were in youth. It remembers the thousands of hours of football, the
wonderful times swimming the widest rivers, the passion of first love.
And then it's gone. The terrible thing is that while the body doesn't
yearn for the activity and the passion, the mind does, and the body, it
says, go to hell." Steinbrenner chuckled and Mohammed joined in.
"See," said the professor, suddenly serious, "that's why I don't mind
if you kill me. My body has been in charge for too long now, and my
mind is ready to surrender."

"Who said anything about killing?" The black man squashed out
his cigarette on the dirty white-tiled floor and lit another. "You're too
important to be dyin'. At least right now."

The old man nodded, not in agreement but comprehension. The
thick chain shackled on his left foot rattled as he shuffled toward a
small bookcase near the kitchen. He placed his coffee on the top shelf
and looked at the titles. "Your only problem," he said, "is that you
spend too much time in those progressive bookstores on DuPont
Circle."

"My problem," said Mohammed as he blew a swirling wave of smoke into the room, "is that the white motherfuckers been stickin' it to the black folk for too long."

"For instance?"

"You built this roach-infested country on our bloody backs, then deny us the same economic opportunity that lets every other white mother get ahead. You seen the shit where we live at over on the Northeast side. Black kids going to bed with rats and shit. Slaughtering each other for a few grams of crack and maybe some airplane glue."

"Not all blacks live that way."

"Sure!" Mohammed blew another cloud of smoke. "Sure, not the motherf'n tokens you bring out and parade through the media. The mothers who make up your success stories, who climb above their poverty to sing like Whitney Houston or box like Mike Tyson. Nothin' but entertainment."

"How about Senator Pierce, one of the finest statesmen in America."

"As white as snow. Fucker's so white, even his dick's shrunk."

Steinbrenner studied the books to let the remarks pass. There was no conversion in sight for Mohammed, at least not now. He picked the least offensive book from the shelf, a selection of essays by academicians with the lusterless title *Revolution: Central America.* The chain clanked as he moved back to the bed. "It was thoughtful of you to provide the books," he said.

"They're always here. This is a safehouse, where we bring colleagues on the run—for protection and shit."

"But I imagine I'm about the only white man in the building. Surely I stand out."

"Nobody's seen you. We brought you up the cargo elevator in a piano box."

"Not creative, but adequate." The professor thumbed through the pages of the book, stopping long enough to read the chapter headings: "The Origins of Crisis"; "The Reagan Debacle"; "The Diplomatic Answer." "How long do you plan on holding me? At least until you kill me?"

"There you go talking 'bout death again. You know, you got a one-track mind."

"I figure it must be information that you want." Steinbrenner snapped the book closed and looked at Mohammed on the other side of the room. He had the appearance of a college boy, skinny in his suit and lean through the face, a kid who did not understand the real philosophical issues that dictated his actions, but who was simply going along for the clichés. "You know I cannot give you anything. And you know that every second you hold me, you and your people are one second closer to being caught."

"I follow my orders. But nothing's going to happen to you."

"A myrmidon," the professor said under his breath as he returned to the bed.

"What's that?"

"Nothing."

Mohammed stood up quickly and rushed toward him. "No, mother-fucker, what'd you call me?" He reached down and took Steinbrenner by the collar and drew him nose to nose.

"A myrmidon—a faithful follower who carries out orders without question. The Myrmidon—legendary Greek warrior people of Thessaly who followed their king, Achilles, on his expedition against Troy."

"Don't be callin' me that." Mohammed dropped the professor back onto the bed, lit another cigarette and returned to his chair. "I'm just holding you until another guy gets here, a guy who wants to ask you some questions."

"And you think that if I refuse to answer they're going to let me walk out of here."

"Shit!" Mohammed exploded in laughter, ignited by his rationale. "You're the man who wants to die."

Steinbrenner stared at him.

"I'll promise you one thing—the way our boy's going to ask you the questions, you're going to see death as a fuckin' friend."

The professor drew a deep breath, and closed his eyes. "Do you know the man?" he asked.

"No. But I seen him work once. He's a bad mother—peeled a guy's face right off. I never seen anything like it before. Skin peels off like a banana—you know that?"

Don't even answer, Steinbrenner told himself, *and don't let this boy see he is affecting you.* He opened his eyes and looked at Mohammed.

"All you got to do is take a razor and cut the skin just below the hair, down the sideburns and ears, over the jaw and under the chin. Skin will come right off—like a Halloween mask—over the nose and everything."

"I never knew I would be so important."

"It's not you that's important. It's what you know. You know—knowledge is power."

"Something like that," Steinbrenner said. "What's the man's name?" He did not mind asking the question. The boy had been free with all his information so far, a definite sign that there was no way the scientist would be allowed to leave the tiny room alive.

"Why's that important?"

"It's not important, really. But maybe I know him."

"Oh, I'm sure you know him," Mohammed said in a voice that taunted Steinbrenner and delighted him. "He's known real good here in Washington."

The expression on the professor's face begged for the answer.

"Chances are you've had dinner with him. Maybe you even picked up the bill."

The professor's brow wrinkled into a thousand creases.

"Frankly, he's our most important man in Washington. Maybe our most important man in America—maybe even the world."

"Then I *should* feel important.

"Yeah," Mohammed grinned, "yeah, I guess you should. If I was you, I'd—"

Before the Muslim could finish his sentence, three distinct knocks sounded on the door. Suddenly, a Browning 9-mm appeared in his hand and Steinbrenner was not sure how it got there. He thought it must have come from under the suit coat, but that made little difference now, as the black man moved to the door and ordered: "Who is it?"

The professor heard a faint reply, something like "Charlie," but he was not sure. He had guessed correctly when he thought earlier of yelling for help, but believed the walls were probably insulated enough that his cries would not be heard, at least not before they were stifled.

The boy smiled and asked: "Are you alone?"

There must have been an answer because the smile broadened and Mohammed unlatched three chain locks and twisted the deadbolt. The door opened and one of the most beautiful young girls Steinbrenner had ever seen walked into the room carrying a box of Popeye's chicken.

"Love ya, Charlie," he said, taking the carton from her hands and placing it on the cabinet in the kitchen.

Steinbrenner only stared as the woman in a black silk blouse and green leather miniskirt followed him into the kitchen area. Her shining coal-black hair was cut short and slicked back against her scalp. Her legs were tanned and smooth and stockingless. She wore black pumps, and moved like she was born in them.

Where do they come from? he asked himself. *How do they find such people—a woman who could have everything? Is she motivated by altruism, or is it the excitement and intrigue of the lifestyle that attract her?*

"He's awake," she said, and the professor noted her thick and formal English accent.

"For about forty-five minutes now," answered Mohammed.

"Has he talked?"

"Hell, yes, he's talked."

"Anything important?"

"Shit," laughed the boy, "you're too caught up in the drama— watched too many spy shows—'Has he talked?' You and me wouldn't know what he was talking about anyway."

"The hell I wouldn't," she argued. "I've been briefed on the operation." She pulled three plates from the cabinet over the sink.

"We don't need no plates," said the boy. "Let's just eat out of the box."

"My mother would kill me."

"If she knew what you was doing she'd kill you anyway. Let's eat out of the box. No mess. No dishes."

"So did he say anything about SDI?"

"Forget SDI. Let's eat."

"At least I must put his chicken on a plate." She turned to Steinbrenner and smiled a college girl smile, a smile the professor had seen thousands of times from the young students who charmed his old ego. Sure they were after grades, still they made him feel good. "Would you like white or dark?" she asked, and her voice filled the room like sprightly music.

"White, thank you," he answered and studied her form as she turned back to the counter.

"I love the dark shit," said Mohammed.

"Figures," said the woman with a laugh. "Helps you keep your color."

"And what do you eat?" joined Mohammed. "Snowballs?"

The woman delivered the plate to the professor. "You've not eaten anything for some time now. I suggest you eat slowly. If you should like more than these two breasts and the biscuit, I would be happy to get it for you."

"This is enough, thank you."

Charlie smiled politely. "Can I get you anything to drink?"

"I have coffee over there." The physicist nodded to the bookcase, and the woman retrieved the Styrofoam cup.

"It's not all that hot anymore."

"It will be fine." The physicist bit off a small piece of meat and chewed slowly. His empty stomach was already reacting to the flavor, growling for more. He took a bite of his biscuit, washed it down with the coffee and could not remember when he had tasted anything so savory. "So you want to know about the Strategic Defense Initiative," he said as he took another bite of chicken. "There is not much I can tell you. I am only the President's scientific advisor. You think they would trust such information to a man as old and broken down as I am?"

Charlie settled into the recliner, and her skirt slid up on her thighs as she crossed her firm legs. Steinbrenner's heart beat a little faster. "Would you please pour me a cup?" she asked Mohammed, who was still standing next to the stove, and then she turned back to Steinbrenner. "We know better, Dr. Steinbrenner," she said. "We have it on very good authority that you are precisely the man in charge—that you are the man who frequently briefs the Senate Intelligence Committee on the Initiative." Her teeth were white and perfectly aligned as she smiled. "I'm really not trying to flatter you, professor, but you are much more important than you think. I almost insisted that they bring you here, to my safehouse."

"Yours?"

"I run it, anyway. So while you are here, consider yourself my guest."

Steinbrenner was self-conscious under the woman's gaze, and he rubbed the age-spots on his forehead with his right hand. It was greasy from the chicken. *What do you care what she thinks about you, you old bastard?* his mind scolded his vanity. *She wants one thing from you and it certainly is not your impotent virility.* He tried to rub the grease into his forehead, but believed he was only smearing it, and was embarrassed.

"We move very carefully," she continued. "And I can assure you that before we risked such a daring abduction, our people would be certain that we were taking the correct person."

"Your people?"

"We're fuckin' everywhere," said Mohammed as he moved from the kitchen area to the recliner. Charlie gave him a disapproving look.

"You can clean up your language," she said and then turned back to Steinbrenner. "You see, doctor, one of your people offered you as a sacrifice before he was killed."

"A sacrifice?"

"He made the mistake of talking—perhaps thinking it might save his own life."

Steinbrenner realized immediately that she was referring to Senator Watenburg. He took another bite of chicken, trying to act unaffected by the information. "I don't know of whom you are speaking, but I assure you he must not have been as informed as he, or you, thought."

"He was well informed," said Charlie.

"And like a fuckin' capitalist, he sang like a canary when his life was threatened."

Again Charlie looked disdainfully at Mohammed. "I have to apologize for my associate," she said. "I've been working on his manners, but have made very little progress."

"Fuckin' A—" Mohammed laughed and walked into the bathroom.

"I really do apologize," said the woman once the bathroom door closed, and Steinbrenner nodded his acceptance. Everything about her bespoke sincerity, and he understood that she was a warrior of altruism, one who literally believed the egalitarian myth of communism.

Bar political circumstances and Steinbrenner believed she would be the wife of a wealthy man, a woman whose life would be like virtu crystal, adorned and protected. Her elegance would grace the polo fields of Europe and sit in the company of royalty. But somewhere along the timeline of her life, she was influenced by the humanitarian deceit of the revolutionary left, and now a woman who once would have loathed the violence of espionage was an adherent to moral compromise for political purposes—a woman who believed that in the advancement of her revolution any means is justified.

"I've heard college students with far more foul mouths." He took another bite of chicken.

"Yes, I am sure you have."

Steinbrenner was aware of how pleasant her voice sounded, the long English vowel and mellifluous intonation.

"Your colleague has said I will be questioned by someone—a leader of yours."

"Yes, I think you will quite like him," she answered. "His name is Thompson, though I have never met him."

"Thompson?"

"Yes. And from what I gather, he is quite an authority on your hierarchy here in America. He must be awfully reassured that you are the right man."

"Why do you say that?"

"Because we have been told he cut his European holiday short so he could visit with you." Charlie stopped speaking long enough to bite her biscuit. "He has been vacationing in Spain, I think they said. I am looking forward to meeting him myself."

"Your friend says he has worked with this Thompson before—that he is skilled with the knife."

"I believe Mohammed exaggerates. No one will hurt you."

"You really believe that, don't you?"

"Of course I do." Charlie placed the drumstick on her plate and stared at Steinbrenner. "Don't you?" she turned her head softly, and her eyes held the emotion that the old man had missed since Ida's death.

"Perhaps I'm a little more pragmatic about these things."

The sound of the toilet flushing and Mohammed opening the bathroom door put an end to the dialogue. Charlie returned to her chicken and Steinbrenner watched the man move past the bed toward the stove.

"You know, your chain's long enough to reach the john," said Mohammed. "But I guess you can keep goin' in your pants if you want to."

"That's uncalled for," Charlie snapped even though she had a mouthful of chicken. "One more remark like that and I'll report you."

Steinbrenner felt the heat of his blush and tried not to look at the woman.

"We're out of coffee," said Mohammed as he threw the empty Folger's bottle into the trash. "If I gotta stay here tonight, I want more coffee."

"I'll pick some up after class," Charlie said as she wiped her mouth.

"Fuck that. I want it now."

The woman stood and walked to the kitchen, placed her plate in the sink. "You really are impossible."

"I been here two days. You dance in and dance out, and act like you're some motherfucking queen, or something."

Steinbrenner watched as Charlie turned red and spoke through clenched teeth. "First of all, I cannot be a motherfucker," she yelled. "That's anatomically impossible."

Mohammed laughed and lit another cigarette.

"And second, I swear, you get out of line once more, and I will have your head floating down the Potomac!"

Steinbrenner brightened up at the imagery and watched as Mohammed blew smoke into the woman's face.

"I will get you your bloody coffee—"

"Watch your language." Mohammed cackled even louder, and Charlie, now beyond rage, kneed him in the groin. As he buckled over in pain, she ripped her knee into his forehead, and he collapsed on the floor.

"Fuckin' bitch," he screamed as she grabbed her keys off the tile cabinet and rushed out of the apartment, slamming the door. "Ahh, shit!" he said and flicked glowing ashes off his neck. He scrambled to his feet and moved to the door.

Hold on, old man, the professor said to himself. *These two amateurs are going to create such a disturbance that you will be found yet.*

But no sooner was the thought complete than the boy stopped before he opened the door, appeared to regain his composure, and latched the three chain locks and flipped the deadbolt above the knob.

"Bitch," he said as he turned to Steinbrenner. "Fights like a fuckin' nigger. Ain't proper for an English bitch."

The professor only nodded and took another bite of chicken. It was getting cold now, and the emotion of the disturbance made his arms and hands weak. "I'm full," he said and held his plate and coffee cup out for Mohammed.

"I'm your maid?" Mohammed dropped into the recliner. "Put the dishes in the sink yourself." He examined his cigarette. "She's too damn beautiful for her own good."

Steinbrenner slid painfully off the bed. The chain rattled as he moved toward the sink, but stopped taut when he was six feet away.

"I'm sorry. I can't reach the sink."

"Then make like a basketball player."

"Excuse me?"

"Throw them into the sink. Shit! They're only plastic."

"I'm afraid I would make a mess." The professor placed them on the floor and returned to the bed.

Chapter Twenty-Three

The woman in the Seát 600 was not attractive. Her features were masculine, and her hair was coarse and dull and brown. She wore a beige broadcloth shirt, under a green wool sweater, and baggy corduroy trousers. She was not Mediterranean, too pale and large, with freckles on her hands, nose, and cheeks. The Uzi in her lap did not soften her image, and neither did the recollection of how she used it only moments ago. Robert thought she looked like her male companion, brother and sister maybe, except she was more masculine. Even her movements were strong and anxious as she looked about the car, then fumbled for something beneath the sweater and withdrew a pack of unfiltered Celtas.

"You scared the devil out of those old men," said the driver in English with a thick Spanish accent. That he spoke in English confirmed to Robert that the woman was not from Spain.

"Where did I place my lighter?" She patted her pockets, and the Uzi tumbled off her lap onto the floorboard. Robert tensed, but the gun did not fire, and he watched her open the glove compartment and shuffle through a half dozen maps.

The man reached into the breast pocket of his shirt, pulled out a matchbook, and handed it to her. "I have never seen *dominós viejos* move that quickly"— he laughed —"jumping to the ground. You made them remember Franco and the war, holding their berets, keeping their heads low, yet curious enough to want to look."

She lit and puffed a gray cloud into the car. "Did I kill any of them?'' she asked with a shrug, and Robert knew she was not American, but he could not place her accent.

"Luckily, no," said the driver.

"Lucky for them," she corrected and turned to face Robert. He wanted to say something, to ask who they were, where they were taking him, but he thought she was going to speak first, and he was grateful for the rescue and believed that he should remain in silent gratitude at least until the car was a safe distance from the battle site and everyone was more relaxed—especially himself. For a moment, he thought she was going to speak, but her face was expressionless, and the silence continued.

The Seát veered right around a hairpin turn split by the odd-shaped wedge of an elegant gray stone hotel, the kind built in the gilded twenties when luxury was ornate and ostentatious and people were proud of it. The car was now moving west on the coastal boulevard, and Robert recognized the pier and beach he visited the night before. It seemed so long ago. He tapped the notebook in his back pocket to reassure himself, and looked out the rear window to see if they were being followed. There was no police, no chase car, but he counted at least seven Seát 600s and realized he was in the care of professionals. The little cars looked like undernourished Volkswagen Bugs, and they were the most popular car in the country, nondescript and swarming from the Pyrenees to the Mediterranean.

Maybe Julia's people, he thought, reasoning they were not communist or they would not have killed their own. *They are not American— not CIA. I can spot CIA from fifty paces, and these two don't fit the mold. They must be Julia's people.* He settled into his seat painfully aware of how uncomfortable the rear of such a small car was, especially for a man with a broken rib.

The Seát raced by the Almería docks, where a merchant ship flying the Japanese flag was tied and unloading cargo. A tin roof covered the concrete platform for about one hundred yards, and thirty or forty longshoremen with manual dollies stacked the cargo boxes in a dozen straight rows. Farther down the road, Robert saw the whitewashed gypsy cliffs on the right and the majestic castle where he spent the night, and suddenly the coastal city was behind them. The traffic thinned out, and the driver pulled the Seát two car lengths to the rear of a bus.

"This is a safe speed," he said, and the woman grunted her approval.

She kicked the Uzi forward on the floor, rolled down her window and flipped the cigarette onto the road. Shadows of dusk played off the mountains, and Robert saw the sparks scatter as the cigarette hit the pavement. The mountain dropped another two hundred yards from the highway on the left, and the torches of a small fishing village burned along the beach as the weather-tanned men pushed their ponderous boats into the surf. One fisherman had already hoisted his lugsail, but it only flapped in the gentle breeze.

The odor of tobacco in the car made Robert's stomach growl and his head ache, and he wondered how much longer they would travel in silence. The passing lane was clear and the driver forced the Seát into third gear; it lurched forward, and soon the bus was fading in the rear window.

"This is bad mountain road for the autobus," said the man, and a road sign read: MÁLAGA 78 KIL.

"Are we going all the way to Málaga?" Robert finally spoke, and the woman glared at him. He could think only to nod and return a self-conscious smile. "You can tell me where you're taking me—can't you?"

"Where you will be very safe," said the driver. He returned Robert's smile, and gentle reassurance filled the journalist.

"Málaga?" he asked again, and the woman looked at the driver then back to Robert and nodded.

He wanted to ask if they were associated with Julia, but he believed if they were not, it would place her in jeopardy. He studied the woman's eyes and asked, "Who are you?"

"We cannot answer that," she answered. Her voice was flat and final, and for the first time he detected a German accent.

"At least give me a name. I'd like to know who I owe my life to."

"Call me Paco," said the driver as he looked at Robert in the rearview mirror.

"And you can call me Conchi."

"Well, thank you—both of you—for what you did back there."

Paco responded pleasantly. The corners of his eyes creased with deep lines that made him look rugged and handsome, and Robert was a little self-conscious. His own skin and hands were soft, his face was lined only by time, not weather and sun. *Less masculine*, he thought. "I saw you in the bar. You were waiting for me, weren't you?" "We had our orders," said Conchi.

"You can't tell me who they came from?"

"I wish we could," said Paco, and Conchi lit another cigarette. She handed the pack to Robert. "Do you smoke?" she asked, and when he shook his head, she placed the pack in the glove compartment.

"Conchi smokes like—you Americans say—a chimney," Paco laughed. "I smoke too, but only because my father thought it killed worms and cleaned the lungs. Only because all men smoke."

Robert smiled. "You're Spanish, then?"

"*Vasco*," said the man proudly.

Conchi laughed for the first time and smiled at her colleague. "Vasco, he says, and while his comrades are tossing bombs and fighting in the streets for liberation, he is down here in Málaga tossing bombs and fighting in the streets for—" she paused and took another drag.

"For?" Robert's smile faded. Impulsively, he wanted to take his notebook out and begin writing.

"*Nada*," said Paco. He was the only one left smiling.

"I have never seen Paco smoke." Conchi changed the conversation. "He says he does, though, and I have no reason to doubt him, except that he is awfully concerned about his macho Iberian image." Her eyes brightened as she looked at him, and Robert was taken by how appearance can change with disposition. She looked prettier now, and he believed there might be more than a professional attraction between the two.

The highway drew deeper into the mountains, away from the sea, and through a narrow valley, now and then, Robert could see the shadow of water in the settling dusk. The car passed through a small village with white stucco *casitas* trimmed in red and surrounded by low trees and bushes common on the dry, rocky terrain.

A fat old woman dressed in black cotton hung bed linens from a clothesline next to the roadside market, a stone fence away from the highway. She was oblivious to the passing traffic, concentrating only on that which was important to her, and Robert thought about how simple her life must be and found it strange that when one person can be overcome with crisis, others carry on—just another day. *It's that way with death*, he thought, and was overcome with the picture of Senator Watenburg's family, even Julia Peterson. In their case, it was he who had carried on, unaffected by the tragedy, pursuing his story, and thinking nothing more of the murders than how they fit as pieces into the puzzle *he* was putting together.

He remembered what Julia had said on the telephone: Journalists have only one loyalty. To themselves. They serve no one else. It embarrassed Robert to admit that she was right, but he knew it was true. Since Woodward and Bernstein ushered in the era of superstar journalism, the hounds of hell could not keep the throngs of college kids away from the campus newsrooms. Overnight, journalism was a celebrity industry filled with coveted front-page bylines, book contracts, and Pulitzer Prizes that played like Academy Awards in the self-aggrandizing profession.

Take egoism out, and you'll castrate the benefactors, Robert thought and laughed silently at the words of Emerson. He both enjoyed and detested these moments of self-revelation, because, while his honesty was brutal, he also believed he was in part motivated by scrupulous and humanitarian objectives. *The media are society's watchdog*, he thought. *Our duty is to make the uncomfortable comfortable and the comfortable uncomfortable, to shake up the status quo and ask the questions that make mankind dig deep into evaluating its progress and objectives and inhumanities.* Those were the desires that motivated Robert when he argued with Harper about journalism school. But the old man knew the perils of the power journalists held with the printed word.

"The press controls the mind of America," Harper once said. "I think, like most of the gosh-damn politicians who've run us into hell, the press, after a while, loses its own focus. They bullshit and hammer, bullshit and hammer, until even the tiniest fact becomes a crisis, and everyone starts doubtin'. And they got no pride in the flag. Think they're all too smart for that. Smarter than you and me, boy—smarter than the President. Then they forget they're supposed to be reportin', and they start tellin'. They start opinionatin'. Every country's got problems, but they don't spread them out on the front page like the signs over Subic Bay whorehouses. Here in America, the reporters advertise the problems. And the worse thing is that they're smilin' inside when they do it."

Harper usually complained in this manner when the journalists reported a story he did not agree with, or when they criticized America. Harper was not political, but he loved his country.

"You be different, boy. You be honorable."

Robert was glad Harper was dead when he broke the MX story. He was not glad that the man he loved had died, but rather that he was not around to see his boy play a pawn in the political chess game that destroyed the credibility of the missile system and landed him in prison on contempt charges. He had won a Pulitzer, probably more because of the notoriety from prison than because of the five-part series report. Either way, it was a Pulitzer, and Robert was not content to stop with one.

A dirt road broke from the main highway as it twisted back from the mountains toward the sea. Paco pulled the car onto the road and drove until he was out of sight from the highway.

"I must change the *matrículas*."

"*Matrículas?*" Robert asked.

Conchi turned around. She had lighted another cigarette, but lost in thought, Robert had not noticed until now. "The license plates," she said. "In case anyone was quick enough to get our number."

Robert nodded. "Can I help?"

Paco made two clicking sounds with his tongue and teeth that Robert took as no, and looked back to Conchi. "Then do you mind if I get out and stretch my legs?"

The woman looked at Paco as he took a screwdriver from under the seat and opened his door. He shrugged his shoulders, and the fact that the two had to consider the request made Robert nervous.

"Yes. Fine," said Conchi, and she opened her door to get out with him.

Robert heard the clack of metal and turned to see that she had taken the Uzi off the floor and held it tucked under her armpit.

"There's nowhere to run," he said and bent over to pick up a rock.

"Only a precaution," she said. "We do not know if we were followed."

"Look," Robert lowered his voice so Paco could not hear. "Do we have a mutual friend?"

"What do you mean?" She looked down the mountain to the black sliver of sea that could be seen through the gorge.

"I mean, did anyone ask you to find me?"

Conchi looked at Paco, whose head was bobbing up and down as he twisted the screws on the rear license plate. Then she looked back to Robert. Her eyes were soft and seemed at odds with the rest of her face. A faint smile creased her lips, and she nodded yes.

A church bell chimed nine times as the pale blue Seát rolled over the cobblestone Calle Calderón de la Barca and parked in front of brownstone building number thirty-nine. Robert was more relaxed now, even excited, knowing who had orchestrated his escape. The night was cool, but once the small car descended from the mountains to the shoreline and passed the docks of Málaga, he had rolled down his window and breathed deeply. His headache cleared and his mood brightened as his mind played with the image of Julia, and he thought about seeing her again.

Through the rear window, he saw the illuminated clock on the spire of a city cathedral. The moon was rising behind the belfry and the shades of night were haunting. No one walked along the street, and Robert thought of the sharp contrast from the night before when the sidewalks of Almería were filled with life. He dropped his head low to get a good view of building thirty-nine through the front window. It looked to be seven or eight stories high. Lights on half of the floors still burned, and he wondered which apartment was hers.

Both Paco and Conchi sat still. Robert waited for their lead. Finally, Conchi turned and said, "Floor four, *piso B*."

"That's it?"

She smiled and nodded, and suddenly Robert felt like a teenager on a blind date, dropped at the door by the couple who arranged the meeting.

"Aren't you coming in?"

"You need my help?" Paco said gruffly and began to laugh. Conchi wheezed along, and Robert slowly opened his door. He looked at the two windows four stories up. Only one was lighted, and he wondered what Julia was doing right then. Was she waiting for him? Was she anxious to see him? Her kiss was tender. She had saved his life, not once, but twice.

He closed the door and walked to the portal. An intercom on the right offered two buttons for each floor of the building. He pressed 4-B, and before anyone spoke, the door buzzed and Robert gently pushed it open and stepped inside.

The stairs wound like a nautilus around the walls to a skylight above the eighth floor. He expected to see Julia peering over the fourth-floor balustrade, and when she did not appear, he felt a sense of loss and continued.

You're embarrassing. He mounted the stairs and tucked in his shirt with each step. *You stink. You're dirty. You look horrible, and you're vain enough to think this woman rescued you because of your charm. All she wants is a story—a story to exonerate her husband and to nail Bo Thompson.*

Maybe you're right.

Of course, I'm right. And what about Diana?

Diana?

Remember—yesterday's infatuation?

I'll call her first chance I get.

Sure you will. Hell, you haven't thought about her since Conchi broke the news about Julia an hour ago. You're so damn fickle, you have about as much chance of getting married as Teddy whatshisass.

Don't start talking commitment.

You mean the C-word?

You know what I mean.

You got a character disorder, pal.

That's exactly what I mean.

Robert knocked on the door and imagined the glowing face of Julia on the other side. It opened quickly and he looked up from where he thought Julia's face should be to the startling face of a black man who stood almost seven feet tall.

"Come in," said the man with a brilliant smile that seemed to obscure the rest of his face. "You must be the writer."

"Malibu," Robert said, shaking the man's huge hand. The fingers seemed to wrap twice around his own hand, and he was immediately self-conscious. The man was dressed in a tight yellow sweat outfit. His body exploded from the waist like an inverted pyramid and perspiration soaked his brow and dripped into a full beard. Robert never realized that the body of Michelangelo's David was modeled after a black man.

"I'm Bond."

"Sure," Robert must have said incredulously, but purely by accident. He would never openly doubt a man who could maim him with a stare.

"Really. My parents even named me James. They weren't too creative, but I gave up on that shit years ago. You can call me Jerry."

"Jerry." Robert took his hand back and inadvertently checked it as if to make sure it was all there.

The man moved gracefully through the entry hall, past a bedroom, to a narrow sitting area on the left. "Have you noticed that everything in this country is small?"

"I imagine," said Robert and then quickly added, "Yes." He followed Bond's lead and sat slowly opposite the big man on the far end of an anorexic sand-colored sofa. It was uncomfortable and, like Bond had warned, small. "You're a friend of Julia's."

The big man gestured yes and then quickly stood up. "You want a brew, or something? We got something in the box."

Robert let out a sigh of relief. "I'd love anything. Whatever you got without alcohol."

Jerry walked across the hall, and Robert heard the suction of the refrigerator open as he stood up and looked around the plain room. "Do you mind if I browse?" he asked. "It's an occupational disease."

The sound of two bottle caps popped, and Jerry's form filled the kitchen doorway. "Make yourself at home. It's not my place." He handed Robert a Coca-Cola and kept a Michelob for himself.

"American beer."

"And God bless it." Jerry tipped his bottle for a toast.

The Coke stung at first and then danced joyously down his throat. "Where do you get it? The Michelob?" he asked and then suddenly the pieces meshed into a troubling puzzle. "Don't tell me—you're CIA."

Thunderous laughter spewed beer from Bond's mouth. "Shit, no!" he said with a grin. "I imagine it comes from the American base in Rota. Probably black market shit. I don't know. I said this isn't my place."

"It doesn't look like it belongs to anybody."

Bond nodded. "It's a crash pad."

"Or a safehouse."

"Maybe, yeah," he agreed and took another swig of beer. "I stay out of that spy shit."

"But you're a friend of Julia's?" Robert asked again, begging for a little better explanation.

"I run in strange circles, though."

"Where is she?"

"Julia?" Bond said, and then answered, "She's in the shower. We just got back from jogging." He gulped again, and Robert saw that he had already siphoned off two-thirds of the beer. "You never met a woman as physical as she is."

Robert swallowed on the Coke and tried not to appear shocked by the insinuation.

"She can keep up with me stride for stride. And I haven't lost much since '88."

"Eighty-eight?"

"The last year I played ball."

"Jerry Bond," Robert said matter-of-factly. His memory opened the drawer marked trivia, and facts began to take shape and spill through his head. "New York. You played nine years. Defensive end." His excitement and desire to make an impression with his facts ran faster than the sensitive side of his brain that governed social consciousness, the side that remembered which facts were okay to voice and which were better left unsaid. "You were All-Pro four straight years. Then something happened," his voice trailed off as the facts stormed out of his brain and to the tip of his tongue. "And you were gone," he said softly and took an uneasy sip of Coke.

"Six years," Jerry said and finished his beer. The bottle clinked against green marble as he placed it on a side table. "I was All-Pro for six years, then I got hung by the rules of '88."

"I remember, now," said Robert apologetically.

"I was a three-time loser. And the funny thing is, the day I closed my locker for the final time—I've never put the candy up my nose since."

"That was a bad year for the league."

"But they were right, you know." Jerry stared out the window as if he could see all the way to the Meadowlands and feel the pain of being knocked from the apogee of success over and over again. "I remember what I would've thought if Olsen or Grier or my heroes had used the shit when they was playin'. My heroes. All I wanted to do was be like them. Shit, it took three seasons to get me to play in white cleats. But success has to be sexy, don't it?"

He looked back at Robert, who only nodded.

"You like Dave Grusin?" Bond asked suddenly, and his face lit up, taking the pressure of a response off the journalist.

"Yeah—sure I like Grusin. Ritenour and Rangell."

"That's right. I got some great Grusin discs."

"I haven't listened to him for—it must be years."

"And you cannot listen to him now." The voice of Julia broke into the reanimated conversation.

Robert turned around and was captured by her naked beauty, fresh and clean and without makeup. She wore a large white terry-cloth bathrobe, and a white towel was tied like a turban around her wet hair. Her features were so fine and dark that for a moment he imagined he was staring at a portrait, alive and flawless, painted by a man in love with his subject. Then he realized he was staring and glanced away, conscious of how terrible he looked in the same filthy clothes he was wearing the last time they saw each other.

"As you can see," he said with a faint smile, "I didn't get back to my hotel."

"We have plenty for you here, don't we, James?"

"Maybe a little big. But what's mine's his," Jerry said with a smile.

"I bet you would like to take a shower and sleep in a real bed, wouldn't you, Mr. Hamilton?"

"Bob," he corrected, then agreed with every one of her suggestions.

"Robert," she said with a sly, almost sexy, smile. "I like Robert."

Chapter Twenty-Four

Winter rain fell in heavy sheets across runway nine as Pan Am flight 347 touched down at Washington's Dulles International Airport. Bo Thompson could not see the terminal from his window, but knew that it had to be out there somewhere beyond the black flood that had swallowed the 747. The cabin was still dark, and though most people had awakened for the landing, it was still silent, and blue blankets were scattered from seat to seat.

Bo had not even closed his eyes. Two hours into the flight, he tried to empty his mind with the transatlantic movie, but even the plot bothered him, about a Cuban military attaché in the London embassy who opened fire on a Sunday afternoon street corner at Piccadilly Circus.

From that point on, Bower tried not to pay attention, but gathered from the pieces of the film he caught as he looked up from the magazines that the plot twisted like the Thames, hinting at one outcome and then another. First it appeared the Cuban had acted in self-defense, that he was being followed by the CIA. Then there was a hint that he was insane and acted on his own, and finally it was an assassination attempt on a former Cuban intelligence officer who had defected to MI5. The hitch was, the officer did not know he had assassinated the man. He really believed he was acting in self-defense.

Bo was certain the plot was by LeCarré. No other Cold War novelist was as complex. Life certainly wasn't.

"Ladies and gentlemen, welcome to Dulles International. Please stay seated with your seat belts fastened until the plane has come to a complete stop and the captain has turned off the seatbelt light. Local time is 10:48 PM. The temperature is forty degrees, and I'm sorry to advise that rain has been drowning this poor city for the last two days.''

Bo looked at his wristwatch and moved the hour hand back from 3:48 AM.

"On behalf of your flight crew, I would like to thank you for flying Pan Am, and hope you will fly with us again, soon. For those of you on our frequent flyer program, this is still double mileage month, and if you forgot to have your totals readjusted at the ticket counter, one of our flight attendants would be happy to help you at this time. If you are interested in the program, Wendy, in the fore-cabin has our new three-step application. You can fill it out before you deplane, and we'll even throw in the miles on this flight.''

Bo reached beneath the seat in front of him and pulled out his saddlebag briefcase. *You were smart to get out of Spain as quickly as you did*, he said to himself as he unbuckled one of the compartments and withdrew his Daytimer. *Smart and lucky.* He flipped it open to the address book in back and looked under the Cs.

CHARLIE—555-1455

He was tired and did not want to make the call before dawn. He had not slept in his Georgetown home for two weeks, and his mind that had been awake over forty-eight hours, now, was ready for his king-size Stearns and Foster. But the last order he received before leaving Sevilla was to contact this Charlie.

He's not going to be happy when I jerk him out of bed, he thought and shoved the Daytimer into his hip pocket. *That's what I hate about this business. So many people, so many names, you never know who you're talking to until the conversation's over and you've either hung yourself or earned a promotion. Charlie could be anyone from the epaulet-laden chief of the Second Directorate of the GRU in North America to some college bagboy who runs pieces of information between illegals. But more than likely, Charlie is an illegal himself, a GRU officer living undercover with forged documents and a professional front.*

Bower unbuckled his seatbelt and reached over his head to the storage compartment. A stewardess had already opened it, and he took down his hanging bag. He learned early on never to check luggage, but to bring it on board. You were always guaranteed to have it stowed away once on the plane, but you were never guaranteed to see it again once it was checked, and when you had to move quickly, the distinction between the two became even more pronounced.

"Young man, could you please hand me my cosmetic case?" asked a fragile old lady sitting across from Bower on the aisle row in the center section of seats.

He nodded and gently handed her the pearl-colored case. She had deep rouge on her checks, and it flushed scarlet and swelled as she smiled in gratitude.

"Thank you," she said.

Bower did not reply, but stepped into the aisle and began inching his way to the door. When he finally stepped into the people-mover, he felt the early morning chill and wished he had not packed his jacket. The little lady sat next to him on a fold-down bench seat and patted the sides of her gray hair. The creases in her face were deep and powdered.

Shoot me before I get that old, Bo thought and looked out the rain-streaked windows of the giant vehicle. It always seemed to take longer to get from the airplane to the airport in the people-movers than it did getting from city to city in the plane.

"Would you kindly help me claim my bags once we're inside the airport?" asked the woman.

"There'll be a skycap." Bo answered sternly without looking at her.

She drew a nervous breath and fumbled with the handle on her case. "You were just so kind to help me on the plane."

He looked at his watch. "It's late, and I have to make a call."

I hate this blind-acquaintance spook detail. How do I know this old bag isn't Charlie?

"Do you live in Washington?" she asked.

"Yes, I do."

"Do you work for the government?"

For two of them, he thought but answered only "Yes."

"What do you think of President Satterfield?"

"I work for Senator Boyd Ashworth," he said as if it answered her question.

"That's nice. I love President Satterfield."

She's not Charlie.

"I'd love to see him dead." Bo said and the woman gasped. His mind was tired and irritable. He did not care what she thought, only that she shut up.

The people-mover docked, and Bower walked quickly to the telephone bank at the right of the customs counters. Four officials were on duty, and the lines were short and moving quickly, given the late hour for international flights, but Bo wanted to make the call before checking through.

He dropped a quarter into the phone and dialed the number.

A deep, tired voice answered, "Yeah?"

"Charlie?"

"What?"

"This is Thompson calling for Charlie."

"Yeah, uh, hang on." The man's receiver dropped away from his mouth, and Bower could hear him trying to wake someone up.

Can't even keep the fags out of espionage.

He heard the phone exchange hands and was then surprised to hear the sensual, awakened voice of a woman he guessed to be in her thirties.

"Hello, this is Charlie." It carried a melodious English accent.

"I'm sorry to wake you, but I just landed."

"Mr. Thompson?"

"Yes." Bower heard her cup the receiver and tell the man something, but could not make out the words.

"Hold one minute, please," she said and then spoke to the man again. There was a moment of silence before she returned. "I'm sorry," she said to Bower.

"Are you alone now?"

"Yes, now."

"I was told to call you."

"Did they tell you why?"

"Something about the Project," Bower said and watched the little old lady shuffle past him toward the far counter.

"We've set up a meeting with the Architect." Charlie emphasized the last word.

"What!" Bower blurted in surprise. "This wasn't supposed to happen—not so quickly."

"Yes. We've got him under control. Under my control."

Damn bureaucracy—more chaotic than the Kremlin itself.

"Where is he?" Bo asked but knew she was too smart to answer.

"Meet me for tea."

"With a book?"

"Upstairs. Tomorrow morning—10:30."

"Maybe we better meet tonight," Bo said. He knew the woman would object, but it was a game he learned on Capitol Hill to gratify his ego, to demonstrate that he was more dedicated than anyone else. *Play the strong man*, he thought. *The dedicated. Besides, this girl isn't going to tell you when and where to meet.*

"I can't meet now."

Probably sleeping with the director. "Why?" he pressed.

She sighed objectionably. "I guess it's a matter of priorities. You wake up the Architect at this hour, and push him the way I've heard you push, and he'll die of a bloody heart attack. And no matter who you are, despite your reputation, that wouldn't be good for your career."

"What do *you* know about my career?"

"Family talks," she said flatly.

"What family?"

"To some of us, this is more than a bloody hobby. It is a cause, and we are tremendously dedicated."

Bo could feel pressure mount on the back of his neck and into his head. He pressed his big toe down on the tiny plastic pouch in his left shoe. "I think this conversation's gone as far as it's going tonight. You won't meet with me—fine." He closed his eyes and imagined the thick down pillows on his bed. *That's what I need. Screw this bitch.* "It's your *bloody* decision," he mocked.

"Ten-thirty!" she said and hung up.

Bo did not bother putting the phone back on its cradle, but left it hanging by the cord. He moved quickly past the customs agent who took one look at the red passport carried by government officials and waved him through. From the counter, he moved to the restroom across the hall, locked himself inside a stall, and took off his left shoe. Suddenly his body was settled. Even before he opened the pouch and snuffed the white powder, his head was calm, his mind relaxed, and his mood spirited.

Thank you, Bolivia, and may your shrubs always blossom above Cochabamba.

Bo folded the bag, placed it back in his shoe, and looked at his watch. The time was 11:20, and he wondered what clubs would still be crowded with the people he wanted to see. "Now I remember why I'm in this business," he whispered, throwing his hanging bag over his shoulder. "It lets me feel so damned wonderful."

He remembered meeting Dr. Semenovich in front of the John Adams building of the Library of Congress, and on his coke high, he idolized the illegal. It was Semenovich who recruited Thompson into the GRU more than a dozen years earlier, when Bower was a second-year legislative assistant in Ashworth's office.

Before I became so fucking cynical, he thought as he walked to the escalator. When my letters back to Wichita were still paraphrased from *The Federalist Papers.*

Semenovich looked innocent enough, in his floppy hat and well-worn wool sweaters. Thompson had never met a man so intelligent, especially one who took such interest in him. For three months, the two met weekly for lunch at the Pizza Cellar on Pennsylvania Avenue. The professor said he was on sabbatical from Charles University in Prague, doing research on the United States media representation of the 1968 invasion of Czechoslovakia.

"I guess the Soviets have a right to secure their satellite countries just like America has." Bower encouraged the professor and demonstrated himself to be open-minded enough for further indoctrination.

"This is what Brezhnev said," Semenovich taught, "that there is a limitation of sovereignty of communist countries, which have only the right to self-determination so far as it does not jeopardize the interests of communism in their own countries, or in any other state in the Communist Commonwealth."

"Like we did in Nicaragua—in El Salvador."

"Exactly," Semenovich smiled and took the methodical next step, inviting Bower to his 12th Street apartment, where the boy eventually rolled his first tube and succumbed to the induced nirvana of cocaine.

The professor was too gentle and trustworthy to be doubted, and Bower dared not object when Semenovich slid the mirror with two lines across the coffee table.

"This is why America is great," he said, handing the young man a dollar. "Meese and the drug czar—I always laugh at how your politicians use the word 'czar'—they will never stop the good drugs from coming to America. It will be like turning the tide back with a teaspoon. With drugs you can smile at violence. With drugs you can laugh at class distinctions. And with drugs you can sop the wounds of poverty. Your ghettos need drugs like Russia's need vodka—to keep the masses from rising, to keep their heads on the tables and their minds numb. People who feel good never revolt."

Young Bower reluctantly objected, and pushed the mirror back to Semenovich.

"Wisdom only comes through experience," the professor encouraged and gently slid it back. "There is nothing to fear."

"I do a joint now and then, but that's as far as I go."

"Everything is fresh to an enlightened mind."

"What do you mean?"

Semenovich straightened out a line with the razor blade. "One snuff and you will know exactly what I mean."

Unconsciously, Bo had rolled the bill into a tube, looking from the mirror back to the halcyon face of his mentor. "It's late," he said.

"Just one line, and your mind will run brilliant for hours."

"One line?"

"Of course, but only if you choose."

"I've always been scared to death of getting addicted."

"What do you call—a wives' tale."

"My dad was an alcoholic," he tried to objectively explain his rationale, "an obsessive, and I've always wondered if I have the same tendency."

"I understand," said Semenovich, moving the mirror back to his side of the coffee table. He opened the drawer and began to place it inside.

"No, no," Bo retreated, feeling suddenly guilty that he had offended his host. "I mean, I understand what you're saying. I've always believed that the best and the brightest were elevated to higher levels of consciousness by something, maybe drugs. But I—"

"Don't worry." The professor closed the drawer, stood up and walked into the kitchen.

Bo stared through the table and imagined the white lines reflecting on the mirror in the drawer. He pulled it open and looked—looked at the tube, then back at the coke.

"Why not?" he said quietly and lifted it to the table. Out of the corner of his eye, he could see the shadow of Semenovich standing in the door frame as he inhaled one line and then the other. Shadows can't smile, he thought, but he knew Semenovich was.

"You opened my eyes, Fedor," Bower said as he rode the escalator to the ground floor, where baggage was claimed and two lines formed for taxis. The old woman from the plane was sliding her suitcase along the day-worn floor. Pulling then resting. Pulling then resting. He walked up behind her and placed his hand softly around hers that gripped the handle. She gave way and he smiled. "Are you catching a cab?"

The woman nodded and primped her hair again.

"To the city?"

"Arlington," she said. "I've an older sister who lives in Arlington."

"I'm right across the bridge in Georgetown," Bower smiled. "Let me see that you get home."

Chapter Twenty-Five

Sergio's back, chest and shoulders itched beneath the damp burnoose, and he could feel that, despite the protective layer of thin cotton cloth from his hospital gown, the flax and hemp robe had irritated his areolas to open wounds. His hair beneath the hood was dirty and matted to his head from the river and rain. The boots, only uncomfortable at first, had produced blisters under the ball and lateral arch of both feet. His face was scratched, and crusted blood covered the wound from the thorny overgrowth in the garden, but this did not bother Sergio since it was the same overgrowth that protected him from being captured as he made his way from the garden over the wall into the brush beside the white stone sidewalk along the bank of the Tiber.

He was almost caught once. In the beginning. The voices of two orderlies, profaning the rain and mud and thorny brush, stirred Sergio from his daze after he fell from the window. They were only feet away, but the cloud-blackened night and the bushes concealed the quarry.

"*Porca Madonna*," said one as Sergio listened. "It matters little who the man is, nothing is worth going out on a night like this."

"A while longer," said the other, "then we can return and report that we found nothing."

"I say we return now. I can already feel *polmonite*. And I have family—four boys."

The other laughed. "*Amico!* You will not die from pneumonia. We have looked only ten minutes. Ten minutes longer and we will return."

Sergio heard a branch break only inches from his head. The pain in his back was insufferable, but his senses were completely awake and his whole body ached—except for his hand. He could not feel his hand, it lay motionless at his side, out of sight, and he tried to remember if it still held the broken glass.

You dropped the glass when you climbed to the window, he reminded himself and at once felt vulnerable. Then he sensed the pressure of another shoe step on the hem of his burnoose and held his breath.

"If my pneumonia does not kill me, perhaps the patient will." The voice was directly over Sergio, now, and he strained to see the face, but could not as the heavy rain fell hard against his eyeballs.

Do not look down, he mentally commanded the man standing above him and wanted to pray but decided against it.

"Maybe you are right," said the other man. "He has left by now. And I have children of my own—I am almost sure of it."

"Sure of what?" asked the man above Sergio as he stepped off the hem. "Sure that he has left, or sure that you have children?"

"Both," laughed the orderly.

Sergio's pain abated with the ebullience from the man's retreat into the brush. He breathed a sigh of relief, and just as quickly as the pain had abated it returned with even greater force, causing his body to quiver. He listened to the voices, the profanity and laughter, fade until he was certain of being alone. Then he moved slowly, pressing his numb hand into the mud and using it, and then his arm, to prop himself up. He gathered his feet under him and stood cautiously, straining his eyes in the darkness to see where he was. The brush and blackness were too much, and he could not see more than a few feet in any direction.

In the beginning, his steps were quiet and deliberate. Step and listen. Step and listen. Then he quickened his pace until he was moving as fast as his pain allowed. The thorns and branches surprised him, whipping against his upper body and often in his face. He tried to whack them away, swinging his numb hand and arm as a man in the jungle would swing a machete, but it was impossible to deflect them all.

He could feel the warm blood flowing down his forearm to his elbow, and he wondered how badly damaged his hand was. *You will have plenty of time to nurse yourself once you get away*, he encouraged. *Now, put the pain and fear from your mind.*

With another step, he broke out of the garden and found himself balancing on a stone wall precipice with an eight-foot drop. Beneath was another steep slope overgrown with greenery. *They might be waiting for you down there*, he thought and listened. Except for the falling rain, he could hear only his heavy breath. The distance between the top of the wall and the ground decreased as it ran northward. He turned and walked, not quickly but with determination, toward the northwest corner where the drop was about five feet. He looked at his numb hand. It was a bloody pulp, but he sighed after counting all five fingers. *It is repairable.*

If you do not first bleed to death.

Such thoughts are dangerous. Put them out of your mind. You will not bleed to death. You have seen much worse.

But I was younger then.

Die now, if that is how you feel.

We are too old for this. I should be with Gabriela, living in America—in New York—watching movies and plays, listening to music, and growing old with children. Celebrating Christmas with my children.

Gabriela is dead and you have no children. Now you are the father of revolution.

For what, this revolution? I am old and expendable. Ask Basalobre.

Basalobre?

The name generated a bolt of excitement that began in Sergio's heart and flooded to his extremities. For a moment he even thought he could feel his damaged hand. Once again, he had a sense of purpose.

He sat on the wet stones and carefully swung his legs over the wall. Then, lying on his side, he tried to drop his feet as low as possible so his landing would be light. He fought the pain in his back, biting his lower lip to stifle a scream. Then he dropped, and this time he could not hold back his cry as he crashed through the brush. A branch gashed his left cheek just below his eye, then his feet hit the slippery slope and sank into the mud over his boots. After two or three steps, he found moving in the mud too strenuous and looked wonderingly at the flowing black surface of the Tiber, just over the white stone walkway.

Its flow was not too rapid. It would be cold, but he could stand the cold. It might even be comforting, and all he would have to do is stay afloat, allow the current to carry him downstream. He knew where he was now, on the Isola Tiberina, the small island in the Tiber that holds the great hospital originally dedicated to San Giovanni di Dio. It was linked to Rome by two ancient bridges, the Ponte Fabrico being the oldest, built sixty-four years before Christ.

Sergio remembered from the map that the metro station Ostea Lido was just four bridges down river, only blocks away from Ponte Testaccio. From the station, he could catch the subway to the main terminal, where, if he evaded the carabinieri, he could catch a train to Naples. He patted the money purse tied to his belt. From Naples, an Alitalia flight would take him to Málaga. There he could finish his business with Basalobre Libertad.

The water will also clean the blood and mud from your clothes. You will not be so offensive, so suspicious looking, he thought as he slipped from the bank into the river and gasped from the freezing water. Posted lamps lighted both sides of the Tiber, and Sergio could see the first bend to the right. He also saw the lights on Ponte Cestio, the second island bridge, just before the church, St. Bartolomeo, and delighted that age had not yet robbed him of his keen sense of direction.

After floating about two hundred yards, his body swept through the rapids and rammed into several large boulders left by the 1850 landslide that closed the upper river to navigation. The water numbed the pain, but the anticipation of hitting other boulders made him tense. He cleared the gray stone-cut bridge and a minute later was out of the rapids.

Immediately in front of him was the brightly-lit Ponte Palatino. Within moments, he was swept beneath its shadow. Again, he feared rapids, but there were none as the river grew deep. In the distance, he saw the lights of the third bridge and began to relax. Then he turned and looked behind him, at the two ancient bridges growing smaller as he floated southward, and for the first time he noticed the pulsating lights of police cars barricading the hospital entrance on both sides of the river.

His damaged hand felt cold, and heartened by the feeling, Sergio sank beneath the surface and felt his body purged of filth and perspiration. He agitated the burnoose, breaking the caked mud from the coarse fibers, and resurfaced. The tension in the muscles of his aching back began to unwind and the pain completely disappeared.

Maybe you should stay in the river until it empties into the Tyrrhenian Sea, he thought and then dismissed the idea as foolish.

Just get to the fourth bridge, Ponte Testaccio. The train will take you to the coast.

Suddenly, he was covered by a shadow and realized he was coming upon the third bridge, Ponte Sublicio; the final bridge was about ten blocks away. He had memorized the map of the city, a condition of the assignment, and for this he was grateful.

You are *an old man*, he chided, *but you do have a fine memory*, and once again he completely submerged. This time he pulled the front of the burnoose away from his body and reached beneath it to pull the hospital gown over his genitalia, which were becoming irritated by the heavier, coarser cloth. He tucked the hem of the hospital gown between his thighs to keep it from floating up.

When he finally surfaced for air, he was stunned to see a boat coming at him full throttle. Two men stood on the bow with a spotlight. It had come around the left bend of the river, and the roar of its engine could be heard above the falling rain.

Sergio's first impulse was to get to the river bank. He saw the red strobe lights and derided himself for not anticipating that the carabinieri would be doing more than covering the two bridges.

The boat closed the gap to about one hundred and fifty yards, and Sergio began to paddle himself toward the right shore. Two strokes. Three strokes. Then he understood what the military policemen were doing. By the direction of the spotlight, he could see that they were not looking in the water, but directly at the right bank of the river, assuming the fugitive had already crossed the Tiber and was fleeing on foot.

He broke into a hard swim toward the opposite bank, even using his feet to kick. Pain surged from his lower back to his shoulder and he groaned into the muffling water. His heart pounded, and he felt as if his lungs were going to explode.

"Slow it up," he heard one of the bowmen yell above the engine and rain. The throttle cut back a half, and Sergio lay motionless in the river.

"The man would never have gotten this far," the other *carabiniere* argued. "They say he has not yet come over the bridge."

"We can take no chances, though. We will start here."

Sergio filled his lungs and sank beneath the surface a third time and began to push toward the left bank. He estimated the boat was about thirty yards away, and he determined not to surface until he was safely down river.

At first it seemed easy, and he tried to relax to conserve oxygen. But beneath the surface it felt as if he was barely moving, and after thirty seconds he began to panic.

Keep down. Drown if you must, but do not come up.

But you will not make it past the boat.

You will *make it. Calm down.*

He kicked his feet as much as he could without disturbing the surface of the water.

Hold on! He estimated himself to be even with the boat. He sank further beneath the surface. *Better to die than to return to prison.* His head began to throb and cried out for air. *Breathe!* it demanded. *Breathe!* He responded by forcing himself even deeper into the river. The temperature was getting colder, and his nose teased him that it was going to swallow water. The nostrils flexed, but he kept them from inhaling. Something in the back of his neck exploded and he felt himself losing consciousness.

Get to the surface, he demanded, but believed he could not make it in time. *The boat has passed. Get to the surface!*

He kicked as violently as he could and thrashed his arm against the current. The water grew warmer and then suddenly his head blew above the surface, and he gasped for air until his lungs burned and he realized he was swallowing rain.

Then he heard the engine and felt the kick of the current. He opened his eyes and the tension in his muscles grew limp when he saw the churning propellers only four feet in front of him. One man stood at the stern of the boat and flashed his light on the bank opposite the men on the bow.

Without another breath, Sergio sank into the river, grateful that he had not come up a second sooner than he did.

"God watches over us all," he said as he stepped from the backside of the artisan's shack where he had burrowed a bed in the sand and slept until the morning light awakened him. He was cold, but not sleepy, and wondered how far he had walked after the train dropped him at the seaside village of Pozzuoli. There had been no trouble getting the metro at Ostea Lido, the police were nowhere to be found at the central train terminal, and once on board for Naples everything ran smoothly for two hours, until a tired conductor looked at him suspiciously when he got off one stop early.

"You are boarded to Napoli," he objected. "This is Pozzuoli."

"I want to look at the sea," Sergio said, as he intended to wash in the surf and find another change of clothes before going into the big city. The carabineri in Naples might already be looking for someone of his description, and they, along with their sister organization, the Servizo Informazioni Sicurezza Militare (Service for Military Intelligence and Security), were much more astute due to their responsibility for the huge NATO base nearby.

"There is sea in Naples."

"Dirty sea, and there is no beach—only a big dirty port."

"But I am *Napolitano!*" the conductor said, offended by the insult.

"Then you should clean your sea."

"Peh," he spat and looked at the ragged man in the filthy burnoose, "you are one to talk."

"I will catch a later train." Sergio tried to put a friendly tone in his voice. He regretted his insult and wanted to end the confrontation.

"You will have to pay for another ticket," the conductor said gruffly.

"It was my mistake."

The man shrugged his shoulders. "Your money," he said and walked on.

Pozzuoli was only ten miles up the line, the first cape inside the province of Campania, and Sergio could see the beach as he stepped onto the gravel beneath the track. It was still dark, and he counted five other travelers getting off the train with him. No one spoke as he walked along the track, past the station, and crossed a small plaza with palm trees and a dry fountain. The boots were tearing the skin on his feet and sharp pain returned in his back after the long sit, but he continued to walk until he found the small seaside shack and tried to sleep the remaining hours before dawn.

Now, as he dusted the sand from his robe, he tried to estimate the time and how far he had walked.

More than a mile, he thought and peered around the shack that opened onto the beachscape, rugged with towering crags and coves and sand. Huge white and black boulders bordered the beach and waves the color of the misty gray sky broke along the shore. The air was humid and heavy with salt.

Half a mile down coast, he could see a mountainous white stone castle perched like a foreboding redoubt on the stony palisade rising from the sea. The beaches were empty, but two brightly colored boats bobbed in the surf.

Sergio's feet were blistered and bleeding. His chest and groin were raw. *The salt water will sting*, he thought, *but it will also clean the wounds, help the healing*. He stepped in front of the open-faced shack and was startled by the bold voice of a man.

"*Sostare!*" the voice ordered, and Sergio stopped. He looked back at the ragged image of an old man, with shoulder-length white hair and a scraggly beard covering his chest. His face had the color and texture of tanned leather and folded deeply around the eyes and sunken cheeks and mouth. The next thing Sergio noticed were his hands. They were caked with wet brown clay and appeared to grow from a ceramic bowl spinning on a potter's wheel. The old man's legs were pumping up and down to keep his wheel in motion while he watched Sergio.

"You surprised me," Sergio said, and the old man's eyes narrowed as he studied the burnoose.

"You are not from Campania," he returned suspiciously. "Where?"

Sergio pointed out to sea. "From there," he said softly.

"And now you are going to swim home?" The man smiled and his teeth were bold against his dark skin.

"I was going to soak in the sea."

"What happened to your face?"

"I scratched it in a garden."

"And your hand?"

Sergio tried to hide it beneath his robe. "Some glass," he said. With his wheel still turning, the old man motioned for him to come closer.

"What?" Sergio asked as he took a step toward the shack.

The artisan did not answer but only waved his muddy hand for him to draw closer still.

He took another step.

"Let me see your face," said the man, and he reached up and touched it with his mud, wiping the clay across the wounds. "Does that feel better?"

Sergio nodded that it did.

"The mud is from an Etruscan tomb," the potter said bodefully. "It will purify your blood."

Sergio nodded again.

"Wash your body, but not the mud. And when you return we will care for the hand."

Another silent nod and Sergio turned to the surf. He was careful to keep his head above water as he slipped out of the burnoose and washed it in the waves. The salt stung his raw chest, groin and hand, and the movement of the hospital gown against his body aggravated the wounds, but the cold water soothed his feet, and his back welcomed the lightness of being in the water, and the motion of the waves relieved some of the stiffness.

He looked at the venerable potter behind his wheel and envied the provincial life. "God watches over him also," he said to himself and rubbed his hand softly beneath the gown against his areolas and genitals.

The old man waved, his long, twisted fingers still caked in mud, and Sergio nodded and imagined what a spectacle he must be, first dressed like an indigent Arab and now up to his neck in the sea, being careful to keep the hospital gown below the surface to avoid arousing the potter's suspicions. *As if you are not already suspicious looking,* he criticized. *This ancient will never forget you. And someone will be here asking questions. Somehow he will find out who you are.*

I must move on now.

You know what you must do.

Move on.

You must kill him.

Then they will know I was here.

He lives like a hermit—away from the village.

But he will be found.

And you will be gone. And they will never be certain it was you who killed him, but they will be most certain if you do not.

He has done nothing.

Neither had the viejo in the hospital. You should have killed him, too, but you were weak. Had you done what you were trained for and cut his throat, you would not be in such a position.

The stinging from the salt had vanished with the waves, and Sergio carefully stepped into the burnoose, drawing it up over his shoulders but leaving the hood off his head. He walked to the beach where the damp and cracked-leather boots rested in the sand. For a moment he thought about putting them on, but even the thought made his feet ache, and he decided against it, picking them up and walking back to the shack.

"Feel better?" the potter asked and looked from the boots to Sergio's feet. He grimaced at the sight and kicked off his sandals. "These will be better," he said. The wheel slowed to a stop as he stood up and walked to the back of his shack. Beside his bed was a water basin and towel. After washing his own, he gently washed Sergio's hand, wrapped the towel around it and tied it with a piece of cord. "When you have the chance, you should see a doctor."

"Yes," Sergio replied like an obedient child. Something about the man stripped him of his fear and anger, yet he did not feel vulnerable—respectful, even humble, but not vulnerable.

"Are you hungry?" The potter turned and walked to a rough-hewn wooden cupboard mounted on the wall above his wheel. "I have some hard bread and cheese. And there is some wine on the table over there."

Sergio uncorked the bottle. "*Molte grazie,*" he said and took a long swallow. His throat and stomach welcomed the attention, then quickly tensed as the old man smiled and handed his guest a carving knife.

"Goatshead cheese," said the man as he laid the tray on the table.

Sergio studied the blade of the knife. It was clean and sharp and eight inches long. It was a good knife, an old knife forged in the days when craftsmen rather than machines made knives. The worn handle was carved and smooth and fit well in his hand. "Thank you," he said and watched the man turn again toward the cabinet for bread.

Shamefully, he realized he was studying the back of the old man's neck, the base of the head where the neck meets the skull. *He is a good man*, Sergio insisted. *He is a man of God. A true man of God.*

And you? You were a man of God, too.

I cannot kill him. The blade slid easily through the moist cheese and Sergio tasted a sliver without the bread. His stomach growled, and he realized how famished he was, remembering only the cookies and water at the hospital.

Do not make the same mistake twice.

"Sorry it is only hard bread, but I seldom get to the city."

"Anything is fine."

"Do you eat hard bread where you live?"

Sergio did not answer but received a broken chunk from the potter and gnawed it anxiously.

"I understand your reluctance to speak about yourself," said the man as he placed a stool next to Sergio, "but if I can help you somehow—"

"I need to find clothes," Sergio said quickly and then took another bite from his bread and cheese.

"Mine will fit," the potter answered graciously. His eyes were penetrating, and he tugged at his U.S. Navy-issue shirt that Sergio knew came from the NATO base. "You are strong, but this shirt is big—big enough for two of me."

"I cannot take your shirt." Sergio shook his head.

"It means nothing to me. And my pants, they are only worn dungaree, but you can have them."

"I cannot pay," Sergio said and cut another piece of cheese. Its odor was pleasant, stiff and salty, but there was not much left and he did not want to give the impression that he would eat it all.

The potter dropped his shaking head slowly. "I would never expect payment. In fact, you will need money, and there is money in the pockets. It goes with the pants."

"No," Sergio objected.

"But I insist."

"What would you wear, then?"

The potter looked at the burnoose.

"This garment is rotten." Sergio said. *If you kill him there is no need to bicker*, his mind returned to torment.

But he is so kind—an unusual man.

"It would fit an artist well." The potter offered a feeble smile.

Kill him, take the clothes and be gone.

No, I am finished killing.

Even Basalobre?

No. No. Basalobre needs to die.

Then kill this man, too, and be gone.

Sergio's hand tightened on the knife and he cut another piece of cheese. "You do not even know me, and you would give me your only clothes?"

"They are clean, and they cost me nothing," the potter answered, "and I was going to get new sandals anyway."

"Thank you for your kindness." Sergio said abashedly, as if he were talking to a third person, sitting closer to him in the tiny room.

"But helping a friend is cheap."

"I mean for everything. You have been generous." Sergio paused and looked directly into the man's eyes. "And you remind me of a man I once knew. I mean, you act like him—gentle and wise."

"Oh?" said the potter as he stood up, suddenly remembering something, and pulled an attractive gray-black wool sport coat from where it hid behind the cupboard. "Was he an artist?"

"No," said Sergio softly. "No. He was a priest."

"Then you are a Christian?"

Sergio slowly nodded his head, looked down at the man's sandals already protecting his swollen feet, and gently placed the knife on the table beside the bread and cheese.

Alitalia offered two daily flights to Málaga, one at 10:45 AM and the other at 5:15 PM. Both planes were 727s and stopped over on the island of Sardinia, the morning flight landing in Sassari and the evening flight in Cagliari. Flight time between Naples and Málaga was three hours and forty-five minutes with a half hour layover.

The airport was east of the city, and Sergio did not arrive until noon. His feet did not ache as much in the sandals, but his body was still sore and his movement slower than he would have liked. Once inside the terminal, he purchased his ticket, reassured himself that the Arab's passport—water damaged as it was—would get him aboard the plane, and made several attempts to relax behind a pay television. However, the terminal was filled with carabineri, even State Police, and more than once he felt them watching him. He looked respectable in the sport coat, and his clothes were clean, perhaps a bit bohemian, but they fit, and he believed he played the artisan role well. As much as he could, he kept the bandaged hand inconspicuously at his side, out of sight from the police.

Maybe you are imagining, he thought and forced himself to concentrate more on the inane daily television program.

You cannot assume that.

Then maybe it is the Etruscan mud. He had forgotten about the clay. It was dry and light, and he quickly wiped it off his face. With it gone, he felt more confident and began to relax until his flight was called, but it was not until the plane touched down in Málaga that he felt the muscles in his body unwind and the tight nervous throb of his wounds give way to a dull ache.

The foreign currency exchange booth was located at the bottom of the T-shaped main terminal next to the taxi stand, and Sergio thought from a criminal perspective, while it was convenient, its proximity to the cars and traffic was not the wisest. His mind often worked this way, especially as he waited in lines and cased the vulnerabilities of the environment around him. It was a useful hobby, one he had picked up early on from Marighella's book, *The Mini Handbook of Urban Guerrillas.*

This would be a three-minute strike, nothing more. Another traveler finished his transaction and moved away from the window. The line tightened up a step and, lost in thought, Sergio bumped into the man in front of him.

"*Perdón*," he said, and the man turned to respond politely, but ended studying Sergio's battered face for an uncomfortable moment.

"Está bien," he finally said with a horrible Spanish accent. "It's okay."

Another American.

Again, the line inched forward, and the man moved to the window. He pulled an eel-skin wallet, still shiny and new, from his back pocket, and a skinny notebook stuck to it flipped out and fell at Sergio's feet.

Both men stooped at once to pick it up. Sergio reached it first.

"You dropped this, Mr."— he read the name written in pen on the cover—"Malibu."

Robert nodded, smiled, looked again at the gash under Sergio's eye, the deep scratches on his cheek, took the notebook and turned back to the window.

A minute later, the cashier handed Sergio his own money, thirty-two dollars worth of pesetas, which he shoved into the pocket of his dungarees as he walked through one of three revolving doors and to the first available taxi.

"Calle de la Santa María," he said, and the driver in his black leather coat and green tee-shirt pulled his car around an unloading tour bus, over the access road and onto the coastal thoroughfare. "Do you know where the street meets the Avenida de Picasso?"

The hack nodded that he did.

"There is a cutlery store on the corner."

"Cuchillos de la Costa Sol," the driver responded proudly that he knew the very store.

"Yes." Sergio drew a deep breath. For the first time in days, he felt animated and in control. "Yes," he said. "We need to stop there first."

The "Navaja Toledero" was Sergio's preferred stiletto, a precision instrument handcrafted in Northern Spain, in the city of El Greco. Cuchillos de la Costa Sol had only two in stock, one a five-inch blade and the other seven.

Basalobre's neck is large and fleshy, he thought and slid the five-inch back to the saleslady, an old *mujer* wearing a widow's black patch on her blouse where a brooch should hang. He turned the pearl handle of the stiletto over and over in his right hand, noting the weight and balance.

The woman placed the smaller knife back in the glass case and smiled at her customer, the only one in the store.

"How much?"

"Two thousand pesetas," she answered. "A good knife."

"A very good knife and worth the money." He placed it on the counter and dug two green notes from his pocket.

"Would you like it wrapped," she asked and reached for a piece of newsprint.

"This is fine." The blade snapped back into the handle and Sergio placed it in his pocket.

"Be more careful with this knife than you were with the last." The woman smiled and pointed playfully at his bandaged hand.

Bells jingled on the door as he stepped onto the cobblestone sidewalk. Across the street the evening line was beginning to form in front of movie theater that advertised *Médicos de Muerte*, a movie about zombie doctors and, from what the posters showed, their sexy nurses. He slid into the back seat of the taxi.

"The open marketplace," he ordered.

"*Centro o Campo*?"

"There are two now?" Sergio asked with surprise.

"*Sí*, one in the city and the other by the *barrios*."

"Do you know which one has the *bodega* Vino San Cristóbal?"

"Of course, *señor*, everyone knows this *bodega*. It offers the best wine in the city."

"That is the place." He remembered the image of Basalobre, massive, with a barrel chest and shirts that were always stained with perspiration and had collars two sizes too small. Though he was fat, he was strong and very smart, a leader in the network for many years. For the last dozen, Vino San Cristóbal had been his front, a front that he had run so successfully there were rumors inside the revolution that he had actually retired from the movement. Now he was used as a field director, the middleman who dealt out the assignments and provided the blueprints and financing and alibis. Sergio had not seen him before the Rome mission, only a phone call and a package in the mail with pictures of Peterson and Watenburg, tickets and money, maps and an introduction of his partner—his partner he was ordered to kill. In fact, Sergio had not seen Basalobre since before his imprisonment. *He will be surprised to see me now*, he thought. "How long will it take to get there?"

"Maybe a few more minutes," said the driver and Sergio looked out his window.

Shades of gray were beginning to shadow the streets as the sun set on the other side of the tall city buildings.

"What time does the market close?" he asked.

"It closed at *mediodía*."

"*Mediodía*?"

"But don't worry," smiled the cabbie, "the *bodega*, it stays open until midnight. Spanish men, we need our wine."

"*Sí*," Sergio agreed and touched the hard knife in his pocket.

"I wait for you, or what?"

"No," said Sergio. "I have some business."

"But the rest of the market—it is closed."

"Business with the *bodega*."

"With Basalobre?"

Sergio sat up and fixed his eyes on the reflection of the driver's face in the rearview mirror. "You know him?"

"Everyone in Malaga knows Basalobre. We buy our wine from him, and he is a leading citizen, a member of the city council."

"How is he?"

"You know as well as I do, *señor*, he will live longer than both you and me."

Sergio did not know what to say, and silence filled the taxi until the driver spoke again.

"Is it Basalobre you want to meet with?"

Sergio looked at the statue of Maria stuck on the dashboard and the four photographs of the man's children and wife taped below. *Tell him too much and you will have to kill him as well.*

He already knows too much. When Basalobre is found dead, he will come forward and tell everything about you.

"Because if it is Basalobre you want, he is not at the *Centro bodega*. At night he goes home to Carrus."

"Carrus?"

"A rich part of the city on the other side of the *plaza de toros*."

"Please take me there." Sergio said, and his mind exploded with the awareness that now he would have to kill the driver.

It never ends, he thought. *Why can it never end!*
Because of the choices you made.
I was young and in love.
But they were your choices, and now you will live with them.

"You sure you want to go to Carrus? I mean not to offend, but your dress is not for Carrus. People will think you are a criminal. They are that way in Carrus—very suspicious, and Basalobre lives in a towering *piso* in the modern Villas Cielos, with a doorman and neighbors and old ladies. They are all without shame and angry gossips."

"Take me to the market," Sergio said regretfully as he looked at the faces of three young children and a beautiful dark-eyed woman.

"Taxi for Basalobre," Sergio said as he brushed by the doorman, who had stepped aside for an elderly couple dressed in evening gown and tuxedo. He turned his head to keep the battered side of his face out of sight.

"Maybe we could share a driver," said the woman, tugging at her husband's elbow.

Sergio slowed his pace, but did not stop. There were two elevator banks on either side of the ornate lobby, and he could see that those on the left were for floors one through eleven. The opposite side ran from twelve to twenty-three, and he walked in that direction.

"You know Basalobre," the old man in black said sternly. "It will take him too long to get down here."

"Juan!" she gasped.

"*Bien*," he said. "If another cab does not come first, we will go with Basalobre." He turned to Sergio. "*Hombre!*" he shouted, "the other side. Basalobre is on the seventh floor—seven-thirteen."

Without acknowledging, Sergio turned, stepped between the open brass doors of the elevator, and within a minute knocked on door 713.

"*Quién es?*"

He immediately recognized the voice, deep and grinding, and he turned his face so it would not be fully seen through the peephole. In his hand, he held the stiletto.

"Taxi," Sergio shouted back, certain Basalobre would not remember his voice.

"I am going nowhere."

"You called for a taxi."

"I called no one."

"You are Señor Basalobre, of the *bodega San Cristóbal?*"

"*Sí.*" The voice was now immediately on the other side of the door.

"I am sorry, *señor*, they said you called for a car."

"There must be a mistake." A chain slid and the door opened slowly, with difficulty. When the opening was sufficient for Sergio to move, certain that it could not be slammed shut, he stepped forward to let Basalobre see him.

"No mistake," he said and moved through the door quickly, pushing it all the way open and shocking himself by the sight of the once powerful man now confined to a wheelchair.

"Armando!" Basalobre gasped and slumped back into his chair.

Sergio nodded his head and tried to clear it of the sudden confusion. A *wheelchair!*

"You are alive." Basalobre looked at the knife. "*Gracias a Dios!*"

"*Gracias a Sergio.*" He stepped into the entry hall and closed the door behind him.

"And your mission was successful."

Sergio swallowed hard. "All but you. You failed."

"I failed."

"You left me to die."

"A lie!"

"You made me kill the German, the American and my own colleague. I was foolish to think you would not kill me. I remained the only link to you and the people for whom you work."

"Lies!" Basalobre wheeled quickly backward, and Sergio kept pace with each stroke on the wheels. "There was no reason for such secrecy."

Sergio took another deep breath, still overcome by the vulnerability of the man he had come to kill. "Then who ordered the strike? Tell me."

"The regular—"

"The regular?" Sergio mocked. "I do not kill for the regular." He lifted the knife and waved it in the air like a viper. "And you should have seen how I killed. Everything you taught me. Skill and cunning. I was brilliant. But maybe I can show you."

"I—I," Basalobre struggled for his words.

"No argument. Do not even think. Just tell me."

"Moscow."

Sergio sliced a quick straight line down the left sleeve of Basalobre's shirt without drawing blood. "It will be very painful, Basalobre Libertad." He spoke the name as if it were sacred.

"Washington."

Sergio sliced open the right sleeve.

"No—I mean it—I mean Washington. People in Washington, Thompson is his name. One of our own—with such deep cover that secrecy must be maintained."

"Even by killing our own?"

"I do not make the rules." The man's voice was defeated and it cracked with fear. Tears began to form. "I do not make the rules. *Oh, Dios.*" He stopped rolling his chair and resigned himself to the fact that he was going to die. "*Oh, Dios mío,*" he sobbed.

"You taught me much of what I know," Sergio said softly. "You were my hero, a revolutionary with a cause that was greater than any of us. Never did I think that cause would one day force you to kill me."

"I had no choice," the words were muffled as the man had dropped his face into his hands. "I swear it, Sergio, *por la Madre María.* I had no choice." His head shook slowly from side to side and his back quaked as he cried. "The orders are in my library safe—thirty-twenty-one-twenty-four-thirty. If you want—you can read them. Never—never would I cross you."

"But you did," said Sergio as he stuck his stiletto into the base of Basalobre's skull.

"No—" the man cried out, gasped and fell from his wheelchair onto the marble floor, and Sergio watched the blood stain the pearl handle. His impulse was to reach for the knife, to wipe off the blood.

But you will need it no more, he told himself, *Basalobre was the first man to see you kill, and now let him be the last.*

Chapter Twenty-Six

Four Avco Lycoming turbofan jet engines screamed against the dense sea-level air as the British Aerospace 146 raced down Málaga's southeast runway. At lift-off, the G-force pressed Robert into his seat with greater force than he normally felt on a commercial flight. He looked across the aisle at Julia, her white-knuckled fingers gripping the armrests.

"Ever flown before?" he asked with a smile.

"Of course." She stared intently at the cockpit door, as if she could see right through it and watch Jerry Bond and his associate, Borsman Michaels, command the aircraft through the night sky.

"Ever fly with Jerry before?"

"Never!"

"He seems to know what he's doing." Robert tried to reassure her. "Besides, he said he's been flying for years."

"He's a maniac."

Robert laughed and dropped his head back into the seat. "You know him better than I do," he said and looked out his window. In the distance, he could see the luminous Torremolinos, like a diamond cluster, and follow the flood of lights along the Costa del Sol shoreline as it appeared to lap gently against the onyx sea. The aircraft was climbing quickly, and the lights continued to fade beneath its wings as the scream of the engines abated to a deep, lulling whistle. "Well, if you get too nervous," he began again, "I'd be happy to hold your—" he looked at Julia, who was now fast asleep "—hand."

Her expression was peaceful. Her hands relaxed. The dark, rich tone of the leather upholstery set into the complexion of her tanned face and long neck, and Robert could not remember when he had seen anything as beautiful, feminine and gentle, even vulnerable. The thought of her being vulnerable bestirred his masculine ego and flung open the floodgates of a warm, yet titilating, sensation that embarrassed him. When it came to romance, his mind was as capricious as a schoolgirl, and he figured that to be a major reason why he never married. No one could fall in love so completely, so deeply, yet with so many—at the same time. The problem was not a failure to fidelity, to devotion, rather that he could be faithful and devoted nine or ten times in a single year. And it was a good thing that he came of age in the free-loving sixties, because at any other time he would have been shot, sued or both!

Harper usually got the blame on those rare occasions when a black mood descended on Malibu, and he tried to analyze why he was the way he was. Harper never committed to one woman either, and he taught his boy the same. But for the old sailor it was not a romantic thing, rather a need to be free. It was more a life-or-death proposition, the latter almost certain if Harper lived in captivity, shackled to one woman. Robert, on the other hand, knew he could settle down, some day, if the right woman pressed all the right buttons. But even he did not know what those buttons were.

Julia shifted in her seat and Robert quickly averted his stare. The jet had leveled off and a blanket of clouds now covered his view of the ground.

"She's out cold."

Robert looked up to see Jerry closing the cabin door, then he looked back at Julia.

"A couple of minutes now."

"I'm glad she's not a nervous flyer. You know, sometimes these smaller jets can be a little scary."

"She looks fine to me."

"Damn, she is about as beautiful as they come, isn't she?" Jerry said wistfully, but before Robert could answer he asked, "Are you comfortable?"

"It's like traveling in my living room."

"Yeah, I kinda like this plane myself. In fact, you know the Queen of England's got one just like it, except hers is an SRS 200. This is a 300.''

"You and the Queen.''

"Well, this isn't mine, exactly, but both planes are a lot alike—modified for private use.'' Jerry sat in the chair opposite the table from Robert.

"Who does it belong to?''

"Well, Bors is the pilot. He's pretty good, too, don't you think?''

"Very good,'' Robert nodded and Jerry's smile broadened ear to ear.

"Actually, *I've* been flying up 'til now.''

"Yeah, I think Julia was saying something about that.''

"Put her right to sleep.'' Jerry looked across the aisle and shook his head.

"You've known her for a long time?''

"Maybe five years. I've helped her out a couple times.''

"With what?''

"What's that?''

"You've helped her out with what?''

"Well, like now, you know, getting her from place to place. Shit, about two years ago I brought her out of Istanbul at three o'clock in the morning. Crazy Turks were shootin' at my tail section and everything.''

"Did you know her husband?''

"The German?''

Robert nodded his head.

"Maybe once or twice I met him. Nice enough dude.''

"Why isn't she more emotional about his death?''

"Shit, you *are* a hard-assed reporter.''

"You haven't wondered?''

"Well, actually, I asked her the same thing, yesterday.''

"And?''

"She said the hurt's gone from the pain.'' Jerry reached up and turned off the overhead lamp. "I guess I understand what she's sayin', that after a while you gotta separate the private life from the professional life. And one thing about her—she's a professional.''

"But she told me she hasn't engaged in field work for seven years—that she's at some desk for Mediterranean—Mediterranean affairs.''

Robert thought about her second lie, that she had never flown with Jerry before, but he did not want to mention it.

The big man shrugged his shoulders. "Like I said, I pulled her out of Istanbul about two years ago. The guys who was after her didn't look like they was collectin' a delinquent phone bill."

"So you think she's still active?"

"I don't ask questions. Frankly, I leave people alone and they leave me alone. If I can help them, I fly in and fly out. Like I told you last night, a lot of us travel in the same circles."

"There's no compensation involved?"

"In-kind, I guess, no money, if that's what you're askin'."

"What do you mean, in-kind?"

"You know, in-kind, favors and shit. Sometimes they're there to help me out. But like tonight, you guys have to get home to the States. I'm headin' back to the States, after I make a visit—a short stop—and if I can help you out, that's my contribution."

"Where are you stopping?"

"Now that's one of our rules. We don't ask each other questions. But I'll let that one go because I know you're a journalist and you ask those kinds of questions." He smiled. "The next one, though, and you take a walk out my aft door."

Robert returned the smile. "Agreed," he said.

"But I will tell you that in about two hours we'll be over Italy."

"Italy?" Robert said with surprise.

"Like I told you, this is a great plane. Travels economically at over seven hundred kilometers an hour, that's at thirty-one thousand feet. But the really great thing is that it can land on a dime. Almost doesn't need a runway."

Robert realized that Jerry thought his surprise about Italy had more to do with how quickly they could get there rather than why they were going in that direction. But no sooner had the explanation been offered about how the jet needs little runway when Robert understood the business his newfound friend was in. The aircraft was modified with the first quarter section being cockpit and executive cabin, complete with a telephone, television, VCR and Fax machine. The rest of the fuselage was blocked off by a door, and Robert now knew that it was one very large cargo hold.

He also understood that Jerry did not care if Robert knew he was a smuggler. Going over Italy meant that they were either on their way to the Adriatic Sea or into Central Europe. And there was only one reason Robert knew of to go in that direction under the cloak of darkness in a cargo plane.

"Tell me about your fuel capacity," he smiled and Jerry laughed.

"What do you mean?"

"How in the hell are you going to get into Yugoslavia or Bulgaria or Romania or wherever we're going and then get out to get fuel?"

Jerry laughed harder and Julia stirred but did not awaken. "You think you're a genius, don't you?"

"I'm not slow, anyway," Robert laughed.

"What I'm doing is important shit."

"Oh, yeah," Robert nodded, "but I'm not asking any questions. You know—the rules—and the door."

"That's right," Jerry reached across the table and slapped Malibu's shoulder. "Smart man, but I gotta tell ya—this bird—this bird—she can fly for days without setting down. We got integral tanks in the wings and wing center section. We got auxiliary tanks in the root fairings. And then we got another six hundred gallon reserve in the hold. Next time we fill 'er up, it's gonna be in Venice."

"Venice?"

"That's right. And they got a great duty-free store there, too. Get ready to spend some cash."

"I imagine," Robert could not keep from grinning, "I imagine you got a great duty-free store right here on the plane."

"Me?"

"Well, you know—" he said sheepishly.

"Shit. We just zip in—we zip out. Nothin' to it!"

"Romania? Hungary?"

Jerry shook his head. "Yugoslavia," he said as if he were a general ready to lay siege on the country. "And now you know too much," he added.

"You're going to have to kill me?"

"To the door!"

Robert winked. "We did violate the rule."

Jerry's expression turned serious enough that Robert grew nervous. "But if you can't trust a man whose life you've saved, who can you trust?"

"Spoken like a statesman," said Robert in a hushed tone.

"Besides," Jerry's voice faded, "it's not part of your story."

Robert motioned to Julia. "She told you about that?"

"She said you were doing her a big favor."

"Maybe. Unless I'm just another pawn in a bigger game."

"Brother," said Jerry, "we're all pawns. But when we play right—when we play fair—everyone of us eventually gets ahead. I don't know much about Julia. I know she's a very dedicated lady, a professional. Tougher than hell and willing to do anything to get the job done. I guess in a way she reminds me of my mother"— his face lighted up —"with a few noted exceptions. But she has the same sense of dedication—of being involved in something bigger than life. If she told you one thing, and now you think she lied, it's probably because she's trying to protect you—not her."

"Protect me," Robert blurted. "She about got me killed!"

"Think about it. Did she about get you killed, or did *you* about get you killed?"

"She didn't know that—" Robert thought about Bower Thompson. There was no way Julia knew the two men were acquaintances. Her design was to meet him in Almería, to point out Bower Thompson, to tell him what she knew about her husband's death, and then to have him write the story. It was on his own initiative that he sought out the administrative assistant, talked to him even before he talked to Julia. Then the next move, the move that almost killed him, was Bower Thompson's. "I guess you're right," he concluded.

"Like they say, she's tough but fair. And in her business that ain't easy."

Robert was going to agree, but before he could say anything the cabin door flew open and Borsman walked to the table. He was more cartoon character than human, with a rolling chest and stomach tucked tightly into a green tee-shirt that ended with a crescent-shaped hem above his bellybutton. His eyes drooped and his cheeks weighed heavy around his nose. His chin doubled and even tripled into his neck, a neck that Robert estimated to be thicker than his own thigh. Even walking from the cockpit to the table put Borsman out of breath. He pulled up the brim of his New York Yankee baseball cap and wiped perspiration off his forehead. His Levi jeans were black with grease and oil, and Robert realized that he was more than a co-pilot. He was also the mechanic.

"She's flying auto," he said in a voice that sounded like someone rode a bicycle across his neck. "Should be over Sardinia in twenty-three minutes. Once we get to the coast, we've got to drop her down below radar. Weather's looking good, and I figure we'll be in and out inside of ninety."

"Sound good to me, mans," Jerry said in his best Jamaican accent. "I'll tell you, Bob, Bors is the best damn runner in the world." He looked back at his co-pilot. "What's it been, sixty runs this year?"

"Sixty-eight. Tonight's sixty-nine." Borsman smiled. His teeth were stained with chewing tobacco.

"He started with a Cessna Caravan, running imitation Peruvian artifacts into Mexico during tourist season. How much were you making back then?"

"Two-fifty a trip."

"Can you believe that, flying over Cocos Ridge in a single engine for two hundred and fifty bucks a trip?"

Robert tried to flatter the funny man by shaking his head in disbelief.

"They said he could make more money in dope, but—"

"Forget that shit," said Borsman.

"See what I mean. He wouldn't touch the stuff. So he flew wood carvings for two-fifty." Jerry slapped the man on his leg. "But you're doing better now, ain't ya, Bors?"

"Yep."

"But we still gotta get you some nicer clothes. And maybe a little deodorant." All three men laughed. "Shhh," Jerry said, "let's not wake up Sleeping Beauty."

"Well, anyway, I'm going to check the cargo," said Borsman. "Once we get to the boot, we gotta take her off auto and drop her down. Won't have time to ready the load."

"If I didn't know the rules, I'd ask what cargo you're carrying," said Robert.

"Damn good thing you know the rules," said Jerry as he stood up. "I'll check it with you," he said to Borsman, then turned back to Robert, "and you stay put."

"Sure." Malibu watched the men open the cargo hold door. He turned back to the table and the phone. "Would it be okay if I made a call? I'll reimburse the cost."

"No problem, mans," said Jerry, "and don't worry about the cost, it would only confuse my taxman." The two passed inside, closing the door behind them.

Robert turned back to the phone. He did not want to make the call all at once, but savor each step and allow his ego the gratification that he was not a man possessed. He placed his hand on the red receiver and studied the push-buttons as a man would study a piece of abstract desk sculpture, unaware of its entire meaning yet gratified by the possibilities.

An instruction card adhered to the phone read: CELLULAR COMMUNI-CATIONS. DIAL DIRECT IN THE UNITED STATES OF AMERICA—AREA CODE AND NUMBER. FOREIGN TRAVEL REQUIRES OPERATOR ASSIS-TANCE—COUNTRY CODE AND "O." BE PREPARED TO PROVIDE THE AIRCRAFT CALL LETTERS—SXBDA.

Robert punched 39.

"Operator," a man said after two rings.

"Yes, I need to place a call to—"

"What is your call number?"

"X—S—I mean S-X-B-D-A," Robert answered and then realized he had not opened his notebook for the phone number. Quickly he withdrew the spiral pad and flipped it open.

"The city, and phone number please."

"One minute—" Robert searched through the pages until he found what he was looking for. "Yes—please dial 99-23-99."

"City, please?"

"Italy—uh—Rome." *So much for my ego,* he thought, *for being too collected, for taking my time.*

He heard the six clicks and then the line began to ring. Once, twice, "*Albergo Cicerone!*" The connection was not good, hollow and filled with static.

"Yes—please connect me with the room of Diana Sillito."

"One moment, please." The call was placed on hold, but just as quickly the voice returned. "I am sorry, Ms. Sillito has not come in yet this evening. Do you wish to leave a message?"

"She's never in!" Robert said in frustration. "What am I going to do with that woman?"

The hotel operator laughed.

"Sure, I'll leave a message. Tell her that with how unavailable she is, I'm surprised she ever scores."

"Excuse me?"

"It's an inside joke."

"A joke?"

"You know, a personal thing. She'll know who called. Tell her I miss her—terribly."

"Yes, sir."

"Oh—and—ah—tell her that I'll be in Washington, back at my place, if she ever cares to look me up. My name's in the book."

"In—the—book," repeated the operator as she was taking down each word. "Is that an *inside* joke, also?"

"No—no," Robert laughed, "it's a cliché, but she'll know what it means."

"Thank *you*, sir. Is that all?"

"Yes."

"Thank you."

"Thank *you*," Robert replied and hung up the phone.

He relaxed back into the seat and looked out the window, though there was only darkness beyond the flashing white strobe at the end of the wing. The thought of rejection began to taunt his mind as he wondered what Diana was doing out so late. But then he reassured himself that such hours were indigenous to her lifestyle, a part of the romance and a requirement of the job. The after-hour networking that moved careers was only one more similarity between show business and politics. Whether it was on Pennsylvania Avenue or Rodeo Drive, fortunes were made and broken at the cocktail party.

"Who were you trying to call?" Julia asked in a weary voice.

Robert looked at her eyes, moist from sleeping. "I didn't know you were awake," he said.

"Barely." She offered a half smile.

"I was calling a friend in Rome."

"Rome?"

"You didn't know we're taking the long way home."

"Knowing Jerry, I am not surprised." She closed her eyes again and leaned her head back into the seat.

"And evidently you know him better than you let on."

"What's that supposed to mean?" She looked back at Robert.

"I think it's time we're honest with each other."

"You mean that I am honest with you."

Robert shook his head, "I mean—"

"That's exactly what you mean. You weren't about to tell me about your relationship with Diana Sillito—"

"You heard."

"Nor about your friendship with Senator Watenburg."

"How do you know about that?"

"You weren't going to tell me about your stint in the National Security Council, nor about your time in prison."

Three lightning strikes. Robert was confused and feeling vulnerable. At first he believed the jolts were prompted by her interest in knowing about the woman he was calling, but now he realized it had nothing to do with lack of knowledge or personal interest at all.

"Nor," she looked wide awake now, "did you tell me that you have been fired by your newspaper. You did not tell me about any of that! So, Mr. Hamilton, who is keeping information from whom?"

"How do you know so much about me?" Robert now regretted digging into her relationship with Jerry, but his professional instincts told him that in confrontation it is better to smite than be pummeled. Unfortunately, however, at the moment he was not feeling too confident about his instincts. This woman was a formidable match for any one.

"Information is as important to me as it is to you. The only difference is that in gathering mine, I am not driven by my ego."

"But you can certainly be as biting—as cruel."

"You would know. Journalists *are* the leeches on misery."

"So—answer my question. How do you know so much about me?"

"All your questions? It seems that I have everything to explain and nothing to gain."

"You'll get your story," Robert said coldly. "That's why you saved my life, isn't it?"

Julia did not answer, but looked out her window.

"Isn't it?"

Still she said nothing.

"Well, don't worry. It will get into print. Maybe not in the *Post*, but you'll get what you want. Your vengeance will be satisfied."

Julia looked back. Her expression was condescending. "You people are always unerring, aren't you. You comment on the weaknesses and failures of others after the blood has dried, after the emotions have been drained, lives and fortunes lost. You place the foibles of man up against some ideal standard that is understood only by you, by your editors and publishers and people who know nothing of common reality. Life doesn't happen only in Washington, Mr. Hamilton, or in New York. It also happens in mud huts in Nigeria, where Marxism threatens to exterminate millions just as it did in Ethiopia. It happens in Berlin, where my husband's parents were caught behind the Wall while he was studying in Stuttgart. He never saw them again, afraid to go in, afraid of being trapped, because he, too, was from Neuenhagen. And they were never allowed to leave. And, Mr. Hamilton, life ended in that hotel room in Rome because two men believed in something, because two men believed they could offer a deterrent to nuclear war, a way for the West—the good guys, remember—a way for the West to break free of nuclear blackmail.

"People who engage in life are never absolutely certain of what they do. A man's decision is proven right or wrong by history. And there are times when real people—there are times when real people have to compromise for a greater purpose—a strategic compromise that says when history *is* written, the means will justify the end. I believe that end is democracy, Mr. Hamilton, and I believe we have to stop awarding ourselves sins that we have not committed. We have to stop judging ourselves as defendants who are automatically guilty in the court of world opinion. And, above all, we have to stop blaming ourselves because another power is working to destroy us."

"You were in Rome, weren't you," Robert said flatly, appearing to be unaffected by her words.

"No," she shook her head, "no, I was not in Rome. I was working in Almería, just as I told you." She took a deep breath. "But I was working closely with my husband. I was working closely with Grayson. And when Grayson discovered Hans" —she paused and took another deep breath— "he called me, first. And it was *our* decision to call you."

"I don't under—"

"Listen, and I will tell you everything. Then the decision of what you do is up to you. When we land in Washington, you can do as you please. You can walk away, or you can—"

"Compromise."

"If that is what you want to call it."

"Isn't that your word—*strategic* compromise?"

"I guess it is."

"Oh, but please continue," he said insolently, and reached for his notebook. "Don't let me interrupt. I'm just a damned jackal that's been brought out of mortality to play chess with you gods of global politics."

"Are you going to take notes?"

"Isn't that what you want!" Robert's face flushed and his temples began to pulsate.

"Settle down," Julia demanded. "And understand we couldn't tell you. Senator Watenburg told me about your sense of ethics. He told me you went to prison rather than betray a source. We needed someone with that sense of noble purpose. And believe me, our objective is as honorable—worthy of you and your conscientious standard. But we also understood that journalists do not make the news. You report it. And we tried to approach from that perspective, knowing that any other way you would have refused."

"Refused?" Robert repeated in disbelief. "Hell—I would have—"

"You would have reported about us, rather than go after the story."

"What story? It's a game, and now you've made me a player. I can't believe I trusted you. And I should have known better than to trust Senator Watenburg—again."

"Game?" the woman shouted. "My husband's murder was no game. Senator Watenburg—his was no game. The story is about who killed my husband."

"Did Grayson tell you that this is the second time he set me up? Did he tell you it was because of *him* that my career ended at the National Security Council? Did he tell you I've worked like hell to put my life back together and now you—your manipulating, devious—" Robert lost his thought. "I've lost another job because of you and your people—and your *strategic compromise*."

"I can understand your—"

"You can't understand anything," Robert said, but a tinge of guilt followed when he remembered that this woman had just lost her husband. *Who can't understand whom?* he chastised himself. *The sacrifice she offered at her altar of freedom sure as hell outweighs your miserable job. You couldn't work with Simon, anyway. And*

*getting fired was going to happen. This just made his job easier. It
gave him a reason.*

"I understand that there was no other way," she said.

Robert lowered his voice to a rational level and said, "In your world
you could have knocked Bower Thompson off without suspicion.
Tweeking is as easy for you as chewing gum. You didn't need to get
me involved."

"One man, perhaps, but what we're after is an entire infrastructure—an infrastructure that we believe knows too much about an issue
so sensitive it could spark nuclear war."

"Spare me the drama." The journalist looked away. "Besides," he
added, "the Cold War's over."

"Believe me," Julia said sternly. "I won't lie to you anymore."

"Then I was right in Almería. Star Wars is more advanced than
people believe—despite the peace."

The woman agreed softly. "Now more dangerous than ever."

"How advanced?"

"I don't know everything. My husband—he didn't know everything. But there is more than research and development."

"You mean deployment?"

Julia nodded again.

"Good lord! Do you know what that means?" Robert's voice was
filled with disbelief.

"The drama is real, Mr. Hamilton. If Bower Quincy Thompson
were to die, we would never know how deep his network goes. We
would never know how much he already knows, or how much his
comrades know. We assume they don't know everything, because they
killed Hans and Grayson—probably for information. The senator told
you about the sulfazine?"

"Yes. He said—"

"And you do not torture a man by cutting off his ears if your only
purpose is to kill him."

"Then why don't you people simply pick up Thompson?"

"For what? There's no on his hands. He's been on vacation. The
rule of law still applies to our trade, especially when the objective
would be prosecution."

"But—"

"But your profession is filled with speculations and allegations. If we can put Bower Thompson on the front page of a major newspaper, your Justice Department will have to act. And its investigation will expose his associates and end his hunt for information concerning SDI."

"That won't stop him from passing his information. An investigation will take months."

"You can't understand how difficult it is to engage in espionage. When your cover is suspect, it becomes almost impossible. And stopping him now, before he makes another move, before he gathers more information, would be better than giving him even another day. There is no telling what he could do." She paused, but Robert said nothing, so she continued. "Later, once he's exposed and information about his activities and associates has condemned him, then he can be tried for the murder of my husband."

"I can't figure what's more important to you," Robert said much too insensitively, "your husband or your job."

"They're synonymous, Mr. Hamilton. Life for one is given meaning through the other. You probably can't understand that—never having loved, perhaps anything."

Robert shifted quickly in his seat, prepared to pounce on her audacity, but on second thought considered her response an appropriate comeback to his brazen attack.

"You seem to know a lot about me," he said inoffensively. "Some things truer than others. For example, how did you know the *Post* let me go?"

"That I cannot tell."

"You promised to level with me."

"Not when it comes to putting other people's lives in danger." She shook her head. "On that there is no compromise."

"Whose life would be in danger? Not too many people know, just Jed and Simon, and they don't know you from"— at once Robert remembered— "Andy—Asp—enu, or Apsenu, or—"

"I do not—"

"His last name was Niccolini. He was CIA, in Italy. He was in my hotel room. It had been ransacked. He admitted to being CIA."

"He said he was CIA?" Julia asked, her voice more animated than before.

"With counterterrorism at Langley. He was Italian, but from Washington. He lived in Washington."

"Americans need to be more circumspect."

"Then it was Andy!" Robert paused for emphasis. "You people are incredible."

"Who did ransack your room?" Julia asked without regard to Robert's insult.

"I have no idea."

"Then you really must be a terrible investigative reporter."

"Is that supposed to hurt?"

"Think about it. Who were you with the night before?"

"Like I told Andy, it's none of your business."

"I don't need to know, but you should scrutinize your own life as passionately as you scrutinize others'," Julia said. "Try to draw parallels, like who you told you were going to Spain. Who you told you were staying at the Hotel Libereros. Bower Thompson even knew the room number. And think about who you just left a message for—a message that you were on your way to Washington."

Rage swelled inside Robert's chest, in his heart and lungs and into his shoulders. He was going to burst and strike out. There was no other recourse because his conscience agreed with what Julia was saying, and no other hurt was as powerful as suppressed truth released like sudden thunder. His next inclination was to not respond, to let her warning drop as if he had not heard it, as if he refused to give life to her speculation. And then finally he questioned the motives of his anger. Was it provoked because Diana had betrayed him, or was it from personal embarrassment that his ego had allowed him to be duped by a beautiful woman?

"How long have you known about Diana?" he asked and was startled by how humble his voice sounded.

"Andy spoke with Ambassador Markum. We've known for a day or two."

"Why did you—"

"Keep it a secret?"

"Why didn't you tell me?"

"Then you would know our motive for involving you."

"Of course," Robert said silently. "Of course." He looked out his window. The strobe appeared to flash stronger now, more pronounced, as if it engulfed the entire aircraft, holding it captive inside its light.

"Maybe I should have said something sooner."

"The sooner I would have thrown in the towel."

"Then you're not going to—" Julia was interrupted by Borsman bursting through the cargo door and huffing his way to the cockpit.

Robert jumped to his feet in surprise, but was pushed back into his seat by Jerry.

"Hang tight," said the big man. "We're in luck."

"Luck?" said Julia.

"We heard over the hold squawk box that a Jugoslovenski 2H9 is on its way out of Rome to Belgrade. I haven't had this much luck since I took a shit-load of Barbie Dolls into Karaganda."

"What do you mean?" she asked.

"Normally we got to drop down below radar when we fly into a country's air space. Sometimes that means a thousand feet, which gets sticky when you got two thousand foot mountains."

"I see what you mean," said Robert.

"But if you can fly in the shadow of a commercial flight going your direction, you got no problem. Radar sees what it's supposed to see— one blip, not two."

"Wait a minute," said Julia. "You mean we are going to fly directly beneath a huge airplane."

"A little behind it to be exact," said Jerry with a smile. "Beats hell out of walkin'."

"And when you have to leave your—" Robert began.

"We call them our shadow."

"When you have to leave your shadow," he continued, "don't you defeat your purpose. Radar picks you up again."

Jerry laughed. "Hell, no," he said. "You pull back your throttle and jam your spoilers. You drop so fast, the dude watchin' the screen in Belgrade thinks it's time for a coffee break."

"And you plan on doing this tonight?" said Julia rhetorically.

"You two just fasten your belts. Hold your breath. I don't know what's gonna be more fun, diving into Zadar, or trying to catch the jet to Belgrade."

"Surely the Jugoslovenski flight will see us coming," said Julia, and Robert looked back at the strobe lights, which immediately cut off as if cued to her comment.

"Bors just turned the lights off," Robert blurted incredulously.

"We're a ghost now," said Jerry. "He also shut down our transponders. You guys'll love this. It's gonna be great!" He turned to walk into the cockpit, then stopped at the door and looked back. "But remember to cinch your belts."

"Every time he puts me through this," lamented Julia. "He does it to me every time, and I never learn." She gripped the armrests, and Robert realized now that her nervous reaction when the jet first took off was due more to her memories of former flights with Jerry than with spontaneous anxiety.

He could hear the engines accelerate. The whining intensified, and the craft gained altitude.

"It's going to be okay," Robert tried to assure and then was startled by an excited shout from inside the cockpit. "I imagine we're in the shadow, now."

Julia did not respond, but remained in white-knuckled silence, and Robert wondered how a woman who could be so calm under fire, as she was in Almería, could be so afraid in what he believed was a less dangerous predicament. *It must be that the circumstances are out of her control,* he thought. *Maybe if she were at the stick, as she was when she had the gun in her hand, she'd feel better. Some people are just that way.*

Time passed as the turbofans droned on. At one point, Robert caught himself slipping into the starry, somnolent state that finds sleep a welcome relief, but he could not push himself over the edge. Several times he looked back to the woman, her eyes focused on the cockpit door, and her breathing like a boxer between rounds. He was still feverish about being set up, but for some reason—maybe because the present situation placed a universal perspective on things—his violent anger had given way to an unyielding chagrin that he allowed himself to be used by Diana. This bungle he could not forgive.

Without warning, the engines wheezed and the aircraft lunged forward. Julia gasped, but still said nothing.

"It's going to be okay," Robert said as if his command would make it so. The silver and blue 146 dropped like a wounded bird from the shadow of the Yugoslavian airliner. The G-force pushed him hard against his seat, and his stomach felt like it was oozing into his chest. Pressure around his eyes quickly turned into a headache and his ears crackled as the craft fell ten thousand feet per minute. Julia's eyes were closed tightly, her face frozen, and the last thing Robert felt before the plane leveled out at one thousand feet was her soft hand grabbing his wrist for strength.

Another shout exploded in the cockpit, and then Jerry appeared at the door. "I got some good news, and I got some bad news," he said.

"The bad news is over," Julia said sternly, finally letting go of Robert's wrist.

"Maybe I'd better start with the good news," he continued. "We're where we want to be. We're holding over our landing field."

"And the bad news?" asked Robert.

"We're not in what one would call a state of normalcy."

"What do you mean?" Julia demanded.

"Things look too good down there."

"What do you mean?" Robert looked out his window and saw the well-lit dirt runway, with aluminum-reflected bulbs on either side. At the ends of the runway were two large spotlights. "Everything looks fine to me. I don't see anybody, but everything looks fine."

"You're not supposed to see anybody. Just the lights. The folk we're supposed to meet hide in the shadows, just in case."

"In case of what?"

"In case things aren't normal."

"In case of what?" Robert repeated.

"The only place I have problems is in Yugoslavia."

"Don't say that, Jerry," ordered Julia.

"This is Yugoslavia," said Robert. "What kinds of problems?"

"Well, I haven't had problems, exactly. My people—they've had problems."

"What kinds of problems?"

"I may be overthinking this. Maybe nothing's wrong."

"What's wrong?" Julia's tone pressed for an answer.

"The field's too well lighted."

"Too well lighted?" scoffed Robert.

"We never had spotlights before."

"Maybe your friends are doing you a favor," Robert suggested.

"Maybe," Jerry conceded, "but I got this feeling."

"Then don't land," said Julia. "Go back to Italy."

"We've gotta land."

"Jerry, you don't *gotta* do anything," Robert corrected. "You're a free man now. Do you know what that means—to be free? You don't have to do anything you don't want to. Ninety minutes, and bang, we're back in Rome—or Venice. Hell, Julia and I'll go anywhere you want."

The woman nodded as aggressively as she could. "Nothing you have to deliver could be so important as to put our lives in danger," she added.

"What are you delivering?" Robert added.

"I can't implicate two friends," said Jerry. "If I told you, then you'd be accomplices—or something." He dropped into the seat across from Robert. "Now look, I'm not going to stick around to see who gave us the spotlights. I should have been told about 'em before now. But I do have to leave the cargo."

"What are you saying?" asked Julia.

"Normally, I set down, take my time dropping the booty, bullshit for a while, even get some fuel. Tonight we're talking touch-and-go. We're not gonna stop the plane, just keep moving along the strip. But I'll need your help."

"What did you just say about implicating us?" Robert asked with a smile.

"I gotta ask you two to help me in the cargo hold. We've got about a hundred and twenty boxes lining both sides of the fuselage, and the second Borsman touches dirt, we've gotta start dumping them on the runway, and keep dumping until every box is gone. If we don't get 'em all out before Bors takes off—keep dumping them from the sky."

"You're certain about this?" asked Julia.

"It's my job," replied Jerry as he stood up and moved to the cargo hold. Robert unbuckled his belt and went after him. Julia followed last.

Walking room inside the cargo hold was tight for the three of them, and Robert wondered how Jerry and Borsman managed to move around before they organized the unmarked cardboard boxes into the two lines. Jerry flipped the lock that fastened the red handle on the compartment door. All three lost their balance when Borsman banked sharply to the right on his approach. Julia fell onto a stack of boxes and the top crushed beneath her weight but did not open.

"Putting our lives on the line, and you're still not going to tell us what's in these boxes," said Robert half humorously. He regained his balance and looked out the hold window. The plane was perpendicular to the landing strip. "Those spotlights are bright," he added.

The plane began to drop.

"Bors is takin' us in." Jerry shouted as his grip tightened on the door handle. His other hand gripped a safety bar. "Steady yourselves, and the minute the gear touches, let's throw this shit out."

Julia sat back on the crushed box and leaned against the fuselage wall. Robert grabbed the railing with his left hand, but before his right made contact, the wheels hit the ground, bumped once, and then hit again. Julia rolled off her box when Borsman jammed the engines into reverse thrust, and Jerry sprang the door and began rolling boxes off the bay onto the dirt strip. Through the open door, Robert could see the makeshift runway lamps flashing by like a narrow line of fire.

"Five, six, seven," Jerry yelled as he tossed the boxes. "Come on, man," he shouted at Robert. "Push some more my way. We don't got time—"

The solid line of fire began to break and split into individual lamps as the 146 slowed down. Robert shoved a stack of boxes toward the door. They were lighter than he expected, and he was embarrassed that he did not take two stacks.

"Push 'em out," said Jerry as he ran to the front of the hold for another stack. Robert let all five tumble at once.

Julia followed with a stack of her own, and Jerry pushed fifteen at once.

"Fifteen it is," Robert said to himself and threw his weight behind three stacks. The aircraft slowed down, and with the door open the engines roared as Borsman turned on the end of the runway.

"It's a short field," Jerry yelled as Robert pushed his cargo out and returned for more.

Julia moved another five, but Robert pushed two more stacks into her path and got behind the load. They pushed together, but it was Julia who froze first when she saw the men running out from behind the lights. Robert let the boxes fall and then he saw them, and their machine guns, but by that time it was too late. A burning slug burst into his chest, next to his shoulder, and sent him spinning back into Jerry's boxes. They crashed all around as Robert fell hard against the forward door.

"Jerry!" she screamed.

"I see—" he said in a panic and reached for the microphone. "Bors," he shouted, "Bors!"

"I know, I know." Borsman's voice was sharp. "Fucking spotlight's in my eyes."

"Get us up."

"Got three jeeps heading straight for us—blocking takeoff."

"Jerry!" Julia screamed again and pointed to the cargo door where a man dressed in a dark green uniform was trying to get enough leverage to climb aboard. With a single motion, the big man dropped the microphone and kicked the Slav in the mouth. The man groaned and fell backward onto the strip.

"Robert's hurt!" Julia said after she took up communications with Borsman.

"Dead?"

"Unconscious. Get us up. Please!" she pleaded.

Another trooper tried to board and Jerry shoved his boxes out on top of him. "Tell him to turn the other way," he ordered the woman and Julia responded.

"Turn the other way," she screamed at Borsman.

"It's too dark. I can't see."

"Tell him to do it, before they pierce our fuselage."

"Do it!" Her words did not invite argument, and the plane began to turn. Jerry piled out another three stacks, careful not to expose himself to the men outside the door.

"Help me with the boxes," he yelled at Julia.

"Forget the boxes. He's hurt." She sat next to Robert and placed his head on her lap.

"Now's no time for maternal instinct!"

Three soldiers ran around the jet as it turned and one fired a fusillade through the door.

"Damn the boxes," Jerry agreed as the bullets burst like pock marks into the cargo. He dove to the floor, where Julia was cradling Robert's head. She had ripped off her blouse and was pressing it into the wound; but it was already soaked with blood. "Is he dead?" Jerry asked.

"Not yet," she said, her expression filled with concern.

As the aircraft lunged forward, vibrating violently over the rocky black ground, and the engines groaned to pick up airspeed, Jerry realized it was safe to close the door. Only the jeeps could keep up with them now, and moving as fast as the craft was, the men would not be able to shoot straight. If nothing lay in the jet's path, it would be in the air within seconds, and Jerry could not remember anything—trees or boulders or ravines. Other than rocks and brush, the ground was flat. He crawled across the floor. Two streams of light from the jeeps' headlamps raced along the ground beside, but he could not see the jeeps themselves. He slammed the door and shoved the red handle forward. The turbofans roared and the aircraft strained skyward.

Chapter Twenty-Seven

The efficiency apartment was cold when Dr. Steinbrenner awakened. The window over the dining room was wide open and Mohammed, with the omnipresent cigarette propped in his mouth, stood in his wrinkled suit looking at the street below. The morning sun was more golden than yellow, and the professor figured the time to be well before eight. The rush and horns of traffic, clattering trash cans and the noise of garbage truck compressors were the only sounds he could hear. Absent was the whistling teapot from the day before.

"Damn bitch," Mohammed said once he saw that Steinbrenner was awake. "I knew she'd skip without bringing the brew." His face was tight and angry as he left the window and walked to the bed. "Now I can give you no coffee. Damn bitch. She never came back."

"I am sure something happened," the professor said in Charlie's defense.

Mohammed shook his head. "Ain't no way. She's just like that—into herself."

"It sounds like you might be taken by her." Steinbrenner tried to roll to his side, but his body hurt worse than the day before, and he resigned his attempt.

"Fuck that!" the Muslim snapped angrily. "One more comment like that and there won't be nothin' of you to find when the bitch comes back." He stopped beside the bed and spoke down on the professor, spitting his words. "But that's what you want, isn't it, Doc? To get blowed away here in this greasy apartment. Like you said, end your miserable life. Well, I wouldn't make it so easy, you can be sure of that!''

"I am reassured," Steinbrenner said softly. "Besides, what would Al-Ghazzali say?"

"Who?"

"This is what I thought," Steinbrenner closed his eyes. "Muslim, indeed. I would suggest you are more of a faddist."

"Al-Gonzo—faddist—what religion's that?"

"Al-Ghazzali was an orthodox Islamic philosopher. You should know that. He wrote of benevolence, of prayers and fasting, that through them the final intuition of God could be attained.'' Steinbrenner opened his eyes and looked directly into Mohammed's. "And a faddist is one who knows nothing but following fads—one who has never in his life known the joy of an original thought. One who serves as a lackey for others, whether they be peers, promoters or merchants. I would suggest you sustain all three."

Mohammed slammed his fist into Steinbrenner's head, leaving a dull, painful ache. "Shut up!" he ordered. "Fuckin' bitch—and now you." He stormed into the bathroom and threw the door closed. "I don't have to take this shit!" he shouted. "You got no right talkin' to me like that. Charlie's got no right fuckin' with my brain. She knew she was supposed to come back with coffee. She knew it. But she didn't—the bitch! Thinks I'm shit to be stepped on—to be left behind and ignored. I'll show her." The toilet flushed. "I'm no nigger—no Uncle Tom to be used by white trash. You bitch!" he screamed, as if he saw Charlie in the distance, and then he returned to the bed, holding a roll of gray duct-tape.

"What are you—" Steinbrenner began to question.

"Goin' after my own coffee," interrupted the boy. "Now lift your head."

"Please close the window, first. It's cold in here."

"Get pneumonia and die," was the harsh response and the Muslim slapped the tape across Steinbrenner's mouth, around the backside of his head, and wrapped it twice. "Now let me see your hands," he ordered and then quickly taped them together at the wrists. "Nobody cares about me—I don't give a shit 'bout them. All I care about now is my coffee." He walked to the kitchenette, filled the teapot, lit the stove with his cigarette, and placed the water to boil. "Forty-five minutes—that's all it would've taken the bitch. Then none of this would have to happen." He walked to the door, threw off the chains and turned the deadbolt. "Forty-five fuckin' minutes!" He opened the door and slammed it behind him.

Steinbrenner's arms struggled against the tape on his wrists, but his muscles ached. *You cannot even turn over in bed,* he derided his feeble attempt, *and now you attempt to break these bonds?* He looked about the room, to see if there was an instrument within reach that would help him cut loose. But there was nothing, only books on the shelf. *And what will you do when you are free from the tape, still shackled to the radiator?* He swung his feet off the bed, but jerked them back when he heard the key in the door. His abdomen strained with the movement.

"It's me they'll kill if anything happens to you," said Mohammed after he entered the room. "If you're going to get pneumonia, let it be on the bitch's watch, not mine." He marched across the room and slid the window shut. "Save my black ass," he said and left the room without another word.

My work is done, Viktor, Steinbrenner thought as he moved his feet to the floor against the will of his aching stomach. His knees cracked as they straightened to support his weight when he stood. *Only I am responsible for my existence now. I have lived to life's expectations— to the destiny that you gave me. And now the time has come to shed my guilt.* He turned and took the blanket from his bed. It weighed light, polyester and cotton, but heavy enough to do what he intended.

The chain, however, weighed heavier than he remembered, even from the day before, as he dragged it across the floor. *You age ten years in a single day,* he insulted. *Do nothing, and you may die anyway before he returns.*

Mohammed had not bothered to pick up the plates and Styrofoam cup Steinbrenner placed on the kitchen floor the evening before. The breastbones and crumbs from the biscuit still sat on the greasy plastic. With his left foot, he rigidly swept them to the side and then took a stance like a man at a pistol range, his feet spaced evenly apart from the center of his body.

Holding to one corner of the blanket, he let the bulk unravel onto the floor. Then he took a deep breath.

I miss you, Ida, he reassured his decision, took aim, and then using the blanket like a bullwhip, snapped the teapot forward on the stove. It moved eight inches and he struck again. Four more inches. On his third attempt, it crashed to the floor and the water began to drain from the spout in undulating motion. The boy had paid little attention to the flame when he lit the stove, and Steinbrenner was grateful as it burned at full height.

One more strike from the blanket and the flame was gone. A hissing sound filled the room, and within seconds the professor could smell the odor that accompanies gas. He took another deep breath and tried to fill his lungs, expecting a burning sensation, but none came. Several minutes later, however, his eyes were irritated and watering, and he knew it was a good sign. Soon his legs began to feel weak, but he did not want to move from the kitchen area. He sat on the floor, where the plate and cup once rested. Then he lay down, his eyes stared at the grime-covered green ceiling. The gas was beginning to burn his throat and he coughed against the irritation. His head throbbed, and his breathing began to grow irregular.

Inhale deeply, he ordered. *Do not fight it*. He looked out the window in the dining area. The sun was still shining. From all that he could see, it was a beautiful Potomac day, a mild winter morning, far from the vision he imagined of Treblinka when he thought of the torment and death of his parents—a vision filtered through cold and despairing gray—hard and bleak like death was supposed to be. Sunshine is inappropriate for death, he had once believed. Though today it seemed fitting. He closed his eyes and tried to think only of things pleasant.

Ida died when the sun was shining, he reminded himself, then was startled that he could not hear the hissing of gas. But it soon returned and he realized he was slipping from consciousness. *Ida died on a beautiful day—a day like today*. He thought. *God I miss you, Ida*.

I am proud of you, Rubin. At first he heard Ida's voice and he was not certain whether he was still conscious, though escaping gas continued to hiss and the room filled with the sharp odor.

Then he saw the image, in the distance, small and bright, but he was certain who it was. The light gained, and the vision of his faithful wife became more pronounced as it moved closer to him, until she stood within reach, her hair was snowy white, and the smiling lines of her face were softened by time. Finally, the odor of gas was gone and all that remained was the floral scent of her sweet perfume.

Ida? the old man began to cry. *God I missed you, Ida.*

I am proud of what you have done, Rubin. We are all proud. You have carried on. You have carried on for me and for Abrham and Pani, for Viktor and Marc. They love you, too, Rubin.

It's over, Ida.

Oh, Rubin, it is not over, he heard her say. *It is never over. You are not the only one who kept our love alive. I have always been present in you, and you in me. Now we will be together for eternity.*

The hissing started again.

Please, Ida, stay with me. God, please let her stay with me!

I am here, Rubin, she answered softly.

Don't leave me. Don't ever leave me.

Never again. Never again. But this time you must come with me. You have done what you were to do. Abrham now waits for us.

But it has been so long.

No, Rubin, not long, but as it should be.

Then I did have a destiny, he cried.

Ida shook her head slowly and stretched her arms to her husband. *Not a destiny, Rubin, but a noble calling.*

Then Viktor was right.

Yes. Yes, he was right, but now you must come.

As Ida took his hands in hers, the hissing stopped for good, and the pain of age drained from his body as he felt suddenly light, floating and spinning through darkness, staring only at the comforting image of his wonderful wife, calm and unencumbered. Then he was gone.

Mohammed found his Folger's Instant Coffee at a 7-Eleven on 14th Street. The wind was blowing and litter stuck to the west-side buildings and chain link fences surrounding construction sites as he walked back to the efficiency. Three old men, only one dressed for winter in a wool green army surplus overcoat, bundled together for warmth and shared the dregs of a Jim Beam bottle. Parked at the curb in front of them was a white Cadillac with golden wheels and a custom grill. Two strongmen, one in a Zoothat and the other in a cashmere overcoat, stood outside the passenger's door talking to the driver. Across the street, a black lady and her teenage son waited at a bus stop in front of an experimental theater with a broken window. Gypsy cabs buzzed north and south along the street as their drivers were the only hacks who would brave the area. Drivers of company cars knew better than to go any farther north than N Street, as one of two things was bound to happen, and neither of them good. First, there would be no return passengers for round-trip fare, and second, the driver would become a prime victim for robbery, murder or both.

"What'cha got in the bag?" yelled the bum in the green coat as the other two stirred and then nestled back into him.

"Nothin' you'd be interested in, old man," Mohammed replied without breaking stride and then looked at the two men standing at the car. The man in the hat glanced back at him, and Mohammed threw his cigarette to the ground and picked up his pace. Though he was reassured by the 9 millimeter he carried beneath his suitcoat, he was nervous in this part of the city. He was from the northeast side of Washington. He knew the projects well, and though this was only a dozen blocks away, it may as well have been another country. On this side of the city, the people had not resigned themselves to poverty, and those who could not make it straight—those who roamed above N Street—pursued the American Dream through pimping, whoring and dealing drugs. If a man was killed in his neighborhood, it was generally assumed he deserved to die, that he was tangled up in a drug war or hanging out with the wrong people. But here a man could get killed just for being in the wrong place at the wrong time, and Mohammed wanted to get back to the apartment.

"I'll never let you do this to me again, Charlie," he said under his breath as he turned left at the next corner, but his pace did not slow down, nor did his breathing return to normal until he saw Malcolm X Park and a dozen Howard University students racing on foot and bikes to and from class. The trees in the park were gray and barren, though the bushes remained green, and at the far end, beneath the statue of the black Muslim leader, sat a young student and his girl, reading a paperback book. Mohammed stopped and tried to read the title, but could not see it from the distance. With his free hand he placed another cigarette in his mouth and tried to strike his Bic lighter. Once, twice, three times, then he cursed that he was out of butane and should have picked up another at 7-Eleven. He walked out of the park and crossed 16th Street.

"Beautiful day, but it's cold out there," said the doorman in his lime green coat with golden epaulets. On his head was a cap that looked like a doorman's but still had the Greyhound insignia above the brim.

"Tell me about it, Homer," replied Mohammed without expression. He knew the crusty-skinned old man really was not the doorman, but a tenant who had nothing better to do than sit in the lobby, listen to talk radio all day, and try to start conversations with people as they came and went. He took two steps past the man, then stopped. "You have a light?"

Homer searched his pockets and opened the drawer in the small desk that held his radio. "Sorry," he said with apologetic eyes.

"Then you're not really good for anything, are you?" Mohammed insulted, turned away and finally smiled to himself for putting the man down. He skipped up the four steps leading toward the hall and the elevators, leaving loving Homer with a long, sad face.

"Got no right to talk to a man like that," said the gray-bearded doorman as the boy got on the elevator. "Got to get some kindness back into this world. Just ain't right people hating people for no good reason at all."

The doors closed and Mohammed nursed on the filter of his cigarette as he watched the lights climb to number six. When the doors opened, a man dressed in a purple Nehru jacket and African beads stood with a bag of garbage.

"Gotta light, man?" asked Mohammed.

The student smiled a foreign, I-don't-understand smile.

"A light," repeated Mohammed as he pointed to his cigarette.

Suddenly, the man shook his head, set down the garbage, reached into his jeans and took out a pack of cigarettes.

"Close," said Mohammed, "but no cigarette." He made a striking motion with his free hand against the bag with the coffee and pretended to light his Winston.

"Oh—fire!" said the student with a thick Nigerian accent.

"Yeah, that's it, fire."

The man nodded in comprehension and again dug into his pocket.

There was only one match left in the book and Mohammed did not bother asking the friendly kid if he wanted it. Rather, he struck it against the pack, but instead of lighting, the damp head came apart on the board.

"Been sweating?" Mohammed asked caustically.

The man found the situation funny and laughed as he stepped by the elevator and opened the door to the garbage chute. The bell on the second elevator sounded as it arrived on the floor.

"Funny as hell," said Mohammed, and he turned and walked down the hall. "I'll get my own match," he said looking back. A woman in her late thirties was stepping onto the floor, and he watched as the man asked her for a light and she stopped to comply.

The man shouted at Mohammed, who was now at the end of the long hall, and waved his lit cigarette triumphantly in the air. "Fire!" he shouted.

Mohammed rolled his eyes and fumbled in his pocket for the apartment key.

"Fire!" the shout came again.

Mohammed unlocked the door, but not until it was opened did he realize something was wrong. The odor was so pungent that at first he could not place it, then suddenly his mind registered gas. He rushed into the room and looked first at the bed. Then he saw the chain stretched tight across the floor. He raced, coughing, into the kitchen and flipped the dial to cut the gas. Trying to hold his breath, he reached down and took Steinbrenner under the arms and dragged him into the dining room. The dead weight was heavy, and moved slowly, and the chain wedged beneath the cabinet, straining Mohammed's back when it jerked taut. He gasped again. Tears filled his eyes, and the gas choked him into a hacking cough. With a hearty yank, he pulled the chain from beneath the counter and jumped back to the professor.

It was then he heard the word that froze him in terror.

"Fire!" yelled the Nigerian, now only a step away from the door.

"No!" screamed Mohammed, but it was too late. The windows shattered and the walls heaved as the tiny room exploded into a ball of fire.

Chapter Twenty-Eight

President Satterfield's private office was a stark contrast to the regal Oval Office it adjoined like a dark closet. But Satterfield liked the room, thought of it as a refuge, off limits to everyone but the First Lady, a place where he could rest and think and work without the bothersome interruptions of his staff, an office akin to the hideaway he enjoyed in the basement of the Capitol when he served in Congress. Both were small and warm, and held the same sense of security that a child loves in his playroom when he can shed his best behavior and act and think and do as he pleases.

At the moment, he was looking at a picture of his wife on the credenza behind the desk. She was a remarkable woman who maintained any semblance of stability that he could boast in his own life. From his first days in law school when her quiet determination insisted he at least muddle through the year of fear before calling it quits, through his exhausting congressional campaigns and the turbulent years as secretary of defense, her strength was always supportive but never overbearing. He depended on her heavily, some might say too heavily, and though he would like to think it was different now that he was self-inspiring and methodically driven, she was still his anchor and alter-ego, and his impulse was to call her into the present crisis, get her reaction, her positive reinforcement.

On the desk in front of him was an untouched plate of scrambled eggs with french fries the way he liked the kitchen to prepare them. Idaho russets cut an inch thick and fried crisp in peanut oil—not healthy but delicious. Today, however, they, too, sat untouched.

His left hand still rested on the receiver of his secured line and his mind was ablaze with incendiary information that had been pouring through the phone all day. Uncertain of which facts were relevant to Dr. Steinbrenner's abduction and the murders in Rome, he felt unable to piece the bits of information into any analytic equation, and his head throbbed. His senses were numbed by lack of sleep and a stifling habit he called overthink.

Now he was being told that a gunfight in some Spanish hotel was suspected of being connected with the imbroglio, which seemed to be evolving exponentially.

He glanced from Pamela's portrait to the walnut bookshelves lining the walls of what at the moment seemed more like a pseudo sanctum, and his eyes fell automatically on John Kennedy's *Profiles in Courage*. He believed there should be strength to draw from JFK, from the crises the young President faced in his own career, but found it difficult to draw consolation from anyone right now. *Hell,* he thought, *even with the missiles in October, Kennedy knew who he was dealing with. He could pick up the phone, call Khrushchev and negotiate leader to leader. I got nothing but riddles.*

He looked at his wrist watch. The time was a quarter past ten, and Skillman had just called to tell him that the Council was waiting in the basement. Softly, he touched the glass of his wife's picture as if to stroke her cheek. The gravity of his dilemma overwhelmed his emotions as he considered their relationship, how much he loved her, and how that love could be lost if he made one wrong move, if he sent the wrong signal to Moscow. Death en masse, such as it would be in a nuclear attack, was a callous statistic, but when the mass was considered individual by individual, relationship by relationship—as he considered his with Pamela—it lost the protective indifference that needs to be present when strategic decisions are made.

The President rose slowly and walked to the elevator, knowing that he had to re-establish that indifference before he entered the Situation Room.

"First thing I want when this ordeal is over is to have that thermostat fixed," he ordered with a benevolent smile to the officer on watch as he walked into the bunkerlike room. Keeping with his character, Skillman had not overstated the facts—every member of the Security

Council, with the exception of the national security advisor, Rich
Spencer, was present, and their attention focused on Satterfield as he
took his seat at the end of the conference table. "Before I begin," he
said looking away from his advisors to the three communications
officers sitting behind their high-tech bank of computers, receivers and
transponders, "I want to thank each of you for staying on duty. I hope
you've been able to get some rest."

Each of the four nodded in gratitude, and Satterfield turned back to
Skillman. "Where's Rich?"

"There's been an incident," Tab began.

"An incident?"

"At a suspected Soviet safehouse up 16th."

"On 16th Street?"

"Yessir."

"Damn communists got balls of iron," Satterfield said as he rocked
back in his chair. "First they build their embassy two blocks away
from the White House, and now they got a snuggery of spies up the
street? As if they didn't employ enough in the embassy. We got to
move to a better neighborhood," he quipped, but received only a
courteous response. "What kind of incident?" he said with regained
seriousness.

"At first report—a fire."

"At first report?"

"FBI responded first. It's their arena—"

"And?"

"Central Intelligence followed up, and Spencer's men moved as
quickly as they could. We haven't heard from them since Rich left
over an hour ago."

"Nothing?" The President rocked back in his leather chair.

General White leaned forward and said, "We assume, sir, that Rich
has been busy taking charge of the situation, as it could possibly be
related to our present condition."

"I imagine it's a bureaucratic nightmare," said Tab, "Metro Police
hustling the firemen out of the area, FBI hustling Metro out, CIA
hustling FBI and Spencer hustling CIA—"

"I get the picture." Satterfield turned to Secretary of State Parryman. "What do we know about Spain."

"That they're not ready to cooperate." The reply was unvarnished.

"Not ready to cooperate?"

"Señor Hernandez has stated officially that two citizens of the Soviet Socialist Republic were killed by an American in the coastal city of Almería. That's all we got. No names. No titles. They won't even give us the hotel registration to check who the American was, if he was registered in that hotel."

"Then who linked it to Steinbrenner?"

"That's my theory, sir," said Doland Rheem. "As you know, we've got the smaller phased-array tracking system under construction in Almería. Add two dead Soviets—"

"Soviets killed by an American," Skillman broke in.

"But surely we'd know the man on our side." Satterfield's voice begged for a better explanation.

"That's what concerns us," Tab continued. "We don't know."

"It appears we've got—" Rheem began again but did not finish.

"Another unaccountable, unsubstantiated, unknown factor that, frankly, we can't afford." The President's voice was angry.

Both Rheem and Skillman sat back in their chairs.

"Again, it's only a theory," Parryman added softly. "Until Madrid will let our people in to investigate, we won't know for certain."

"Somebody's got to know," said Satterfield. "Spencer or Central Intelligence—somebody. American tourists don't go around shooting damn Russians."

"Frankly, Ambassador Holmes is surprised no one has come in to one of our consulates seeking protection," the secretary continued. "Whoever it is, he must be running scared."

"Or he's a professional," said Skillman.

"Or," Satterfield said, as if just enlightened, "he's not really an American."

"That's a possibility, sir," said Rheem, "but given the coincidence of the radar system and Señor Hernandez's statement, I believe we better consider it a strong possibility."

"So then all we've really got is the same damn story—no new information—Steinbrenner in hostile hands—"

"If things don't check out up the street," Skillman said, and Satterfield was at first offended by the obdurate inference that Steinbrenner's death would somehow resolve the most pressing equation in the crisis, though he, himself, knew it would.

There was a cautious pause, and before the President could continue, Tab asked the next logical question. "Did you get through to Senator Ashworth?"

Chief of Naval Operations Jules Morrow and Marine Commandant Raymond Bradford looked at each other and shifted uneasily in their seats.

"I did," Satterfield answered. "He says he left his briefing book on the table—that he didn't even open it."

Skillman offered a skeptical expression that only the President could see.

"That's what he said," Satterfield continued, looking away from his chief of staff, "and I have no reason to doubt him."

"With respect, sir," said Rheem in his commanding voice, "we've already reached the conclusion that he took the book. The man's a politician, do you expect him to tell the truth?"

Everyone looked at everyone, unsure of what to expect from Rheem's last comment. Skillman looked at the President who was trying to maintain a straight face.

"You just remember what Truman did to MacArthur," Satterfield smiled, and the room rocked with laughter.

"But MacArthur's bullheaded advice was dealing with the communists," Rheem responded with a smile, "not someone as dangerous as Senator Ashworth."

Laughter continued until Skillman said seriously. "The problem is, we can't be certain."

"And," Rheem added, "we can't discard the possibility that he took the briefing book as we decide our course of action."

"Granted," said Satterfield.

The army captain sitting behind the communications desk left his position and walked to Satterfield's chair. "Yankee Clipper on one-three, sir," the officer said and looked at General Rheem as if waiting for approval. Everyone at the table knew Yankee Clipper was the code name for Rich Spencer, but the captain knew better than to breach strict emergency operating procedures.

The President pressed line thirteen on the phone in front of him. "Rich," he said and looked at the men sitting around him. "Hang on, I'm going to put you on the speaker." He turned to the captain who pressed the intercom button. "Can you hear me?" he spoke in an unnaturally loud voice.

"Yes, Mr. President, but be advised I am not on a secured line."

"Thank you." Satterfield looked into the eyes of the men around him to reinforce the fact that they should use caution as they spoke. "Where are you?"

"In my car."

"What do you know?"

"It's as we expected, sir."

Satterfield looked directly at Skillman.

"I'm following the ambulance," Spencer continued. "I've ordered that the body be taken to Bethesda Naval, to remain under our supervision."

"Anything we should know?"

"Nothing right now—I'll be in the office by three—four at the latest."

"We'll talk then."

"Yes, Mr. President."

A deep hush fell over the room as the captain pressed the release button on the phone and returned to the communications desk.

Skillman was the first to speak. "Now our only problem is knowing whether or not he talked."

"Good lord, you're a cold sonofabitch," Satterfield said trying to get his point across without sounding too offensive, because he, too, agreed with the premise of Skillman's remark, and he knew the other men were thinking the same thing.

"I'm sorry, Mr. President, I appreciated the good professor as much as the next guy, but if he talked, we have only one alternative. And we'll have enough time to reverence his passing when, and if, we get out of this sauna."

"We have to increase our military alert status," said Secretary of Defense Ned Bart, speaking for the first time, and Satterfield agreed.

"God, why does this have to happen on my watch," lamented the President. "Once we increase the defense condition of our forces, it's going to be detected by the Soviets, and they might raise their own alert status—we're bringing the bear to the board."

"There's no other way, Mr. President," said Chief Morrow. "We have their submarines miles off our coast. On the General Secretary's word, our silos and major cities have roughly eight minutes."

Satterfield bit into his lower lip and looked deep into the eyes of Skillman, who nodded only slightly.

"What if they're not thinking about a preemptive strike?" the President asked, knowing he was contradicting what he told Tab the day before on the South Lawn.

"Then you should be getting a phone call," said Parryman.

"But Moscow won't call if they're going to strike," Rheem added. "The gamble we take if we don't increase Defcon, is that either the professor has not talked, the briefing book has not been passed on, or either way, the information has yet to reach the Kremlin."

Satterfield closed his eyes. In the glory of the convention, when the delegates stormed to their feet in applause and it appeared that all America was on his bandwagon, he never dreamed that he would find himself in this confrontation. "How do we explain to the Soviets why we raised our alert status if they don't have any knowledge of what the hell's going on over here?" he asked. "Our Defcon hasn't been raised for over sixteen years, since Cap Weinburger accidently raised it when Hinckley shot President Reagan."

"Tell the General Secretary it was another mistake," said Skillman. "Hell, we haven't been in office long, and we deserve one or two."

"There is an alternative," said General White, and the sudden change of expression on Satterfield's face welcomed his opinion. "We can send a message to our field commanders, informing them of the situation in Washington, but keep our strategic forces in their normal defense condition."

"But our strategic response is defensive in nature," argued Rheem. "Our silos can't withstand a nuclear strike, the only way to make the Kremlin back off is to show them that we're ready to launch our payload—to retaliate inside those eight minutes. Our message, Mr. President, has to be clear and unmistakable."

"Assuming that Steinbrenner did not talk," Tab began, but the President cut him off.

"I thought you said we have to assume he talked."

"I said we have to prepare for the contingency. But in the event that he did not talk, we have to get our hands on the briefing book."

"And what do you propose, storming Ashworth's office?"

A devious smile spread across Rheem's face. "I've got just the men," he said.

"I bet you do," Satterfield chuckled, and found it ironic that in such critical moments humor was not only enjoyable, but an effective tool to clear the mind and mounting tension and to allow the decision-making processes to flow naturally.

"We can't get a warrant for search and seizure without compromising national security," said the President. "And even if we got the warrant, if Senator Ashworth doesn't want us to have the book, we're not going to get the book."

"Do what Lincoln did," said Skillman with a smirk. "Assume additional executive powers and have his offices searched without a warrant."

"Lincoln didn't have to worry about the damn networks," said the President. "We do that and we'll be top story on tonight's edition of 'Nightline.' "

General White sat forward. "Can't we explain the ramifications to the good senator?" he asked. "Surely he must understand that the book threatens to compromise our security."

"I tried," said Satterfield. "He agreed with me—said the whole damn SDI system threatens to compromise our security—but still insisted he doesn't have the book."

"Jackass's motivated by politics—not reason," gushed Rheem.

"What if he doesn't have it?" asked Bart. "What if Steinbrenner did take it for some reason?

"As a matter of practice, our people will be searching the professor's townhouse," said Skillman. "And I imagine if Rich found anything with the body, he would have mentioned it."

"If he found anything more than ashes," said Parryman.

"That's a point," said the President. "If the doctor had the book in his possession when he was abducted, then—"

"He more than anyone knew better than that," said Skillman, and again Morrow looked nervously at Bradford, uncertain that anyone should interrupt the President. "There's no way he would have taken the book to the Press Club."

"Excuse me for being so brash," said Parryman, "but he was getting old."

"A brilliant man doesn't compromise his life's work with stupidity,'' Skillman objected. "No, I think we can be certain he didn't have the book when he was taken. Now, whether or not he had the book when he left our meeting, well, that's another possibility altogether.''

"Either way,'' said Rheem, "we have to go on the assumption that it's fallen into hostile hands.''

"Just as we have to go on the assumption that Dr. Steinbrenner talked before he died,'' concluded the President.

"To what extent are you willing to go to get the briefing book from Ashworth?'' Rheem asked. "If,'' he added sardonically, "he actually has the book.''

"When Spencer gets back and has a chance to debrief, I'll have him take care of it.''

Rheem grinned. "I thought we had problems about a warrant,'' he chuckled.

Satterfield's eyes beamed in return. "If I remember the Fourth Amendment—and heaven knows I should—it protects against *unreasonable searches and seizures*. And quite frankly, there's nothing unreasonable about what Spencer will do. We'll have the book back in no time.''

"And what about the incident in Spain?'' asked Skillman.

"I'm not going to worry about that until Señor Hernandez wants to get serious enough to do more than issue *official* declarations.'' His tone on the word "official'' was sarcastic. "Just because two Soviets died, we can't assume the integrity of our SDI secret has been compromised.'' He looked at Rheem. "Though I do agree with you, General, I believe it has more to do with this nightmare than we realize.''

"And what about our defense condition?'' Rheem asked. "Do we raise Defcon, or do we alert our field commanders like General White suggested?''

"In principle, I think you've got a great idea, General,'' he turned to White, "but I'm afraid the Soviet Union has one recourse, and one recourse only, to the news that we've got our satellites in orbit, and that's a preemptive strike—to hit us before our system is activated. In this case, any specific orders to our field commanders would be moot against a nuclear confrontation. Consequently, we have to move ahead as if a nuclear attack upon the United States or our allies is imminent.''

"Are you saying State Scarlet?" Parryman asked in a hallowed, disbelieving voice.

"Good lord," said White, "that would give your authority to use our nuclear weapons to the Unified and Specified Commanders."

"Don't jump ahead of me," Satterfield said stiffly, "but I do believe our condition has surpassed the first two stages of strategic alert. We were through Condition Blue and Condition Yellow before we knew what in the hell was going on." He paused to take a deep breath. "Gentlemen," he continued, trying to hold eye contact, "I do believe we're one step away from State Scarlet. We're in State Orange, and if the Kremlin wants an explanation, we'll know that we planned for the worst—that they don't know everything we're giving them credit for knowing. And I'll do my damned best to lie like a sonofabitch. If, at that time, we have the briefing book in our hands, and if we've accounted for the incident in Spain, we'll all go home, eat meatloaf and sleep like we did back when we earned honest livings. But right now, gentlemen, I'm declaring our condition State Orange."

Chapter Twenty-Nine

The Cause was an underground bookstore in every sense of the word. Even its entrance was underground on DuPont Circle, and the store's clientele was a group of hold-over hippies from decades gone by who were, as the store's name implied, looking for new causes to champion. Unlike their previous era in the sixties, when they were raggedy, motley, dirty children, riding motorcycles and injecting drugs with infected needles, today they were intelligent, articulate, well-dressed activists, educated with the money of their rich parents at America's best universities. Most of them were involved in left-wing politics, representatives of political action committees, lobbying groups, and throw-away newspapers that stood fast against nuclear defense, zealous pro-lifers, conservative members of Congress, and President Delbert Satterfield.

Like many bookstores catering to the radical intelligentsia, The Cause offered a tea and coffee shop upstairs, overlooking the main floor. Most of the time, homosexuals who frequented DuPont Circle passed away the hours in the small room, sipping tea and nibbling biscuits, but not always. After the phone call the night before, Bower Thompson knew Charlie was not gay, and as he saw her for the first time when he rushed into the tearoom, thirty-five minutes late, he realized what a shame it would be if she were. Her beauty was stunning, and for a moment his composure, and the high hand he had gained during their previous conversation, evaporated as she stood to greet him.

"Mr. Thompson," she said, hurriedly extending her hand.

He acknowledged and sat down, studying the details of her eyes. "I'm sorry about the time. I had to park about a mile up the street," he said. "It seems like each time I come to this plaza it gets more crowded."

"Yes—" was all she could say before it finally dawned on Thompson that something was terribly wrong.

"Is everything okay?" he smiled doubtfully as he watched her ravishing presence decompose in front of him.

"No," she said. "No, it isn't." Her face strained to maintain a vestige of professional aplomb. "I am afraid—"

Immediately, Bower felt his arms grow cold and the muscles in his hands ached. "Not Professor Steinbrenner," he shook his head.

"I tried to call you an hour ago. There was no—"

"Not Steinbrenner," he repeated.

"Yes," the word exploded like a child's tearful confession.

"What? What happened?"

"He—he is—"

"What?" Thompson said viciously and caught the attention of neighboring patrons. "What?" He reached across the small round table and grabbed her arm.

"Dead!" she cried. "He's dead!"

"No!" Bower's fingers turned white as his grip tightened. "No, no, no, no."

"Sorry," she sobbed. "I am so, so very sorry."

"Sorry?" Thompson yelled in disbelief, and the man behind the counter put down his cleaning rag and moved as if he were going to quiet the commotion. "You're sorry?"

"Please—"

"Come on," he ordered as he stood and pulled her out of the chair and toward the stairs.

"My coat—"

"Forget it." His command was unrelenting as he hustled her across the main floor and out the door.

A cold northeaster nipped his face while they made their way up the street, and he was sure the woman was freezing, dressed only in a white silk blouse, blue leather miniskirt and black pumps.

"Please," she said, "my arm—you're hurting it."

"You're lucky it's not your neck," he said and then shoved her in front of him. "It's the red Nine-eleven on the next block. Wait for me there." He disappeared into an international newspaper and magazine shop, broke a dollar buying the *Post* and went to the pay phone.

His anger was so intense he misdialed twice before getting his party on the line.

"You know who this is," he said when he recognized the voice on the other end.

"Yes, I know."

"You've heard about Steinbrenner?"

"I have heard."

"It ruins everything. The amateurs your people gave me—they ruined everything."

"No. Not everything."

"Except for the information I got in Spain, we're no closer than we were a year ago. And we had the scientist in our hands. In our hands. So close."

"Wrong. We are much closer."

"How do you mean?"

"Base London has informed us that only an hour ago your President raised his nuclear commitment to level three."

"What?"

"Apparently for no reason at all, he is preparing for a nuclear confrontation."

"A nuclear confrontation? Why?"

"This is the question for today. Why, when the world is more at peace than it has been in recent decades, does he do this? There is no troop movement. No preparation for conventional war. Only a dramatic increase in your nuclear commitment."

"As if he's assuming we may discover something—something perilous enough to our defense that we'd launch a first strike."

"You have become enlightened over the years. I am proud of your progress."

"Then you think it's Steinbrenner?"

"We can only speculate it relates to the demise of Professor Steinbrenner. If this is true, then the assumptions we have used this year have been correct."

"But we still don't know how far the Initiative's progressed."

"At least not yet, no. Our people, however, are preparing to respond to President Satterfield's hysteria. Until we are certain what his motivation is, Moscow has committed to a strike.''

"And when we find out why?"

"Moscow will respond accordingly."

"Then what do you want me to do?"

"See what your good senator knows."

"Ashworth?"

"Of course. See what he has been told."

"How do you know he's been told anything?"

"Our sources tell us he flew home from Italy earlier than expected to attend a White House meeting—a meeting that was also attended by Dr. Steinbrenner."

"I'm on my way to the office now."

"Good."

"Oh, and what about the girl."

"She failed us. So did her underling, Mohammed."

"And?"

"You know what to do."

"Not me. Not here in Washington."

"Put her on the 1:25 Metroliner to New York. Amtrak to Penn Station. How do they say—life is cheap in New York. We will have someone take care of her there. She will never be traced back to you— or to us. Now go. You have been good for us. People are pleased with you. I am pleased with you."

"Okay," said Bo.

"And be certain to get back with me as soon as you get any information from your senator."

"Okay," Bo repeated and hung up the telephone.

Charlie's eyes were filled with tears when he joined her at the car. Her arms were wrapped around the front of her body, trying to shield away the wind.

"I am so sorry," she said.

"Get in," Bo unlocked the car and opened the door. She obeyed without a word. "You should have thought about it last night when you were getting off with whomever it was that answered your phone."

"I did not think—"

"You're not paid to think," he said negotiating the car into traffic.

"You're paid to carry out your orders. That safehouse was your responsibility, and you failed."

"But Mohammed—"

"Forget Mohammed. He wasn't in charge. He was nothing but an ideological bootblack. You should have never left the apartment."

"I know that now."

"Now is too late." He turned off Connecticut Avenue onto H Street, then took a right on 13th.

"What will happen to me?" she asked.

"Our people don't correct their mistakes," Bower said bodefully. "They bury them." He looked out the corner of his eye to see her expression, but she only stared straight ahead, looking at the traffic as if it were a hypnotist's soporific pendulum.

The car turned left on Pennsylvania and moved slowly toward Capitol Hill.

"Are you going to kill me?" she finally asked, and Bower was taken by how calm her voice had become, as if she had resigned herself to the fact that there was no recourse available to save her.

She was looking at him, and he glanced at her several times before answering. "It would be a tragedy to kill something so beautiful," he said, forcing his voice to sound as compassionate as possible, and he offered a congenial smile. "No, I am not going to kill you—though I've never disobeyed orders before."

Charlie's eyes brightened. "I will never fail again," she promised him.

"I believe you," he said and turned the car left on North Capitol Street. "But unfortunately, we have people within our ranks who wouldn't be so sympathetic."

"I know we do," she quickly agreed. Her tears dried, and she finally brushed the windblown hair off her forehead.

"So I suggest you get out of the city. Change your name if you need to. Start a new life."

"I will." Her gratitude swallowed his every word like a rushing vortex. "Thank you. Thank you so very much."

Bower could not remember when he last saw eyes so grateful and inviting. "Do you have money?" he asked and turned the car into the cul-de-sac in front of Union Station.

"In my coat pocket," she said apologetically.

"Back at the bookstore?"

"Yes."

"Don't worry," he forced another smile, "I'll take care of it." He parked the car in the unloading zone and led her into Union Station's expansive hall.

The two walked through the marble-adorned lobby, with its statues and inlaid floor, and moved past the designer boutiques to the ticket counter.

"I feel so very fortunate, Mr. Thompson," she said as they stepped up to the counter. "Not everyone would have been so understanding."

"I know," Bower nodded and blinked his eyes slowly. Then he handed the ticket agent his American Express card and said, "One ticket, please, on the next Metroliner to Penn Station."

Carla Baker looked surprised when Thompson entered the dark wood-paneled reception area outside Senator Ashworth's office.

"How are you, sweetheart?" Bo forced a smile as he moved past her toward the tall door leading to Ashworth.

"I'm," she began nervously, but paused without answering. "How are you?"

"Never better."

"Bo—I think—"

"Is he in a good mood?"

"Horrible mood," she said.

"Nothing's changed, then."

"He's irate with you."

"Like I said," Bo continued, "nothing's changed." He opened the door and stepped inside the office.

"Where in hell's name have you been for the last two weeks?" Senator Ashworth stormed as he took a pair of half-cut spectacles off his nose and threw them on top a pile of mail.

Bo closed the door and looked about the office. It was a cluttered room, overrun with gifts and plaques and photographs and books, and it stood in need of a good dusting, but the old senator would not allow the cleaning lady inside. For that matter, he would not allow anyone inside except Bower, who made certain the staff worshipped the senator more as an imperial officer than a steward of the people. In this regard, the office was a monument of Ashworth's unyielding ego

rather than a place where work was accomplished, and as far as
Thompson could control the staff outside the senator's door, he built a
kingdom of his own where he reigned as the surrogate senator, acting
in Ashworth's name whether the latter knew it or not.

"It's been ten days, Senator," answered Bower with a smile, "and
I've been on vacation. You knew about it."

"World's coming to an end, and you're grab-assing on vacation."
The senator dropped into his thickly padded black leather executive
chair and rocked back. "And now here it is—" he looked at his watch
"—past noon and you come waltzing in like a prima donna. Remember who runs this show, Bo."

"Who put the caffeine in your coffee this morning?" Thompson
tried to joke.

"Dammit to hell, Bo," the senator's eyes were scorching, "I'm not
playing, I've been trying to get a hold of you for the the last two
days."

"I understand," Bower said soberly. "I've been in transit."

Ashworth turned around in his high-backed chair and looked out the
window at the dome looming behind the barren trees on the Capitol
grounds.

"What's wrong?" Bo ventured when the senator did not speak.

"I don't even know if I can tell you."

"Then why's it been so important that I get home?"

"Contemptible country's going to hell. Damned people out there—
you think they care—you think the governed care about government?
Hell, they're so damned oblivious to what we're about. They haven't
the slightest notion what we're about. Lady in Falls River once complained to me that the garbage man wasn't collecting her trash. Three
times I told her that was a local issue. I'm not in charge of the garbage
collectors, ma'am, I said as kindly as I could. I said I was responsible
for federal matters—for foreign policy and national laws. But it's not
getting picked up, she said the fourth time. Finally I told her she ought
to talk to the mayor or the city council. You know what she said? You
know what she said, Bo?"

"No, sir."

"She said she didn't want to go that high up. She didn't want to
bother the important people."

Bower laughed.

"It's not funny, Bo," Ashworth said solemnly. "It's not funny at all. You think those people care about government? Maybe as long as their trash gets picked up, but no more. Hell, not even fifty percent of them vote. They put a sniveling idiot in the White House who'd just as soon terrify the fucking communists as he would sit down with them at a peace conference. You know what he's done, Bo? You know what's he's done?"

"No, sir, what's he done?"

"I can't even tell you. It's so damned despicable, I can't even tell you. The haughty bastard. And his arrogant assholes. But we're going to get the last laugh, Bo. Teach them a lesson."

"What are we going to do?"

"Mercurial citizens," Ashworth ignored Bower's question as he continued his sophistic oratory. "Force history down the throats of your illiterate children, but when it comes to participating in history, to influencing history, leave it to the ungodly assholes in government." He spun back around in his chair. "Well, that means you and me, Bo. The making of history falls into our hands. Damn Satterfield and his assholes. When the footnote of history is written, our names will be in bold, Bo. They'll be in bold—honored by generations to come."

"Sir?"

"What I'm going to tell you—what that damned President of ours has done—you can tell no one."

"Of course."

"They would say it's illegal for me to do what I'm going to do. But the lawless bastards know so damn little about morality. It falls on us to do what's right, doesn't it, Bo?"

"Of course," Bo repeated.

"We're talking about fate, about the future. We're talking about America, aren't we, Bo?"

"Yes, Boyd, we're talking about America," Bower answered as the dogmatic facilities of his mind became aroused by what Ashworth was leading to. *It's going to be so easy*, he thought. *Ashworth is going to hand me what I need to know.* "And you and I are the last people to stand aside and let those iconoclasts destroy everything our forefathers worked so hard to build."

"Damn right we are. We've gone too damn far to do nothing."

"So tell me what the President told you."

"He tried to—" Ashworth paused. "Wait a minute, how did you know I spoke with him?"

"Well," Thompson groped for an excuse, "I—you sounded as if you've spoken with him."

"Yeah. Yeah. I guess so," Ashworth agreed. "But what I'm about to tell you now doesn't go any farther than that door, at least not until we've discussed a proper plan of attack."

"Of course."

"Used right and we're going to bring down this administration and destroy their party until well into the next century. We're going to make Watergate and the Iran-Contra scandal look like damned games. What do they call the game when you sink the guy's—"

"Battleship."

"When we expose this we're going to make Nixon and Reagan look like they were playing Battleship. If a bunch of Cubans breaking into a hotel is enough to bring down one President, what I'm about to tell you will kill Satterfield, Bush and Reagan—a fucking conspiracy that's been brewing for twelve years."

Thompson nodded, unable to think of another appropriate reaction that would be suitable without looking overeager.

"Open my safe. On the second shelf there's a briefing book marked EYES ONLY. Get it."

Bower obliged by walking to the senator's private bathroom where the safe stood in the corner under the sink. He dialed the combination, opened the heavy door and looked inside. Next to the Smith and Wesson .357 Magnum that Ashworth kept for as long as Bo could remember was the red-and-white-striped folder.

"Eyes only, folder number three," Thompson said to himself as he pulled it from the safe. His heart beat faster, and he could feel his stomach begin to flutter. "This is it," he said and opened the folder to read the title: "Strategic Defense Initiative Final Phase Briefing for the National Security Council."

"Forget the combination, Bo?" Ashworth shouted.

"No, I got it." He slammed the door, turned the crank, and spun the dial. "I got it right here." He walked back to his chair.

The senator pointed at the briefing book. "That's not to leave this office, do you understand?"

"Sure." Bower dropped back into the seat, surprised by how

relaxed he felt. This was his answer. *We don't even need Steinbrenner*, he thought, and handed the folder to Ashworth.

"This briefing has everything we need to hang Satterfield and his party from the dome. But we have to be wise, Bo, you understand." Ashworth smiled for the first time, though it was only a sly smile, and Bower responded in kind.

"So they've moved ahead on the Initiative without congressional approval?" he ventured a guess.

"Bo, they've finished the bastard. It's a done deal."

Any feeling of self-possession that Thompson found himself enjoying seconds earlier vanished like steam with the senator's words. He sat up straight. "Done?" he blurted.

"The satellites are already up there. Thirty-six fucking satellites—launched."

How are you going to explain this? Bower's mind involuntarily began dredging up questions that he did not want to entertain, at least not at the moment. *How are you going to explain that while you were passing along technological information—elementary information at best—you were being blindsided by your own government? While you were still talking about research and development, the Initiative was being deployed.* "How could it be done?" he asked. "Nobody knows it's gone that far!"

"Settle down, Bo," the senator said with concern.

"Settle down? This is impossible. It's impossible that the satellites could be up there. Absolutely—"

"Well, they are!" Ashworth said angrily. "And I'm as upset as you are, but don't lose your head over it."

"Okay." Bo tried to relax into his chair, but the muscles in his back remained rigid. "How, Boyd? How could we not know about it?" *I failed. I failed.* His mind taunted him and thought about Charlie, about the naïve look she had when he walked her to her train, about the grateful kiss she gave him as she left. *Charlie failed, and now I've failed.* "You sit on the Intelligence Committee—on Armed Services—how could they do it without us knowing?"

"The best I figure is that after the launch gap created by the *Challenger* disaster, they fired enough ABM satellites into orbit that neither Congress, nor anyone else, noticed. This, and they must have used our civilian space program."

"That's ridiculous," Bower retorted. "Impossible."

Ashworth shook his head. "It's not impossible at all, if you settle down and think about it. First, we were using all the wrong assumptions. You and I, and all those good-for-nothing scientists we employ in our Office of Technology Assessment. In the beginning we figured—because we were being told—it would take twenty-four hundred satellites at forty-thousand tons apiece to do the job—to hold a linear accelerator big enough to generate the neutral particle beam necessary to stop a Soviet launch. Come to find out, we don't need even a hundred satellites as long as they're in the correct orbits. And we don't need forty thousand tons at all, but twenty-five tons—even less."

"Certainly we, or the Soviets, would know what kinds of satellites were being launched."

"They're still dark," Ashworth tried to explain.

"Dark?"

"The Pentagon hasn't activated the system yet. Until they do, it's impossible to determine what kind of satellites they are. As far as anyone knows, those satellites are nothing but space junk."

"It's not activated?" Bower said flatly.

"No," Ashworth shook his head. "Not yet. Steinbrenner said it's going to take ninety days to do it, too. You realize what the Soviets could do in ninety days?"

It's not activated. Bo tried to reassure himself that he may have earned a reprieve. If he could get the information to his people before they discovered it elsewhere—if he could explain how it happened without his knowledge, without Ashworth's knowledge—if he could explain that the system would not be viable for another three months. *But you can't call from here,* he thought. *You've got to get out of the office—and you've got to take the book with you. Your people will need proof.*

"You're sure about that?"

"Of course, Bo. I've read this twice, all the way through." Ashworth waved the book. "I was as incredulous as you at first. I figured there was no way they could have launched without our knowing. But you'll see it here. Do you realize that for a viable deterrent we need only thirty ABM satellites in orbit. That's how sophisticated the system is. Put five or six in what they call Molnya orbit, where they spend twelve of their thirteen hours over the northern hemisphere. Put another dozen in low-earth orbit, and a dozen in mid-earth, and you've got the Initiative. And after the launch gap, we were putting up well over a half-dozen satellites a year on our shuttles alone."

"Who knows about this?" Bo said gravely.

"About what?"

"The system. That it's finished."

"In short, nobody but the damned Security Council. Maybe a handful of scientists."

"You know about it."

"I think Satterfield believed if he could win me, his battle would be over." Ashworth rocked back in his chair. "Well, his battle hasn't even begun." He flipped the folder across his massive desk and Bower picked it up.

"I don't see that there's much we can do," Bo said, trying to prod the senator into explaining what he intended. "This is an EYES ONLY document. We can't take it to the press."

"I got it, didn't I?" Ashworth said critically. "Damn Satterfield called me personally. Asked me if I happened to notice who, of those attending Steinbrenner's briefing, might have walked out with a book. What an asshole."

"What did you say?"

"I told him, no, I didn't happen to see. And I didn't. I didn't see any of the others walk out with a book."

Bower tried to grin.

"But you're right. We can't take it to the press. We've got to be more circumspect. That's why I don't want the book to leave this office." Ashworth stood and walked around his desk. "I've got a leadership meeting this afternoon and tomorrow morning. In fact, we'll probably go as long as we need to, tomorrow, until we iron out the chairmanships and the majority leader slot before we convene in January."

"So what do you want me to do?"

"You've got to go after the numbers."

"The numbers?"

"The money spent on the entire program." Ashworth said in a patronizing sort of way. "Where's your mind, Bo?"

"I'm just thinking about"— *no wonder the President raised the nuclear commitment. He thinks Steinbrenner talked before he died. And he's wondering who's got his book*— "about—nothing, Boyd."

"Listen, before I leave you with the damn briefing book, I want to be damn certain I got all of you back from vacation."

"I'm all here," Bower reassured.

"Never have I trusted someone with so much in my life. One wrong move and both our careers are over."

"I understand."

"We've got to do this just right. We can't take the book out of this office, but we can use it to find where they got money for the program. When you get into the economic tables in the appendix, you're going to be surprised to find where those creative bastards took billions from important programs and funneled it into SDI. Damn breach of public trust. I want you to work over the figures. Get the specifics on appropriations. Prepare a case. Then we've got to find additional sources where we can get the same information. We can't attribute it to the book—but to independent reports. It's got to be on record some- where, if not within the individual program budgets. We'll use that to hang Satterfield."

"I understand."

"Good." Ashworth walked to the door. "Now take off your coat and make yourself at home. If you need anything, a sandwich or anything, use Carla. I don't want the book to move. And, Bo, until you've outlined a full report, I don't want you to move. I want you to give this your undivided attention. Understand?"

"Oh, you can count on it," Bower said, standing to see the senator out of the office.

Chapter Thirty

Night had fallen inside the Colosseum, though it was only twilight over Rome. The shadows cast by the five-story wall made the bowl inside the magnificent red-stone amphitheater dark, and the crowds of tourists had dispersed leaving behind only the spirits of a thousand gladiators, a thousand Christians, and Teddy Silverman.

The agent stood in a stone-hewn tunnel beneath the floor of the stadium and looked at the vestiges of the ancient elevators that once carried the Christians to the floor where they met their deaths with either the lions or bulls or gladiators.

Over three hundred elevators once hoisted the scenery from the labyrinthian dungeons to the floor of the Colosseum. Along with the Christians and the lions, the elevators lifted hundreds of tons of sand, if the spectators wanted a desert scape, or thousands of palm trees if they wanted a jungle. But now the elevators were gone and only the pillars remained in a pit that sank two stories beneath the floor.

When he was certain the last of the tourists had gone, and the gates were closed, Teddy moved out of the tunnel, into the pit, and tried to imagine what it was like in ancient times, to step into the arena with a hundred thousand bloodthirsty Romans screaming for the lions to tear you apart on the hot summer sand. He imagined what it was like to run from the lion until your breath was gone, then to baste it when it attacked, but knowing all the time that your fight was in vain, that never would you be allowed to leave the Colosseum alive. He could imagine the blood on the sand, the limbs being ripped from their sockets, and the powerful beasts feeding on flesh in their frenzy.

Something about the scenario appealed to him, to the constant baying of his orgiastic instincts.

You would have made a good Roman, he thought and looked at the wall rising behind him, to where he imagined Caesar must have watched, surrounded by his young lovers and smiling at the carnage in the round. Bloodsport was exciting, titillating emotions that no other sport could.

Behind the emperor's box, the faint light of the setting sun fell through the top row of portals on the wall. Down in the pit, the only colors of light remaining were shades of blue and black. Teddy looked back to the ground and moved carefully over the weeds and boulders toward the east wall, stirred by the emotions of what once had happened on the ground where he stood. He took three easy steps then stumbled over a rock hidden beneath a clump of grass and fell forward, catching himself on a pillar. The palm of his right hand tore against the sharp stone and left a swipe of blood. It hurt. But it was also energizing, as Teddy felt he had somehow consummated his swelling sexual desire, spilling his own blood in the icon of his passion.

He licked the blood from the palm of his hand and smelled the cold, musty aroma of the ancient rock. The evening air was chilly and he took another step, then another, licking the blood from his palm whenever there was enough to lick. Finally he could see the black opening of the east tunnel, where the meeting was to take place. The pit was completely dark now, the only light coming from the bright stars in a cloudless night sky. Moving more cautiously, he waved his hands slowly in front of him like a blind man groping in a strange room, and placed each step with care. The danger and the pain aroused him, adding a sensual delight to his environment and the anticipation he felt about meeting his lover.

The two men had been separated more than a month, while Teddy was on location with Diana, though they had spoken three or four times a week, and Teddy was delighted when a change of orders demanded that they meet in the romantic city.

It was his idea that they reunite in the Colosseum, and even then he had not fantasized that the ambiance would be so stirring.

Moving more quickly now, anticipating the reunion, Teddy considered their relationship that spanned three decades and withstood their countless professional conflicts. His arsenal of memories opened with vivid pictures of their myriad passionate moments, and he quickly remembered why it was easy to endure the comparatively inane conflicts.

He looked back at the west wall. The sky was so dark he could not see the imposts of the portals. Suddenly, he slipped again and reached out for a pillar, but caught a hand instead.

"Careful, Ted," said a familiar voice.

"Dwight?"

"Of course, who else would be in this morbid place after dark?"

"Dwight," Teddy said gleefully and wrapped his arms around Dr. Sillito. "I've missed you, so—"

"How's Diana?"

"Haven't you missed me?"

"Of course, Teddy, but how's Diana?"

"As spoiled as ever. Obstinate. Out of control. And irresistible."

Dr. Sillito chuckled. "I'm glad she's still happy," he said and returned Silverman's hug.

"It was genius putting her on that journalist," said Teddy. "You were right that he would dig up the information we needed. He was the first person Senator Watenburg called, he hasn't stopped running after the story since, and we've been able to follow him all the while—as if Diana's in heat and he's the only dog in town—he's been calling, telling us where he is, where he's been, and where he's going. And it sounds as if he's as close to getting the story as our people. He's a good backup in case our man fails."

"Our man won't fail," said Sillito. "He already has the information we need. Besides, Hamilton has been too thorough."

"Our man has the information?"

"He needs only to pass it on now. We'll have everything we need. We'll know exactly where the Americans are with the Strategic Defense Initiative."

"Then we won't need the journalist?"

"Not after our man passes a copy of the SDI briefing book to Ambassador Voroshilov."

"Then Hamilton's no good to us anymore?"

"No," Sillito answered pensively. "No, but after what happened in Spain—we need him dead."

"Well, with the bitch in heat, that won't be hard at all."

Dwight Sillito stared disapprovingly at Teddy. "I wish you wouldn't talk about her like that."

"Don't start with me. You know you've haven't cared for her, not since you were a frat-house bastard and got her mother pregnant to prove your manhood. Since she was born, I've loved her more—spent more time with her than you."

"I'm her father."

"You're her pimp." Silverman spat the word, and Dwight hit him with an opened hand. "Do you feel better?" Silverman continued. "Does that somehow exculpate you from the past?"

"I'm sorry," Sillito said breathlessly, "I didn't mean to do that." He rushed forward and embraced Silverman. "I've never cared for anyone as much as I've cared for you. Please forgive me."

"I know, Whitey. I know, Baby. I'm just so happy you came."

"Let's go to your hotel." He kissed Silverman on the forehead.

"I'd rather stay here."

"Here?"

"That's why I asked you to meet me here—I've had this fantasy."

"Fantasy, Teddy?"

"It's stimulating, don't you think?"

"It makes me uneasy. Let's go to your hotel."

"I do have the penthouse. And it's beautiful."

"Diana won't see us, will she?"

"She's at a party, where else? She'll never know you were here."

Teddy noticed how striking Dwight Sillito was as the two men walked leisurely down the Via Filorentino to the Cicerone Hotel, and he remembered why Diana was so beautiful: she resembled her father.

The pale yellow light from the street lamps blanketed his lover's silver hair and made it glow like the moon, and the angular features of his face were tanned by the Southern California sun. In Dwight's countenance, Teddy found the masculinity that he longed for, the strong, Roman godlike quality that had drawn him to the boy so many years ago.

When they were together, Teddy could feel that masculinity. Vicariously he, too, became macho as he drained the masculinity from his lover. Nothing was as fulfilling as being loved by someone he desired so completely, someone who represented everything he wanted to be.

They walked across the plaza in front of the brightly lighted Tomb of the Unknown Soldier, the bleached white monument that looked like a city-block sized birthday cake and held the eternal flame, guarded by two soldiers in dress uniform. The tomb was rococo, a winding, twisting, fanciful architecture, but massive and bold, and Teddy saw it as a fitting symbol of his lover.

"How about here?" Teddy asked and tugged at Sillito's sleeve.

The professor laughed, "You're sick—you know that—don't you."

"Right on top." Teddy laughed and pointed up at the crest of the monument. "Right up there—our perspiring bodies going at it."

"The hotel will be fine—"

"Last chance," said Teddy as they crossed the street toward the Cicerone. "I'll never be this kinky again."

"You're always kinky."

Teddy squeezed Dwight's arm. "I'm so happy you came."

They entered the spacious lobby of the Cicerone and Dwight immediately looked at the gold and crystal chandelier hanging above the red velvet room. "Remember when we were kids," he said with a nostalgic voice, "remember the Quimby Hotel down by the wharf. We'd sit on those big chairs for hours and blow spit wads at its chandelier."

"What were we, twelve—thirteen?"

"Remember when we got caught?"

"You mean I got caught," Teddy laughed. "I couldn't run as fast as you." He paused, "But you came back for me—I'll never forget that. I'll never forget—you came back. I loved you even then." He put his arm around Sillito and squeezed, but the professor quickly shrugged it off, keeping with the pact the two had made never to display public affection. "We're on floor sixteen," he continued in a sterner tone to disperse the uneasiness he felt for breaching the pact.

Sillito nodded and followed him into the elevator.

"How are we going to get rid of the journalist?" Teddy asked once the elevator door closed and they were alone.

"It shouldn't be our problem, but that's why they sent me here, to meet with you. Since we got Hamilton involved, I guess our people see it as our problem."

"At least they know we're responsible. Killing the wetback wasn't our problem," Teddy said, "and it never got done."

"Interesting choice of word for a terrorist."

"Terrorist?" Teddy scoffed. "An old man. Completely expendable."

"Who didn't die when he was supposed to."

"Maybe we could use him to kill Hamilton."

"Are you kidding," Dwight scoffed, "at the moment we're *persona non grata* as far as he's concerned."

"He has nothing against us," Teddy objected. It's—" he paused, struggling for an answer. He did not know who was ultimately responsible for the orders they were receiving. "Who is the man?"

"I don't think anyone knows, for sure." The elevator stopped on the sixteenth floor, and Sillito looked up and down the hall to make certain they were alone before he continued. "I've figured it must be someone in a very strategic, a very sensitive position in government, to get his hands on the information he's supposed to have—the information for Voroshilov. You and I—we get our marching orders from the West Coast consulate, not from Washington. I also know there's someone else—someone here in Europe— who works as sort of a clearing house. But I don't know who he is, either."

"I hate not knowing." Teddy inserted his key card in the door. The light flashed green and he turned the knob. "It makes me feel so unimportant."

"We are unimportant." Sillito laughed and followed the agent into the room. "Twenty years ago things were different, but we made the choices to remain on tier two—to pursue our own careers and remain involved with the cause only passively."

"You call what we're doing passive?" Teddy threw his fur coat on the bed and helped Sillito out of his camel-hair jacket.

"We're not as involved as we could be. This assignment, for example, it was shadow only, to follow up on the initial objective of getting Watenburg and that German—"

"Peterson," Silverman interjected.

"To get Watenburg and Peterson to talk. Now our job's done."

"And we can celebrate." Teddy walked to the liquor cabinet and pulled out a bottle of champagne.

"You celebrate for anything. You celebrate rain, you celebrate sunshine. You celebrate pain, you celebrate health."

"I love pain," Teddy said as he turned to walk into the bathroom.

"But tonight we're both going to celebrate love, and we're going to start in the sunken tub. It's got the cutest little mirrored—" suddenly he was silent.

"You and your mirrored ceilings," Sillito said with a smile and poured himself a half glass of brandy. "One thing I can say about you, Teddy, you *have* kept our relationship exciting and alive." He sat down on the side of the bed and kicked off his shoes. "When are you going to run the water, Teddy. I could use that bath." He sipped his brandy and looked at the time. It was thirteen minutes past seven. "You know my flight time wasn't bad." He stood up and walked to the television. "That Concorde II amazes me—that you can get from the East Coast to Rome inside four hours. From now on, the 747's a relic for the Smithsonian." Dwight sat back down, then stood up again. "Teddy, what about the water?" He walked toward the bathroom. "What kinkiness are you up to now?" He turned the corner in the dressing room and saw his lover sitting on the edge of the tub, staring at the corner of the room, his face as white as the bathroom tile. "Are you okay?" He placed his glass down on the dresser as Silverman looked at him with a blank stare.

Then he saw the man's image appear in the door frame. A Tokarev 7.62 pistol was pressed in his right hand.

"Who the hell are you?" Dwight asked.

"You will not ask the questions, Dr. Sillito."

"How do you know me?"

"Your picture—it was in the safe—in the safe of Basalobre."

"Basalobre?" Sillito asked and looked at Silverman sitting, quaking helplessly on the edge of the tub. "I don't know a Basalobre."

"Your curriculum vitae was in his safe. Yours and Mr. Silverman's. The two of you left me to die."

Like a cold rushing waterfall, the information suddenly took logical shape and poured into Sillito's mind, and then he, too, was scared. "We had nothing to do with—nothing to do with what happened."

"Then you *do* know what happened?"

"We weren't responsible."

"Who was?"

"We don't know."

Sergio nodded almost imperceptibly, then kicked Sillito in the left knee. It cracked like a branch, and the professor fell to the floor screaming. Silverman jumped up, but Sergio turned the gun on him and he quickly retreated.

"I have no time to waste," Sergio said with a warning voice.

"You're going to kill us anyway." The professor could not move his leg. His chest heaved and his arms trembled.

"Then why die as heroes, when you can die painlessly?" asked the terrorist. He reached into his pocket and withdrew the razor. "Have you heard what I did to the senator?"

"Watenburg?" Dwight groaned.

"Yes—to Senator Watenburg. Have you heard what I did? It was masterful."

"Please leave us alone." Teddy pleaded and tears began to flood his eyes. "Please let us be."

"Then you have heard," Sergio smiled proudly and flipped open the blade.

Sillito tried to use his good leg to push himself away, across the dressing-room floor, but even its muscles would not respond. Sweat was breaking on his forehead, and he felt feverish. Then he saw the blood on the floor, under his leg. He felt the back side of his blue wool trousers, at the knee, and touched the bone sticking out of the skin in a compound fracture.

"I took the senator's ears, but not his nose," said Sergio as he stepped toward the professor. "I do need a nose." With a deft kick to the foot of the broken leg he made the man scream again. "Scream louder. No one will hear you. Scream!" He kicked again and then again.

"Stop it!" Silverman yelled. "Please stop it. I'll tell you. I'll tell you everything I know—everything we know. Oh, please, please, stop it."

"Good," said Sergio as he turned around to face Silverman. "Good, because I believe your boyfriend has lost consciousness."

Silverman strained, his eyes wet and red, to see his lover's inert body on the floor, blood smeared across the rose-colored carpet where Sergio had kicked the leg around.

"Like you," Silverman began, his voice unsteady. "Like you, we don't know who's at the top."

"Basalobre called him Thompson, but that is all. There was nothing about Thompson in the safe. Only about you and him," Sergio motioned to Dr. Sillito, who was beginning to moan again, "and about the operation—the operation here in Rome. There was nothing more, Mr. Silverman. Nothing more. Which makes me think that we all were sacrificial warriors. Sooner or later we would all be killed and the operation would never have occurred. Everyone—our superiors in Washington—every one of them would be safe, and we would pay dearly for their safety."

Silverman tried to fight back his tears, glancing occasionally at his lover, who was still prone on the floor.

"Well, they messed with me, and that was their most serious mistake—that they did not kill me. Now tell me what you know."

"I don't know—I don't know who this Thompson is. I'm unfamiliar—unfamiliar with the Washington people. We—Dwight and I work from California—and we don't know Thompson."

"Who ordered my death?"

"I don't know. We don't know."

"But you knew they were going to kill me?"

Silverman looked at Sillito again without responding.

"You knew they were going to kill me?" Sergio repeated and Teddy finally nodded without looking up.

Segio's grip tightened on the gun. "Did you know that I was to kill the German and the senator?"

Again Teddy nodded. "That's why I had to follow the journalist."

"The journalist?"

"My order was to shadow you—to make sure you accomplished your mission. We knew"— he looked again at Dwight —"he knew that the journalist would pursue the story. He knew that through him we could follow the progress of the operation—possibly use him to gather information as well—to expose the story and embarrass the United States government."

"Answer my question—what journalist?"

"Hamilton. His name is Hamilton. Robert Hamilton. He works for the *Post*, and he's been following the story from the beginning." Silverman paused and took a deep, unsteady breath, his chest huffing as he inhaled and then exhaled. "He would know more than us."

"Robert Hamilton," Sergio repeated approvingly. "Where is he?"

"Back in Washington," Silverman answered. "He's gone back to Washington."

"Perhaps he knows Thompson."

"Please don't kill us," Teddy pleaded. "Please let us be. We meant no harm to you."

"You knew they were going to kill me. You were my shadow. Did you tell them they had failed?"

Teddy said nothing.

"Did you tell them?" he yelled.

"Yes," Silverman said quietly. "I read they had found you in the park, and I reported it to the consulate officer."

Teddy Silverman offered his last words and did not feel the pain of the razor as it cut across his throat. He fell back, into the tub, and Sergio kneeled beside Dwight Sillito, placed the blade next to the unconscious man's jugular and with one precise stroke put him out of his misery.

Chapter Thirty-One

"*. . . to repeat our top story, Dr. Rubin David Steinbrenner, science advisor to presidents, is dead at the age of eighty-six.*"

The radio newscast awakened Robert first, and though the room was pitch black, it seemed familiar, the position and tone of the radio, the firmness of the bed.

"*A three-alarm fire early yesterday morning at the Westminister House on 16th Street claimed the life of professor Steinbrenner, father of the hydrogen bomb and well-known proponent of the Strategic Defense Initiative,*" the broadcast continued. "*Official word from the White House says President Satterfield mourns the loss of a, quote, special friend and trusted advisor, unquote, but remains ambiguous on the mysterious details surrounding the death of the famed scientist.*"

Robert tried to sit up, and the right side of his torso exploded in pain. He gasped, dropped his head back into the pillow, and touched the thick elastic wrap that bound his shoulder, chest and ribs.

"*We go now to Miles Johnston standing by at Bethesda Naval Hospital where it's been confirmed that government officials took the body of Dr. Steinbrenner. Miles?*"

"*Yes, Jason, I'm still here, surrounded by an assemblage of what must be two hundred reporters, camera crews and photographers, each waiting for a word, a clue, a hint about what's going on inside. It's after midnight, now, so it can be said that this is our second day, and still no real answers have emerged, and mystery continues to surround this tragedy. Several high-level officials have come and gone throughout the day, all without comment, and it's speculated—but not verified—that the President's national security advisor, Rich Spencer, was the administration official who brought the scientist's body to the hospital yesterday morning.*

"Miles, is there any guess at what the scientist was doing inside the Westminister House in the first place?"

"Well, as you know, Jason, the political pundits and media watchers have been speculating on this for a day now. The high-rise apartment complex is, for the most part, a residence for Howard University students. But why Dr. Steinbrenner would be there so early in the morning, when his own home is in Georgetown, is leading, as you can guess, to a passel of rumors, the most popular being that perhaps the scientist had a girlfriend. His own wife—"

"At eighty-six?"

"Stranger things have happened, Jason. Remember, the professor's wife passed away some time ago."

"Why then this shroud of government secrecy?"

"Well, Jason, that's of course the sixty-four dollar question."

"Have you received any further verification that President Satterfield has raised the nation's strategic alert status?"

"Again, all we have right now are rumors. That one came in sometime yesterday afternoon. It persists. One minute we hear a report that it's factual, that our country has entered what's known as State Orange, or the third of four levels in our strategic nuclear commitment. The next minute such a rumor is laughed away as hysteria that often accompanies a loss of this magnitude."

"You mean Professor Steinbrenner?"

"Exactly. When a man like Dr. Steinbrenner is killed, and the circumstances surrounding the death are obscured, it's not uncommon to react in an exaggerated fashion—preparing for every possible rationale for the death, from natural causes to a terrorist attack. One thing's for certain, however, President Satterfield better line his ducks quickly and speak to the American people. Until he does—until questions are answered—the situation remains both dubious and dangerous."

"Thank you, Miles, we now go to—"

Robert tried to move again, this time more slowly, but a gently placed hand took hold of his arm.

"Be still," came a soft command.

It was Julia's voice, and he craned his neck against the pain to look back but could see only her black form behind him in the bed.

"Where are we?" he asked.

"Your place."

"In Washington?" he said with surprise.

"Yes."

"When did we get here?"

"Late last night."

"The last I remember is Yugoslavia."

"You were shot."

"That's the part I remember." He tried again to sit up. "What time is it?"

"You mustn't move," she warned and then reached up and turned on the bedside lamp. "Two in the morning."

"We *are* in my place," Robert said as he looked about him at the floor-to-ceiling walnut shelves that surrounded his bedroom walls and were laden heavy with an unorganized collection of books. "How did we get here? How long have we been—"

"Jerry," she answered, "and we landed yesterday night."

"I mean into my apartment?"

"Once we landed at Andrews, we got your address from officials there."

"Andrews?" Robert questioned. "How did Jerry land at Andrews? That's an air force base."

"Did you hear the news?" Julia asked.

"About Steinbrenner?"

"Things are happening faster than we anticipated. They were only rumors earlier. By this afternoon, the press was reporting it as fact."

"They said the President may have raised nuclear readiness."

"According to my sources, he did," she answered plainly.

"I've got to sit up," he said and began to lift his head.

"Carefully," Julia added as she helped him. "The doctor said you must—"

"Doctor?" Robert asked. "A doctor's seen me?"

"He had to remove the bullet. It pierced your pectoralis, broke the rib below your clavicle. Luckily, it somehow became tangled in your intercostal muscles before it could puncture your lung. He said you are a very strong man."

"I hope you put it on my Blue Cross."

"They took care of it at Andrews."

"There you go again dropping that like I'm supposed to know what you're talking about."

"When the time comes, everything will be explained."

"I think the time's come." He looked at her, still dressed as she had been on Jerry's plane, but with blood stains covering her blouse that he assumed were from him. She looked tired, her deep eyes bloodshot with the lines around them more furrowed than usual. "But you can start by telling me what you're doing in my bed?" He offered a gentle smile.

"Somebody had to stay with you, and better me than Jerry." She looked away. "Maybe you are disappointed."

"Not at all," he said. "Thank you."

"But not to worry. Your virtue is still intact."

"Now I *am* disappointed." His smile widened.

"Since you are awake, I think I'll take a shower and change." She walked to the bedroom door.

"I want you to tell me about Andrews," Robert said. "And I want to know how the two of you got me into my apartment. Every government official from Barcelona to Los Angeles must be looking for me. They know who I am. They got my wallet and ID and everything."

"I will. I promise. But in due time," she said, leaving the room.

The muscles in Robert's right shoulder and chest were stiff to the point that he could not easily move his right arm. He stood up and noticed for the first time that he had been changed from his clothes into pajama bottoms. The drawstring was tied tightly around his waist.

"I wonder if Jerry did this?" he asked himself and shuffled out the bedroom to the bathroom door. "Where is Mr. Bond?" he yelled because Julia had already turned on the shower.

"What?" she returned.

"Where's Jerry?"

"I will tell you when I get out."

"Tell me now."

"I can't hear you."

"Bullshit."

"What?"

Robert moved from the door through the living room, where a blanket was spread over the sofa and a pillow had fallen to the floor. *Jerry must be around here, somewhere,* he thought. *And I'll be damned if I'm going to let these two play me out of their little game— not after I've come this far.* He stepped into the kitchen and opened the refrigerator. The acrid odor of sour milk filled the air and he slammed the door shut. It was then he noticed the Chinese takeout food on the counter and assumed the unopened cartons were for him. One was filled with chicken and cashew nuts, the other with sweet and sour shrimp, and he recognized the red dragon design on the boxes from the restaurant on the street below his place. Jerry and Julia had evidently eaten already, and though the food was cold, it took Robert no time at all to finish his meal.

"I hope you don't mind me borrowing your shirt," Julia said as she entered the kitchen while he rinsed his plate in the sink. She was running a comb through her wet hair.

"It looks better on you than it does on me," he said and glanced at the beautiful shape of her legs.

"I haven't unpacked yet. But I will, just as soon as I get to my hotel."

"Hotel?" Robert asked.

"There isn't room for me here," she said. "In fact, I can't remember when I last saw a flat so barren."

"Barren?"

"You've got no furniture—a bed and sofa and all those books. Jerry thought you had been *ripped* off." The way she said ripped sounded artificial, as if she was repeating exactly what she heard Jerry say. "And what is the meaning of the poem in your bedroom?" she asked bluntly.

"The poem?" he questioned shyly, understanding full well what she was talking about. He had not anticipated being carried unconscious into his apartment, allowing these people the freedom to open up his life and look inside without his guiding participation, but that is exactly what they were able to do, and apparently it's exactly what they did.

"On your wall, in calligraphy," she answered.

"It's by Edgar Allen Poe."

"What does it mean?"

"You read it," Robert said. "You tell me." He threw the empty food containers into the trash and walked to the living room. It seemed juvenile to still have the poem on his wall. But then he had had it for so long, since he was a child, that he could not easily part with it, and in fact believed it served as a poetic description of his life, an emotion that Poe tried to convey that Robert understood only too well.

"From Childhood's hour I have not been as others were," she began to recite carefully, as if she had placed the words sequentially into her brain. "I have not seen as others saw. I could not bring my passions from a common spring. From the same source I have not taken my sorrow; I could not awaken my heart to joy at the same tone; and all I loved, I loved alone."

"I see you know it well."

"I must have read it a hundred times while you slept," she answered. "And memorization is good for my English."

"Then you know what it means," Robert said.

"Not to you. What does it mean to you?"

"Why do I get the feeling you really don't care?"

"I'm only asking."

Robert pulled a Diet Coke from the fridge. "I guess Poe and I just have a lot in common, that's all. Maybe he just intrigues me."

Julia stared without speaking, without moving. Her eyes were a mixture of understanding and boredom.

"We share similar obstacles. I know how he felt when he wrote the poem—his emotions and everything," he continued, speaking as if Poe were only out to lunch and not dead. "And"— he paused— "we're both alcoholics." Robert looked at his bare feet, planted deep inside the plush beige carpet. "He died drunk, in Baltimore, in the street. Alone. And I'm"— he paused uncomfortably—"I try to remind myself that I don't want to go the same way."

"Not alone?" Julia asked with a hint of compassion.

"Not alone," he said. "See, neither Poe nor I—neither of us knows where we came from. We just exist. He had no beginning that he knew about. And neither do I."

"Everybody knows where they came from," Julia said.

"I don't—not until Harper."

"Harper?"

"A nice old sailor—down in Norfolk. He's dead now."

"I'm sorry."

"It's been awhile," said Robert. "But he adopted me—in a way. He raised me. I've always thought of him as my father, but I never knew for certain." He looked away. "It was important for a few years, I guess. I thought life was difficult, trying to do something, go somewhere, place a direction and perspective on things, without knowing who I was, or where I came from. For a time I tried to find out. Nobody ever wanted to know anything as badly as I wanted to know about me." He looked back into her deep, emotion-filled eyes. "Harper would never tell, and when I left home I tried to find out on my own. Maybe that's why I was attracted to journalism—to investigative journalism. I don't know. But it doesn't seem all that important anymore." He paused and shrugged his shoulders. "Call me Robert," he said, and then laughed alone. "It's a joke," he said. "It's the first line to—"

"*To Moby-Dick*, I know," she interrupted.

"Well, you've got to draw parallels in life, and I'm in good company: Ishmael and Edgar Allen Poe. It seems like all my heroes are self-destructive men."

"I don't find that funny," she objected.

"Sure it is. You've got to laugh about it."

"So you don't cry?" she asked.

"No, but how many people do you know who live a life without existence? I save a ton of money at Christmas."

"That's horrible. And I don't have to listen to it." She walked out of the kitchen. Robert wiped his hands on a towel and followed her into the living room.

"I don't want your sympathy," he said. "In fact, all I want right now is the story." *So close, but so far*, he thought and grabbed her elbow and turned her around to face him. The motion ignited a pain in his chest that made him grimace. "I'm not going to let you and Jerry count me out of this game."

"Game?" she snapped her head around and glared at him. "There you go, again, calling it a game. Is that what you really think, that this is nothing but a game? For one who has worked on the National Security Council, you *are* an idiot. Either that, or you've completely lost your perspective on what is and is not important in this life. If a byline is all you want, well, Mr. Hamilton, you have your story now.

You have all you need to know. And as far as I am concerned, you
have all you are going to know.'' A wet strand of hair caught on her
cheek, and suddenly Robert remembered the street in Almería, how
beautiful she looked then, with her rain-soaked hair clinging to her
face when she kissed him to elude the police. He remembered that he
owed her his life, not once now, but twice. However, even the most
pleasant memories—memories filled with romance and gratitude—
could not erase the spite and malaise that infected his heart and mind
because he had been used, because his professional ethics had been
compromised by spooks, the very people he had learned to regard with
cynicism and suspicion. Now, as he looked at her, he tried to imagine
her more as a pathetic creature than someone to be desired.

There were moments of attraction, yes, like the one aboard the
aircraft, and only minutes earlier when she stripped away his emotional redoubt and asked about the poem. But now he had to force himself
to remember that this woman was nothing more than what he had
learned to despise, that, despite the attraction, he had to focus on his
objective. He had to get the *whole* story. As far as he was concerned,
there was no such thing as a strategic compromise. Means were not
justified by the end, and despite the consequences, the public has a
right to know.

''You're not taking a step without me,'' he said with the conviction
of a king issuing a decree.

''Without you? Who do you think you are?'' She jerked her elbow
from his grasp and walked into the bathroom, locking the door behind
her.

''You heard me,'' he shouted.

''Your job is finished, Mr. Hamilton.'' Julia yelled back. ''Every
move I've made, you've exposed me. You drew those people to me in
Almería—''

''You asked me to come to Almería.''

''I did not ask you to tell your treasonous, girlfriend.''

''You can't talk about her like that,'' he stridently objected.
''You're not certain—''

''You made her job so easy. She ought to pay you. Now she's even
called you here—yesterday night—then again tonight. They know
where you are. They know where I am. And now that I know you'll
live, I'm leaving.''

"I'm not disposable," he said angrily. "And I'll be damned if I'm going to be used by you, or by anyone like you—like Jerry, who is anything but a two-bit smuggler. I'm not going to allow it. I'll find out, and I'll write the story. So you'd better tell me everything, now. Who is he, Julia? Smugglers don't land at Andrews Air Force Base. They don't get chased out of Yugoslavia by the army. And the two of you work too well together. You two work so well together, I'm surprised your husband ever let you out of his sight."

"Oh, no." She opened the door slowly, and tears began to glisten in her eyes. "Oh, no." She shook her head, and Robert quickly felt like he had once again overstepped the bounds of propriety that govern even the most impassioned arguments. "No, he is more than a smuggler," she said. "He's one of the few patriots your country has left."

"Touché." Robert turned away. Then he faced her again. "I'm sorry," he said. "I don't mean to be so cruel."

"You and I both have professions that make being cruel very easy," she said.

"But I can't let myself be used again," he said. "You have to know what the NSC did to me before to understand why I feel the way I do. I don't owe anybody anything. Allegiance requires allegiance."

"You can still have your story about Bower Thompson."

"Bower Thompson is the tip of the iceberg, and you know that. So with or without you, I'm going to break this story. I'm going to break the whole story—not just the part that you and Grayson intended."

"And you are apt to destroy civilization in the process."

"Oh, I highly doubt that," he said. "You've got to remember I've lived in this town too long. I know the art of fear and intimidation—the art of exaggeration. You want to stave off an investigation, you make everyone around you believe it will touch off a nuclear holocaust. You want to win an argument, you convince your opponent since he doesn't have sufficient need to know, since he doesn't have the insight and security clearances you have, he'll never understand just how correct you are. Don't bullshit a bullshitter, Julia."

"You really don't understand, do you?" she asked sternly. "Well, there's one thing for certain, I am not going to be the one who tries to explain it to you." She closed the bathroom door. "I saved your life. You owe *me*." she shouted. "I brought you here only for one reason, to write the story about Thompson. And now my job is finished!"

Parking was always heavy in Old Town Alexandria, even on week nights. The waterfront city was one of America's oldest, and a wonderful preservation project had rebuilt the cobblestone streets, renovated the red and yellow brick storefronts, and insured that the quaint city would remain quaint into the future. Many of the small buildings that were filled with blacksmiths, coppersmiths and markets when George Washington lived in nearby Mount Vernon, were now designer boutiques catering to the new gentry. Now Old Town was a nighttime hotspot, filled with theaters, restaurants and bars, where colonial charm mixed with modern money to produce more than a city, but a feeling—a feeling where romance and creativity lurked together down the narrow cobblestone alleyways lined with adventure.

Earlier in the evening, Jerry Bond had found a parking space two blocks away from the German restaurant where he was scheduled to meet Djian Gatian, an associate involved in the smuggling operation the former athlete operated in the Eastern Bloc.

Gatian was a native of Czechoslovakia who had supported the communist overthrow in 1948. For two decades he worked as a state policeman, and when the conservative Stalinists were driven from power in 1968, and replaced by the reform-minded party members, Djian, still a purist, left the country for the Soviet Union. In Minsk, he joined the KGB as a clerk, but soon worked his way through the ranks until he was sent to the United States to work in the Czechoslovakian embassy.

The pantheon of communist gods smiled upon him when it was believed that Djian's support of his own country was overshadowed by his desire to please the Soviet puppetmaster, and he earned the reputation honestly. Many of his activities included supplying the Russian embassy, and subsequently the Kremlin, with information about covert political activities among the leaders of Czechoslovakia.

In 1981, information he supplied about national leaders who supported Charter 77, calling for open debate on the observance of human rights in Eastern Europe, resulted in arrests throughout the Soviet satellite countries. Thirty-six of his own countrymen were jailed in the biggest roundup of dissidents since 1971. Their only crime was supporting Charter 77 and the Polish labor union.

Despite his allegiance to the Soviet party, Djian Gatian, like countless communist leaders, was enchanted by the wealth of capitalism and involved in the black market. His superiors knew of his involvement. They, too, were a part of the system, and it was through this illegal corporate structure that Jerry Bond broke into the ranks of Eastern diplomats, received protection and information, and provided Langley with priceless information. He often called what he did the most legal illegal occupation in the world, sanctioned by the leaders of both countries—Americans who gained covert access to foreign operatives and Soviets who lined their pockets while they rhetorically railed against the very free-market system the smuggling operation supported. Men would indeed do anything for information and money. Jerry knew this to be true, and he prospered because of it.

The last time Bond had seen Gatian was while the latter visited him at his estate on the island of Zante, off the coast of Greece. They had communicated several times since, but never made personal contact. On this evening, however, Jerry recognized his friend quickly as the Czech sat at the bar drinking a Bloody Mary, and he was surprised by how the man had aged in two years. Djian, who once appeared strong, with a thick head of peppered hair and a body resembling an old icebox, short and stout, was now bony and feeble, hunched over and using a cane.

Jerry smiled and greeted the man with a warm hand around the shoulders. "Good to see you," he said.

The Czech placed his glass on the bar. "And you, Jerry. It is always wonderful to see you." He stood slowly. "Come. They have held a table for us. A private table," he whispered. "Upstairs, where we can talk." He pointed at the ceiling with his cane.

Bond felt sympathetic toward the old man as he assisted his climb to the second floor. In the past few years, he had felt his own physical prowess wane, and he understood, as well as anyone could who had not experienced old age, what it must be like to lose stamina and control, to lose the edge that stature and strength afford men. His desire was to say something to the wheezing old man, to tell him that he understood what he must be feeling, but he remained silent.

"I guess you want to know what happened in Yugoslavia," Gatian said after he was seated and comfortable. "Before we begin, however, let me assure you I had nothing to do with the attack on your aircraft."

Bond was surprised his friend already knew about the incident, impressed that Djian was so informed. "I'll tell you—" he began to answer, but was cut off.

"Things are not as they once were," Djian said and waved the waiter to the table. "Give me a Bloody Mary," he said. "And get my friend here a—"

"Dortmunder Union—"

"A Dortmunder Union beer," Djian repeated with an impressive German accent. "And are you ready to order?" he asked Jerry.

"I'm not hungry."

"Sure you are. He will have your thickest steak and a baked potato. And I," his eyes brightened, "I would like Wienerschnitzel mit Bratkartoffeln."

"That's very good this evening," said the waiter.

"I know," Djian answered. "I had it for lunch."

"Glad to see you still have your appetite," Jerry laughed, and wondered where the old man put the food.

"Good Wienerschnitzel is not easy to find, and when you're my age, you take it whenever you can get it."

"I've always felt that way," agreed Jerry.

"What are you waiting for?" Djian asked the waiter. "My Bloody Mary. I am counting—one, two—" The waiter placed the order at the bar then disappeared into the kitchen. "Now where was I—oh, yes, things have changed in the Old World. No longer can we count on envy and greed and all those other virtues that once moved the communist hierarchy. Today they have been replaced with words like *glasnost* and *perestroika* and opened markets and media. And the politicians—they are not as secure anymore. Look at what they've done in Czechoslovakia, Poland, East Germany and even in the Soviet Union. It's all coming to an end, Jerry. Once, the politicians had to worry only about offending their colleagues and superiors. Today they must worry about offending the people. The people—" he repeated, twisting the expression on his face. "After a half century, it is as if they discovered the people for the very first time."

"It was too close in Yugoslavia," Jerry said. "Too close for my liking. I gotta start thinking about getting out of the business."

The waiter returned with the drinks and Djian took a big gulp. "Good thing," he said with a tomato-juice mustache covering his upper lip. He wiped it away. "It is a good thing, Jerry. With the way things are going, soon Levi 501 jeans will be manufactured in Gorky. No one will need your services." He paused and looked around before whispering, "No one except your government." He winked and Jerry took a swig of beer.

"I can always nurse on the federal tit," he agreed.

"Just as I have." Djian lifted his glass in a gesture of approval, and Jerry noticed, for the first time, that the man's fingers were swollen, crippled by arthritis. "We are men of information, and that is good, Jerry. Information is good. Very, very valuable."

Jerry nodded. He appreciated the old man. He appreciated the directness and winsome charisma that dynamic people cultivate as they grow older and the emphasis in their lives changes from appearance to personality. "That's why I wanted to meet with you," Jerry used the Czech's last comment as an opening. "I need some information—some very important information."

"Okay." Djian waved the waiter to the table again. "Where is the food?" he asked. "I am still counting—one million, three-hundred thousand—"

The young man gasped in dramatic disbelief and then assured him the orders would be delivered shortly.

"They take too long to prepare the food here," Djian said when the waiter left. "But that, too, is good. This is the best food in the city. The best German food. They stole our recipes during the occupation of '39. I swear to you, Jerry, many of the meals I eat here I ate in mother's kitchen as a young boy. They should pay me a royalty, don't you think?"

"I'm surprised by your nostalgia," said Bond. "I thought your life was the Soviet Union."

"I *have* been accused of being too Soviet, yes," said Djian. "But I believe one gets further ahead by being on the rising tide of revolution. You surf, or you drown."

"And you're a surfer."

"Of course. Though I have never liked the Beach Boys. But know this, Jerry—in my heart, Prague is my city—not Moscow—not Washington."

"But tell me, Djian, do you believe the revolution continues?"

"Don't you?"

"I guess it's an academic question now," said Jerry.

"All I know is that I am old now." Gatian took another large gulp. "I am old and tired."

"No regrets?" asked Jerry.

"Show me a man with no regrets, and I will show you a boy who died in childhood."

"I know what you mean." Jerry tipped his beer to the wisdom.

"So what information do you need?"

"First, tell me one of your biggest regrets."

"That I never wore boxer shorts until I came to America."

"I'm serious," Jerry laughed.

"So am I," said Djian, "I could have avoided years of chafing and discomfort." He lowered his voice to a whisper. "Nothing's worse than Russian briefs. Except, of course, Russian toilet paper."

Both men laughed until Bond, with renewed seriousness, asked, "Would you like to make up for every regret you've ever had? Would you like to do something that is so important it would benefit not only the United States and the Soviet Union, but the world?"

"Is it dangerous?" Djian smiled. "I am getting far too old for danger. I have killed my last man."

"No one will die—if we succeed."

"I love intrigue."

"I'm learning to." Jerry grinned a wide, toothy grin that contrasted his large white teeth against his chocolate-colored skin. "And you're the only friend I have who can help."

"How is that?"

"By giving me information about a man named Steinbrenner."

"Dr. Steinbrenner?" Djian's voice was animated by surprise. He made a disapproving, hissing noise and shook his head. "I don't know anything about him."

"Come on," said Jerry. "You know a hell of a lot more than I do."

"He died. That is all I know. And I am very sorry."

"He didn't just die," said Jerry. "He was fucking blown to pieces, and you've got to tell me who did it."

"You ask the impossible."

"No," Jerry said and looked up at the approaching waiter.

The young man put the plates on the table. "So how high did you count?" he asked, but Gatian did not answer.

"Thank you," Jerry said softly, and when the waiter retreated to the bar, he turned back to Djian. "It's not impossible, and you have to help me."

"I am old," Gatian answered without changing the spiritless expression in his eyes. "Since Gorbachev, the old warriors we have not—"

"Don't tell me that," said Jerry. "Some things never change. And some things change more slowly than others. In the world of espionage, the internal structure changes very, very slowly, and I need to know who was holding Dr. Steinbrenner. He was too important to be kidnapped without the word coming from the top."

"Besides," Djian continued as if he had not listened to Jerry, "whose side do you think I'm on?"

"You and me," answered Jerry, "we're proverbial citizens of the world. You've played politics on your side, I've played on mine, but we have always understood each other because our allegiance has been to a value that knows no national boundary or politics. Money has always been our common ground, but now, Djian, now we're into something much more important than money."

The Czech looked silently at his food. "I am too old, even for money," he finally offered. "I can say nothing."

"You've been in this city too long," Jerry continued, seeing that he was pricking the old man's conscience. "You know your people from the top down, and you know who ordered Steinbrenner's kidnapping, just as you know the consequences if the Kremlin gets the information they're after. You know it, don't you. You know President Satterfield has already raised the nuclear alert status. You know time is short. Now, I need to know who."

"Steinbrenner—he did not deserve to die," Gatian said reverently.

"Of course he didn't," Jerry agreed.

"Like me, he was old—too old to dance this dance. He served his side well. He did many wonderful things for his side, as I hope I have done for mine. The time came for his life to end. Like me, I am certain he looked forward to his rest. But he did not deserve to die the way he did. No one deserves to die like that. He deserved a noble death. I can hardly walk before noon, do you know that? My life is finished, like the professor's. But no one deserves to die the way he did."

"You *do* know more than you're willing to say."

"Only a fool would admit that—a man rich in ego but poor in brains. Wise men are discreet, and discreet men live long." He paused and then returned: "But I have lived long already."

"So now isn't it more important to be wise, than simply discreet?"

"How do you mean?"

"If you're so wise, then you know what's happening, and you know the consequences if we don't succeed."

"Yesterday, I was not sure. There were only rumors. Scary rumors."

"But today—you know how serious it is, don't you?"

"Only if the professor talked before he died."

"We'd be foolish to assume he didn't."

"Yes," said Djian. "And we are not foolish. We are wise men."

"You'll help me."

Gatian took a deep breath. "I can see no other way," he looked solemnly at Jerry. "If we leave the matter to our presidents, we are all dead."

"Then you *do* know."

Gatian nodded. "Our people have long suspected that America is militarizing space, in violation of our treaties. I know that is an arguable point, but I make it anyway. I must somehow appease my sense of loyalty before speaking any further—before compromising our intelligence network—so please do not argue it. It is Moscow's belief that you have violated the ABM agreement, and you have begun deployment of your Strategic Defense Initiative. You understand the strategic importance this has for us—for our people. Many years ago we placed an agent—or recruited an agent—to monitor the United States, knowing that anything your country does must be reported to the Senate Intelligence Committee—"

"You used Bower Thompson," Jerry said.

"He directs our operation, under the immediate supervision of Voroshilov."

"The ambassador?"

"When you successfully place a spy so close to your adversary's center of power, you trust no one else. He reported to the ambassador."

"Then Thompson ordered Steinbrenner's capture?"

"Of sorts, yes. Senators on the committee are not permitted to report on intelligence briefings. So there was only so much information Mr. Thompson was receiving. However, he did know that Steinbrenner was briefing the committee with increasing frequency. The Kremlin also noticed a dramatic increase in payload launches—''

"Launches carrying satellites,'' Jerry clarified.

"Yes, but there was no certainty as to what was being carried into space, and assuming the need to make up for your dearth of launches between 1983 and 1988, no one would dare accuse the U.S. of launching antiballistic satellites—such a claim without evidence would be enough to discredit the Soviet Union. We assumed, however, that the secret satellite aboard your space shuttle *Atlantis* in November of '88 was related to the Initiative, but again, the successful blackout concerning the operation left us with nothing tangible—nothing to hang our hat on. All we knew, for certain, was that you were completing your radar stations in Spain and Iceland, and that those facilities were part of a complex ABM network. However, there was nothing we could say about that, because we had our own such installations. You see, without more evidence—evidence that the U.S. was beyond laboratory research and development—there is nothing we could do. Without firm evidence, the U.S. would only have to deny the satellites' existence. The issue would be put to rest until sufficient evidence was gathered, and the fear was that by that time it would be too late, the balance of power would be disrupted enough to render the Soviet Union vulnerable.

"So Thompson had Steinbrenner kidnapped,'' Jerry said.

"Not that easily. He had to first find a secondary source leading to Steinbrenner. Senator Ashworth is the most useful idiot the Soviet Union has on the Intelligence Committee. In no way did we want to compromise his integrity, and because he is the most—as you say liberal—we wanted to avoid any suspicion of his involvement—especially his connection with Bower Thompson. The NATO conference in Rome provided the opportunity to solicit information from alternative sources.''

"You call what happened to Senator Watenburg soliciting information?''

"In a most violent way, yes.''

"But you're saying you already knew about Steinbrenner's role.''

"Yes. Senator Ashworth spoke with Mr. Thompson a number of times concerning Steinbrenner's appearances, though he never said specifically what the professor covered in his briefings."

"So those two men were slaughtered for no reason at all."

"To protect the integrity of our network."

"Something you're compromising right now."

Djian looked at his untouched plate of food, and Jerry immediately regretted what he said, fearful that the old man might stop speaking.

"I am only doing what must be done. You said we are both citizens of the world, and the world can ill afford what will happen if my worst suspicions are founded. You see, we play a zero-sum game, Jerry, there are no winners, and if the United States has launched those satellites the Soviet Union will respond. One way or another, it will respond, and we will all lose. We have played into a strategic stalemate and the most explosive component now is information."

"But if it's true—" Jerry began. "If it's true that America has those satellites up there, then sooner or later your people will find out. Sooner or later they will have the evidence they need to retaliate."

"We can be certain of that, but I hope at that time your President will not be as nervous as he is now—one step away from nuclear war."

"Have your people responded?"

"Of course they have. Once yesterday's rumors were confirmed, our military went on full alert. Our foreign minister contacted Secretary Parryman this afternoon."

"And?" Jerry asked.

"Your secretary of state promised an answer by noon tomorrow."

"Noon?" Jerry blurted. "Tomorrow?"

"You see how close we are," Djian said matter-of-factly.

Jerry looked at his cold steak and uncut potato. "What would you do?" he asked.

"If I were you?"

"Yes."

"Stop Bower Thompson from getting the information that will confirm my people's worst nightmare."

"And if he already has the information?"

"Then I would stop Bower Thompson."

Chapter Thirty-Two

The man standing on the street outside Robert's building looked familiar, but it wasn't until the journalist was in a taxicab bound for Great Falls, Virginia, that he realized he had seen the man in the last week, though he could not remember where. When the cab turned off Independence Avenue, passed the Washington Monument, still brightly lit at 2:25 AM, and crossed the 14th Street Bridge, he stopped thinking about the stranger. He assumed that he had seen the man in one of the NATO committee meetings, or maybe at a party. He couldn't recall, and he had to start thinking about Senator Ashworth.

Julia was still in the bathroom when Robert placed two calls, the first to Italy:

"Operator?"

"Yes, operator, I need to call the Cicerone Hotel in Rome."

"You can dial direct, if you wish."

"I know I can, but you take care of it. I'm in a hurry."

"It would be quicker if you dialed direct."

"Dial it—99-23-99—dial it now!"

"Yes, sir." The line clicked, then sounded a distant ring. Once, twice.

"Albergo Cicerone," said a cheerful voice.

"I need to speak with Diana Sillito, immediately," Robert said softly, so Julia could not hear.

"I am sorry. She has checked out."

"Checked out?" Robert said angrily.

"Yes, she has checked out this morning."

383

"Damn it!"

"Perhaps I can be of some assistance."

"Did she leave a message? Where she was going?"

"One minute please."

After an abnormally long pause, another voice came on line, a more powerful, self-assured voice. "Can I ask who is calling, please?"

"Who am I speaking with?" Robert demanded without answering.

"The hotel manager."

"I need to find Diana Sillito."

"Can I ask who you are?"

"My name's Hamilton."

"Robert Hamilton?" the manager asked, pronouncing Robert as if he were going to say *Roberto*.

"Yes—Robert Hamilton."

"She did leave a message for you, but perhaps I had better explain what—"

"Just give me the message," Robert demanded. "I don't have time."

"She is on her way to America. She will contact you soon. Until then, she said, do not come above ground." The man paused. "Do you understand—do not come above ground?"

"She's coming here?" Robert asked, though not necessarily to the man on the other end of the phone.

"As soon as the paperwork has been finished, she will come to America."

"Paperwork?"

"That is what I was going to explain. There was trouble here—not last night but the night before. And she is answering questions with the police. Soon she will be at home."

"What kind of trouble?"

"That I cannot say. I am sorry. Only that there was trouble and she asked to give you the message that she will call soon."

"Is she okay?" Robert asked and then realized that the question was the only one that mattered at the moment. *Julia might be right*, he thought. *Still, there was something special about Diana. He knew it from the moment they met. If she is guilty, as Julia says, then there has to be a good reason.* But Robert knew he was not going to uncover the explanation with this phone call.

"She is fine, Mr. Hamilton. She has been with the police. The trouble was not with her."

Silverman, he thought and a thundering insight from his subconscious confirmed the truth. *It's Silverman. He's behind Diana. It's not Diana who cares about where I am, or what I do, or about this spy versus spy shit. She's not the one spilling her guts out to Thompson and his people. It's the queer.* "Her agent," he ventured with the manager. "Is the trouble with Silverman?"

"Sorry, Mr. Hamilton. I can tell you only that which I have said."

"Thank you." Robert's voice was soft again as he hung up the telephone, feeling that he should write something in his notebook, but instead he dialed another number.

The Ashworth housekeeper answered the phone and refused to wake up the senator, even after Robert identified himself, explained that it was an emergency, and demanded that she had no other choice.

"I wouldn't get him out of bed for President Satterfield," she refused.

"Satterfield wouldn't want him out of bed," Robert responded. "But either you get him up, or I'm coming out there to get him myself."

"And the police will be waiting for you when you get here."

"If that's what the senator wants on the front page of tomorrow's *Post*, it's fine with me."

"You're a crank."

"Right now, you're hoping I'm a crank," he yelled, finally not caring whether Julia could hear him. "In about forty-five minutes, you'll find I'm not!" He slammed the phone down and quickly dressed.

Julia met him head-on as he flew out of the bedroom. "Think about what you're doing," she said. "One way or another, you're going to be stopped."

"Then you'd better get your gun and shoot me now, because next time you see me, this story's going to be in black and white and on every doorstep in America," he said and left the apartment. On the street, he saw the man but brushed by him and walked two blocks to Independence before hailing a taxi. The cab was warm, and Robert felt his painful muscles that had tensed in the cold night air relax until the tension abated, leaving only the pain of his wounds. In violation of the law, the driver smoked a cigar the size of a miniature baseball bat, the kind people buy at carnivals. It looked expensive but smelled cheap, and Robert opened his window a crack to let the smoke escape.

"Light traffic tonight," the hack said as he pulled the taxi off the 14th Street Bridge onto George Washington Parkway. In the distance, the city of Rosslyn looked like a fireworks display of lights rising from the ground. The twin towers of the *USA Today* buildings emerged from the skyline and topped the display with their flashing red aircraft-warning lights for the frequent jets that landed and took off from National Airport a mile down river.

For a moment, Robert wondered if he should try to sell his story to *USA Today*. It was the most widely read newspaper in America, but among reputable journalists it was known only as window dressing, nothing more than shallow reporting on substantive issues and over-flowing with human interest stories. No, he would not sell it to *USA Today*. He would either use it to get his job back at the *Post*, or he would go to *The New York Times*. This story was for the prestige press. Politically, it was more explosive than Watergate, and the intrigue and national security impact far surpassed the Iran-Contra scandal. He pulled his notebook from his pocket and held it tightly without opening it. *This is what Pulitzers are made of*, he thought and tried to force the image of Diana from his mind.

"Are you listening to me?" said the driver.

"Excuse me," Robert fled from his thoughts and looked at the driver's eyes in the rearview mirror.

"I said there ain't going to be no return trip from Great Falls, so I'm going to have to charge you extra."

"No. I'll be returning. I need you to wait."

"Twenty bucks an hour."

"That's fine," Robert said.

"Beats the hell out of me picking up stiffs in the District."

"Excuse me?"

"I got suicide detail. Midnight to dawn. I'd rather wait for you out where the blue bloods live anyway. Every time I pick up a loser in the city, I'm putting my life in their hands. Job's not worth all that."

"No, it isn't." Robert agreed numbly.

"But a man's got to have a living."

"Yes, he does."

"And what do you do to be coming out at this hour?"

"Right now I'm unemployed."

"You got money for this ride?" the driver slowed the car and his eyes narrowed to study Robert's reaction.

"Of course I've got money."

"But you ain't working? Collecting unemployment, huh. Living off the government? I tried to do that, too, but my old lady said she'd walk on me. Leave me with the kids. I was driving a taxi within twenty-four hours. Shit, the stiffs in Washington are easier on me than the kids."

Robert smiled and looked out the window. Across the Potomac the Lincoln Memorial was as breathtaking as ever, a symbol of America's ability to endure just about anything, even stand against itself if necessary. In his final days at the NSC, Robert found himself jogging by the Memorial with greater frequency, stopping and mounting the steps to the magnificent statue of the emancipator still holding vigil over his nation. Lincoln appealed to the idealist inside of him, the fond-feeling character that lurked behind the cynicism of his journalistic ego, the character that often made him get choked up by patriotic beer commercials.

"What did you do before you was milking the government?" asked the driver."

"I'm a journalist. I worked for the *Post*."

"No kidding. A journalist? Do you know Geraldo?"

Robert laughed. "No. No, I don't know Geraldo."

"He's an ass-kicker, Geraldo is."

"My kind of man," said Robert.

"Did you see the show about the punk-rock nuns and their alternative convent?"

"Missed it," said Robert.

"He's an ass-kicker."

"And what did you do before you started driving taxis?" Robert asked.

"Me? I was into property management."

"That's a good field. Why did you leave?"

"Being a security guard isn't all it's cracked up to be. It seems like a good living when you're watching their commercials. You know—join the fast-paced field of property management. And then the guy comes on and tells you how he managed a four-billion dollar office skyrise.

Well, I got a two-story surplus store and they didn't even invite me to the Christmas party.''

Robert watched the lights of the medieval-looking Gaston Hall belfry as the car passed Georgetown University. When he was a young man working his way through state school, he used to look covetously at the Georgetown skyline and imagine being a student in the regal private school where the kids drove cars worth more money than the entire gross national product of some banana republics. But he didn't care anymore. Harper said a man got out of his education what a man put into his education, and looking back on his own life Robert believed the old man. After his Pulitzer, he spent five weeks out of the year lecturing at universities, and couldn't tell the difference between a good student from George Mason and a good student from Harvard.

"The worst part," the driver continued, "was that they made you buy your own gun. Can you believe that? Buy your own gun! Then they wouldn't let you put bullets in it." He turned around and looked at Robert. "What good's a gun without no bullets? Tell me." He returned to look out the front window. "Well, I'll tell you, it's just inviting trouble. You go up against some of these stiffs who can hit the lint out of your bellybutton at fifty yards, and a gun without no bullets is asking for trouble. One day, a fourteen-year-old kid comes into the store with a zip gun—a homemade special—wood block handle taped to a piece of plumber's pipe the size of a .22 load. The firing pin is a carpet tack. Can you believe that? A carpet tack glued to a rubberband. He comes in and holds us up because I got no bullets. So what happens to me? I get canned. I've been fired, too, mister. So don't be feeling bad. I been fired, too. But in my case it weren't my fault.''

Robert smiled at the unwitting insult and opened his notebook:

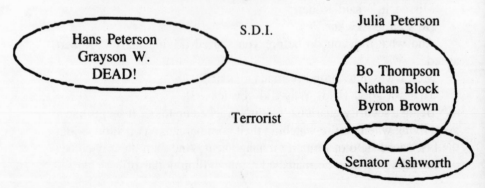

Julia was right. He did have a story. The puzzle pieces fit together nicely, and he did not have to dig any deeper if he didn't want to. He scribbled Jerry Bond's name beneath Julia's and wrote the word "smuggler?"

It would be enough to expose Bower Thompson as a top Soviet agent. It would be enough to tie Thompson into the murders of Peterson and Watenburg, and to suggest that the catalyst was the Strategic Defense Initiative. All the elements were there. It was a story sexy enough to entice the voyeuristic impulses of Americans, one that would encourage and sustain spin-off articles for the next two years, maybe three or four books, even a miniseries. He had most of the elements of a good story, the who, what, where, when, and how. And that was good enough for any normal story; still, he could not acquiesce to Julia's demand that he probe no further. He was uncertain if his drive was fueled by his resentment of being used once again by the government or by his need to resolve the sixth element of a news story, the need to resolve why it occurred.

Why did Bower Quincy Thompson sell out? Why was information about the Strategic Defense Initiative so important that the Soviets would take such risks to expose it? Why was Steinbrenner killed if he was so important to the communists? Robert felt a sudden sense of inadequacy to handle the story. All at once it seemed more like the mythical Hydra, growing two more questions each time he answered one. He wrote Professor Steinbrenner's name beneath those of Hans Peterson and Grayson Watenburg.

"A moment of silence for our brave spies at Langley," said the driver as the taxi passed the CIA headquarters. It sounded like a line well rehearsed, a line the driver used often as he drove people by the area. It probably worked with tourists, but Robert knew Langley too well, and he did not respond, but for some reason the next question his mind entertained was about Jerry Bond. That was one *who* he did not understand, at least not one minute ago. He looked at the forested entrance to the CIA compound off Dolly Madison Boulevard. *Is Jerry with the Company?* he wondered.

There was talk of CIA involvement in smuggling, especially in the late eighties, during the Oliver North trials, and there was little doubt in Robert's mind that CIA could use Andrews Air Force Base. Jerry being with CIA even solved the riddle about why, when Robert left his identification behind in Spain, no one was waiting to pick him up at his apartment in Washington.

Now that you've walked out on Jerry and Julia, his mind warned, *you're on your own, and you'd better watch your back.* For a second he regretted leaving his apartment, challenging Julia to stop him. *You did have enough for a story, so why not leave well-enough alone?*

The press is not to be manipulated. I'm not to be manipulated.

Come on! The press and the politicians feed off each other's flesh— mutual parasites—one dead without the other. You know that. You've worked both sides of the fence. In government, each time you planted a story, you offered your media contacts exclusives if they would march in your direction. You made every one of those journalists who covered the NSC feel he was somehow more special, more important to you, than the others. It was a game. That's the way you played it. Sometimes you offered ten journalists the same exclusive, and never once did you feel guilty about it.

But they used me, too.

Of course they did, but every time they did, you called it a favor and made a mental note to collect one day. That's how you got your job with the Post in the first place. Now you claim there's some double standard, that you compromise your sacrosanct ethics if your objective happens to correspond with theirs.

But they will never let me write the whole story.

They don't know the whole story.

Julia knows enough to say it will destroy civilization.

Then why are you so damned determined to write it?

"This is Route 137." The cabbie interrupted Robert's mental dialogue. "What address did you say?"

"Fifty-two thirty-seven."

"Will you look at those houses!" the driver said aghast. "Look like little kingdoms, all lighted up. Look at that one, it must have a thousand bathrooms. Guy who owns it probably don't have to look at his wife for months—can't find her. And the kids! Can't find them, neither. I'd love a house like that. Except I wouldn't mow that lawn. Take you a year. Maybe seven. Have to get some goats—some goats or some cows. Cows eat grass, don't they?"

Robert knew which home belonged to Senator Ashworth before he read the street number. He recognized the midnight blue Jaguar SJ-12 convertible, the same car once featured on the front page of the *Times* over an article about U.S. senators who blast foreign imports in floor oratory about global competitiveness, but who still drive foreign cars.

"It's the one on the left," Robert said, and the driver pulled into the long semicircular driveway.

The home was off the set of *Gone with the Wind*, a magnificent white mansion with marble pillars and a huge golden chandelier that hung beneath the porte-cochère. Behind the house the lot was wooded, and Robert estimated the land to be seven acres.

"You got some rich friends," said the driver.

"He's not a friend."

"Then I'd make him one—real quick like."

"Wait here," Robert ordered and stepped slowly from the car. His chest had stiffened up again, and his movement tugged at the wounds and made breathing difficult. He pressed his hand against the bandage to reinforce the support and walked across the asphalt driveway.

It appeared that the only light in the house that was on was the light in the hall behind the front door. Robert stood on the porch and paused before ringing the bell. He took a deep breath, but before pressing the button the door flew open and Ashworth stood in the frame.

"What in God's name are you doing out here?" he demanded angrily.

"Good evening, Senator," Robert said methodically, trying to take the bite out of Ashworth's anger.

"Good evening? It's three o'clock in the morning!"

"Good morning, then," Robert corrected and took a step forward.

"You've got a lot of nerve threatening my help."

"I didn't threaten anyone but you, senator," Robert said. "And I think once you hear what I have to say, you'll be thankful I came to talk to you before I wrote my story."

"Well? Go ahead. Tell me."

"Not here. It's a long—"

"Well, I'm not inviting you inside, if that's what you want."

"Like I said, senator, this isn't necessarily what I want. I think it's what you'll want once you're enlightened. However, I'm not going to stand here and freeze to death. So if you're not inviting me inside, I'll write the story that Bower Thompson, your administrative assistant, is a Red spy, and you have no comment." Robert turned back to the cab, but before he could take a step Ashworth grabbed his shoulder. The pain made him wince, but he was encouraged by the reaction.

"Wait a minute," said Ashworth. "Bower? A spy?" he scoffed. "That's ridiculous."

"Is it?" Robert faced the man. "Three days ago, I got the shit beat out of me in a Almería hotel room by him and two of his foreign leg-breakers. He admitted to me that he was GRU, and then he gave me a reading on Sun Tzu."

"Sun Tzu?"

"The Chinese military leader."

"I know who Sun Tzu is. I taught Bo everything he knows about Sun Tzu." Ashworth's face turned from angry red to defeated white. He stepped aside and allowed Robert to pass into the house.

"Well, you should be proud, then, he's putting it to good use. Unfortunately, however, he's working for the wrong side."

Ashworth shook his head and walked slowly into his rich, wood-grained study two rooms to the left of the ballroom-like entrance hall with its encircling staircases. The senator turned on the green-shaded banker's light atop his desk and dropped into a burgundy leather sofa. Robert sat down next to him.

"I can't believe what you're telling me," Ashworth lamented. "I can't believe Bo's involved." He turned to face Robert. "He's like a son to me. A son, do you understand that?"

"More than you'll ever know," Robert answered softly. "But I've got two witnesses. Two people who know what he's doing."

"I taught him everything. He started in my office years ago as an intern—an intern. He drove my car. I taught him everything."

"I understand," Robert said, "But—"

"I don't believe he could betray me—betray my trust—betray his own country."

Color began to flush back into the senator's face and Robert believed he was gathering steam for another storm. At the door, something Ashworth knew must have testified to the accusation Robert was laying before him, but now it appeared the senator was trying to rationalize, to refuse to accept the story. Maybe he was thinking about the repercussions to his own career, and in refusing to accept them, he was groping for any explanation, logical or otherwise, to exonerate his assistant. Whatever the reason, Robert wanted to push back the storm before it blew, he wanted to keep the senator submissive to the facts and willing to cooperate with his investigation.

"Do you know anything about the Strategic Defense Initiative?" he asked.

"What do you know about it?" Ashworth shot back. The red had returned completely.

"The question, Senator, is what does Bower Thompson know about it?"

Ashworth looked away and then stood up. He walked to the black leather judges' chair behind his desk and then to the far end of the office, never looking back to Robert, but the journalist continued speaking.

"There is even speculation that Bower had something to do with Dr. Steinbrenner's death," Robert said.

For a moment, Ashworth stopped pacing long enough to stare out the plate glass window behind his desk at the bare-branched forest between him and his neighbors. He shook his head slowly. "I'm going to have to ask you to leave," he finally spoke.

"You don't want me to leave. You know that I'm right, and your best friend right now is a well-informed press. Any other way and people are going to assume that you had something to do with Thompson's activities."

"I said you'll have to leave."

"Is that really what you want? You want me to write that Senator Ashworth refused to comment. Once this story breaks, people are going to formulate their opinions, and anything you say after that will be seen only as damage control—not as the truth."

"Get the— Get out of my house!" Ashworth screamed and pointed at the door.

Robert used the arm of the sofa to help himself stand, and then he straightened his body slowly to ease the pain. "Senator," he said after taking two steps toward the den door. "I understand how you feel. It's late, and I know you're tired. But I do know that Bower is involved with the Soviet GRU. I know that he's not only involved, but he has some substantive rank within the organization. And if what I've been told concerning the SDI project is true, then he's not only in a position to compromise our national security, he's in a position to incite a nuclear confrontation. It may be too late already, depending on what he knows, on what you know, and on what you've told him.''

Ashworth dropped his head into his hands. His voice abandoned all emotion when he said: "Get out of my house. Just leave me alone.''

Robert saw himself out, leaving the silhouette of a powerful man standing in the shadows of the den. He opened the car door and slid carefully into the back seat.

"That was quick," said the driver. "Too quick. Now I got to go back and pick up stiffs.''

"Not necessarily," Robert replied. "I want you to pull your car about a quarter mile up the road, where the house is still in view. And we'll wait there.''

"For how long?''

"For as long as it takes.''

When the car pulled out of the driveway, Senator Ashworth sat down at his desk, stared at the green lampshade, and tried to take control of his emotions. His body refused to relax, to give his mind the respite it needed to consider the predicament he was in. One overpowering thought, however, was that Bower was guilty as Robert charged, and Ashworth wondered why he had not allowed himself to believe it earlier. He wondered why he abandoned his suspicions, suspicions that plagued him often over the years when he watched the young man he raised professionally—politically—make decisions and associate with people who he considered un-American.

Time after time, he dismissed Bo's actions as youthful indiscretion, perhaps left-wing indignation. The boy never seemed to step over the boundaries of propriety, but still there was a pattern, and Ashworth was tormented by the brazen fact that he, too, had been boiled in Bower's cauldron. He, too, had been used, not once but perhaps hundreds of times as he trusted the young man and nursed him on an insatiable diet of sensitive information.

And now there was the Strategic Defense Initiative. In his overwhelming passion to bring down President Satterfield and his administration, Senator Ashworth had crossed over the boundaries himself. Bower had the briefing book, and what he had done with it during the past fifteen hours, Ashworth did not know. He looked at the clock above the fireplace mantel. The time was 3:05 AM, and the awareness of the hour seemed to click a switch in his mind. At once he felt tired, and the specific elements of his dilemma began to cloud into a damp but imperious conundrum. He knew, however, that he did not have time to be tired. He had to act at once, to assess the damage of his own indiscretion.

Senator Ashworth picked up the telephone and dialed Bo's home number. The assistant answered on the first ring.

"Yeah?" he said in a groggy voice.

"Bo?" Ashworth was torn between love and rage, and his voice reflected the conflict.

"Yes, Senator."

"I thought I told you to stay in the office until you found what we were looking for."

"I barely got home—but I did as you said."

"Well, I need to see you. Immediately."

"About what?"

"Immediately, Bo."

"Yes, sir—but about what?"

"Meet me in my office. Forty-five minutes."

"It's three o'clock."

"I said meet me in forty-five minutes." The rage was beginning to get the better part of love.

"Yes, sir."

The senator hung up first, turned off the desk lamp and walked up the winding marble staircase to his bedroom for his shoes. The handsome Mrs. Ashworth was still sound asleep on her side of the bed. The light from the bathroom cast a soft golden tint on her brown hair and striking features—her small, straight nose and full lips. She looked peaceful, the only calm Ashworth could feel at the moment.

Slung over the top of the wing chair beside where she slept was a sequined gown, and he pondered the romance only hours before as they returned from the ballet, not a care in the world, except to climb into each others arms and await the morning.

He pulled on his socks and slipped into a pair of Allen Edmonds wingtips, the shoes he had worn earlier to *The Nutcracker*'s opening at the Kennedy Center. The senator took the tuxedo jacket from the walnut hanging board on his side of the bed and walked around to kiss his wife.

"I love you, Ann Marie," he said softly. "I love you more than anything in this world."

She responded to his kiss without awakening. Ashworth put on the jacket and left the house without another word.

"Stay on the tail of that Jaguar and there will be another fifty bucks for you," said Robert to his driver as the senator pulled the midnight blue car onto Route 137.

"The guy's going ninety miles an hour, and that's coming out of his driveway."

"Stay on him, but don't look like you're following. Understand?"

"That's a Jaguar. I've got a Plymouth."

"Hundred bucks," Robert finally gave in and watched the speedometer climb from zero to ninety-five inside two minutes.

"But it's a customized Plymouth," the driver admitted with a grin. "Bought it at a cop auction. Paid top dollar. Wanna hear the siren?"

"No—no," Robert answered quickly. "That's fine. Just follow him. My guess is he's on his way to the Capitol."

"Then why the tail?"

"Because it's only my guess."

Chapter Thirty-Three

"Do you have any idea what time it is?" President Satterfield's eyes strained against the light in the private White House sitting room that adjoined the bedroom. His hair was tossled and he tied the belt around his heavy navy-colored terry-cloth bathrobe. "It's three-thirty in the morning."

A house steward handed him a cup of hot coffee.

"A little milk and sugar," he asked politely. "Especially this early." He sat down across the coffee table from Tab Skillman and CIA Director Maurice Sidey. The former looked as tired as the President; the latter as upset as a sinner on Judgment Day. "Tab said you needed to see me now," he continued once he was comfortable.

"Mr. President," said Sidey, his words cut short and his breathing was irregular. "I don't know where to begin. Earlier this evening, I received some very disturbing news, sir, and I wanted to verify it before I—before I—"

"Say what's on your mind, Maury," the President stirred his coffee and looked at Skillman.

"Before I tendered my resignation."

"Resign, Maury?"

"Yes, sir. If what I've been told is verified by you."

"Okay." Satterfield shifted his shoulders uncomfortably beneath his robe and looked at the director, who spoke through taut lips to hide his bad teeth. "What have you been told?"

"I know you and I have never seen eye-to-eye on a lot of things, that you felt you had to appoint me to pay back a chit to the party chairman,

397

but I'll be damned if I'm going to let you degrade Central Intelligence without regard to the law and security of America.''

Skillman shrugged his shoulders, and the President took a sip from the china cup.

Satterfield looked back to his chief of staff. "I don't know what we could have done to degrade Central Intelligence," he said. "If it's serious, though, I'm happy you came to me."

"Came to you, sir?"

"Before you went to the press, like some of your people often do."

"I have tremendous respect for you, Mr. President. I always have."

"And I appreciate that you've always been a team player."

"Then why not tell me about the Initiative."

"Initiative?" asked Skillman with sudden interest in the conversation.

The DCI did not look at the chief of staff, but kept his eyes on the President. "The Strategic Defense Initiative," he said. "You've held, what, two or three meetings with the Joint Chiefs and members of the Security Council, but you've excluded me. I don't understand."

The President leaned forward and placed his cup on the coffee table. His mind was groggy and he did not want to deal with the confrontation, exert the energy he knew it would take to mollify his director. He began slowly, deliberately, drawing the argument from his mind like a master painter carefully finishes a canvas, stroke by stroke, blending logic like colors into an appealing sense of acceptance. "Let me first apologize," he said with the humility of a God-fearing man at confession. "You know I've never been good at sharing secrets. When I was over at the Pentagon, there were things I never told President Bush. When I was in Congress, there were things I never told our party leader. In this city, information is power. Knowledge is security. And closely held information and knowledge become powerful security, especially when it has to do with defense and foreign policy."

"Like SDI?" asked Sidey.

"Like SDI," Satterfield agreed, but did not want to add any more information until he was certain of how much the director knew.

"But I sit on the National Security Council, Mr. President. I am the operative branch of the intelligence community."

"But you're surrounded by a group of—a group of—"

"Cutthroats," Skillman offered and the President cut him off.

"Not cutthroats, but operatives who—"

"Talk too much," said Skillman.

"I've got some good men," Sidey objected. "Better men than some," he looked at the chief of staff.

"Of course you do," said Satterfield, "but intelligence gathering was not a priority for us—at least not in this situation. We didn't need intelligence. We needed complete secrecy, and you have to admit that Langley is not always known for its discretion."

"Who did you think I would tell?" Sidey asked, his voice betrayed his mounting anger.

"Maury, it was not a question of who you would tell, but a question of who needed to know."

"Besides," offered Skillman, "you've been in Hawaii at some soldiers of fortune convention. We wanted to have you in attendance," he lied, "but you're never around when we need you."

"It was the annual Conference of Western Intelligence Communities," Sidey corrected without looking at Tab.

"Same thing," said Skillman, and he stood to get coffee off the dolly.

"And if you're upset about the two meetings in the Situation Room," Satterfield continued, "well, again, I apologize, but, frankly, Maury, I saved you and your boys a lot of time. Rich took care of everything."

"Rich is not operational," said Maurice. "He does not have operatives. CIA and the Defense Intelligence Agency, they are your information gathering services. No other agency can conduct that activity, not Rich's, not Tab's, no one."

"I don't have an intelligence agency," Tab said flippantly, "but I'd like one for Christmas."

The President tried to contain his laugh but could not. Sidey jumped to his feet. "Damn it," he said, his façade finally melting away like celluloid film stuck in front of a hot bulb. "You know what I mean."

"Come on, Maury," Satterfield said. "He's only playing with you."

"Well, I'm finished, Delbert. I'm done. Through. You can deal with your crisis any way you want. You can walk over your future directors, but not me. And I'll tell you another thing, the way you're going—the loose cannons in your administration—you're going to live in infamy—the President who started the big one.''

"Hey!" Skillman shouted. "That's uncalled for.''

"Your judgment on SDI is going to bring the superpowers to war,'' Sidey continued as if he had not heard the chief of staff.

"For what?" Satterfield asked. "For having Dr. Steinbrenner brief the Joint Chiefs? That's hardly worth war.''

"For launching the damn satellites without congressional approval.'' Sidey finally blurted what Satterfield wanted to know: how much information was on the streets.

Out of the corner of his eye, the President could see Skillman staring at him. Trying to maintain the unaffected expression on his face, Satterfield tipped his cup uneasily to his mouth and swallowed hard, maybe too hard, and he wondered if Sidey detected his concern.

"What do you know about it?'' he asked as plainly as he could.

"You didn't think I knew anything, did you?'' Sidey asked. "You thought all along that I was just offended—that my ego had been busted—because I hadn't been invited to your meetings. That's what you thought, wasn't it?''

"How much do you know?'' Satterfield pressed.

"Just about everything, Mr. President.''

"How much?''

"That we've deployed some ABM satellites in violation of our treaty with the Soviet Union. That the murders in Italy and the death of Steinbrenner were a result. That we're in Code Orange, and Parryman has until noon today to explain what in hell's going on around here before Moscow determines retaliatory measures. And more importantly, I know, because of the damned bungling of this crisis, the Soviets already have the information.''

"What the hell are you talking about?'' Skillman dropped his cup on the dolly and moved nose to nose with the director.

"Back off now!'' ordered Sidey.

"Come on, Tab,'' Satterfield said. The President could feel his insides turning. The acid in the coffee, especially on an empty stomach, was tormenting his already turbulent nerves and he was feeling sick. His face became drawn, and he asked sternly: "What do you mean, they have the information?''

Maurice pressed Skillman away with his stare, then turned back to the President. "Just what I said. A Soviet agent is in the position to know everything you've done—the status of SDI—everything."

"You don't know what you're talking about!" Skillman challenged.

"Hold on, Tab," Satterfield commanded and calmed his voice when he said to Sidey: "How do you know, Maury?"

"Everybody knows," the director said indignantly. "You people lock yourselves in this ivory tower, you look out at the bag people across the street, sleeping in Lafayette Park, and you think you control the world. Well, Mr. President, it's all coming to an end."

"Fuck you!" Skillman yelled and threw himself at the director.

"What's going on here," asked the sweet, morning voice of Pamela Satterfield as she walked from the bedroom into the fray.

Skillman withdrew his attack and stepped back, embarrassed. He looked at the President.

"Nothing, sweetheart," Satterfield tried to reassure.

Pamela poured herself a cup of coffee. She took a sip and looked at the three men, all of them silent, like actors waiting for a cue. "I can see that whatever it is, I'm better off in the bedroom." She retreated without another word, and Satterfield looked disapprovingly at the two men.

"Listen," he began, "we *have* had our differences, Maury. I'm the first to admit I've made some terrible mistakes. I've allowed this infighting to go on too long. You and Tab have been like pit bulls since I appointed you despite his objections." He turned to Skillman, "And you've poured salt into old wounds for too long, Tab. I'm not saying now's the moment to bury the hatchet. We don't have time for that. But what I *am* saying is that there's a much more important dilemma that we've got to resolve despite all this." He motioned for the two men to sit down and stared at the director. "I need to know where you got your information."

"Are you ordering me to tell you?" Sidey asked.

"Do I need to?"

"I want to know if it's an order."

"Maury," the President said, "let me explain something. If the law's been broken, and I guess one could make a pretty damn good argument that it has been, and if treaties have been broken, which, again, one could argue—"

"It's nothing the Soviets haven't done," Skillman interjected.

"One could argue that they have, I am not the lone accused. Everybody from Reagan on has to share this burden with me. Frankly, I think we've done nothing more than protect the best interests of our country. And actually, I'm proud of what we've accomplished. But I agree, we're in one hell of a mess right now. The three hours I've slept tonight are the first in the last three days, and despite all the infighting that's plagued Tab and you and me, I need your help. Do you understand that?"

"Yes, sir," Sidey said with a shade of contrition.

"I don't want your resignation, Maury." The President caught Tab's sudden glare. "Quite honestly, I won't accept it, and I promise, Maury, once we're out of this nightmare, you and Tab and I will put things straight."

"Yes, sir," the director repeated and looked blankly at the President's coffee cup on the table between the two men.

"Now tell me what you know."

"The day after Senator Watenburg's death, one of my men, Niccolini, in counterterrorism, interviewed Robert Hamilton."

"The journalist?" asked Satterfield.

"He's been fired from the *Post*. But Watenburg called him in on the Peterson murder. Later, he returned to find the senator."

"Then the press has been involved from the beginning," Satterfield said.

"Hamilton has."

"But he's not the Soviet agent," Skillman said bluntly. "Talk about the Soviet."

"Hamilton's involvement is very important, too," said Sidey, and the President agreed. "Irresponsible journalists are more dangerous than communists."

"He's a good journalist," Skillman objected.

"He's an egomaniac who will do anything to get his story—to get his job back. He's already admitted that to one of our operatives."

"You've got an operative involved?" the President asked, and Sidey nodded.

"An informant of our own and an allied operative."

"Allied operative?" asked Skillman.

"Julia Peterson, a German."

"Peterson," said Satterfield, "related to Hans Peterson?"

"His wife."

Satterfield shook his head slowly. "It's out of control," he said and looked despondently at his chief of staff.

"She's a good woman—good bona fides—a dedicated Christian Democrat, and her husband was one of the ardent European supporters of the program. He single-handedly convinced the chancellor to endorse the research and development." Sidey paused and looked at Skillman. "But, of course, no one knew about the deployment."

"Don't get off the point," said Satterfield. "So this Peterson and Niccolini—"

"No, Niccolini was working another angle we thought might be related to the murders, but we haven't verified it—not yet, anyway. He was checking on a man named Silverman, a real sleaze, who we think is somehow involved with the communists—an informant of some kind. But that's another story altogether. The operative involved now is Jerry Bond. He accidentally found himself in the middle of the case when the Peterson woman contacted him to fly Hamilton and her out of Spain."

"Spain?" the President exploded.

"They were on the run. Hamilton—or the woman—killed—"

"Two men in a hotel room," Satterfield mumbled and glared incredulously at Skillman. "Why didn't you bring this in earlier?" he asked.

"Because I wasn't invited." The director looked spitefully at Skillman. "And because we were still gathering information. Bond wanted to meet with a covert contact of his, some man who has kept him effective over the years. They met earlier this evening."

"Where?" asked Tab.

"Somewhere in Washington."

"Then Hamilton's here?" asked the President. "He's in Washington?"

"With Bond and the woman."

"Where?"

"We don't know right now. Peterson said he placed a call and left the apartment in a hurry."

"Where's Peterson right now?" asked Skillman.

"Langley—with Bond."

"So we have a journalist with the whole story running loose somewhere in the city, and we—" the President stopped speaking, and thought about the implications. In his mind, the journalist was as dangerous as the Soviet spy. "Tell me about the mole," he said, and Sidey shifted uncomfortably, then stood and began to pace behind the sofa.

"I'm a little embarrassed he's been allowed to operate on my watch," he began with a sigh, "but I guess if I use your logic, I'm to share the blame with the last six directors, because he's been in position for fifteen years."

"Fifteen years?" Satterfield groaned.

"Where?" asked Skillman.

"In the Senate."

"What?" the President screamed. "A senator?"

Skillman's face drained to a pale, waxy white as he looked at Satterfield.

"Not a senator—an administrative assistant."

"To whom?" asked Satterfield.

Sidey looked at both men. The President looked as if he had only moments ago witnessed a terrible accident. "Ashworth," he said. "To Senator Boyd Ashworth."

"Good God," said Satterfield as he closed his eyes and dropped his head back into the chair. "It can't be. It can't be."

The President did not want to look at Skillman. He wished the chief of staff would excuse himself from the meeting, leave the room, leave the city, and not come back until the predicament they were in was over and the tensions and emotions had evaporated safely into history. Skillman had warned him about involving Ashworth, about inviting the senator to the Steinbrenner briefing. Skillman wanted to fight the decision, but Satterfield had not allowed it. Instead, he had eaten dinner. He had eaten dinner alone and not given a second thought to Tab's furious objection.

"It's on good authority. Bond got the word from his contact."

"Maybe the contact's bluffing," Skillman offered, but Sidey shook his head.

"No," said the director, "no, the contact knows the repercussions if this crisis is not resolved by noon tomorrow. He knows that now is no time to bluff, and he compromised a fifteen-year plant because of it—perhaps the most strategic plant the Soviets have ever achieved."

"Who's the senator's administrative assistant?" Satterfield asked without opening his eyes.

"His name's Thompson," said Skillman, "Bower Thompson."

"I want him picked up immediately. Do you understand that. I want him in front of me inside twenty minutes."

"Sir," Sidey objected, "if it's information you want to get out of him, I have men who can take care of that."

"I don't want your people to have this kind of information. That's what I've been trying to tell you. The dissemination of information is our number one problem right now." The President stood and walked behind his chair, then he gripped the leather back and dug his fingers in as far as he could. "What you're telling me is that two of your operatives already know. A damn jackass journalist. Some hidden contact on the other side. And maybe even the Kremlin—for all I know. I don't want just anybody talking to him."

"The Kremlin doesn't know. Not yet, anyway," said Sidey. "They're only speculating right now. They think they know, but then they've been thinking that since Reagan started the program."

"Are you certain?" Skillman asked.

"According to Bond's man. He told him that he didn't know if Thompson even had the information yet."

The President eased up a bit and walked to the phone. "Get me Rich Spencer," he told the operator.

There was a pause and Maurice Sidey walked to the coffee dolly and poured himself a cup.

"Rich," said Satterfield, once his security adviser was on the phone. "I need you in the living quarters, immediately . . . You'll have to drop that . . . Tell Parryman he can handle it on his own . . . Hurry." He hung up the receiver and turned to Skillman. "He's on his way up."

"Where is he?" asked the director.

"Situation Room," said Skillman.

"He and Parryman are going over the options for the foreign minister." Satterfield looked at the wall clock. "They've got to have a plausible explanation for the Code Orange in eight hours." He turned toward the table and took up his cup. The coffee was lukewarm, and after a sip he placed it back on the table and turned toward the bedroom. "I'm going to leave the explanation in Parryman's hands now," he said as he moved to the door. "Rich has to make sure this Thompson doesn't get his hands on the briefing book."

"What briefing book?" asked Sidey.

Skillman took a deep breath and let it out slowly. Satterfield stopped and turned back to face the director. He did not want to tell him about the book. He did not want to acknowledge how foolish he had been, first to invite Ashworth into the meeting, then to let the book slip out of the conference, and finally to hesitate in getting the briefing book back under NSC control. But Maurice Sidey had been helpful. The director's anger had subsided, and Satterfield believed his bruised ego had been put on hold in deference to national security. His willingness and concern merited honesty and candor, no matter how difficult it would be for the President.

"In an attempt to assuage the Democrat Party's hostility to the SDI project—especially its congressional leadership—and knowing the time would come when Congress would have to be briefed—I invited Ashworth into the first meeting. The one with Steinbrenner. When you were in Hawaii." The President fought for his words, for a logical explanation that would permit him to save as much face as possible. "Tab, here, thought it was a bad idea. In hindsight, I have to agree with him."

"But we had no idea about Thompson," Skillman added to ease the burden on the President, and Satterfield was grateful that he spoke in first-person-plural, as if to include himself in the final decision.

"Of course we didn't. But the fact is, *I* asked him to attend. He did and flew into a rage when Steinbrenner explained that the Initiative was complete—that the necessary satellites were already in orbit."

"Then it *is* done?" asked Sidey, and the President looked surprised.

"I assumed you knew," said Satterfield.

"That some satellites were deployed, yes," said Sidey, "but not that the Initiative was finished."

"Almost finished," said Skillman. "Right now it's not even engaged—activated. In case of a nuclear attack, we couldn't even begin to use the system."

"That's months away," Satterfield added.

Sidey collapsed into his chair. "No wonder you're in Code Orange. You're worried about a preemptive strike."

"I thought you knew all this," Satterfield said.

"Bits and pieces," Sidey answered. "But not everything. I don't think anybody believes we have a complete network up there. It's inconceivable. Absolutely—" he paused and changed the direction of his thought. "How could it happen with absolute secrecy?"

"Sometimes the system works," said Satterfield.

"But even—"

"You didn't know?" said Skillman.

Maurice put his hand over his mouth and shook his head. "But that may be good news," he said as if he had just received a second wind of thought. He looked up at the President. "Bond's report was that the Soviets only suspect deployment—deployment of a few satellites— maybe only one. If the entire network is inconceivable to me, it has to be out of the question for Moscow."

"That brings us to the hard part," said Satterfield. "One of our briefing books, detailing the entire Initiative, is missing."

"Missing?"

"Gone," said Skillman.

"Wasn't it EYES ONLY?"

"Of course—" the President began but was cut short by a knock on the door. "Come in," he said, and Rich Spencer walked into the room. "Thanks for coming," Satterfield continued and shook the man's hand. "I'm telling Maury about the briefing book. Any word?"

"I plan on visiting Ashworth first thing this morning. If he has the book, I'll get it," Spencer said confidently. "If he doesn't, I'll get it, anyway." He smiled.

"Well, we've got another problem," said Satterfield. "According to Maury, Ashworth's administrative assistant is a Soviet mole."

"A spy?"

The President nodded and turned to Sidey.

"According to a strong source, he's been feeding information off the Intelligence and Armed Services Committees for years," the director said. "As far as we know right now, he's the highest placed active spy in America. And if what you're saying about this briefing book is correct—that Ashworth took it—he's going to make the Walker family ring look as ineffective as Maxwell Smart."

"Do we know who he is?" asked the NSC director.

"Name's Thompson," answered Skillman. "Bower Thompson."

"Let's pick him up," said Spencer as he looked at Maurice Sidey.

"I said I want him here in twenty minutes," Satterfield added.

Rich picked up the phone. "Give me extension 213," he said.

"I'm getting dressed." Satterfield opened the bedroom door. "Give me fifteen minutes."

"This is Spencer," Rich continued into the phone. "I need Anderson and Haddow to meet me at the north gate in five minutes—that's 3:48. And I need a complete printout on the name Bower Thompson . . . No, I don't know his social security number, but he works for Senator Boyd Ashworth—Senator Ashworth, yes. I need his address and everything your computer has on him. Five minutes." He hung up and looked at Satterfield.

The President's eyes were tired and sunken, and circular lines ran from beside his nose to the outer edge of his eyebrows. Only four hours before, it had been Rich who demanded that the President get some sleep, at least a few hours in case he had to negotiate with the General Secretary before the present crisis came to an end. He wanted the commander as crisp as possible, mentally alert. But now as he looked at Satterfield, the President's face betrayed his concern and fatigue.

"We'll get Thompson, Mr. President," Spencer said and patted Sidey on the shoulder. "However, with all due respect, sir, we won't bring him here. But we will find out everything he knows. That I promise. And don't worry, Mr. President, everything's going to be okay."

Chapter Thirty-Four

The garage beneath the Hart Senate Office Building was deserted and dimly lit as Senator Ashworth turned his car off C Street and drove down the ramp, passed the half-dozing Capitol Hill police officer in his booth, and parked in his stall. The Jaguar looked a deeper, richer blue, wet from the rain that had started to fall in the streets. He unbuckled his seatbelt and stepped out of the car, slamming the door and sounding an echo like a gunshot in the empty garage. Jumping in his chair, the guard acknowledged the senator's presence.

Ashworth did not wave back, but looked at the concrete floor as he walked into the basement of the building and thought about what he had considered his entire trip into the city: how he was going to confront Bo.

The boy is weak, he thought and determined that the only course of action was to break him down, convince him to confess his espionage involvement and take the fall alone, persuade him not to mention that the senator had given him the stolen SDI briefing book. This was important, and the senator believed he could successfully prevail upon Bower to make the right choices and limit the damage that would otherwise occur. As early as 1986, Ashworth had been successful in defeating legislation that would provide the death penalty for those who knowingly compromised national security. Never did he consider that one day he would personally benefit from his adamant position.

Bo would not have to die—especially if he was not directly responsible for Steinbrenner's death—and consequently Ashworth knew he might be able to convince him to give himself up, to answer for what he had done, to pay the price and then start over again. He was willing to help Bo start over again. While his own political career might come to an end after the revelations about his assistant's involvement with the GRU, Ashworth knew he would not fall in disgrace, especially if he could get the briefing book back to the President with the assurance that neither it, nor its contents, had fallen into hostile hands. If this could be done, he would be able to recover, and he could then help Bo.

But the decision is up to the boy, he concluded and stepped into the elevator.

Lights were off on the first floor and the Calder abstract sculpture, the sharp black mountains rising into the foreboding black clouds, that filled the center of the building's atrium, loomed like a dangerous shadow beneath the predawn-lit skylights. Each step echoed in the empty hall as Ashworth walked to his office at the corner of the building, wedged between Second and C streets. Trees surrounded the sculpture and generally gave the atrium a warm, foresty feeling, but Ashworth could not feel it, not now, as he stopped at the double glass doors leading into his office. Only half the lights were on inside and the doors were locked, but with a turn of the key, and without turning on the lights, he walked directly to the safe in his office bathroom.

The pine-scented aroma of cleaning solvent still hung in the air as he knelt down and dialed the combination, missing the first and second times, and finally hitting it the third. Inside the safe was as dark as a cave. He could not see the book and tried to feel around, but it was gone. "Damn you, Bo," he muttered and reached up to turn on the bathroom light to check again. Clicking the switch, nothing happened. Three, four times, still nothing, then he remembered that he had not flipped the master switch inside the front doors. He turned and then froze.

"Looking for this?" Bower pointed the .357 in his right hand at Ashworth. His left was hidden on the other side of the door frame.

"My heavens, man, you scared me."

"Are you looking for this?" Bo waved the gun.

"You know what I'm looking for."

"This?" Bo exposed his left hand. In it was the briefing book.

"Thank God, you haven't done anything foolish," Ashworth sighed in relief.

"I didn't leave your office, just like you ordered me. I never left, until I found what we wanted."

"Put down the gun."

"I found what we wanted. They robbed a dozen worthwhile programs to fund their project."

"Look, Bo, we don't need—"

"There you go again, using the imperial 'we.' You once said to shoot you if you ever became so arrogant that you used the imperial 'we,' like some ordained leader."

"You're making me nervous, Bo," Ashworth said and stepped toward his assistant. Clicking metal as Bo pulled back the hammer made him stand still, even take a careful step back. "What are you doing?"

"You know damn well what I'm doing," Bo said. "Why did you want me here this time of the morning? Why are you looking for the book?"

"I just wanted to see—"

"You wanted to see if I'd turned it over."

"I don't know what you're talking about."

"Who talked to you?"

"What?"

"Who spoke to you?"

"Bo, son, I really don't know what—"

"Don't lie to me, Senator. Don't patronize me with a lie."

"I don't know—"

"Of course you do."

Ashworth could feel the perspiration breaking on his upper lip again as he probed the eyes of his assistant to see if he could find even a trace of compassion. Certainly the boy would be tormented by conflicting emotions. Certainly his mind would not justify turning on a man to whom he owed so much. But there was no compassion, and Ashworth knew that Bo knew exactly why he was in the office. "You know we can get out of this. You've done nothing yet, Bo, and we can get out of this mess, together, and save our careers."

"Our careers?" Bo scoffed. "That's all you worry about, isn't it—your career. Time after time, I've put my career on the line for your career. I've lied for you, and stolen for you, and cheated for you. All for your career. Well, this is my career now. It's my career."

"It's not a career, Bo. It's treason."

"Treason?" Bo laughed. "To you who taught me about Sun Tzu? It's not treason. It's war. Remember. It's war. When murder is committed in attacking a country, it is not considered wrong; it is applauded and called righteous. It's war, and I am an agent of fore-knowledge, an agent in that war. Remember, Senator? Remember what you taught me about Sun Tzu and foreknowledge? That it can't be elicited from spirits, nor from gods, nor by analogy with past events, nor from calculations. It must be obtained from men who know the enemy situation."

"You're lost," Ashworth said defeatedly.

"I'm not lost, Senator Ashworth," Bo mocked. "I'm not lost at all. History rides proud with the victor. Had the English not blundered, we'd celebrate Benedict Arnold as the father of America."

"Do you understand what that briefing book can do?" Ashworth tried to plead with Bo's sense of concern for humanity. "Do you know what will happen in the event of nuclear war?"

"That's no concern of mine, remember: Set your men to their tasks without imparting your designs—"

"That's enough—"

"Use them to gain advantage without revealing the dangers in-volved. It's Sun Tzu—remember? Throw them into a perilous situation and they will survive; put them on death's ground and they will live. For when the army is placed in such a situation it can snatch victory from defeat."

"There will be no victory," Ashworth said sullenly.

"Of course there will, Senator, but first things first." Bower waved the gun to motion him out of the room.

"Where are we going?"

"Downstairs."

"Into the catacombs?"

Bower nodded an evil smile. "To your private office."

"Think about what you're doing, Bo. You don't have to—"

"I know exactly what I have to do."

Malibu crouched in the shadow behind the fourth leg of the moun-tainous sculpture and watched Bower Thompson walk the senator from the office to the elevator bank. Ashworth's face flushed as he moved reluctantly along the north wall. Light from the ceiling windows reflected off the white marble walls and cast a haunting blue-gray hue into the atrium and made the sharp features of Bower's face look like Ichabod Crane three days dead. Robert studied the man's movements, the control he had over the senator, and that was when he saw the gun and wished he were armed with something more than his notebook. The situation made him think of the cab driver's gun with no bullets, he wanted to smile but could not, certain Bo's gun was loaded, and he remained still, propping his right shoulder against the cold black iron mountain.

Capitol Hill police officers were certain to come along any minute, of this Malibu was sure, since they got rid of the patronage positions, sent the students who once worked as cops back to night law school, and hired professional officers. He looked at his watch: 4:18. *Maybe not,* he thought and moved stealthily to the back side of the sculpture and watched the two men. *The officer you snuck around was asleep in the garage booth,* he reminded himself. *Maybe they ought to bring back the school kids.*

Elevator six, marked FOR SENATORS ONLY, opened immediately and Thompson pushed Ashworth inside.

Up or down, Malibu asked himself as he scurried across the floor and pushed both buttons. The elevators were government contract low bid and consequently did not have the visual bank monitor to show where the six elevators were positioned, where they were moving.

Down, insisted the logical side of his brain. *They're going into the garage. Thompson knows he can't kill the senator here. He has to get him off Capitol Hill, into Anacostia or onto 14th Street, where his death will have less of an impact, be less suspect.*

But that's only if Thompson plans on sticking around Washington after Ashworth is dead, he objected. *He knows that you are on to him as well, and his best bet is to seek asylum. It has probably been arranged already, through the Soviet embassy, and in that case his safest bet would be to kill the senator in the basement, in the catacombs, in his soundproof, bug-proof, private office, and not chance going past the guard in the garage.*

Check the garage anyway.

I know they're going into the catacombs.

Check the garage.

I'll lose time. They're going into the catacombs. I know it. They'll never be found down there. It's never patrolled, and if Bo's plan is to kill the senator, Ashworth's body won't be discovered in his office, at least not for a day or two.

Neither will yours, the cautious part of his brain objected. *Call security and let them handle this. After Ollie North, Washington doesn't need another hero.*

But it's my story, and I'm going to finish it.

Dead men don't write news.

You said that before. I didn't listen then, and I'm not listening now.

Elevator three opened. He stepped inside and pressed the button. Senators had their private offices in the basement. Malibu remembered interviewing Ashworth years ago, about the MX story, in his basement hideaway. But could he remember where it was? Wandering yellow and green-tiled subterranean tunnels connected a dozen block-sized buildings on Capitol Hill in a Byzantine maze of offices and restaurants and stores and post offices and printing shops and carpenter's closets and hidden passageways, marked chaotically by cryptic signs and arrows that often confused more than helped. And the most powerful senators did not mark their doors. Many never even told their staffs where their Capitol offices were located, and disallowed anyone except families, spouses and lovers to grace the inside of their sanctum doors.

Subway trams stood abandoned on the tracks that connected the Senate office buildings to the Capitol, and only one of every eight neon lights was on and filled the tunnel beneath Constitution Avenue and the Capitol lawns with a cold, liquid green color. Malibu shivered as he inhaled the greased-iron early morning air and watched the tracks wind right and disappear around the wall past the Dirksen Building. The scene was lifeless, as he expected, and he strained his ears to listen. At first, he heard nothing and turned back to the elevators, finally conceding that the two had gone to the garage, one level above. He pressed the button and the bell rang as the doors opened. That was when he heard the footsteps, running away from him in the tunnel. Without giving himself a moment to think, to consider what to do, he turned and ran down the subway tracks to the point where the Dirksen wall jutted out like a seashore cape, and he stopped to carefully peer around the wall.

"Who's there?" Bower yelled as he held Ashworth like a shield in front of him with the barrel of the gun buried in the senator's white hair over the right temple.

Malibu was silent.

"I said who's there?"

"It's me, Bo—Robert Hamilton."

"Why the fuck don't you die?"

"I know everything, Bo. I know more than the senator. In fact, I was the one who told the senator what he knows."

"Is that true?" Bower demanded from Ashworth, and the old man mumbled that it was.

"Then his blood's on your hands," Bo screamed at Malibu.

"You don't have to kill him."

"What do you know?"

"That you don't have to kill him."

"Listen to him, son," Ashworth pleaded breathlessly as Bower held his neck in a stranglehold with his left arm. His hand still gripped the briefing book.

"Back off, or he goes right here," Bo ordered, and Malibu leaned back against the wall to take a deep breath and consider his alternatives.

"Who else have you told?" Bower demanded.

Again Malibu was silent.

"I said who else have you told, asshole?"

"I've already written the story, Bo," Robert lied. "It's already written. The part about you is already—"

"Where?"

"In a safe place. But I'll give it to you—I'll give it to you if you let Ashworth go. He's got nothing to do with—"

"I've got all I need," Bo shouted. "I've got everything—the book—the senator—the gun. Show yourself, Hamilton."

Robert did not move away from the wall.

"You've got to three. One—two—"

"Wait!" Robert's hard command stopped Thompson momentarily.

"Wait, Bo, consider what—"

"I'm finished considering. I've done what I've been ordered to do. My name will be worshipped. I don't need the senator and I sure as hell don't need you."

"But you need to get out of here, and unless you let the senator go, I'm turning back to alert every police officer on the Hill. You'll be in the middle of a beehive of blue uniforms. And if you even hurt Ashworth, they'll blow you three ways to hell. You know that. You know that, don't you, Bo?"

"Foolish move, Hamilton," Bower said confidently. "You think they'd try to stop me as long as I have the senator? Hell no."

Malibu knew Bo was right. Pressed tight in front of him, with a pistol muzzle against his skull, Ashworth was Thompson's trump card, and as long as he held the senator, he called the shots. Malibu also knew that in the maze of hallways, and close quarters, even a special response force could not get into position to take Bo without killing Ashworth. It was not like they were in an office building with over-sized windows, well-lighted rooms and open spaces for sharpshooters to draw their beads and drop their mark before his crooked finger flexed the trigger. Any response would have to take place within feet and inches, not yards, and Hamilton knew that under those conditions Ashworth would have to die before Thompson was taken—if Thompson were to be taken.

Go for the police and you've lost the story, Malibu's ego warned even before he consciously considered turning the situation over to those more skilled at handling hostage situations. *They'll never let you write it, in fact, you'll probably be extradited back to Spain to stand trial for the hotel deaths. You know your only defense is your article, for you to explain everything that happened, to use the media and take your case to the people.*

"I'm counting," Bower shouted.

"You're not going to kill him," Malibu said. "Not yet. You still need him. When he's dead—you're dead. And you know that."

"But if I go, I'm taking you and him with me."

"Bo," Ashworth began feebly, "you don't—"

"Shut up." Thompson tightened his hold. "Listen to me, Hamilton—you turn back, and I'll drop this old man and you before you get to the elevators."

Malibu looked behind him and estimated the distance. If the elevator were still on the floor, he might be able to make it—if the doors opened quickly. If not, then Thompson was right, and he could kill both men.

"I see that you have only one option," Bo continued, "and that's to show yourself."

"Don't do it," Ashworth objected as forcefully as he could. "Don't listen to him."

Thompson increased the pressure on his elbow and the senator began to choke. "Shut up, or I'll break your fucking neck."

"Then it's over, Bo," Malibu warned.

"Don't do it," Ashworth repeated. "He still has the briefing book." He coughed violently. "If he passes it on—if he passes it on—it's all over."

"I said shut up!" Bower screamed, and Malibu sensed that he was distracted, perhaps concentrating too much on the senator.

He took the split-second opportunity, hurdled the rail between him and the nearest subway car and slammed against the control panel next to the conductor's seat in the middle of the car. Pain exploded in his shoulder and ribs. His head grew light and he saw speckles of stars, like phosphorescent dust swirling in the air. Jerking his head from side to side, like a boxer throwing off a punch, he tried to clear away the pain, but it did not vanish, only turned into an aching, throbbing, tormenting grip that paralyzed his upper back, and he worried that he had torn open his wound. He would have stopped, screamed out, and perhaps even fainted if the adrenaline of fear had not taken over and systematically placed his motor skills on automatic. Next, he turned the key and heard the spark on the electrical rod. Leaning back against the booth wall, he tried to arch his back to relieve some pain. Still, it did not abate. Two lights, one red and the other green, began to flash. He pushed the green, shoved the throttle stick forward. The door slid shut and the tan car began to rock along the tracks, slowly at first and then with speed.

"What the fuck are you doing?" Bower screamed. "I said I'd kill him." He shoved the senator face down on the concrete walkway and fired the gun into the aluminum-sided door.

The metal melted like butter as the white hot lead blew through it and into the control panel. Robert's ears hurt from the echo of the shot. He looked at how close to his head the slug had struck. *Three inches,* he thought and realized that had he not been arching his back against the pain, he would be a dead man. His next worry was about the damage to the panel, but the train kept moving.

"Get up!" Bo screamed at Ashworth. "Get up, dammit." He
grabbed the senator by the collar, and the anger in his muscles lifted
the old man off the floor in one fluid motion. "Run toward the
Capitol."

Ashworth stumbled and fell forward. Bower threw him into the tile
wall, and his nose began to bleed.

"I said run!" Bo fired another shot into the car as it passed by.
Again the lead buried inside the control panel with no apparent damage
as the train continued to pick up speed.

"Keep going," Malibu coaxed the train in a whisper and discovered
himself rocking softly forward, trying to give the car as much help as
he could. "Get to the basement of the Capitol. There has to be a cop on
watch at the entrance." *If he's not asleep,* his mind offered cynically
and realized the pain was fading, leaving a headache in its wake.

The car was now down line from Thompson and Ashworth, following the track to the right and then veering left on a direct course to the
Capitol basement, and Malibu heard the sound of their footsteps about
ten yards back. Cautiously he peered above the metal siding and
looked out the plexiglass window to the guard desk almost a quarter
mile down the hall. His vision was blocked by four giant concrete
pylons that separated the subway landings from the three sets of tracks
that arrived at the Capitol from the Senate buildings. Finally he saw the
desk and no one was there. He looked to both sides of the tracks and
moved his head, straining to see around the pylons. Then he saw the
man in the dark blue uniform, running full speed toward the sound of
the gun. One of the officer's hands was resting on the gun in his
holster, the other holding onto his hat.

Malibu wanted to scream out, to warn the man that Thompson had
the senator, that he had a hostage and human shield, and that if the
officer got too close he would be an open target, but he knew his
warning would be too premature. It would also warn Bower that an
officer was on his way. So he held back until Thompson had come
around the final left corner and was in range.

"He's got the senator!" Malibu yelled, and the policeman fell to the
floor with his gun drawn.

"How many are there?" the man shouted back.

"Just one. But he's got the senator." Robert watched the officer
aim at the moving target and realized there was nowhere for the man to

hide, only the open walkway and subway tracks. The pylons were the closest shelter and they were twenty-five yards behind him. "Get behind the pylons," he shouted and pulled back on the throttle, but the train did not stop. "The pylons," he shouted and pointed toward the concrete braces. Again he yanked at the throttle, but the train continued. He pressed the red button, but nothing happened. "Please, no," he said and looked at the rapidly approaching iron and cement bump-guard at the end of the track.

The man in blue, finally understanding what Robert was trying to say, realized the compromising position he was in, unable to shoot at a man who held a hostage, especially a hostage who was a senator, and himself being completely unprotected, jumped to his feet and turned toward the nearest pylon on the right side of the tracks. He took two steps before Bower fired a round that hit behind the left kneecap and exploded out the front. With a lunge, he skidded across the slick concrete just as the subway slammed through the gate, into the solid barrier, and folded like a foil airplane.

Crashing into the flexible plexiglass window saved Malibu from being thrown from the car, but his shoulder and back spasmed in pain, and he found it hard to move as he tried to maneuver himself from the wreckage. Carefully he slid over to the door and stepped as far as he could away from the electric track, though he found it impossible, with the pain, to walk straight.

Unable to get back on his feet, the officer was sliding himself along the pavement, still holding fast to the gun, and with one leg useless. His progress was slow, and Robert tried to get to him as quickly as possible. Thompson and the senator were still about fifty yards away. Bower fired another round as Malibu grabbed the policeman under the arms and strained against the pain to pull him to the other side of the pylon. But it was not until he sat the man against the huge vertical beam that Robert saw the officer had been hit in the middle of his shoulders. The wound in the back was small, but the hollow-point punched a fist-sized hole out the front. Through it all, a bloodless right hand still gripped the .38 revolver, and Robert pried it from the dead fingers.

Hanging the gun in his hand on the outer edge of the pylon, he fired a round into the wall twenty feet in front of Thompson.

"Stop right there," he ordered, and Bo pulled the senator back, closer in front of him.

"You're not going to shoot me," Bo said. "You'd kill Ashworth."

"Shoot him," Ashworth said. "Shoot—" he coughed and Bo jerked his neck and head back into his shoulder.

"You've got two shots left," Robert advised. "One for the senator and one for me. You'll never get out of here alive. Give yourself up and—"

"Surrender and I'm dead anyway."

"Nobody's dead yet," Malibu lied as he looked down at the officer's pale face.

"Bullshit. I caught him in the left shoulder blade. I saw it. His heart's gone."

"No one's dead, yet," Malibu repeated.

"Then have him talk to me. Have him say something."

"He's unconscious."

"Bullshit." Thompson took another step forward, making sure to keep himself well protected behind the senator. "I figure you've got one move, Hamilton. Throw down the gun and come out here."

"You're banking on the fact that I'd rather die than see Ashworth blown away. Well, understand this, Thompson, I'm no patriotic Capitol cop. Now you have two bullets left and I've—" he quickly calculated, trying to remember if the officer had fired "—I've got five and the odds."

Thompson took another step and Malibu tried to draw a bead from around the concrete but could not get enough target in his sight. "Dammit," he spit the word between his teeth and backed up against the pylon. Again he reminded himself that as far as anyone else was concerned, he was just as guilty as Thompson, and would not be allowed to walk away from the Capitol, despite the outcome. If he accidentally killed the senator, there would be no way to explain the story, especially now that he had alienated Julia, his only link to the truth.

"Go ahead and try," taunted Bower as he moved Ashworth closer to the pylon. "Go ahead, Hamilton. Drop the senator and you'll be dead before you hit the ground."

Robert looked at the panel of glass doors opening into the Capitol at the top of the escalators leading up from the tracks. At the early hour, the escalators were still and he wondered how fast he could get inside those doors. He wondered if Thompson would take his second to the last shot. *It would be an easy shot,* he thought, estimating that Bower was now only fifteen feet away. *There's no chance of making it. But you have no other choice,* he insisted.

Shoot Thompson. If you kill the senator, it's a risk you take.

Nerves tumbled inside his stomach and felt like they were sucking his heart and lungs down into the emotional pandemonium.

Shoot Thompson, his mind ordered, but he doubted he could even steady the gun, remembering how inept he had been in Spain. *Shoot him.*

Again he hung the gun to the left side of the pylon and looked around the corner just in time to hear the blast and feel the intense pain in his hand and wrist as Thompson's slug struck the pylon next to the .38 and the cement exploded. One large chunk caught Malibu's thumb with such force that it dislocated, and the gun dropped onto the open walkway.

"No—please, God," said Ashworth with resignation as Robert grabbed his hand and snapped his thumb back into the socket. Flesh was torn away from the soft inside palm where the thumb met the pointer finger, and he tried to stop the bleeding.

"Now come out," Bower said frankly. "And kick that gun to me."

Robert raised his hands, and blood began to cover the injured palm and run down his wrist and soak the sleeve of his shirt. He kicked the gun to Bower, who carefully tucked the briefing under his armpit, picked it up and fired a round into the wrecked subway car to see that it still worked. A smile creased his lips.

"Sometimes even I can be lucky," he said. "Now let's finish our trip to the office."

"Just kill us here, boy," said Ashworth.

"They can't tie the cop to me, but they sure as hell wouldn't have to guess about the two of you. Now, do as I say." He shoved the .357 into Ashworth's back and the old man led them up the motionless escalators, through the glass entrance, into the maze of halls, turning half a dozen times before stopping in front of an unmarked door. "Open it!" Bo ordered.

"You want it open, you do it," Ashworth refused.

"Go to hell," said Bo as he fired the .357 into the senator's heart.

"Now get the keys," he ordered Robert, and the journalist bent down slowly.

"You're out of your mind," Malibu said. "You're so far gone, I—"

"Open the door."

Robert obeyed.

"Bring his body in."

"You'll never get the blood off the cement. They'll find him now. You know that."

"Of course I know that. I could have waited to get him inside here, but what the hell, I didn't kill him, anyway. You did."

"Me?"

"Two guns," said Thompson. "Two guns and two men. One of you killed the poor, interfering bastard out there, then you came in here and killed each other."

"You're sick." Robert placed the senator's body on the sky-blue carpet, stained with a red trail leading from below the doorframe to where his body now rested, with blood still pouring from the open wound.

His shoulder and chest cried for mercy as he straightened up, fighting diligently against the stiffness. He did not want Thompson to know he was in pain and tried to control his expressions accordingly.

"Not sick," Thompson argued. "Perhaps dedicated, but not sick. You see, I know the future."

"The future?"

"Yes—the future. And I refuse to be on the side of the vanquished. It was a decision I made while still a boy, and one I've never regretted. Your country doesn't even know its own folly, how sick and vulnerable it is from inside, like an apple rotting from the core." Bo drew a deep breath through his nose. "The rabble is restless, and like sheep they listen and watch you media types while they lie in bed, hoping, praying, they'll make it through one more day. Praying the federals won't foreclose on their farms and the taxes won't choke the life out of their kids' college funds and inheritance. And then they listen to you people tell them how it's all going to hell anyway—how their investment is fueling fifty percent pay increases for assholes like him." Bo waved the gun like a wand over the dead senator.

"Just like the people in the Soviet Union," added Malibu.

"Maybe—yes—but at least their government takes care of them, and they're not mocked like your people."

"Just get this over with—" Malibu began to object.

"I'll finish when I finish."

"You're a sellout, Thompson, a selfish, cowardly sellout, and nothing you say—no excuse—is going to suffice."

Malibu stepped back and estimated the distance to the hall, then he looked at the barrel of the gun leveled on him. Three steps, maybe four, and he was out the door. Then there was the tunnel, empty and long, and chances were Thompson could fire off a round or two before Robert even got out of the office.

But it's worth the chance, he thought. *Anything's worth a chance, now. Give up and die—or fight and die.*

For the first time I can't argue.

Like a bull through the rodeo gate, he bolted suddenly. His upper torso lunged, and he could feel his wound tear open, but the pain only quickened his pace as he slammed the door. Two holes burst through the metal reinforcement and tiles cracked as the bullets burrowed in the wall across the hall. He turned left and ran with all the energy he could muster, but his legs felt weak, heavy, and his overwhelming sensation was that he ran in slow motion, fighting against an invisible wind, straining every muscle to break through and run free from his aggressor, but try as hard as he might, the barrier was unbreakable. Twice he wanted to turn into recessed doorways, but to do so would only prolong the inevitable. The only option that remained was the end of the hallway, where three other tunnels met in a fork.

If you can only— he thought but was cut short.

A blast from Thompson's gun shattered two of three water bottles that rested outside another anonymous office door.

Don't stop, ordered his mind. *Run. Just keep moving. Either way you're going to—*

Another blast hit him in his wounded shoulder and sent him spinning into a vintage wood-grained filing cabinet that was waiting to be moved. The cabinet tipped over and he tumbled headfirst into a pile of plastic trash bags filled with computer printouts.

It's all over, he conceded and started to get up slowly when he saw the shadow appear in the third tunnel marked TO CANNON HOUSE OFFICE BUILDING. Next he saw four flashes from the end of a gun. No sound—only four flashes. He turned back in time to see two of the four shots burst like blood-red novas in Thompson's forehead. In slow motion, the blood flooded his face and covered the front of his oxford cotton shirt. Then Thompson fell, unnaturally, without bending at the waist, like a tree, and Robert heard the thump and the clatter of the gun as it spilled from Bo's hand onto the floor.

He turned to look at the shadow. It stepped from the dark hallway into the lighted tunnel, and the journalist finally remembered the face—the face he could not remember earlier in the evening when he left for Ashworth's home. He remembered the Spanish man from the airport at Málaga—his dark eyes—his scabbed face and hands. The man who had picked up his notebook and returned it to him.

But who is he? Robert's mind probed. "Who are you?" he asked and then closed his eyes when he saw the man aim his gun again. He took a deep breath and waited, almost feeling the pain and impact the bullet would make when it entered his head as it did Thompson's. Then suddenly, without explanation, he thought of the only other Spaniard he could remember involved in the story—the unidentified dead man in the hotel room with Grayson and Hans Peterson. This was the terrorist. He closed his eyes tighter, waiting, waiting, regretting the many wrong decisions he had made, realizing the insignificance of the story when it was wrapped inside the overwhelming perspective of life. Then he was taken by the one simple fact that when time comes for all the regrets a man stores away in his life, the regrets he plans to do something about some day, there is never enough time.

At least you can die like a man, he thought and opened his eyes. Sergio continued to hold the gun leveled at his head, and without a word he moved passed Robert, pulling a knife from his pocket. There was a click, and Malibu saw the blade in the shadow-filled hall. His stomach tightened, but then he realized the man was not going to use the knife, not on him anyway. Sergio knelt over the body of Thompson, and in one sweeping movement, graceful like a ballerina, but in what seemed like slow motion to Robert's fast-moving mind, he sliced off Thompson's ears. First the left. Then the right.

Malibu wanted to turn away, to throw up in revulsion, but fear and fascination would not allow it.

Sergio wiped the blade of his knife on Thompson's shirt and picked up the right ear. Keeping his gun on Robert, he buried both in the pocket of his jacket. "If you leave through the tunnel I entered, you will be free," he finally said without the inflection of emotion. "There are two dead officers, one at the other end and one at the entrance to the building.''

Robert looked from Sergio to the briefing book resting on the floor outside Ashworth's office. Suddenly his mind, unencumbered by threat, concentrated on his wound. Pain flared from his shoulder into his chest and down the rib cage and he wondered if the shoulder was not disconnected or separated from its socket. *Forget the book,* he ordered himself, drawing a wild, aching breath, but still he could not put it out of his mind. "Then you're not going to kill me?'' he gasped.

"You want me to?'' Sergio raised the gun.

"No. No. Hell, no,'' Robert blurted and fell back toward the wall, trying to force the tension from his body.

"I have no reason to.'' Sergio shoved the gun next to the stiletto and ear, stepped over Thompson's body and within a heartbeat disappeared down the tunnel.

Robert wiped the perspiration from his forehead and gave himself a moment to settle his heart and regain his composure. Supporting his bad arm, he stood slowly and staggered toward the tunnel opening, then he stopped and turned back to Thompson, to the briefing book. *Your ship comes in once in a lifetime,* he rationalized. *Most of the time you have to swim out and meet it. But not this time.*

Epilogue

Lake Powell was everything Robert had heard it to be, a magnificent red sandstone pool in the southern Utah desert. In December, the wind whistled over Navajo Mountain, beneath a cloudless sky, rushing northward, up the gorge and into Monument Valley where the towering natural arch of Rainbow Bridge stood high above the lake. A bridge built by God. Tied to the dock, beneath the sandstone rainbow, was a sixty-foot lake yacht christened *Balzac* by its owner, Robert's agent, Jed Morehouse.

Christmas music played softly on the radio, broadcast from the Hopi reservation across the border in Arizona. Sitting behind the kitchen table, alone on the yacht, with one arm in a sling and his hand bandaged, Malibu lifted his glass of ginger ale in a melancholy toast to the special day and then turned back to his Macintosh. The cursor flashed and Bing Crosby sang and Robert was caught in what he referred to as dead time, that helpless moment when the mind refuses to engage in the creative process of writing, when it finds it easier to sit numb and mellow and feeling sorry for itself.

This was the third week of his self-imposed exile, when Jed helped smuggle him off the East Coast and into the sanctuary of Utah where he could work, first to finish reviewing and proofing his book galleys and then to begin work on the SDI story, to make sense of his notes—of his notes and the briefing book.

He looked at the EYES ONLY folder sitting on top of a table covered with technical books Morehouse had sent over the weeks, books on nuclear defense strategies, SDI, and the first kiss-and-tell of the Satter-field White House that provided the biographies and color of the characters in his administration. Next to the table, on a chair was a manila envelope overflowing with news articles covering the deaths of Steinbrenner, Ashworth, Thompson, and the Capitol Hill police offi-cers, as well as articles about Professor Silleto and Teddy Silverman.

The irony was that Thompson was made out to be a hero, another valiant American who suffered and died at the hands of a terrorist, just as Senator Ashworth, and even Professor Steinbrenner had. "Tragic Holidays Fall on Washington," read one of the articles which outlined an erroneous, but logical succession of events that culminated in the deaths. Another, "Massacre Beneath the Dome," highlighted the fact that with such a brutal attack in the Capitol of America, no one was safe from the ruthless fist of terrorism, no longer was it confined to Third World reactionaries functioning in distant lands, but it could happen anywhere and at any moment, like these random deaths.

But not here. Robert thought and kicked back in his chair to look out the side panel windows at the beautiful red stone rainbow. *Nobody can find me here, and it's a good thing.* He glanced at the folder next to his computer, not as thick as the envelope containing the stories about terrorism. This one had articles about him, some that went as far as suggesting that he was an accomplice, somehow related to the attacks, fleeing from authorities and wanted in connection with the Spanish incident. Simon Levin was having a wonderful time with sensational leads and dramatic headlines, and Robert was surprised how many of the news services were reprinting the *Post* stories verbatim. He knew only too well where the information was originating. He, too, had once been responsible for planting stories, and it appeared that with the help of Julia and Jerry, the CIA was doing a first-rate job. So far, however, they had failed in their attempt to locate the journalist. And that was good. The way things had ended, he was the only man left to tell the tale, and the authorities were doing their best to discredit him. He was also certain they were doing their best to find him.

Robert took a handful of pistachio nuts, turned back to the flashing cursor and read the lead of a story he had revised eight times already. The first few days he was determined to tell all, regardless of national security and felt that he had little to lose in so doing. But the story he wrote he could not publish, not without tremendous repercussions. He knew that, and so he began the first in a series of edits that culminated in journalistic pap. Then he tried again. And again. Now he was depressed, and Bing Crosby stopped singing.

Dead lead time, widely associated with smaller radio stations, filled the air for a few seconds, long enough for Robert to hear the distant drumming noise. At first he thought it was a large boat coming up the channel, but it was growing much too loud, much too quickly. The Mormon Tabernacle Choir began to offer its version of Handel's *Messiah*, and Robert sprang to the stereo and turned it off. It was not a motorboat, but a helicopter. Not *a* helicopter, but two helicopters. Then he saw them come over the sandstone peak, and their volume increased as the noise of the rotors shattered the calm environment, beating off the water and echoing off the lakeside cliffs.

Watching the gray and white Jet Rangers descend like slow, huge snow geese from the northern sky, he picked up the briefing book and rushed into the stateroom, where he yanked Jed's top drawer from the chest. Socks and underwear spilled onto the cabin floor, and dropping on top of them was an old Army .45. He picked it up, shoved the briefing book beneath the chest, and ran toward the bow of the yacht, stopping behind the sliding glass doors that opened onto the deck.

The first chopper touched down on the cape beyond the pier. White caps whipped against the dock and sand filled the air. Then the next settled down behind it. Roaring engines began to die, and the rear door of the first Ranger opened.

Robert had never met Rich Spencer personally, but he knew who he was the moment he stepped from the helicopter onto the rock. Following Spencer came Maurice Sidey, of the CIA, and a third man who Robert speculated was an operative, maybe even a hitman. *But why bring out the brass if you're going to make a hit,* he thought and slid the glass door open.

"Mr. Hamilton," yelled Spencer, "is that you?"

"It's me."

"You have a gun."

"Of course," Robert lifted it slightly with a twist of wrist.

"You won't need it. I promise."

"You promise?" Robert scoffed. "I know all about your promises."

"But you've never dealt with me."

"I've dealt with your kind."

Spencer nodded his head understandingly. "Okay, you can keep the gun, but please be careful. We need to talk."

"About what?"

"We're here on your behalf."

Robert stepped from the doorway, taken by Spencer's trust that he would allow the journalist to keep the gun. Reassured, he placed the .45 on the railing leading to the gangway. "What do you mean, my behalf?" he yelled over the roar of engines.

"You know very well what I mean, Mr. Hamilton. The dangerous story you have—the one you could write."

"It's finished."

"No," Spencer shook his head. "We've come out here on the assumption that it isn't finished—that maybe we could persuade you—"

"I'll do what I need to. I can't be persua—"

"We have someone who would like to speak with you. Then we'll go away. We'll leave you be. I promise."

"You'll never leave me alone. You know that."

"The past is the past, Mr. Hamilton. Nobody says there were no mistakes. Nobody says this administration is perfect. But we need your help, and *you* know that."

"From what I've been reading, you people think I'm a criminal, that I've—"

"We don't think any such thing. We know the truth. Trust me. But what are we supposed to say? That Bower Thompson just about gave the most explosive information in history to the Soviets? That the Initiative is launched? Do you expect us to give the Soviet Union all the information it would have received from Thompson anyway? You, more than any other journalist in America, should know the danger of the information you have."

"Information?"

"The briefing book, Mr. Hamilton. Look, I'm straight with you, and I demand the same thing." For the first time, Spencer's voice reflected anger. "We know you have the briefing book. You took it from Senator Ashworth when he was killed by Thompson."

"Then you know Thompson killed him?"

"Of course we know. We even know you encountered Sergio Castillo Armando."

"Who?"

"The terrorist, Mr. Hamilton. The man who let you live." Spencer took a step forward. "Look, can I come on board?"

"Who's the man with you?"

"Director Sidey."

"No. I know Sidey. Who's the other man?"

"Don't worry. He's my confidential assistant—not armed," Spencer folded his arms and drew a deep breath. "Can we come aboard? Or do I have to continue to shout above the motors."

"I don't know." Robert took a step backward and looked at the gun resting on the rail. "What more do you want from me?"

"The briefing book and the promise that you won't write absolutely everything you have, that you'll leave out the information about the status of our Initiative."

"The public has a right to know."

"The public has a right to live peacefully, safely. You know that."

"They have a right to know when their government's lied to them."

"Not everyone understands national security, Mr. Hamilton. Most people don't want to. If they have worries and concerns, they want them to be about their families, their small businesses, their homes. They don't want to know about nuclear tonnage and how our boys suffer on the 38th Parallel to keep democracy in South Korea. That's our responsibility, and the decisions we make—the consequences of those decisions—well, they're our responsibility as well. The time will come, Mr. Hamilton—the time will come when our people will know—but for their own safety—now is not the time."

"I'll think about it." Robert picked up the gun and turned to walk into the cabin.

"Wait a minute," yelled Spencer. "If you won't let us come on ship, there's someone here who wants to talk to you." He waved at the second helicopter. The door sprang open, and Diana jumped onto the rock and began moving toward the yacht. Robert's stomach filled his throat as he watched her move toward the dock. A shiver ran up his spine, and his chest and shoulders began to tighten. At first he wanted to turn away, to close the doors behind him and lock her permanently out of his life. She had betrayed him, and even the emotions he held deep inside his heart could not dispel that betrayal in the rational recesses of his mind. Logically, he wanted to ignore her. Emotionally, he simply wanted her.

Stopping short of the door, he placed the gun inside, then turned and watched as her hair fluttered under the wind of the rotors. Her unbuttoned navy-blue blazer flapped around her, but she did nothing to protect herself, her hair and appearance from the turbulent air. Rather, she walked with her arms to her side, open and honest, with a fresh and confident look that defied Robert's logic, and he turned toward her. His wound throbbed as he walked to the edge of the gangplank to help her climb aboard.

At times, the depth and power of one stare can replace a year of candlelit dinners and crackling fires, and this was the stare that caught the two as they met on the bow of *Balzac*. Beyond containment, Diana hugged Robert until he winced in pain, and then she fell back with tears in her eyes.

"I'm so sorry," she said slowly with a soft, hoarse voice. "I'm so sorry for what I did to you."

Robert did not respond, only looked into her eyes and tried to take control of his conflicting impulses. They were more understanding than he ever remembered anyone's eyes. They seemed to invite him inside, innocently at first, inviting him to open up, to trust her and join her in a communion of emotion, and then they seemed to swallow him whole, to take over his emotions and welcome him from within, spirit to spirit, until, without another word from her, he was captivated by her stare.

"I could ask for your forgiveness," she said. "I could beg you to feel about me the way I really—deep inside—feel about you," she wiped the tears from her cold, red cheeks, "but I wouldn't expect you to forgive me. Not now. After everything I've done."

"I wish I could say I haven't thought about you," Robert began stiffly. "But that would be a lie. This whole story—I can believe everything—except for your part. I can't believe your part. I—"

She began to cry. "You don't ever have to forgive me. You know that, I'll never expect you to forgive me. But sometimes we inherit things from our parents that exist in us, that we're powerless to fight, even to understand. They aren't actually alive in us; but they hang on so damn tightly all the same, and we can never rid ourselves of them."

She sniffled against her tears. "I don't expect you to understand," she offered. "But I couldn't let everything end—I couldn't allow you to go on believing that I openly betrayed your trust—your trust and my emotions."

"I'm trying to," Robert said, moved by her sincerity. "I really am trying."

"I guess you and the President and everybody thought I was some kind of Theodora."

"Theodora?"

"The dancing girl who became queen of Byzantium by her deceit."

"No. I never thought that," said Robert. "I only thought—"

"But I didn't want anything for myself—only for my father. I loved him so much." Her tears flowed more passionately and she reached out for Robert who took her in his arm.

"And he loved you," he whispered. "And I know how damned easy that can be."

"What?" Diana asked, looking straight into his eyes.

"It's just that I know how easy it would be to love you," he said carefully.

"Did I ever say that you talk like you write?"

"I think once, yeah," Robert smiled. "It's useful when you have to get out of uncomfortable moments of—well, you know, embarrassment."

Diana laughed through her tears. "Like now for example?"

"Yeah, like right now." Robert felt himself beginning to perspire despite the winter wind.

"Can anything be made of this?" she asked looking away at the silhouette of Rich Spencer in the helicopter.

"I don't understand?"

"Act three, scene four from *Othello*. Desdemona is searching for—"

"Didn't she love Othello?" Robert asked and Diana nodded slowly as she turned back.

"But he was too foolish to believe, despite what it appeared on the surface, that she loved him as intensely as he loved her." She paused, and then with a devious grin added, "And that is portentous."

"What do we do about them?" Robert nodded toward the idle

choppers. "If they leave, you won't see civilization for another two weeks, until I finish the story."

"Must we espouse our fathers' sins?"

"What play's that from?"

"You know what I mean. Everything I've done can be atoned for if you can see your way to not writing the article."

Pleasantries melted to concern in Robert's eyes. "Is that why you came here?"

"Don't be foolish. I'm here because I want to be here—for no other reason. And whether or not you write the story, my feelings for you won't change. Unfortunately, though, the man I flew out here with isn't quite as passionate as I am—I mean when it comes to you."

"Spencer?" Robert asked.

Diana shook her head no and looked back to the helicopter. Rich Spencer disappeared into the hidden chopper, and the next person Robert saw was President Satterfield, flanked by his Marine with the black briefcase and a young man in a tapered suit. "Him," she said with an uncertain smile.

"They're taking all this seriously," Robert understated. "Should I invite him aboard?"

"It's up to you, but he is on the 'A' Party List."

Robert chuckled and waved to the President, who readily accepted the invitation, leaving an agitated Secret Service agent on the dock and bringing only the Marine with the doomsday football. Both men shook hands as Satterfield cleared the plank.

"Mr. Hamilton," the President acknowledged as he straightened his red tie, known commonly to politicians and their fashion consultants as television ties for their bright and captivating color, especially when combined with the power navy-blue suit that Satterfield was also wearing, complete with a silk red kerchief tucked into the pocket over his left breast.

Robert felt self-conscious in his tan crew-neck sweater, faded jeans and leather topsiders on sockless feet. "Mr. President," he said and tried to stand as tall as possible with the pain in his shoulder.

"How are you feeling?"

"Well, sir."

"You'd better not tell me the name of the physician who helped

you. You know what they did to Dr. Mudd when he set Booth's leg."
He grinned a self-deprecating, Jack Benny grin.

"I hope I'm not thought to be John Wilkes Booth," said Robert.

"No," the President continued to smile. "Not yet, anyway. But
we've been hunting for you for what—three weeks now? And you
know the security of America—of the free world—sits in there on your
typewriter. You know that, don't you?"

"I know that—" Robert began.

"—the public has a right to know," Satterfield finished his remark.
"I know, Spencer told me what you said—that the public's got a right
to know."

"Yes, sir."

"Well," Satterfield looked thoughtfully out at the lake, to the red
cliffs that towered five hundred feet above the water, "let me add that
just as certain as their right to know is your responsibility as a
journalist. You understand, Mr. Hamilton, that I'm not alone when it
comes to providing for America's security—for the security of our
allies. You share that responsibility with me, and you accepted it the
day you picked up your pen—the day you determined to make journalism a career." He walked pensively across the bow to the lake side of
the yacht. "You know in antiquity—before the written word—news
was shared and history kept by storytellers—men who had the enor-
mous responsibility of recording events in their memories and sharing
them with tribal councils and small societies. The responsibility for
recording a people's precious history was passed from father to son,
from generation to generation. But just as important as memorizing the
history was the responsibility for choosing which facts remained to be
told and which remained to be forgotten. Essential to the process was
the security of their society, the well-being of their people. Under no
circumstances was that to ever be compromised."

"You're right, Mr. Hamilton." The President looked back at Robert with a penetrating stare that made the journalist even more self-
conscious. "The public does have a right to know. They have a right to
know just as they did when Washington, Madison and Franklin locked
themselves in secrecy inside the State House in Philadelphia with the
other delegates and hammered out our Constitution. Some people
weren't happy then, either. Thomas Jefferson himself was over in
Paris and outraged by the news that even the windows would be closed

with guards at the doors. It was abominable—unjustifiable in a land of open dialogue and public debate. But it worked, Mr. Hamilton. It worked because the rationale of those men was not for individual political gain but for the welfare and future of a nation. And that's all that motivates us now. I promise you. Just as the time came when those proceedings were known and our Constitution revealed, the time will come for the world to know of SDI. But as it was with the Philadelphia convention, timing is everything. So right now, I'm asking you to set aside personal ambitions."

Satterfield gestured toward the first helicopter. "But as my security advisor promised, it's your decision. I want you to know that the events have run their course. We know of your involvement, just as we know of your innocence. And you're free to do whatever you'd like— whatever you think is best. I'm glad the shoulder's healing, and I meant no offense by my reference to Dr. Mudd." He turned and smiled at Diana. "Well," he sighed, "I guess that's all I had to say." Without another word he turned, stepped from the yacht to the pier, and proceeded to the helicopter.

"You think he rehearsed that?" Robert asked, somewhat bewildered.

Diana started to laugh. "I guess when the President speaks, you just listen." She paused and studied his perplexed expression. "The rest is up to you."

"It's the story of a lifetime," he said.

"I know it is," she agreed.

"I'll never forgive myself if I let it go."

"I know you won't."

"But I'll never forgive myself if I write it."

"I know," she said finally as he disappeared into the boat and then emerged with the briefing book in his hand.

"Here it is," he offered and felt suddenly cold. "You can give it to him. Tell him that everything I've written is pabulum anyway, and he has nothing to worry about."

"You give it to him yourself."

"Me?"

"Of course." Diana kissed him on the cheek. "I'm going to go inside, kick off my shoes, make a cup of coffee, and look forward to staying away from civilization for the next two weeks."

Author's Note

Works of fiction seldom carry acknowledgments. *Strategic Compromise*, however, would still be locked in the circuits of my word processor without a handful of military and scientific experts to whom I will forever be grateful. Their eyes brightened as my ruminations, guesswork, and technical investigation zeroed in on a program that has captivated their hearts as well as expertise.

I am also indebted to Senator William V. Roth, Jr., a statesman and teacher who has broadened my political perspective, supported my endeavors, and given me an appreciation for the challenges inherent in leadership and the courage needed to overcome them.

Concerning my literary pursuits, I'm grateful to my parents, William L. and Carol Holladay Nixon, lifelong supporters of my dream to write; John Henry Irsfeld, my mentor and friend; Jim Stein, my agent at William Morris; Sandy Richardson, my editor; Drew Hiatt, Bill Simmons, John Bennett, and Rob Wilkins, constructive critics and trusted friends.

Finally, I wish to acknowledge Viktor Frankl, a man whose genius and spirit fill large portions of this book.

ABOUT THE AUTHOR

William Nixon was a staff speechwriter for President Ronald Reagan and has worked extensively in Western Europe and the Far East on Strategic Defense Initiative matters and other aspects of military policy. He was formerly editor of *American Times Magazine*, and continues to write articles for magazines and journals throughout the nation. He lives and works in the Washington, D.C., area.